THE PILLARS OF SAND

Book Three of
THE ECHOES OF EMPIRE

MARK T. BARNES

47NORTH

Published by 47North, Seattle, WA

www.apub.com

Amazon, the Amazon logo, and 47North are trademarks of Amazon.com, Inc., or its affiliates.

ISBN-13: 9781477819548
ISBN-10: 1477819541

Cover illustration by Stephan Martiniere

Library of Congress Control Number: 2013953970

Printed in the United States of America

To the people who love me, and support me in my passion. You make the world a better place, and I adore you for it.

SOUTHEASTERN ĪA

YEAR 495 OF THE SHRÍANESE FEDERATION

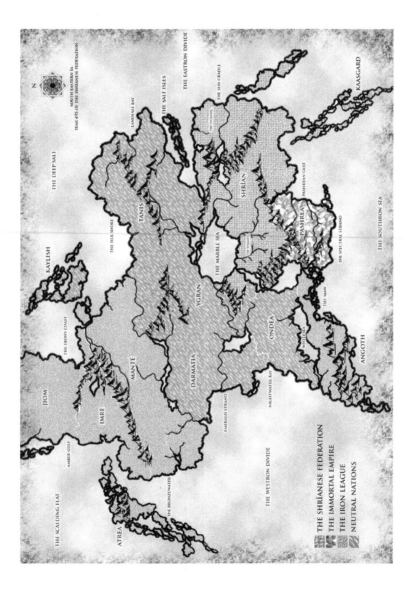

SHRĪAN

YEAR 495 OF THE SHRÍANESE FEDERATION

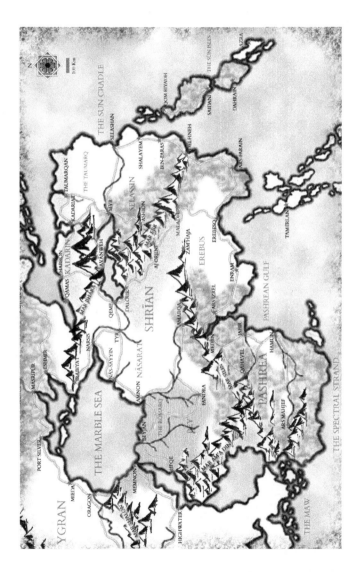

BEFORE

"THERE ARE THREE GREAT RIVERS: THE PAST, THE PRESENT, AND THE
FUTURE. NEITHER THE PASSAGE OF TIME, NOR OURSELVES, ARE
CONSTANT. WE, LIKE TIME, ARE SUBJECTIVE AND VIEWED WITH AS MANY
LENSES AS THERE ARE PEOPLE TO SEE. WE, WITHIN TIME, ARE AT ONCE
THE INITIATOR AND OBSERVER OF PASSING EVENTS, SAILORS ON A RIVER
OF CAUSE AND EFFECT: THE MOMENT WE HAVE CAUSED AN EVENT, OR
WITNESSED ITS EFFECTS, WE ARE SWEPT AWAY BY THEM AND LEFT ONLY
WITH IMPERFECT MEMORIES OF THE SMALL PART OF THE WHOLE WE
HAVE SEEN. NO MATTER HOW MUCH WE TRY, THERE IS NO GOING
BACK, AND THERE IS NO SEEING EVERYTHING THERE IS TO SEE.
NOR CAN WE BUT GUESS AT WHAT IS TO COME."

—From *The Three Rivers,* by Ahwe, scholar, philosopher, and explorer
(First Year of the Awakened Empire)

It has been almost five centuries since the formation of the
Shrīanese Federation, an alliance of the surviving six Great Houses
and the Hundred Families of the Avān, who fled the fall of the
Awakened Empire.

The land within and around Shrīan was littered with the detritus of past empires, echoes of glory and the high watermark of civilizations lost to time, internecine war, and blind ambition. Set
against Shrīanese imperialism and the return to days of glory was

the Human-governed Iron League, an alliance of nations set on ensuring no new empire rises to seize control. The Humans, also known as the Starborn, remember their days of servitude and are unwilling to bend their necks again.

Rahn-Erebus fa Corajidin, the leader of the Great House of Erebus, and leader of the Imperialist political faction, was dying, his body failing as his soul succumbed to its own poison. Terrified of meeting his demise before reaching the heights expected of a leader of his family, Corajidin began a civil war in order to gain access to the ancient treasures and knowledge he needed to stay alive.

Set against Corajidin was Indris, former Sēq Knight. He was drawn once more into Shrīan's political conflict, when Vashne and Ariskander asked his help to locate and return Far-ad-din: the one person who could possibly reveal the extent of Corajidin's false-hood, and corruption. In this new purpose, Indris found himself an unlikely ally.

After she had witnessed the lengths to which her father had gone to achieve his ambitions, Mari, Corajidin's daughter, found herself conflicted. Her duty to, and love of, her family was clear. But her duty to her nation, as well as her duty to herself, was not something she could ignore. After her father had Vashne assassi-nated and Ariskander abducted, Mari was confronted with a dark-ness in her father she had not wanted to see.

As Corajidin continued his drive for power, Mari and Indris joined forces to oppose him. Indris and his comrades set out into the monster-infested Rōmarq, the marshlands that held the ancient ruins of lost civilizations, to rescue Ariskander, while Mari remained in Amnon—a spy in her father's own household—with newfound allies who fought with her to maintain order.

After they had faced the many perils of the marshlands, Indris and his comrades arrived too late: Ariskander had been executed, and his soul was bound into an Angothic Spirit Casque. Indris managed to recover the casque, and denied Corajidin his prize. Corajidin escaped to Amnon, with Indris and his comrades in pursuit.

Corajidin refused to admit defeat, and formulated a plan for his colors to make a stand elsewhere. Before he would leave Amnon, Corajidin was betrayed by Thufan, his own Master of Assassins. Corajidin was nearly killed, but not before he saw his beloved son, Belamandris, mortally wounded.

Though Indris, Mari, and their allies were victorious, it was not without cost. Mari was cast out from her family: a family that faced an uncertain future on the political stage due to her father's failed schemes. There was no clear candidate to lead Shrīan, and the Iron League saw a weaker Shrīan easy to conquer. The Great Houses and the Hundred Families knew their struggle had only begun.

Camped far from Amnon, Corajidin was introduced to the Emissary—Anj-el-din, Indris's wife, who had been presumed dead—a servant of powerful and enigmatic Masters. The Emissary promised Corajidin much: power, majesty, and long life. But the price of these things was not discussed, and in desperation, Corajidin did not think to ask.

Shortly after the events of Amnon, in the Shrīanese capital of Avānweh, came the New Year's Festival, and the time of the Assession when the new government was elected. Acts of violence attributed to Iron League forces, and the return of the Exiles—political criminals who had been banished by the late Asrahn-Vashne—threatened the balance, and gave Corajidin the support he needed to continue his play for power.

Indris, Mari, and their friends were enlisted to help discover what Corajidin had planned, and to end it if possible. The brief peace Indris and Mari had hoped to enjoy was broken by their call to duty, and by the ghosts of their own pasts. For Indris, it was the threat of the Sēq that loomed largest, and their continued interest in his growing abilities; and the pressure from his cousin, Roshana, to serve their House and see to its advancement. For Mari, it was the presence of her family and their agendas, the pull at her own ambitions and duty, and the arrival of an old lover who had taken a position in her father's household: a man who promised danger was coming.

In return for significant portions of the Exiles' wealth, and their vows of allegiance, Corajidin bound the Exiles to his purpose and began anew his plans for ascension to the role of Asrahn. The Emissary tempted Corajidin with the help he needed to realize his goals—though her help came at a price. The Emissary claimed to be able to deliver that which Corajidin desired most: the return of his son, Belamandris; to be crowned as Asrahn; and the restoration of Corajidin's dead wife, Yashamin, who haunted his visions with whispered messages of vengeance. Blinded by his ambition, with the hope he could control his circumstance, Corajidin agreed, and Belamandris was restored to health as the first of the Emissary's promises.

Worried by Corajidin's very feasible grab for the highest office in Shrīan—and by the presence of the Exiles and their agenda—Indris, Mari, and their comrades discovered what they could by following the Exiles and those who wore their colors. It became apparent that the Exiles had planned significant military action, bolstered by the arcane support of witches, Nomads, and bound daemon elementals.

In the ruins of the Mahsojhin, where the Emissary labored to free the witches, events came to a head when Corajidin learned from a Nomad that it was Selassin fe Vahineh who had murdered his late wife. Further shocks came as Corajidin was elected Asrahn, and as a manipulative Rosha, and not Nazarafine, was elected to lead the Federationists.

Pressed for time and short of options to check Corajidin's influence, the Federationists decided to Sever Vahineh from her Awakening, in order to have another Federationist rahn raised to the Upper House of the Teshri. However, during the process, a faction of the Sēq led by Master Zadjinn interrupted the Severance and took Indris, Femensetri, and Vahineh captive. Indris's comrades were unaware of the Sēq's involvement, and came to the conclusion that Indris, Femensetri, and Vahineh had been taken by Corajidin. Corajidin, who had requested Vahineh be handed over to stand trial for murder, believed the Federationists had plotted to protect Vahineh, and rob him of vengeance. A parley to determine the truth of the matter, and to forge some kind of peace, was ruined when assassins tasked by Roshana attempted to kill Corajidin. Corajidin used the treachery as justification for further aggression, in order to bring the Teshri under his control.

Meanwhile Indris, imprisoned by the Sēq, was tortured for the truth about his unaccounted-for years. Indris was unable to give the answers he did not know. However, it was a moot point: The Dhar Gsenni, a powerful faction within the Sēq, and led by Zadjinn, wanted Indris for their own ends. Indris managed to free himself and Vahineh, and they both escaped the Sēq. Returned to the outside world, Indris was reunited with Mari and his comrades. Knowing Avānweh was too dangerous a place to stay, they tried to escape, but were harried at every turn. Infuriated by the violence in his city, the Sky Lord demanded that Roshana, Nazarafine, and Siamak leave Avānweh. Likewise, Indris and his comrades were banished.

However, before they could leave, daemon elementals were set free in the city at Corajidin's order. As the city was distracted by the mayhem, Corajidin politicized the violence and used it as a justification for his own plans, part of which was to demonstrate how the Sēq were no longer relevant, and could be replaced. The Mahsojhin witches were put to dual purpose: those selected to be part of Corajidin's future were used to put down the havoc that Corajidin had started; the others were sacrificed to occupy the Sēq so they were unable to defend the city.

In the chaos, Indris, drafted by Femensetri to help the Sēq, was brought face to face with Anj-el-din, who had supposedly returned to help the Sēq in their efforts. Though Indris suspected there was something strange about his returned wife, the battle drew all their attention and he had no time to act on his doubts.

Mari tried to escort the rahns from Avānweh aboard the *Wanderer*, but they were pursued and grounded. Belamandris, the leader of the pursuit, offered Roshana, Siamak, and Nazarafine their freedom, in exchange for Mari and Vahineh, and Roshana agreed to the terms. Hayden and Omen were killed in battle after the rahns fled, while Ekko and Shar escaped. Both Mari and Vahineh were taken captive and brought to Tamerlan: a place of horror from Mari's youth, ruled by her vindictive grandmother, the Dowager-Asrahn.

His son returned to him, a crown on his brow, Corajidin took the final boon from the Emissary: the reincarnation of Yashamin. As part payment for her services, the Emissary demanded that Corajidin leave Mari to rot in Tamerlan.

The Mahsojhin closed, the witches defeated for the moment, Indris and Anj were taken into custody, where Indris was informed he would be taken to Amarqa-in-the-Snows for further questioning. Cautioned against any attempt at escape, Indris elected to go with the Sēq on the promise that they would tell him the truth of his ancestry.

And now . . .

1

"WERE WE COMPLETE, THERE WOULD BE NO NEED FOR US TO GROW THROUGH STRUGGLE OR ADVERSITY. THERE WOULD BE NO TRANSCENDENCE, ILLUMINATION, OR ENLIGHTENMENT. WE NEED TO EMBRACE OUR MANY IMPERFECTIONS, MAKE THEM PART OF US, TO OVERCOME OUR LIMITATIONS."

—From the *Esoteric Doctrines,* by Sedefke, inventor, explorer, and philosopher (901st Year of the Awakened Empire)

LATE AUTUMN. DAY 51 OF THE 496TH

YEAR OF THE SHRĪANESE FEDERATION

The heat scoured Indris to the point where his muscles, ligaments, tendons, and bones thrummed, pushed beyond their endurance. He shrieked until his voice dwindled to an arid croak. The superheated air parched his gums and made his tongue stick to the roof of his mouth. Fire scorched down his throat and into his lungs; breathing was agony. A serpent of energy coiled around Indris's spine, flexing and lashing at the flowering vortices of his energy centers as it strived to inhabit his mind and soul. *My Awakening, desperate for release.* Worst was the stake of pain through his left eye, a jagged thing that had planted itself and grown molten roots inside his brain burning burning burning—

"Enough!" Femensetri shouted. "Enough, or he'll bloody well kill us all."

"Keep going. He can take more," He-Who-Watches, the Sēq Inquisitor, urged.

"Maybe he can," Ojin-mar, the Sēq Executioner, replied. "But we can't. His jhi-reflex has pretty much destroyed this room, too, save the parts where we had multiple wards. Femensetri, you say there were seven others like him?"

"Eight special children were chosen for the Great Labor. But like him?" Femensetri replied. "No, there were none like him."

Indris relaxed as the Sēq Masters stopped their probing into his memories. It took minutes for the pain to subside, while his hearts felt like hooves beating against his ribs. Minutes where even the caress of the air pricked like needles on his skin. The heat in his skull began to cool. He raised shaking hands to push back his sodden hair, kept them over his eyes until his breathing and pulse returned to normal. Indris saw giant flares and coronas swirling on the canvas of his eyelids. As the sear behind his left eye dwindled to a smolder, and his brain felt less like it was boiling in his skull, Indris cracked open his eyes.

The warded obsidian chair in which he sat seemed none the worse for wear. Indris looked down at his naked body, clothing turned to ash, his skin fading from angry red to its natural light olive, marked with its myriad tattoos and scars. The same thing had happened the past twenty-three times the Sēq Masters had tried to unravel the Anamnesis Maze that coiled around the missing years of Indris's life. Around him the rest of the laboratory—a vaulted chamber of cold stone deep beneath the rock and snow of the Mar Silin range—looked like it had been hit with several kinds of natural disaster. Stone furniture had been turned to slag. There were concentric ripples in the stone, each spreading from where Indris sat to the blasted walls. Small pieces of silicate in the rock had been transformed into points of glass, glittering like diamonds.

Where the Masters stood, the room was barely touched. Indris suppressed a smile at how many of their wards had burned away, leaving the steaming brick-red fractals of their inner circuit intact. The Masters themselves were poised, though Indris noted the sweat that dewed some of their brows. A small number of armored Sēq Knights and Librarians, the latter chronicling the proceedings, stood behind them.

Ojin-mar banished the inner circuit of the ward. The air inside steamed as it rapidly heated, forming tiny clouds that drifted toward the ceiling. The Sēq Inquisitor stepped forward, more relaxed than many of his counterparts. A shock of fair hair and a short beard—little more than stubble—framed his lined, tanned face, and long scars drew down over his right eye and down his cheek to the jaw. He rubbed his jaw with a hand missing both the small and ring fingers. Indris spared a glance for Femensetri, who was scraping a thumbnail along a stain on her Scholar's Crook. She avoided Indris's gaze, much as she had done ever since he had been brought to Amarqa-in-the-Snows. He-Who-Watches wiped sweat from his brow with his brightly colored taloub.

"Did you find anything in there?" Indris tapped at his temple and reached for his worn browns and blacks, leaving the Sēq cassock they had brought him where it lay.

"We can't get through the layers of the maze in your brain without setting off all sorts of mystic traps," Ojin-mar said. "Who, in the names of all the hallowed dead, did this to you?"

"Somebody who wanted something forgotten." Indris looked around the laboratory. "You'd better find something out soon, before you run out of places for me to destroy."

"You're not funny, boy." Femensetri's sharp voice cracked the air. "You don't think we've better things to do than this?"

"I'm a little funny," Indris said, more calmly then he felt or she deserved. "I told you I knew nothing about what happened to me, but that didn't stop you imprisoning me and dragging me down here."

"You came of your own free will, remember?"

"There's a kernel of truth in that statement, I suppose. I came in return for the answers you still withhold, and to understand what happened to me when I was on the Spines. And why whatever I found would lead me to Manté of all places. At least one of us was being honest when they said they'd cooperate. Given you've not held up your end of our bargain—and not for the first time—I don't suppose you'd mind giving me Changeling back, so I can leave? I do have other things I can be doing with my time. Like finding my missing friends. And Mari. Especially Mari."

"It's not as simple as that, Indris." He-Who-Watches flicked a quick glance at Femensetri, his expression troubled. He gestured for Indris and the others to follow him out of the ruined laboratory. "Much has happened in the time you've been with us. Our imperatives, as well as our needs, have changed."

"There's a surprise," Indris drawled. "The Sēq have changed their minds because it suits them. If you won't help me—"

"I never said we wouldn't help."

"Then give me access to the Black Archives," Indris said. He felt the tension bordering on pain in his clenched fists. "Or let me out of here so I can do what I should be doing while you nest here behind your walls and wards."

"Watch your mouth, Indris," Ojin-mar warned. "We tolerate much from you, but there are limits."

Limits? Indris suppressed a bark of bitter laughter. *None of us know what my limits are, though you've pushed and pushed and still not found the answers any of us need.*

He shielded his eyes from the sudden glare as they emerged into the open air, high up above the smokey-towered Amarqa-in-the-Snows, first and greatest of the Sēq chapterhouses. Clouds scudded overhead, and farther down the valley Indris spotted the sparking shapes of wind-ships heading toward Amarqa.

"We don't know enough to let you go." He-Who-Watches stamped his feet against the cold. "And can't afford to lose what may be in your head."

"Does it really matter why Sedefke abandoned you?" Indris folded his hands in the sleeves of his over-robe. His breath streamed between his lips, a milky cloud tinted with all the words he did not say. "And why, in the names of all the sacred dead, do you think he'd tell me what he'd not tell his own disciples?"

"That's one of the things we want to know, boy," Femensetri said. "And it matters. Sedefke is gone. The Time Masters are gone. Other than the Seethe, the other Elemental Masters have vanished from the world."

Ojin-mar's shoulders slumped. "And we need to know if we've been left alone, to face—"

"*Avendi!*" Enough! Femensetri snapped in Maladhoring, unaware that Indris could understand her perfectly well. *But how is it I'm able to understand her?*

Indris let his eyes close for longer than a blink, centering himself, overcoming frustration. He had hoped the Sēq would have found a way around the Anamnesis Maze, revealing at least some of what had happened to him during the three missing years of his life on the Spines. Perhaps he might learn what he and Anj had said to each other before his memories were locked away: Almost every permutation of the Possibility Tree told him his wife had other intentions for Indris than telling him the truth. But in his time at Amarqa there had been no progress. In fifty-one days, seven laboratories had been ruined. One Master sent to the Differential Baths in an attempt to save her life. Four knights and eleven librarians not so fortunate as to make it even that far. And they were no closer to finding the keys to what was locked in Indris's mind, or discovering who had locked it away or why.

If Sedefke was alive, and it had been him that had taken the time to tell me anything, why bother locking it away?

"I need to know what's happened to my friends," Indris said.

Femensetri squinted in the glare. "You may as well forget Mari—"

"No. I'll not. Neither her nor that it was your actions, sahai, which led to the death of my friends, Hayden and Omen. To Mari and Vahineh being taken. If I'd been there, things would've ended differently. I've given. Now you must."

"Sounds like a threat, boy." His former sahai's voice was flinty.

Indris shrugged. "It's what you promised. I've cooperated and my jhi-reflex has killed some of you, and wounded a lot more. The results could end up being different next time."

"Let's all take a step back, shall we?" Ojin-mar raised a hand to shade his eyes. "Indris, surely you've been looking into things yourself? I'd be disappointed if you'd not."

"If I knew, would I ask?"

"Of course you would." Ojin-mar smiled. "Otherwise you'd be admitting I was right and you were skilled enough to break through our layers of wards. Which I think you are, and have. We respect you, Indris, and aren't blinded to certain realities about you. Please do us the same courtesy."

"So, if you respect me so much, you'll give me answers? Or the means to get them myself?"

Femensetri looked to the other Masters, then said, "In light of recent events . . . join us in the Founder's Deep, at the Hour of the Hart tomorrow morning. Bring your questions and we'll tell what it's safe for you to know."

"Safe for whom?" Indris asked.

"Us, obviously." Ojin-mar's lips quirked in what was almost a smile as the Masters walked away, over-robes snapping in the chill autumn wind.

❊ ❊ ❊

It had been a frustrating afternoon in the library, Indris leafing through innumerable books and scrolls without finding any answers. The Mah-Psésahen, the high mental teachings, were alluded to but not discussed at any great length. The Deh-Psésahen, the lesser mental disciplines, were examined at great and tiresome length, with an array of theoretical and practical works, none of which brought Indris any nearer to his goal.

In frustration he had gone to the Manufactory to work on his designs for new armor. The Manufactory had been stifling, and Indris stank from his labors. Once he dropped his new journals with their designs in his room, he was looking forward to a soak in the hot springs and a meal at the Black Quill.

"Hello, husband."

Indris stopped in his tracks at the door of his chambers, hearts skipping a beat at the sight of Anj, leaning long-limbed against the wall. It reminded him of the day he first realized he loved her. He drew in a quick breath and held it to steady himself, before covering his lips with the tiny mask of a smile.

"Anj," Indris said. *Where have you been, and who are you now?* He did not step closer to his door, for fear the opening of it would provide an invitation he was not yet ready to make.

"Sure you don't want some company, stranger?" she said with a wicked smile. She came to stand so close to him, he felt the heat from her skin without touching. Her sapphire eyes were preternaturally bright, her skin glowing against the somber black of her cassock.

"Don't know. You look like trouble."

"You could be so lucky."

And here we are. The same words, a different place. Indris had not forgotten what it was like to run his fingers through the silken strands of her quills. To draw her to him. Linger over the taste of her breath, lips almost touching, the anticipation building until—

He blinked and shook his head. She smiled.

"Somebody's being a very bad man." Her voice was low and throaty, almost a purr. "Exactly the way I like him."

Indris smiled and took a step to the side, causing her to frown.

"What are you planning to do now that you're back?" Anj asked.

"I'm here because it's less inconvenient than being elsewhere, to learn what I need to learn. But there are things I need to do before I have anything resembling a plan." He sobered as he thought of his friends. Of Mari, never out of his thoughts, her mortal appeal so unlike Anj's eldritch fascination. *It's been years. I thought you were dead and said my good-byes. Badly, it now seems . . .*

"Need some help?" she asked. "I've the time, and people don't seem to need me around here."

"Thank you, these are things I need to do by myself. Besides, I thought you'd be of some rather profound interest to the Suret."

"Ha!" Her whole torso rocked with the word, which made him smile as it always had. "They're as curious about me as they are about you, but my patrons in the Dhar Gsenni buy me liberties not extended to you." She frowned. "Fascinating as Order politics is, we need to talk, Indris."

"I've tried to find you to talk but you always seem to be somewhere else." Suspicion rose in him, and not for the first time. "Tell me where you've been."

"Here and there. Mostly there. Indris, I've some of the story of what happened after you left. After I . . . You looked for me, you beautiful man. For years. And I've heard about this Avān woman—"

"Mari."

Anj's eyes narrowed dangerously in an expression he remembered well. "Yes. Her. But you thought I was dead. Now you know I'm not. So, we need to talk, you and I."

You may not be dead, but you are not yourself either. He opened himself to the ahmsah and looked at her Disentropic Stain. There it was! The faint blurring, a writhing of shadows around her as if something hid the truth. The same blurring he sensed around the edges of her features, as if this were a painting of the woman he'd known laid over the Anj she had become. He felt the faint oiliness he had come to associate with tainted energy, gone almost as soon as he felt it.

"We do need to talk, Anj. But it's been a long time since we've . . . I was gone three years on the Spines doing Ancestors know what, then two years as a slave in Sorochel, then two years looking for you. Then, enough time to try to find happiness again. Seven years and more was a long time to be parted, and too many years for nothing to have changed.

Anj nodded slowly, her expression still, as if reading his thoughts. "A lot of years have been stolen from us, Indris, and it was neither of our faults. But I never gave up on you. All I ask is that you give us a chance. We were happy, if I recall. And good for each other, when nobody else was."

"Anj, please . . ." Indris looked at the toes of his boots, hiding the doubts he knew would be written on his face.

She moved so close they almost touched. He stepped back, and found himself pressed against the wall.

"Laughing winds of revelry, will you relax? We've waited seven years. We've both been busy this year, with the Masters taking your time, and me away as often as not. What are a few more days for us to come to terms with where we are?"

"Thanks." *I need to know some "what," "how" and "why," before I think too much on "where." You have the answers to so many questions . . . but do I trust you to tell me the truth, whatever you've become, despite what you feel the need to hide?* He leaned forward to kiss her cheek, but she opened her mouth over his and kissed him hungrily. Her tongue tasted of honey, yet part of him sensed that it, too, was an illusion over a rancid truth.

As he took her hands and put them at her sides—more slowly than he should have; her hands were warm and soft and brought back another flood of memories of the sureness of her touch—Indris stepped back and felt his hearts break all over again. If not for the loss of her, then for the doubts he now harbored.

"There are some things I need to know, Anj. About me. About you. About some people I need to find—"

"Including your Avān?" Anj almost spat the words.

Indris frowned. "Including Mari, yes. Let me do these things; tell me what you know about my time on the Spines. Then you and I will talk about us."

"Very well," she pouted, kicking the wall with her heel, arms folded, head turned down even as she smiled dangerously. "Promise?"

"Would I lie to you?"

"Not if you're smart."

"Lucky for us both, then."

❊ ❊ ❊

Steam coiled about Indris's face as he relaxed in the hot springs, sunk so low that only his head was out of the water. Several other students and townsfolk had come to enjoy the water, dancing comically as they undressed in the chill, capering through the snow to plunge into the water. Indris greeted those he knew well, and smiled at those he did not, but all of them gave him distance as they huddled at the far end of the spring.

Indris altered his breathing patterns with the ease of practice and opened his mind. The thoughts of those nearby clamored in his head, quickly isolated and silenced. More distant thoughts were a whisper that he could listen to if he focused, but his telepathy was not so well tuned that it was simple. With part of his mind, he identified and isolated sounds: the chatter of the other bathers, the wind through the pine needles, the slosh of snow from overhanging plants, the players in the Black Quill who entertained the packed house. One by one he found the noises, and moved them aside until there was only—

"Chaiya?"

"Indris!" Her response was quick. *"Your mental voice is getting stronger every day."*

"Exercising it to speak with you since I got here has helped. Is there any sign of Mari, Shar, and Ekko?"

"Of Mari, no." Chaiya's voice was sad. *"But her soul is not with the dead, so I assume she is being warded by mystics. Wherever she is, people don't want her found. But I've heard the dreams of Shar and Ekko. They are sailing southward, with Morne Hawkwood and the Immortal Companions."*

"Do you know why?"

"I'm sorry, no."

"But they're well?"

"As best I can tell." Chaiya's presence in his mind was comforting. *"Their dreams are vivid, and filled with memories both joyful and heartbreaking. They think you're dead, Indris."*

"So I hear," Indris replied. *"It appears the Sēq have been loose with the facts about my untimely demise."*

"Should I enter Shar's and Ekko's dreams, and tell them otherwise?"

"No, though thanks for the thought. Best not to distract them, or tempt them to come looking for me. If they're with Morne, they must be

doing something dangerous. And more than likely reckless. I wish I were with them."

"Searching for Mari, perhaps?"

Indris smiled at the thought. *"There's nothing they can do for me here, Chaiya, and there are things I need to do before I leave. But I do need to leave here, as soon as I have the knowledge I came for. I'll wait a few more days before I finalize my plans."*

"Is there anything I can do for you?"

"Sing to me?"

"Of course, my friend." Indris counted the heartbeats before the gentle choral voices of the dead swelled in his mind, the intricate instruments of the soul that carried across the endless expanse of the Well of Souls.

"Thank you, Chaiya," Indris said as his eyes closed.

❇ ❇ ❇

The Founder's Deep was built into the rock wall at the high end of the vale, overlooking the long stretch of Amarqa-in-the-Snows and the township at the mouth of the valley. A tower of translucent quartz, the Deep was only slightly darker than the snow that huddled in the jagged cracks texturing its surface. Many sets of stairs and the confectionary glitter of *serill* bridges joined the Deep to the buildings around it, high enough to avoid the cold spray of the Anqorat River, if not the stinging spume that flew from it. Gnarled trees clung to the rock, dappling the quartz with swaying shadows.

Indris folded his hands in the sleeves of his over-robe as he walked across a rimed bridge. The jagged *ilhen* lamps that lined the bridge were fitful sparks in the light of the bright autumn morning. Along the ridgeline to the north, he saw the tethered shapes of wind-ships floating like kites. The guards who stood by them wore no livery Indris recognized, nor did the ships fly any of the colors of the Great Houses or the Hundred Families, or any of the consortiums of the Teshri. There were few who would willingly come to the Sēq in Amarqa, and Indris wondered who had been desperate enough to make the journey.

At the doors to Founder's Deep stood two Iku guards, their watchful round eyes set in cheeks like slanted cliff faces, their skin tinted in swirling colored patterns, and their short wings an oily black. A folding fan made of feathers with steel veins was thrust through each Iku's sash, and both had their clawed hands—wrinkled as chicken feet—wrapped around the hafts of chest-height, studded mauls. Indris had seen just how horrifying the kanbōjé—the "falling sapling," as the weapons were called—could be in the right hands. Legend had it that the Iku had been waiting for the Sēq when they first arrived in the forest valley, and had shown them the hidden halls and secret ways of the fortress that would later become known as Amarqa-in-the-Snows.

Both guards nodded respectfully as Indris approached, and he responded with a smile and a nod of his own.

"General Indris," one of the Iku trilled. She looked around, expression content as she took in the clear skies, mountains, trees, and snow that surrounded them. "Nice day for it."

"Aren't they all, Wakanhe?"

"That they are."

"Do you think it'll stay that way?"

"For some."

Indris passed under the jagged quartz lintel. The translucent walls of Founder's Deep admitted a cool, frosted radiance. Firestones set in black iron braziers cast pools of warmer light around the five tall galleries with their arabesqued black marble columns and floors. The Deep was a wide building, hollow from its high-domed roof down to its gravel-strewn floor, and dominated by a tall, eerily lifelike statue of Sedefke, the Founder.

Indris had asked Femensetri once, when he was still a novice, whether the statue was accurate. She had looked up at it with what the younger Indris had thought was love—though the older might say obsession—and said that it was as if the very man himself stood there, made huge in honor of the greatness of his body, mind, and spirit. The statue wore a small smile, as if Sedefke were considering a joke he was waiting for the rest of the room to understand. He wore the buckled cassock of the Sēq, hood thrown back, with a weapon belt buckled about the sash around his waist. A weapon hung there, or at least the hilt and pommel of a weapon, as long as the man's forearm. The pommel was carved into the likeness of a stylized dragon, or a bird of prey, the hilt covered in what may have been feathers, or scales. Yet there was no blade. Nothing to make the weapon a weapon.

The wise man never carries a weapon that can be used against him, Sedefke had been famous for saying, after he and the scholars had helped Näsarat fa Dionwē topple the Petal Empire. The wisest has no need to carry a weapon at all. His comment had led to the creation of the first psédari, the mind blades. Legend had it Sedefke had perfected the technique yet further, creating the kajari, or soul blade, a weapon that reflected the ternary nature of existence, and existed only by the manifestation of the owner's will. A weapon where the hilt and pommel represented the nayu, the shape of the blade was created by the psé, and the blade itself appeared only as manifestation of the kaj—a weapon that was not a weapon without the soul to make it so.

At the bottom of the stair, Aumh, Ojin-mar, and He-Who-Watches stood waiting. As autumn had strode inexorably onward, the butterflies had stopped coming to flutter in Aumh's fern-like fronds, the lush greenery that sprouted from her head and temples turning copper, now dusted with white as winter drew nearer. The flowers that once grew had fallen, leaving tiny brown seedpods. He-Who-Watches silently observed Indris's approach, his almost translucent eyes disconcerting against his dark, tattooed skin, his taloub loose about his neck.

Indris was led into a small anteroom with a single door leading out to the Master's Round. Through the door he could see the assembled Masters in their black cassocks, precious metals and gems for buttons. The Masters made their way to seats on tiers that stepped up and away from the open space at the base of the Round.

"What's this?" Indris asked Ojin-mar. "I thought I was coming here to have questions answered?"

"In a way," Aumh said with equanimity. The tiny Y'arrow woman poked her head out the door, then gestured for her fellow Masters to enter. She turned to Indris. "Raise your hood and don't let our guests see you. Look, listen, and learn. But under no circumstances are you to reveal yourself. Do I make myself clear?"

"Perfectly."

"Hmmm," Aumh murmured. She gestured for Ojin-mar to take Indris to quiet seats where he would not be noticed.

The Master's Round was a tiered well of black marble, each tier set with high-backed wooden chairs, all lacquered midnight. The domed ceiling featured a leaf-and-vine mosaic, from which hung a large *ilhen* lamp like an inverted orange and yellow ziggurat. There were faces from among the gathered Masters that Indris recognized, though more were unknown to him.

The first tier of the Round had ten chairs with black silk cushions on the seat, and glowing witchfire crescents rising from the carved wooden backs. Of the nine Masters who sat there, Indris recognized Femensetri, Aumh, and He-Who-Watches. The tenth chair was left vacant for Kemenchromis, the Arch-Scholar and Master Magnate of the Sēq Order who dwelled in Pashrea with the Empress-in-Shadows.

"Where's Zadjinn?" Indris asked. "I expected him to be all over me like a cheap robe, but he's not shown his face."

"Zadjinn, and those Dhar Gsenni of whom we were aware, didn't come to Amarqa after the Order was exiled," Ojin-mar replied. "I suspect they'll appear again when it's most inconvenient for us. They were always the most secular of the factions within the Sēq, and our isolation wouldn't serve them well."

"They may be gone, but who's that?" Indris nodded toward a strange figure, standing apart from the rest of the gathering. From what Indris could see beneath the iridescent cloak, the folds of which hung like wings and trailed on the floor, the figure was broad shouldered, but lean, wearing baroque armor of interwoven bands and sharp-looking scales. There was no skin to be seen under armor, voluminous cloak, or the spade-shaped, horned, and mirrored mask that covered his face.

Ojin-mar frowned. "Somebody you shouldn't have seen, and are best forgetting, if you know what's good for you."

"I can't believe you really said that," Indris murmured. "Let's assume, just for the sake of argument, that I didn't understand a word you just said. So . . ."

"I'm surprised you didn't give Femensetri a stroke when she was your sahai!" Ojin-mar rolled his eyes at Indris's expression. "We've not done right by you, but I didn't tell you this, should it ever come to light. The . . . whatever it is, calls itself the Herald. It, and a few like it, arrived almost seven years ago. It doesn't say much, but when it talks, the Suret listens."

"The Herald of what?"

"That's a bloody good question."

A low chime sounded and the Masters, some seventy in all—and there were still almost as many empty chairs—quieted themselves. Twin doors of jade-embossed *serill* opened, and four Sēq Knights and as many armored Iku entered, flanking a smaller group of Shrīanese in silk over-robes that swept the floor as they walked. Their hoods were raised, but Indris could see their heads turning left and right, up and down. The visitors were escorted to the center of the Round, where the guards left them before departing.

Indris recognized the rahns, and frowned at seeing them here.

A vulture-faced Master of the Suret inclined his head toward the visitors, extending his hand, the nails of his long fingers polished ebon. "I am Sēq Magnate Bodekian of the Suret. You have broken your fast and drank of our water, and are safe by all the laws of sende for so long as you remain at Amarqa-in-the-Snows."

"Tell us," a portly older man said, "why have you come so far to be heard? Since we were expelled from Shrīan we have had no interest in your affairs."

One visitor drew back her hood, exposing a sharp jaw and high cheekbones. Rosha was leaner than Indris remembered, almost gaunt. Her complexion had an ashen pall. She gestured to her companions, who revealed themselves to be Nazarafine and Siamak, looking equally worn.

"Masters of the Sēq Order of Scholars," Rosha began in a cracked voice, "we, the rahns of the Federationist Party, come to you because we need your help."

"Fah!" Femensetri said sharply. "The Asrahn and the Teshri made it perfectly clear the Sēq were no longer welcome in the Shrīanese Federation. I don't recall you speaking up to change their minds, girl!"

"Awakened rahns are irrelevant," the Herald said in what sounded like multiple different voices, each echoes of the other. "Only the Mahj, and the mahjirahns, are relevant." The sepulchral voices sent a chill up Indris's spine.

Rosha curled her lip at the Herald, but Nazarafine stepped forward before she could speak.

"The Imperialist sayfs control the Lower House of the Teshri." Her voice was hoarse and wet. "But even they begin to question the wisdom of following too blindly a man who will promise all, and deliver only what suits himself. The Asrahn is supposed to be the keeper of the people, not one who straddles their backs as if they were beasts of burden. Already there are abductions, and threats, and violence in our cities. Cesare, the Speaker for the People, has been assassinated. Your absence has left a great rift. And what the witches have—"

"This is none of our affair," Sēq Magnate Bodekian said.

"It could be, if you agreed to make it such." Rosha glared at the old Sēq Master. She gave a great wracking cough that almost doubled her over. Indris rose slightly in his seat, but Ojin-mar held him back, shaking his head.

"How so?" Femensetri asked, leaning forward like a bird of prey, her gaze intent. "And why would we care for the woes of an ungrateful nation?"

Indris's lips twitched in a smile. *Because you miss being the puppeteers, and can't wait to get your hands on the strings again.*

"Corajidin and his colors are not fighting a conventional war," Siamak said. "This is the precursor to Ajamensût, and we all know it. But rather than House against House, or Family against Family, it will be a civil war of assassins, the likes of which we have not seen in centuries! And there are . . . creatures among his ranks that baffle us. The witches have brought strange, unsettling allies with them. Corajidin's forces scour the Rōmarq, digging in the dust for weapons and forbidden knowledge! He has occupied my prefecture, ignores my demands to leave. He tries to provoke a violent response."

"We are beset on all sides, outnumbered and outmatched." Nazarafine's once ruddy skin was sallow, the plump cheeks sunken. "With each day, members of the Great Houses and the Hundred Families go missing. Intimidation has become the norm. And in your absence, self-serving groups have floated to the surface, like the alchemists and artificers, funded by the Banker's House and organized by the Mercantile Guild."

"You'll learn to find your strength where you can." Bodekian waved away their protests. "We've weathered this before."

"Not this," the Herald said. "You are unprepared."

"Corajidin has never been so overt," Siamak countered, looking at the Herald nervously. "This is an Asrahn who has folded back his sheets, and let any who would do his bidding climb into his bed."

"And now," Rosha added, "we offer a unique opportunity to redress what may have been a serious mistake."

"Go on," He-Who-Watches urged.

"Sayf-Ajomandyan, the Sky Lord, is prepared to call for a vote of no confidence in the Asrahn. The Secretary-Marshall and the Arbiter-Marshall are both in accordance. There is growing discontent in the Teshri, and we're seeing the formation of new political parties that may come to challenge the authority of our traditional leadership."

"But there's nothing self-serving about that, is there, girl?" Femensetri's legs were spread wide in her chair, elbows on her knees as she rested her chin on her fist.

"Of course," Rosha agreed. "But better to relieve Corajidin of his power too soon than too late. I would not see us descend into war, Femensetri."

"And who would replace Corajidin?" Bodekian asked.

"I'm the leader of the Federationist Party," Rosha replied with no attempt at humility. "And I'd respect the Sēq, just as my Ancestors did. After all, were the Näsarat not once counted among your number? My late cousin, Indris—may he know peace in the Well of Souls—was a hero of the Order who died for his people. Can't we find a common cause?"

Indris was about to stand, when Ojin-mar grabbed his arm.

Femensetri barked a laugh, and He-Who-Watches shot her an irritated glance. The Masters spoke among themselves, the crests of conversations breaking over each other. Indris drew back into the shadow of his hood, seeing the hungry looks on some of the Sēq Masters' faces. Conversations close by turned to the familiar topics of power and influence, with little regard to the consequences. Indris turned to Ojin-mar, who wore a worried expression.

"When did we lose our way?" Ojin-mar whispered.

"I've never known it to be different." Indris shrugged. "For an Order that's supposed to serve, educate, and protect, there appear to be quite a few of your colleagues interested in leading, controlling, and manipulating."

Rosha's cough sounded wet. Her arms went around her abdomen, and she spat a gobbet of blood and pus into the floor. Drool trailed from her lips as she trembled. By the time she regained her feet, the Round had gone quiet.

"But there is more, isn't there, girl?" Femensetri strode down, cassock snapping around her legs. The Stormbringer took Rosha by the chin, and stared into her eyes. She turned Rosha's head this way and that, and felt her pulse. Indris saw the discolored rash revealed when Femensetri rolled up Rosha's sleeve. The ancient scholar's mindstone flared darkly, became a whirling vortex that cast deep, sickly shadows across Rosha's skin. "You, and the others, you're dying."

"Yes," Rosha said simply. She gestured to Siamak and Nazarafine. "We all became sick about a month ago. And it's getting worse. We need your help, Scholar-Marshall."

Voices rose in hurried conversation as Femensetri gestured for the Sēq Knights and the Iku to take the rahns to the Thaumaturgeon's Hall, where they could be diagnosed and treated.

The Masters continued to debate their place in the new regime, clutching at the straw Rosha had given them. Even in exile, the Sēq had their hands on the fate of the nation, and Indris knew full well that the Sēq let go of nothing lightly.

"PATIENCE IS NOT A SIGN OF WEAKNESS. THERE COMES A TIME FOR ALL THINGS. TO WATCH, TO LISTEN, AND TO LEARN WHEN THAT TIME COMES IS FOUNDED IN BOTH STRENGTH AND WISDOM."

—Bensaharēn, Poet Master of the Lament
(493rd Year of the Shrīanese Federation)

DAY 53 OF THE 496TH YEAR OF THE

SHRĪANESE FEDERATION

"Erebus's teeth!" Mari snapped, as Qesha-rē probed the newly knit bones of Mari's left hand. As much as Mari disliked visiting the surgery, removing the resin-treated bandages that had immobilized her hand was a relief. The hatchet-faced old surgeon's examination, not quite as pleasant. "For the love of . . . Are you trying to stab me with your pointy little fingers? Is this what passes for the medical arts where you come from?"

"No," the surgeon said calmly, ignoring Mari's swearing as she bent the fingers this way and that, examining the nails and using a needle to jab Mari's fingertips to make sure no sensitivity had been lost. Qesha-rē's thin lips twitched as she massaged Mari's hand. "Why do you think I left Pashrea? A goodly number of Pashreans are Nomads, and already far beyond my ability to heal, even for a Nilvedic surgeon. You, however, are somebody I can treat, and Tamerlan is such a vile and violent place that my skills never atrophy. I daresay you'll keep me busy for some time to come, unless Nadir, Jhem, or the Dowager-Asrahn decide to give you to the sea."

"Dowager-Asrahn," Mari snorted. She took her hand back and shook it, making a fist and opening it over and over again. The fingers were stiff, with little more than a residual ache. Both would pass. The bruising had left the skin, though the hand was pale and thin compared to its counterpart. "That old shark is living on past glories. Don't know why my father indulges the malignant crone."

The healer cocked an eyebrow. "That may be so, my dear, but that old shark has her jaws around everything and everybody in Tamerlan, and you'd best not forget it."

"Including Vahineh." *Especially Vahineh.* "I take it she's still in your care?"

"If you mean is she still in Tamerlan, and is she still alive, then yes. Physically she's improved, but I'm sorry to say I doubt she'll ever be in the fullness of her mind."

"Can you get me into—"

"No."

"Please, just—"

"Stop asking," Qesha-rē said flatly. "The Dowager-Asrahn has been quite clear that none, save Jhem, Nadir, or those in their employ, are allowed access to Vahineh. I'm only permitted to ensure she stays alive. Do you know what they're doing to her?"

Trying to steal her legacy, and have her Awaken the Blacksnake so he, like Father, can be a shadow cast across everything they touch. "I'm not entirely sure. But it can't be good, whatever it is. I can help her, you know. Help her escape."

"Like I've seen you help yourself escape? Stabbing that old pervert Xerji in the eye with the nail from your bed was my favorite, by the way. Terribly sad he died from infection—"

"Not as sad that Jhem didn't."

"No. But, resourceful as you are, you're on an island in the freezing Southron Sea and the Dowager-Asrahn can make your life even more unpleasant. You may be able to survive what your grandmother does to you. But do you think Vahineh can?"

I'd smother the old bitch in her sleep if I could, Mari thought, *though killing her with a blade, so she could see it was me, would be better.* "Vahineh has been through enough, but I'm about as frightened of grandmother as you are."

"I'm terrified of your grandmother."

Mari chewed her lip, tempted to fall back on her default bravado. The surgeon had already seen Mari at her most vulnerable. Lies did not seem so appropriate. "As am I. But she'll never know that. I'll ride her shrieking soul to the Well of Souls like a flogged horse if I have to."

"Let's hope it doesn't come to that." The surgeon gestured for Mari to strip. Mari scrutinized herself in the mirror. Her body, always fit and lean, was now thin with protruding ribs and hip bones. Her muscles played under skin turned pink from the heat of the bathwater, but also mottled with old bruises, the red lines of welts, and the paler lines of old scars. Her cheekbones pressed against her skin, and her eyes seemed sunken in their orbits.

Qesha-rē walked around Mari. Peering. Poking and prodding and shaking her head. Muttering under her breath at the many wrongs on Mari's body that offended her. "You're fortunate to be in as good a condition as you are, given what you do for a living, and your treatment here."

"Being good at what I do for a living helps." *And having a lover who could sing mystic lullabies to me, and erase the scars that life has cut into me, then hold me in his arms until I fell asleep. Did Shar and Ekko manage to find you, Indris? I could use some help right about now.*

Qesha-rē stood beside Mari, and took her by the elbow. "If you keep defying your grandmother, she'll—"

"I know." Mari took a couple of steps closer to give her reflection more substance. She had no intention of fading away in this Ancestors-forsaken pile of rocks on the edge of nowhere. "But if I stay here, I'll die anyway. I'd rather my end be on my own terms, and maybe give the Dowager-Asrahn some pause. Besides, I may just get off this dung heap."

Bound-caste servants bustled into the surgery, carrying folded clothes and a small box filled with glass jars. Qesha-rē spared the servants a brief glance, and gave Mari a faint cautionary headshake. Mari knew well enough that her grandmother had ears and eyes everywhere. That lesson had come the hard way when her first escape attempt was betrayed by a fellow imprisoned relative she had foolishly confided in. Nadir and his crew had caught Mari trying to board a wind-galley. She had been dragged back, trussed like a bird for roasting. Her own grandmother had watched, silent and stern, as Nadir had beaten a shackled Mari bloody with a manta ray tail. Mari had fought back when they had released her, splitting Nadir's lip before they beat her unconscious. That had been Mari's fourth day on Tamerlan. Breaking the fingers on her hand had simply been the latest of the Dowager-Asrahn's attempted lessons in obedience.

"There's a celebration on tonight," Qesha-rē said as she put her instruments back into her bag.

Mari stood still as the servants rubbed light oils into her skin, then began scraping away the hair from her torso and limbs with strigils. Their hands were steady and sure, leaving no new marks on Mari's already marred skin. "I've been told I'm to attend."

"I'll be spending the evening in, I think." The surgeon buckled her bag shut and slung it across her narrow shoulder. "Some meditation and reading will do me good, and I've a book by the Nilvedic Scholar Amapursha on the healing practices of the Y'arrow-te-yi that will be fascinating."

"Nothing I can do to tempt you?"

"Not a chance. Besides, the Dowager-Asrahn's entertainments often end up with somebody needing to visit my surgery—if they survive—so it's best I remain where I can be prepared. Try not to get yourself hurt again, my dear. You never know, you may actually find having no broken bones, or cuts from the whip and the rod, quite delightful."

"Oh, you know me," Mari said dryly. "I'm a free spirit."

"This isn't the place for it."

"I couldn't agree more."

❊ ❊ ❊

Mari sat at the high table, and she watched, and she listened. She ate voraciously, but drank only water from the chipped earthenware bowl that made everything taste a bit like mud.

But mostly she sweated. She felt it prickle her scalp, dew her brow, and trickle down the curve of her spine where it pooled at the small of her back. In each of the four walls, fires burned in hearths so large Mari could stand in them. Tall windows of rough glass perspired in the heat, melting the snow outside where it tried to stick to the iron window frames. Hundreds of lanterns in sea-hued glass hung from the domed ceiling. The skeletons of gigantic sharks hung among the lanterns amid the silver- and gold-plated skulls of fallen enemies. The mosaic walls seemed to ripple, giving Mari the impression she was trapped beneath the sea with the drowned, who continued to drink and dance and fight, unaware they were already dead.

The guests at the Dowager-Asrahn's feast were a raucous, mongrel crowd of hard-drinking cutthroats and opportunists, mixed with the rough and ready leaders of the nearby fishing villages and mining towns. Tamerlan was, as best Mari could describe it, a frontier fortress. At one time it had no doubt been glorious, this ancient construct of faceted quartz and polished marble, carved granite and bronze domes that spiraled up and around the mountain. Now Tamerlan attracted those who had nowhere else to go: those too world weary, disenfranchised, or steeped in failure and infamy to be anywhere else. Even the Sea Witches sworn to the Dowager-Asrahn—pale and hungry-eyed, stern in their layers of blue and green and black like deep-sea shadows—seemed poor and rough in comparison to the stark pride of the Sēq, or the red witches of the Mahsojhin.

Mari looked on with barely concealed disgust as the Dowager-Asrahn's colors hooted, shouted, and stamped their approval of the fourth duel of the evening. Two men and one woman were dead already, their bodies given back to the deep to be consumed, as was the custom in Tamerlan. The Dowager-Asrahn's captains and lieutenants moved among the crowd, inciting their hunger for blood. By any other standards, they were common bravos that could be bought for a handful of copper rings, and a lukewarm meal, in the backstreets of any city in Shrīan.

Chief among them was Jhem the Blacksnake and his cohort. The wounds Mari had given Jhem after he and Nadir had taken her prisoner had turned septic, almost killing him. Sadly Qesha-rē had saved his life—at the expense of some of his jaw, the teeth that went with it, and part of both lips. When he was seen in public, it was only with a leather half-mask, studded and scaled, that covered his disfigurement. In reprisal for Jhem's mutilation, as well as for the death of Ravenet—Jhem's daughter and Nadir's sister—her father's two servants made it their mission to make Mari's existence a misery.

Nadir, doubly stung by Mari's refusal to rekindle their lost love, took great pains to torment Mari whenever he could—but it was not without cost to himself. Tonight he slouched on a chair next to the Dowager-Asrahn with the pained expression of a man who had been soundly kicked in the stones. And so he had been, when he had come to Mari's chambers earlier that evening, along with three of his bravos, to give her some bruises before the feast. Nadir was the lucky one: He was still alive. Mari would apologize to Qesha-rē later for giving her the added work.

I'll take your crew away from you, one by one, Mari thought. *And as I plant each one of them in ashes, know that it's one less person between me and your final, humiliating end. When the day comes, when you're alone and friendless, your reputation as dead as anybody who followed you, I'll open you up from stones to throat, and leave your steaming corpse on a midden heap. Right beside that worm you call a father . . .*

A raucous shout caught Mari's attention as a defeated warrior was hurled into a large hole in the floor lined with twisted old blades like the teeth of some iron shark. It was called the Maw of Savajiin and was part threat and part promise to those who displeased the Dowager-Asrahn. It also formed part of what passed for entertainment at Tamerlan. Tonight the entertainment was for Eladdin—the Dowager-Asrahn's own son by her last, late husband—a young man who had not yet reached twenty-five years. Eladdin was celebrating his becoming one of the Exalted Names of Shrīan the only way Tamerlan knew how.

Eladdin, the Sidewinder as he was now named, could almost have been Belam's brother, but where Belam was golden, Eladdin was made of bronze: a little cruder, a little more tarnished. He stood beside the Maw, his long red-blond hair tied in a high ponytail, his eyes like chips of tourmaline. Sweat poured down his torso, shimmering on ridges of muscle. Two long-knives, each with a coiled snake in silver worked into the hilt, were thrust through the sash at his waist. He had already killed three men this evening, hurling their bleeding bodies into the Maw to feed the sharks that circled below.

The Dowager-Asrahn leered at her son from the high table. She threw a handful of silver rings into the air, careless of where they fell, so intoxicated was she by death and drink. The Shark of Tamerlan had seen her centenary come and go decades before. Her eyes were wide and fevered, her mouth hung open to reveal a row of sharpened teeth, light glimmering from a small trail of drool at the corners of her thin, wine-stained lips. She gripped her golden drinking bowl, the plated skull of a treasured enemy, in one liver-spotted hand. A beauty in her day, time had hardened her. Jutting cheekbones. Flinty eyes. A coronet made of a shark's jaw, set with sapphires and gray pearls, sat on her wispy hair. Even her wrinkles looked sharp, as if to run your hand along them the wrong way would open your skin. Her relatives sat to her left and right, stretching in a glittering row to the very edges of the high table, with Mari seated at the far end on a chair that creaked with every move she made. *Even her bloody chairs talk about every move I make!*

Most of the other familial inmates of Tamerlan kept their distance from Mari, no doubt for fear of punishment by association. From time to time, the Dowager-Asrahn's favorites—hard and beautiful—would risk a glance at Mari. As the daughter of the Rahn-Erebus, Mari lived a privileged life with freedoms the others could only have wished for. It appeared to give her gathered relatives some comfort that she had fallen from grace.

The Dowager-Asrahn summoned Eladdin to the high table, then took a flanged iron ball in her hand—the symbol of her authority in

Tamerlan—and started to hammer it on the wood. Those in the Hearthall took up the beat, stamping their feet, clapping in time, or chanting "more" over and over. Mari barely contained her disgust as warriors, already baffled with drink, glared around the room with murdering eyes. She knew it would not be long before more would draw steel and kill, or be killed, for the Dowager-Asrahn's favor.

A man stepped forward, tall and broad, moving with predatory grace. He was relatively new, come from some sun-warmed country from the look of his tanned skin and streaked hair and beard. Mari leaned forward in interest. This one was not like the others. He might have been handsome once, but years of the sun—as well as the scars that crossed his cheek and oft-broken nose, vanishing like furrows into his short beard—had robbed him of that claim.

The nahdi looked around the circle of warriors, all of whom almost trembled with battle fever, before he pointed at the largest fellow in the room, a bullish man, his squared head set directly on vast shoulders. He was the captain of the ragtag Southern Fists Company, come to Tamerlan for the winter. The nahdi who made the challenge spoke with a lilting accent Mari was unfamiliar with. "I'm waiting for you. But not too long. You'll regret it if I have to come looking for you."

Mari froze, the words reminding her of her farewell to Shar, Ekko . . . and both Hayden and Omen, who had been killed. Guilt and sorrow threatened to swamp her. *Indris, if you only knew how sorry I am—*

His opponent gave a stentorian bellow. He stood and upended a mug of beer, most of it washing a face that was already largely covered in beard, dirt, and scabs. The captain bellowed again, drawing a wicked hatchet from his belt. The Dowager-Asrahn screamed in delight as her man charged forward, feet pounding.

The first passes of weapons were fast and brutal, a complex weave of steel and flesh. Weapons and sweat glittered under the lanterns. The audience stamped and shouted and clapped louder, a few even adding brassy horns to the tumult. Neither of the men was a warrior-poet, nor had they the styles of any of the sûks that Mari knew of. Their fighting was brutal, sourced in battlefields, pitched chaos, and savagery.

Like waves against a cliff, both men smashed together, then parted, then hammered into each other again. Again and again in a shrinking spiral of brutality that saw blood and sweat fly. Mari sat on the edge of her seat, ignoring the idiot commentary of her family. There was something about the new nahdi's style, a glimpse here and there in his footwork, or the angle of an overhand strike . . .

Then the captain charged forward, axe a blur, moving faster than his fatigue should have allowed. But the nahdi stepped in, rather than away. He gripped his antagonist's wrist with one hand, then punched his knife through the man's forearm with the other. Turning his back into the circle of the captain's arms, the nahdi swung down and pierced his enemy's thigh, then swung his head back to smash into the captain's face. Calmly he slid forward, and turned to face the captain as the man fell to one knee, nose and teeth splintered. Slowly the bull rose to his feet and staggered sideways, lowing in pain. His hand spasmed open and the hatchet dropped to the red-streaked floor. There he stood, swaying, dripping blood, and waiting for slaughter.

Rather than end his opponent, the nahdi bowed his head, wiped his knife clean, and stepped back. Another man dashed forward—a lieutenant of the Southern Fists—with a raised maul, ready to smash in the head of his captain, and secure his own promotion. But the nahdi grabbed the lieutenant by the wrist and the scruff of his neck as the man dashed past, spinning him around and hurling him into the Maw. The lieutenant screamed as he was lacerated on its iron teeth, the sound becoming a forlorn shriek as he fell into the depths, bleeding food for sharks.

"Coward," the nahdi said dismissively. He sauntered to the edge, carefully picking his way through the sharp sword blades around the hole in the floor. Leaning over, he spat, then said, "If you want to come back up and finish it, I'll wait. But only for a bit. I'll keep a light on."

Mari felt a smile stretch her lips. She tried to catch the nahdi's eye but he had already returned to sit with his companions, who were markedly more disciplined and sober than the bravos around them. She searched, unsuccessfully, for a familiar face among the man's hard-eyed crew. *Surely they've been sent to find me? Are Shar and Ekko also here? Or Indris? She warmed at the thought. How else could the nahdi know the last words I spoke to my friends?*

Members of the Southern Fists came to help their bewildered captain. The Hearthall resounded with derisive laughter, and shouting. The Dowager-Asrahn seemed satiated by the display, emptying her wine bowl, then refilling it to the brim. Mari saw the drunken flush beneath the sweat on the old woman's cheeks. The shark leaned closer to Eladdin, face lit with drunken avarice. When her emaciated hand rested on his bare skin, the Sidewinder's lips curled, then became a hasty and appreciative smile. Eladdin then stared at Mari, his smile widening, his look suggestive. Mari gave an exaggerated but heartfelt shudder.

Turning to Dhoury, a bug-eyed cousin with a soft doughy face, flowering gin blossoms, and thinning white hair, Mari asked, "Do you know who that man was? The one that fought the captain of the Southern Fists?"

"Hmmm?" Dhoury blinked at her, squinting as he tried to focus. Of her relatives at Tamerlan, he was one of the least odious, and most like a friend. Mari had to grab her cousin by the chin and point him in the direction of the man she was referring to.

"Him! Do you know who he is?"

Dhoury frowned with concentration . . . then farted. Mari

almost choked on the stench, leaning back to breath marginally fresher air. The cloud wafted away, causing others at the high table to swear, gag, or both. With a dreamy, self-satisfied smile, Dhoury said, "I think I heard his name was Hawkwood. Marn? Mern? Morne! Morne Hawkwood."

Servants brought guests steaming platters of grilled fish and octopus. A larger platter carried by four tense servants was placed before the Dowager-Asrahn, who grinned in delight. With an ingratiating smile, Nadir removed the shield-sized cover from the platter to reveal a roasted torso and head.

Mari's stomach churned in disgust. She held her hand to her nose, hating herself for the way the smell reminded her of roast pork—even to the hint of apple, thyme, and garlic—that made her mouth water. The taste of the saliva in her mouth made her want to vomit.

Nadir took a small axe and caved in the chest of the cooked torso. The Dowager-Asrahn gleefully reached into the cavity and carved out the hearts, one of which she dropped steaming onto Eladdin's plate, the other she kept for herself. The Dowager-Asrahn then took her preferred cuts of meat, before having Nadir cut portions for himself and those favored ones nearby. The torso was then handed to carvers, who sliced away filets that were passed down the high table to the less-favored family members. Only those most deeply in the Dowager-Asrahn's thrall set to their food with anything resembling enthusiasm. Beside her, Dhoury stared at his plate in horror, jaw clenched.

"You don't have to eat it," Mari whispered to him. The young man picked up his knife and fork in trembling hands. "Dhoury, don't!"

"And become like you!" he almost wailed in misery. He hesitantly cut his meat, eyes fixed. "You rebel and you rebel and we've all seen what it gets you! There is no refusing her, Mari! You either swim with the Shark of Tamerlan, or are eaten by her."

"Sharks die, like everything else."

Dhoury leaned in close and hissed in her ear. "Shut up! She'll hear you. Grandmother hears everything! Grandmother already hates me! I don't need your help in making it worse."

"How can it get worse?"

"She can offer me to the Deep at the Sea Shrine!" Dhoury's bloodshot eyes widened, and he took a swig of his wine. "She's already threatened me with it unless I improve. Old hag says that if I weren't of the Blood Royal, I'd be completely worthless."

"You're a damn sight better than these degenerate halfwits." Mari nodded down the table. "If they come for you, come to me."

"I doubt they'd give me time to run, Mari. And you? Have you forgotten your whippings, or being locked in the Tidal Cage, or the broken bones . . . ? Mari, do you want to die?"

"Once, yes," she admitted.

Mari was about to take Dhoury's plate away and damn the consequences when she noted conversations dying around the Hearthall. Jhem had arrived, gliding through the crowds in his high-collared coat and over-robe of black snakeskin. His masked face turned neither right nor left as he made his way to the space before the high table. Beside him was a tall woman, folded in the swirling thunderhead of her cloak. She was dressed like a Seethe, her frayed clothing tied together with strips of cloth. The blade at her hip was sheathed in jade-tinted *serill*, flecked with red, the hilt wrapped in skin, the pommel in the likeness of a blackened jade octopus. Mari felt a rush of cold as the hooded face turned in her direction, which passed as soon as the other woman looked away. The Dowager-Asrahn's colors gave the woman speculative glances, even called out a few raucous comments, elbowing each other and laughing.

"Sayf-Tamerlan." Jhem's lisping voice was sepulchral from behind his mask, his ophidian eyes dead as stones. Mari's father's Master of Assassins gestured to the woman beside him. "This is the

Emissary. One of the Asrahn-Corajidin's closest advisers. She has come to speak with you."

The Dowager-Asrahn held the cooked heart in her hand and took a large bite. She chewed with her mouth open, a gnashing of pointed teeth and bloody flesh. She swallowed, then wiped the blood from her mouth with the back of her hand. The old woman did not stand to speak. "My son takes counsel from Seethe bitches now, does he? How much further can he fall, Jhem? I will not have this daughter of a degenerate race in my home. Take it out of my sight and give it to the sea. Perhaps my mewling son, who pretends to rule a nation, will choose more wisely next time."

"Khurshad of the Savajiin," the Emissary said in a voice like an iron bar being bent on itself. "You would do well to keep your tongue behind your teeth, and show respect for those greater than you. How is it that you've forgotten those who protected you, guided you and your family down the centuries? Let me remind you . . ."

The Dowager-Asrahn's eyes rolled back into her head, back arching like a bow stave. Her body trembled and glistening bubbles of spittle frothed at the corners of her mouth. Wheezing, struggling to breath, her head lolled from side to side.

The episode was over as suddenly as it began, too quick for anybody to act. The Dowager-Asrahn stumbled from her chair, tottered from the dais on which the high table stood. The skirts of her floor-length silk coat spread behind her in folds of blue and silver, black and red, like bloodied sea foam. She came on uncertain feet to cast herself facedown at the feet of the hooded woman. With trembling hands she reached for the filthy hem of the Emissary's cloak, drew it to her lips, and kissed it. The Emissary stepped back fastidiously, drawing the cloth from the old shark's grip.

"There are those who remember the oldest of ways," the Dowager-Asrahn said in an awed voice. "We still hold to the secret rituals and festivals, and remember the dreams sent to us by She Who Writhes in the Deep, the Black King of the Woods, and the Storm Rider. The Heart Which Burns in the Night—"

"They, and others." The Emissary turned her hooded head, surveying the room. Mari felt the gaze linger on her again, a cold thing that seemed to peel away skin, muscle, and bone to reveal the soul within. The moment passed, though this time warmth was slower to return. "It's good that you remember. Needful, that you remember, so we may do what must be done. There is a Feigning to come, Khurshad. And you have the means for it under your roof. One of your own blood will once more become the progenitor of something new, to last the ages. I will need this of you before too long."

"All I have, and more. Please accept my apologies, and the apologies of all my line. Long have I desired this. Make Tamerlan yours, and when you are ready, tell me how best I can serve you to repay what we have been given."

All were silent. Even the roaring fires seemed chastened.

The Emissary looked down on the Dowager-Asrahn for a long moment, her face obscured by the shadows of her hood. Finally she reached down and helped the old woman to her feet, for now that was all she seemed to be: an aged, frail woman, her best years behind her and her future one of decline. The ruler of Tamerlan shouted for people to feast, and drink, and take what pleasures best suited them, all the while looking adoringly at the woman who called herself the Emissary.

Mari rose from her chair, skin crawling at the thought of anybody, or anything, that could turn the Shark of Tamerlan into what she had just witnessed.

3

"HATRED AND THE MONEY TO MANIFEST IT CAN BE TWO OF THE DEADLIEST WEAPONS A PERSON MAY HAVE."

—Zamathuri, Principal of the Banker's House of Masripûr, 11th Chepherundi Dynasty (494th Year of the Shrīanese Federation)

DAY 54 OF THE 496TH YEAR OF THE

SHRĪANESE FEDERATION

"Every effort is being taken to find these criminals!" Corajidin's voice cut across the din in the Tyr-Jahavān. "I counsel you to patience until we have evidence of—"

"Evidence?" Hadi sneered, his jowls florid with anger. A stalwart of what remained of the Imperialist faction, the older man pointed a trembling finger at Corajidin. "The Iron League has been sniping at us for years. They terrorized us at our New Year's Festival. They tried again before we could vote in our new Asrahn. I say they're the ones who are abducting our loved ones! Tear their embassies apart!"

"Little good it would do you," Ziaire said. "The crown had not even had time to flatten Asrahn-Corajidin's hair before the Ambassadors of the Iron League, the neutral nations, and Pashrea all made themselves scarce. Would you take your unproven vengeance out on a building? Go to war on masonry, perhaps?"

"You of the Peace Faction would do well to remember who it is that protected us from the ravages of the Mantéans!" Karim was a merchant sayf and owner of several pleasure palaces, a pretty man beloved by, and the lover of, a string of influential women and men. Nix, in his anonymous role as head of the newly formed ban-kherife, had informed Corajidin that Karim was high in the ranks of the Malefacti. The syndicate of organized criminals had proven to be surprisingly good allies, undertaking work with which Corajidin could not be involved. Karim sneered at Ziaire. "Asrahn-Corajidin saved us all!"

"This is all well and good," one of the sayfs quavered. "But I want my sister returned to me! Where is the Kherife-General? She should be here to answer our questions."

"She has been missing for some time," Ajomandyan said. The Sky Lord rapped his cane against the floor with a sharp crack. "We have lost many, not the least of whom the Speaker for the People, found savaged and bloodless by the High Weir. And in that time, these so-called ban-kherife, the Asrahn's secret police, have done nothing to—"

"I'm certain the authorities are doing all they can!" Nix said. The little man brushed his greasy hair out of his eyes with a twitching hand. Those sayfs nearby put subtle distance between themselves and the murderer. "We've all lost people. Even the Asrahn has family missing—his daughter, Mari, vanished since the new year. And our friends Jhem and Nadir. But the ban-kherife? From what I understand, they're doing everything the common kherife corps has been unable to do."

"Then why aren't they stopping the murders, Nix?" one of the counselors yelled. "Bodies drained of blood. Some torn apart. We've heard stories of people being found in barrels, their bodies shredded! That's Iron League malice! Nomad malice!"

"Nomads come from places other than Manté," the drunk Martūm slurred on cue. The rahn-elect teetered on the edge of his seat, held up by the latest of his courtesans. "We've ignored Pashrea for far too long! Perhaps we need to turn an eye, and our spears, southward?"

"But the shredded bodies!" Hadi snapped. "That's Mantéan strife! They call it scaling. A body is placed inside a barrel—lined with blades, and filled with razors, nails, and other items both sharp and unpleasant—and thrown down a hill, waterfall, or rolled into a fast river. This is not a Shrīanese punishment."

"Hadi speaks truly," Nix replied. "I've seen it done in Manté. Now somebody is doing it here."

Corajidin hid a smile behind his hand as counselors raised a din, demanding the return of family members, or loved ones, and investigation of the Iron League threat. The insinuation that Pashrea may be involved. It was not the cohesive support for action he had hoped for, but some people were casting their paranoia in the direction he wanted. Counselors gathered in their respective factions, clamoring flocks that went to roost among those who shared their political views. The factions needed to be reeled in before they became accustomed to their political freedom.

Before Corajidin's Accession to the seat of Asrahn, there had been but two parties: the Imperialists and the Federationists. There were always the unaffiliated sayfs willing to be lured to causes aligned with their self-interest, but these were never organized. Since the new year, more political parties had been formed than Corajidin had ever heard of before. Now there were the Freelancers, a collection of wealthy sayfs with strong investments in nahdi companies, organized by Bijan. The Trade Consortium was spear-headed by the gray leech, Teymoud, and sought to band together all the tradespeople and merchants, controlling commodities and their prices. The Lantern Party, started by the witches Corajidin had freed from the Mahsojhin, wanted the eminence of the witches in government restored. As there were no witches as sayfs, they threw their collective will behind young Estelya of Yadhas, who thought herself a promising mystic. There was the Peace Faction. The Unity Circle, the Torchlight Society . . . groups of sayfs backed by those of the middle-castes and their new money and agendas.

The rahns acted as anchors for the parties to hold fast to and so maintain the illusion that the Imperialists and the Federationists still wielded the balance of power. Yet the rahns were absent, which in itself was worrying. Corajidin did not trust Roshana and her allies when he looked them in the eye, let alone when they were conspicuously absent. Only the parasite Martūm, Vahineh's regent, was in attendance. The wastrel was clad in more expensive clothes and jewels each time Corajidin saw him, new courtesans ever in his company. Rahn-Narseh was confined to bed with an illness. With the Federationist rahns absent, it had fallen to Ajomandyan, Ziaire, Bensaharēn, Kiraj, and Padishin to consolidate the opposition to Corajidin's attempts at moving Shrīan onto a war footing.

The abductions of influential Avān had delivered a common threat—as Corajidin had predicted it would. The murder of the Speaker for the People had been advantageous in removing an opposing voice, and leaving an influential office vacant that Corajidin could dangle before those who curried favor. Fear had transformed the counselors into individuals to be bargained with as their self-interests allowed, forgetting the bonds of politics in favor of bonds of blood. Such fear distracted the Teshri from examining too closely the events of the New Year's Festival, and Corajidin's complicity in them. Yet there were still tongues prone to wag. Some of the witches were disillusioned with their lot in the new world and muttered tales to those who would listen. Huqdi, the street dogs bought and paid for to assist in the carnage, had long spent their silver rings and now looked for more to keep their silence. Corajidin turned a cool gaze on the inebriated Martūm, who pawed feebly at the embarrassed courtesan by his side. Martūm had proven he was only as good as the shine of the gold in his pockets, only ever a payment away from spilling inconvenient truths. *It is past time I closed the chapter on the Great House of Selassin*, Corajidin thought. *Nix can have him scaled as an example to others . . .*

Ajomandyan had taken the floor, the Sky Lord flanked by his grandchildren Neva and Yago. Ajo was everything a sayf should be, and stood as an eagle among gulls.

"Since his rise to the highest office in Shrīan, the Asrahn-Corajidin has done little to still the unrest in the country. Indeed, we have more internal strife than at any time in living memory." Ajo leveled his gryphon-headed cane at those around him. "While I feel for those of you who fear for the ones you love, let us not be distracted by the other events we have endured. Let us not hesitate to question truths we accepted so blithely. There are those of us who maintain the Asrahn's involvement in the events of the New Year's Festival—" Shouts rang about the room, both in support and in denial. Ajo motioned for silence as more voices joined in, each new speaker trying to drown out the one before. It was Padishin who wrangled silence with the hammering of his sheathed dion-esqa on the marble floor. Ajo continued unabashed. "As we suspect the Asrahn and his ban-kherife are involved in our current strife."

"We are all of us dismayed at recent events," Padishin said into the silence. Where Ajo flies, the Secretary-Marshall is not far away. "But let's not forget that we are here to speak for the nation. If we suspect something is wrong, this is the forum for it to be discussed."

"It's not only the abductions and murders of our citizens, but the political rivalries that are tearing us apart." All eyes turned to Ziaire as she rose to speak. Corajidin watched in bitter admiration as the Prime of the House of Pearl—and the leader of the Peace Faction—controlled the room. The most famous courtesan in Shrīan positioned herself on the edge of a bar of sunlight: enough for her pearlescent robes and green eyes to glow, contrasting with the obsidian darkness of her hair. "We need the kind of leadership that unites us, not divides us."

Corajidin hoped his smile was not a sneer as the counselors nodded, or clapped, at Ziaire's speech.

Ajo, too, was moved. Face solemn, he appealed to the Teshri in a strident voice. "As much as it pains me, we need to consider a vote of no confidence in Asrahn-Erebus fa Corajidin." Ajo's words were like knives in Corajidin's ribs. "If Corajidin cannot lead us, cannot protect us, then I suggest we find somebody who can."

Corajidin fought hard to unclench his hands as the tumult rose around him.

✳ ✳ ✳

The Weavegate deep in the abandoned halls of the Qadir am Amaranjin oozed radiance the hue and texture of infection. Rather than shine, the light from the Weavegate poured, and clung, curving about objects—or lancing through them. There was the faint wailing of cyclone winds rushing across the cracks in a window. Shadows grew bolder, dark fingers stretching toward Corajidin and—

Soldiers barreled out of the Weavegate, voices muttering imprecations, and the tail end of screams faded into whimpers as warriors found themselves in a place better than the one they had traveled. Corajidin noted their wild-eyed looks, the waxy skin, the glimmers of spittle on slack lips. One of the soldiers fumbled with the buckles of her helmet, but too late, as she spewed through the narrow slit in the faceplate. The woman made an awful, defeated noise as she crashed to her knees to void her belly.

Far too few soldiers emerged from the Weavegate—all of them battered and bloodied—before Sanojé, Nima, and Belamandris raced out. Sanojé was panting, bleeding from a number of shallow cuts. She chanted the quick hex that closed the Weavegate behind Belamandris. Nima hurled the broken haft of his broken sword-staff away. The Widowmaker looked sadly at what remained of his crew with a dour expression that did not fit his face.

Corajidin counted the number of Anlūki that had returned. Of the thirty that left three hours ago, there were but ten remaining.

"What happened?" Corajidin asked. Belamandris stared at him for a moment, as if struggling to recognize his father. The weary-looking Anlūki checked each other for wounds, and called the roll.

One of the Anlūki stood alone, blood dripping from his hands. His body spasmed, head twitching. His mouth opened and closed like a fish gasping for air. A malicious expression crossed the warrior's face. Corajidin took a step back, breath freezing in his throat. The warrior's skin rippled as something moved under it.

Sanojé shouted for everybody to stand back. Belamandris drew Tragedy, his other hand gripping a heavy knife with a hilt guard shaped into steel knuckles. The silvered blade was marbled with black veins: salt-forged steel.

The Anlūki started to shriek, his hands going to his head, pounding against his temples. Belamandris swept in, smooth as silk on the breeze. Tragedy swept through the Anlūki's neck, severing the head. Belamandris's dagger punched through the warrior's armored chest, left and right, piercing both hearts. After Belamandris moved past, Sanojé's voice crackled like burning logs. The wounded Anlūki was lit from within, fire lapping from the rents in his armor, his body engulfed in tongues of flame. From within the body came a bloodcurdling shriek.

A translucent thing, part lobster, part scorpion, part nightmare, scuttled from the warrior's neck. Its clouded chitin was cracked from the heat. It trilled through a sphincter mouth filled with needle fangs. Sanojé pounced, wrapping her tiny hands around it. She muttered another hex, and the monstrosity lashed and writhed and burned until it was reduced to putrid ash.

"What was . . . ?" Corajidin asked numbly.

"The kind of thing you pit me and my crew against, every time you send us through the cursed Weavegate!" Belamandris glared at his father. "I rue the day that Kasraman showed it to you! Worse, that you ignored the warnings about its dangers, all so you could—"

"It's a straggler from the Drear, my Asrahn," Wolfram interrupted. He stared at the ash morbidly. "A parasite that, like so many other creatures from there, must live off of us to thrive."

Belamandris rubbed his face briskly. "What have we become, Father? Are you so driven by your destiny that we forego all bonds of sende, or common decency? You have me and my crew warring, abducting innocents—"

"The times are what the times are, Belamandris. Though I am Asrahn, there are those who would oppose my plans for the nation." *And keep me from what was promised by the oracles! I must regain the trust of the Teshri if I am to become the Mahj that destiny demands of me.*

"Hence the need for powerful allies, such as the Emissary can bring," Wolfram said bitterly. "But we should, perhaps, rethink our course and those to whom we turn for aid."

Belamandris came to Sanojé's side, the two of them checking each other for wounds with an intimacy in their touch that made Corajidin scowl.

"It is time we discussed our next steps," Corajidin snapped, beckoning to his son and Wolfram.

"Including how to best use your hostages?" Belamandris muttered.

"You have an opinion?" Corajidin asked sharply. "A better strategy, perhaps, to get us the strength we need?"

Belamandris lingered at Sanojé's side as Corajidin headed to the door. He turned to speak with her, but Corajidin interrupted. "If I'm not intruding, Belamandris? Your witch and the Anlūki can see to themselves. As of this morning, time is a luxury."

❊ ❊ ❊

"Do not use that tone with me!" Corajidin warned, hand trembling with rage as he pointed at his golden son. A fire blazed in the hearth of his sitting room in the Qadir Erebus, the stained-glass windows turning the afternoon sun to thick beams of bloodied amber.

"What tone should I use, Father?" Belamandris sipped from his third bowl of black lotus wine. "Can you tell me I'm wrong? You want a War of Assassins? Then use assassins! The Anlūki are—"

"Better?" Kasraman said with no sign of mockery in his voice.

"Yes!" Belamandris's tone was iron. "At Amnon I allowed myself to be used in Vashne's murder, because I was led to believe it was a necessary step toward a greater goal."

"And now?" Kasraman asked.

"Look at what we've done, at what we're doing, for Erebus's sake! Some of the Anlūki are warrior-poets. The rest are high-ranking swordmasters. Some have earned their Exalted Name. We've a measure against which we judge ourselves, Father. The traditions of the daishäri were never intended for stealing people from their beds, ambushing travelers, or abducting children to be held against their parents bending to your will. Sende tells us we don't make war on the innocent, and you make a mockery of it every time you send me through the Weavegate."

"And who is an innocent in this day and age?" Corajidin countered. "Why this sudden resistance? You have always been the good . . ." *Son.* He trailed off, seeing the sudden stiffness in Kasraman's expression. Belamandris looked at his older brother with sad fondness before he spoke again.

"Jhem, your Master of Assassins, and Nadir are useless in Tamerlan. We need them here doing what they're supposed to be doing. Part of which is fighting your unsanctioned war and not keeping Mari a damned captive—another thing we need to talk about."

"Your sister's predicament is of her own choosing. But are you seriously blaming the Blacksnake and Nadir for your failure?"

"The Anlūki I killed at the Weavegate was only nineteen years old, Father. If we'd had accurate intelligence rather than just blundering through the Drear—"

"You are blaming others, then."

"We were reliably informed," Belamandris said slowly and evenly, "that Sayf-Yoseq of Kashmar, his wife, and children, were traveling the Faladin Road between Tyr and Näs-Sayyin with a small personal guard. He was going to be invested as the new Prefect of the city, sworn to the service of the Näsarats."

"And?"

"When we arrived, that small personal guard happened to be a score and a half of the Lamenti, led by Bensaharēn himself. And I expect they didn't want to expose old Yoseq to danger, so for laughs there were four squads of the Lion Guard, Father. Twenty of those big bastards all armed to the teeth and eager to let our insides out. We were lucky as many of us survived as we did—"

"Really? One old man, thirty of his students, and some mongrels from the Taumarq drove the great Widowmaker and his Anlūki away?"

Belamandris looked at his brother for support. "Is it just me,

Kasra, or is there no talking to him these days? Seems Mari saw things clearly."

Corajidin bristled. "So. You not only failed me, you—"

"Were outmatched by some of the best warriors in Shrīan—and no, Father, neither I, nor even Mari, are a match for Bensaharēn the Waterdancer on our best day. The rubbish intelligence we had only added height to the steaming turd pile we had to climb. If it weren't for Sanojé opening up a way for us to get out, we'd all be dead or imprisoned.

"And that's another thing. We're even more at risk using the Weavegate than we are fighting your battles. Sanojé says that the more we use it the more we stir the Drear up, and the more the things that live there are likely to notice us. Each time we use it, more of my crew report troubling visions and nightmares. They can't sleep, barely eat—"

"Father." Kasraman held up his hands in a calming gesture. "Belam has a point. The Emissary warned us, all the witches warned us, and I warned you, that the Weavegate was not to be used lightly. We've other means at our disposal. And how can you expect Belam and the Anlūki to execute these missions without the proper intelligence, unrested, and plagued by the visions traveling the Weavegate gives them? Every time you send them out they've no idea what they'll be facing."

"Or if we'll arrive, or who we're fighting, or how many . . . ," Belamandris muttered. He took another sip of wine, then rolled the dewed bowl against his forehead.

"It's true, Asrahn," Nix said from where he was stabbing one of his knives into the tabletop. Corajidin looked at the mad little assassin sourly. *I'll need to get that table sanded and polished. Again.* The greasy lengths of Nix's fringe fell over his eyes as he spoked away at the wood. "Not the bit about not doing it. I'm fine with that. One thing I learned in Tanis is that all politics is red work.

But the Blacksnake is next to useless in Tamerlan. Free me up from leading the secret police so I can take the role of—"

"That will not be necessary!" Corajidin smiled at Nix, taking in the man's fishbelly skin, trembling fingers, and twitching eyes. He remembered Nix's delight in chaos. The little man eyed Corajidin darkly, but held his tongue. "Until Jhem returns we need to continue taking hostages from among the families of those I need to control. You are doing well as the Knight-General of the ban-kher-ife, Nix, anonymous as the role may be. Fear not. Soon enough I will have you step from the shadows into a more public role."

"But scaling?" Belamandris grimaced. "Isn't that a little gruesome, even for you? And what about these other murders? Bodies drained of blood and torn apart. We need to set boundaries somewhere."

"Such are the times," Nix said. "We need to make people so afraid they feel they have nowhere else to turn. Abductions, murders, thefts, threats . . . It's all in a red day's work for my crew. When the time comes, we'll not need to point fingers at the Iron League: I'll have left a trail of evidence so obvious the blind could follow it. The Teshri will beg us to go to war. I've found the Soul Traders to be a great help, and they're keen for an introduction, Asrahn. They're a grisly bunch, but both my father and I have dealt with them for many years. They can be surprisingly helpful, and have access to assets beyond us."

"Pashrea first," Corajidin said. "We need to unite the Avān first." And appease the Emissary. "As for the Soul Traders, Nix, I want you to cease all dealings with them. They are an abomination, and I will not be beholden to those who harvest the souls of the dead for their own aims."

Nix lip curled, and his color rose. "But, Asrahn—"

"Do as you're told, Nix, or you will find yourself outside of my good graces."

"So there are some lengths to which you won't go? I'm surprised.

You damn us all with this, Father." Belamandris finished his drink and stood. He put the wine bowl down with an audible click, tapping his finger against its rim. "We're all of us riders in this suicidal race of yours. It's only a matter of time before we slip, and are trampled."

"Is the Widowmaker afraid of doing his duty to his Great House?" Corajidin regretted the words as soon as they left his mouth. *Have you forsaken me, you, the child I love above all others? Will you, like your cursed sister, lead us to the brink of ruin?*

"Afraid?" Belamandris snorted. "I'd not given the word a great deal of thought until you brought me back from the lip of the Well of Souls. Until you released the witches and made bedfellows of those you should revile. And again, more so, when you started relying on the Drear, and losing sight of what we should be holding as sacred. Yes, I suppose I am afraid, Father. Not of my duty, which I'll always do, but of where that duty is taking us."

Belamandris turned to the door, shoulders slumped with fatigue.

When Corajidin spoke, his voice carried more venom than he intended. "Are you off to the bed of that Tanisian girl, that filthy daughter of Nomads? You were raised for better!"

Belamandris paused, but did not turn. "If you mean Sanojé, no. I'm going to make sure the Anlūki are getting the care they deserve after fighting your battles, while you sit here safely. It's what a leader does, Father." Corajidin drew in a breath to speak but Belamandris shook his head, reaching for the door handle. "I'd not. We've shared enough words that can't be unsaid for one conversation. Besides, it'll be no great revelation how far your hypocrisy goes. You need a different mirror than I to see what you've become."

Corajidin clenched his teeth, white-knuckled fists rapping on the tabletop as the door closed behind his son. He looked at the others in the room, but they turned away, silent.

✱ ✱ ✱

Corajidin stood by the tall windows of his office. Heavy drops beat a rapid tattoo on the glass, forming thick rivulets that trickled down to pool on the sill. The sky was a uniform gray, dull as an old shield, with tiny scratches of light where the sun tried to break the cloud. His breath fogged the glass, despite the firestones that warmed the room. Fog, too, coiled about the monochrome streets of Avānweh, strands of it blending with the platter of the Lakes of the Sky, flattening the world into a bland expanse.

The contents of the reports in his hand were as expected. Corajidin idly scanned the missives from Master Baquio of the College of Artificers and Master Prahna of the Alchemist's Society. The institutions had reproduced and made available for sale scores of inventions, potions, and other useful items. Chemical light globes, healing salves, improved metallurgic techniques, and plans for new and more terrifying siege weapons. However, their progress where it mattered had been uninspiring. A full season almost over and the Torque Spindles remained still. Such phrases as *close to a breakthrough, ongoing testing,* and *promising results* no longer encouraged him. Banker's House, too, were proving recalcitrant. They knew Corajidin was building for war. Knew he needed additional funding. Between themselves, the Mercantile Guild—and their newfound political aspirations under Teymoud—and the consortium of trades from the middle-castes, they were on a course to extort the Crown and State for all it is worth. Unpalatable as their business dealings were, Corajidin's investment would pay off in time. Across Shrīan the industries of violence worked in preparation for the war that would unite the Avān under one monarch, then arm them for their journey of conquest.

Seated at another desk in his office, Mēdēya penned notes on a small mountain of paperwork. Dressed in layers of damask silk, his latest wife frowned at columns of names and numbers as she chewed the end of her ink brush. The frown was little more than a faint line on otherwise unblemished, burnished skin. Her eyes were almost black, her long curls so dark they had a bluish tint. In Pashrea they would have called her Yashamin-Mēdēya, and welcomed her for what she was. Here in Shrīan she was Mēdēya, Corajidin's scandalously young fourth wife. There was little or nothing left of the original Mēdēya save her body—had not been since the Emissary traded one soul for another in the sycamore grove overlooking the Mahsojhin. She was younger, differently alluring than before, and seemed to be Yashamin in most ways. And yet . . . somehow not. As much as Corajidin wanted to welcome his wife back into his heart, there was too much about Mēdēya that was not Yashamin. Caught in the nets of his doubts, he could not call her by that name, which would not taste the same. She looked up, sensing his scrutiny, and smiled.

Ignoring the call of desire, Corajidin sat at his desk. He took an ink brush in hand and had begun writing his response to the artificers and alchemists when a knock at the door caught his attention. Kasraman and Wolfram entered, expressions troubled. Wolfram handed Corajidin a scroll, then took a step away. Corajidin spared a glance at the green and silver seal of the Great House of Kadarin, before cracking it open.

He tapped the missive against the tabletop. "When did this arrive?"

"Mahav, the witch appointed to the Great House of Kadarin, arrived not ten minutes ago from Kadariat," Wolfram said, leaning on his wretched old staff.

Corajidin desperately wanted a drink of something stronger than tea. "This letter is from Pah-Kadarin fa Anankil. He says that Rahn-Narseh took ill almost thirty days ago, and that no treatment seems to work. This at least explains the vague excuses for her not being here to help us in the Teshri. You'll find the symptoms interesting." Corajidin handed the parchment to Kasraman, where he and Wolfram pored over it.

"How did this happen?" Wolfram asked. "You were the first person to present with these symptoms!"

"That's not exactly true," Kasraman said. "Father, do you remember when you were at Amnon, I mentioned that there might have been a way for you to remaster your Awakening?"

"Vaguely." Corajidin had significant gaps in his memory from when his illness was at its worst and playing havoc with his mind.

"There were references to something that matched your illness in one of the diaries of a Sēq Lore Master, sworn to our House before the Scholar Wars." Kasraman paused, clearly choosing his next words carefully. "You were focused on wringing Ariskander's secrets from him, so I did not pursue this any further. Recently though I found mention of it in Grandfather's journal."

"Ancestor's teeth!" Corajidin swore. "My father knew about this?"

"Grandfather died from it," Kasraman said flatly. "He did not last so long as you, but the early symptoms are there. Like you he hid it from the world. Unlike you he didn't find a solution in time."

"None of us ever knew," Corajidin mused. "Father sent us away long before it was obvious he was that sick. Have we any intelligence on whether this afflicts the Federationist rahns, also?"

"Nothing, Asrahn," Wolfram said. "The last we knew the Federationists were ensconced at Narsis. Rarely have we been able to get an operative in there, and when we do they get discovered and disposed of quickly."

"Find out." Corajidin leaned back in his chair, fingers drumming on the tabletop. He felt the comforting weight of the potion nestled in a pocket of his embroidered silk coat. "Call it my urgent need to know. And find me the damned Emissary! I want some answers."

Kasraman and Wolfram nodded, leaving Corajidin to his musings.

Mēdēya stood by the window, a shadow against the glare. "If this is more widespread than Narseh," she said, "the death of the rahns could work in our favor."

She sidled across to where Corajidin sat, her over-robe sliding off her shoulders as if by its own volition. Quick motions of her fingers and her trousers likewise slid down, leaving her in her silk tunic: revealing nothing, but promising everything. She straddled him, fingers entwined in his hair. She smelled of aloe vera and apple. He felt the warmth of her, an almost fever heat, burning through his clothes. Corajidin's lips opened involuntarily, his tongue resting against his teeth. *Ancestor's teeth, she is like elemental desire!* His hearts beat faster with passion as much as a lingering fear of what she was. *This is not the woman I loved and lost. There is something at once more . . . and less, to her.* Like the other deals with the Emissary, this, too, seemed tainted. The Sēq Order, for Belamandris. A stranger, to bring back what he had hoped was Yashamin. And to come, the toppling of others' thrones in order to ensure his own.

"You were talking of the rahns," he breathed into her mouth.

"They aren't necessary for you to become Mahj." Her voice hummed against his throat as she leaned in close. "You can be father of the empire without them. Wasn't that foretold, my love?"

Corajidin allowed himself to melt into her, his inner voice of caution little more than a cry from another room. Her sure hands slid his coat from his shoulders. What Mēdēya said was true. Those same hands reached insistently for the buckles of his trousers. *But why was Narseh sick?* There came the sharp ricochet of ruby and gold buttons as she tore at his tunic. *And why now?*

Mēdēya moaned low in her throat as Corajidin frantically cleared a space on the desk for them, reports falling to the ground, forgotten. Mēdēya took his earlobe between her lips, lightly massaging with her tongue. His hands wandered, lips tracing a warm track down her neck, then her torso, as she urged him downward.

"And Vahineh." Mēdēya gasped, the muscles in her abdomen twitching. He watched as gooseflesh stippled her skin. "Her road needs to end at my hand, as mine almost ended at hers. Give her to me, my love. Give her to me, and I will give you . . ."

Intoxicated by her, all he did was nod.

"Truths can change like the clouds in the sky, as the wind of fact blows them into more meaningful shapes."

—Zienni proverb

Indris ached, sweating from his labors in the Manufactory. With three of the forges and two of the athanors working, the place was sweltering, the air seeming to stick to his skin. He stood and stretched, letting the hammer fall to the anvil, flexing his tired hands.

His drawings hung as layered panels moving sluggishly in the hot air, backlit to reveal a layered three-dimensional view. Above him the completed fuselage for the *Skylark* hung by chains and pulleys from the iron girders that crisscrossed the ceiling. The windskiff looked like the giant glass skeleton of a falcon, with additional struts in the wings and tail. The pilot's gimbal had been installed, as had the mountings for the Disentropy Spools and the Tempest Wheels. It had taken more than a month to construct by himself, in what hours were left to his own devices after he worked with the Masters and spent what had been fruitless hours in the library.

Calming his mind with a quick breathing exercise, Indris used his improving farsight to inspect the contents of the athanor, the specialized furnace removing the impurities in the thaumaturgic gold, silver, and bronze he needed for the circuits of his new Tempest Wheels. Flicking his mind across to the forges, the *serill* sheets and spars were almost done: There were no drakes at Amarqa-in-the-Snows, but the mystic forges generated the heat necessary to make drake glass. Indris dropped his metapsychic vision and called upon his psychokinesis to gently lower the *Skylark* to ground level. As the skeleton settled in to its cradle, Indris took up some of the *serill* panels he had finished, and the vanes of alloyed thaumaturgic metal, and swept them into place with his mind. Just like any other muscle, or skill. The more he practiced, the stronger he became. And since arriving at Amarqa, Indris had taken every opportunity to practice.

"So this is the secret you've been keeping, boy?"

Indris spun, prepared to flee rather than let Femensetri mine his mind for his newfound skills. But she was not looking at him: Rather, her attention was fixed on the *Skylark* as she fanned her face, perspiration beading her brow. After a short bout of cursing, she crooned a canto that surrounded her with a pale nimbus. The redness faded from her features, perspiration vanishing.

"It's loud in here," she observed. "And too bloody hot."

"It's the silence I can't stand"—*because it reminds me of the voices of friends I can't hear anymore*—"and the heat doesn't bother me. What do you want?"

"Relax your sphincter, boy. I was curious what you were up to." Femensetri rested her fingers on the golden vanes that would make the feathered wings of the *Skylark*. She admired the way the light brought out the different colors in the *serill* and the elegant shape and unique design of the flyer. Femensetri stood before Indris's schematics, tracing them with a dirty, broken nail. "It's beautiful. You've been busy."

"Not a great deal else to do while you're holding me hostage."

"Don't start." His former sahai glanced around the Manufactory at the other projects Indris had been working on. "Show me."

Indris leaned against the anvil and gestured for her to help herself, knowing she would anyway. Femensetri closely inspected Indris's other projects. A suit of *serill* scale armor that, save for the final etching of the last glyphs, was compete. A round shield likewise plated with *serill* scales and likewise enchanted. Indris had no doubt Femensetri noted the Maladhoring glyphs on his work and was grateful she did not ask who had done them. She probably suspected it was his own work and was saving him the trouble of lying when he denied it, or her the embarrassment of appearing to be foolish by believing him.

Femensetri picked up a long witchfire staff. The staff changed color from red, to blue, to purple as she moved it around. Radiant motes shone at the heart of the hexagonal blade. Her fingers ran across the tight, neat rows of Maladhoring glyphs that ran along its length, as well as those in High Avān, Seethe, and Hazhi'shi. The latter elicited a surprised grunt. She gave Indris a sideways glance yet kept her silence. There was also a new storm-pistol there with an eight-bolt chamber and a larger bore. Femensetri hefted it, aiming it at a random target.

"Heavy bastard, isn't it?" she asked, putting it back on the table amid the neat rows of bolts Indris had forged for it. "Never was any good with the damned things."

"After Amnon and Avānweh, I figure I needed a bigger gun." Indris nodded to his handiwork. "That'll do for now."

"And these?" She pointed to a few fist-sized spheres.

"Mockingbirds," Indris said. He took one of the spheres and twisted. The hemispheres shifted, and the device began to tick.

Once the two halves reached their original position, the mocking-bird emitted a loud metaphysical wail that reverberated on Indris's Disentropic Stain. "It's for traveling the Drear. Should keep the locals off my back until I get where I need to go."

"I like those!" Femensetri said. "Looks like you're getting ready for a trip. Typical of you that you made a Scholar's Lantern, rather than a crook. You could be a Master by the end of the day if you—"

"I've more work to do, so if you've—"

"I don't like the distance between us, Indris," Femensetri said. "Since Avānweh we've not been as close as we once were."

"And you're surprised?"

She looked over her shoulder, the opal-hued eyes glowing in the light. "I trained you better."

"We are where we are. Every time I believe I can rely on you, you teach me another lesson in futility. Knowing you is . . . instructional."

"Get over it, boy!" Femensetri leaned on her crook, thrusting her chin at Indris. "People use people, the same way we use words, tools, or weapons. You were trained to lead, to rise above, to persevere and be victorious! And I made damned sure you did it better than anybody who had come before."

"And what if I wanted more?" Indris's voice was soft. "What if I wanted to be something . . . other than what you and others had planned for me?"

"Better?" she jibed.

"Different."

"You don't understand!" Femensetri shook her head. "You're not like the others. Nothing like the others, then or now. Indris, we were promised somebody we could follow—" She cut herself short. Indris may have imagined it, but it looked like her hands were trembling.

"Who promised?"

"I've already said too much."

"Then why are you here?"

"Isn't it always the way? We need your help if we're going to save the rahns."

"Right." Indris let the word linger. "And that worked out so well the last time you asked for my help. I'd think you've all the help you needed right now."

"Not by half. You're the only Sēq alive who's been fully Awakened."

"I wasn't fully Awakened."

"Close enough," Femensetri countered. "Your insights may save Shrīan's leaders."

"Every Sēq has been Awakened," Indris said. "It's how we become scholars."

"Yes, we're all Awakened to some degree, but it's not the same as that with a rahn. We've not undergone the Communion Ritual, or Unity—"

"Nor did I."

"But you've had the soul of an Awakened rahn virtually merge with you." Femensetri's face betrayed her wonder and irritation. "You know things we don't. None of us have your experience!"

"No. You don't." Indris turned his attention to the *Skylark*. "Was there anything else?"

Femensetri's knuckles were white where she throttled her crook. "We're treating the rahns with doses of the Water of Life, but it's only a placebo."

"You've seen this before."

"Just come with me, Indris. Otherwise, important people who can make a difference to the future of Shrīan will die much sooner than is convenient. Including your cousin."

Including my cousin. "Not the most compelling reason given our recent history, but I'll come and see what might be done."

❋ ❋ ❋

The upper valley of Amarqa was a faceted, almost haphazard sculpture of crystal towers fused with carved rock faces. *Ilhen* lamps glowed behind stained-glass windows. Streams shone with crescents of moonlight, while snow-laden trees and shrubs bent their heads. Across the valley, a jagged crystal finger pointed into the glittering sky, an obdurate shadow made darker for the stars about it. The Eibon Hoje, the Black Archives of the Sēq Masters. It was the place where the great secrets were kept: thoughts that had raised nations, words that had toppled thrones. Artifacts considered too dangerous for the world, the scribblings of insane oracles and doomsday prophets, and the inconvenient truths of history, all locked away from prying eyes. If the knowledge Indris sought on the lost mental disciplines was anywhere outside of the Pillars of Sand, it would be in the Black Archives.

The two scholars wound up a narrow stair, a jagged thing burned into the rocks, which passed both through and up the cliff face. Indris was glad for the brief respite in those moments when they were out of the pummeling wind. They passed through an ornate iron gate, the fretwork glimmering with ice crystals. A narrow bridge led to a set of backlit doors, where a squad of Iku stood guard. They hopped out of the way as Femensetri walked past them, one remaining to open the door for her.

The tower had no more than a half dozen rooms, guarded by Tau-se. Paneled glass lamps washed the Pashrean rugs with dusty light. Indris followed his former teacher into an oppressively warm suite, the heat slapping him in the face. Short pedestals filled with firestones were placed around the walls. The room had a peaked ceiling, painted with intricate arabesque designs in blue and gold, fiery phoenixes circling each other. Iron couches with overstuffed pillows and blankets surrounded a small table, littered with books, inkpots, brushes, and journals. A well-worn copy of *The Manifold Duty*, the second volume of the Zienni Doctrines, lay facedown beside a half-empty glass and an empty carafe. A four-stringed Ygranian cielé lay in an open case, parchments covered in sheet music stacked nearby.

Femensetri gave Pah-Näsarat fa Tajaddin a curt nod as they passed each other, she entering the bedchamber as he was leaving it. "Excuse me, but my sister is . . . Indris?" Taj stared at Indris. Indris had the best of his elder siblings' features: handsome as Nehrun, but with the planes and angles of Rosha's lithe strength. Above the plain coat and trousers in the blue and gold of his Great House, his over-robe was the voluminous plain gray of the Zienni ascetics, frayed at the collar and cuffs, and travel-stained around the hem. The hilt of a long-knife, shaped like a golden and sapphire phoenix head, poked from the folds. Taj's pale brown eyes widened as he stared at his cousin. "You're—"

"Not dead, no." Indris smiled at Taj. He was surprised to find it felt genuine. "Sorry to disappoint."

"Oh, far from it!" Taj came forward and threw his arms around Indris, who clumsily returned the gesture. "I'm glad you're here! Between Rosha's illness and the friction at court, a friendly face is more than welcome. But we were told you were dead! Your friends looked for you for—"

"You know where Mari is?" The words tumbled out. "Shar? Ekko?"

"I know where they were. The Seethe woman—Shar—and Ekko came to Narsis a few weeks into the new year, demanding an appointment with Rosha. Poet Master Bensaharēn and I met with them, since Rosha refused. Your friends are persistent, Indris: They'd walked out of the Dead Flat, across half of Shrīan, and through Näsarat knows how many raiding parties to find you. When we told them . . . told them you were . . ."

"Dead?" Indris said flatly. He looked to the doorway where Femensetri now stood, her expression blithe. "You only knew what you were told, Taj. But where did they go?"

"They stayed in Narsis for a couple of weeks. I think they were looking for some of your old comrades from the Immortal Companions, so they could go looking for—"

"Mari." Indris finished for him. He took a deep breath, hands shaking.

"And that's a name you'd best forget, boy." Femensetri gestured to the bedroom with a jerk of her chin. "Remember why I brought you here."

"I'm not likely to forget the circumstances that brought me here," Indris muttered. But he joined her regardless, pausing at the door. "Taj? Do you know whether they found anybody to help them?"

"Bensaharēn offered a few of his senior-year warrior-poets, but Rosha put an end to that. I heard that they managed to find a nahdi called Morne Hawkwood? Apparently he had a crew down from the Conflicted Cities, via Masripûr. No idea where they are now. Last word was they'd killed a couple of squads of Anlūki in Avānweh, before they traveled east."

Indris nodded, but could hardly keep the smile from his face. *Morne!* He laughed, a short, cold bark. Femensetri scowled at him. "What's so funny, boy?"

"Depends on who you are as to whether you'd find facing Morne Hawkwood funny or not."

"Fascinating. Now get in here."

Rosha was sitting in a plush chair, bundled in layers of clothing with a sheepskin rug over her lap. The rahn was reading, her face pale and drawn. She glanced up at Indris as he crossed the distance between them, her jaw dropping at the sight of him, the book slipping from her slack fingers.

Hayden and Omen might still be here, were it not for you. Mari . . . Indris's face felt hard, and there was more than just a flicker of warmth behind his left eye as he damped down his jhi-reflex. What he saw was a sick rahn, the symptom of a failing nation. Or, more accurately, it was the other way around. What was it the Herald had said, when Rosha and the others arrived? Awakened rahns are irrelevant. Only the Mahj, and the mahjirahns, are relevant.

"Well?" Femensetri said as the cousins stared at each other.

"Well what?" Indris said.

"Don't test me on this, boy! We need the Federationist rahns to oppose Corajidin!"

"Do you really?" Indris mused. "I don't think so. It wouldn't be the first time the Sēq have stepped up to manipulate a nation, or courses of events. You could take the war to the witches right now."

"And possibly lose!" Femensetri slammed her crook on the ground. Thunder crashed. The *ilhen* lamps flickered, as great storm clouds of shadow brewed around her, and lightning arced in her hair. "Now see to your cousin, like you were told."

Indris came to Rosha's side. She had not spoken a word since he had arrived, the fear in her apparent. He murmured, "I should put you down for what you've done—"

"Indris!" Femensetri snapped. "Open your mind to me, so we can—"

"That's never going to happen." Indris shook his head.

"Do it!"

His smile at Rosha was a thin thing. "Looks like you might be out of luck, cousin. From what I hear, the best the Sēq can do for you is to make you comfortable while your body rots away in agony, and your mind starts to tear itself apart. Until then maybe they'll find an answer." He looked over his shoulder at Femensetri. "Or maybe they won't."

Indris walked toward the door, but Femensetri blocked his way with her crook. "And where do you think you're off to?"

"I'm tired, and I've a lot of work to do."

"Fix her. And the others."

"I don't know if I can, and I certainly won't be doing anything with you in my head. The choice is yours, but it's my way, or no way. And there's a price to pay before I lift a finger to help her or the other rahns."

"You can't be serious!"

"As the civil war that's brewing."

"Then what?" she sneered. "What's the price of patriotism this time?"

"*Faruq yaha,*" Indris swore as he stepped around Femensetri and walked out the door.

"Don't turn your back on me, boy!" his old teacher thundered as she stamped after him. He felt the hairs on his head and arms rise from his skin in the static of her jhi-reflex. His eye began to burn, washing his vision in flame. Taj gave a strangled curse and bolted for Rosha's room, closing the door behind him.

The two scholars faced each other: Femensetri's form wreathed in turbulent shadows and flickering lightning; everything around Indris drying, browning, curling, and smoldering. Flames licked around his fingers.

"What's happened to you?" Femensetri asked. Indris felt tendrils of her thought trying to grasp his mind, but they burned away before they could gain purchase. Her eyes narrowed dangerously.

"You happened to me!" he said. "The Sēq happened to me. The Spines happened to me. Sorochel happened to me. Anj . . .

Mari . . . But it's your lies and broken promises that happened to me most recently. Price of patriotism? Honesty would be a nice bloody start! You holding up your end of an agreement would also help."

"You'd let your own cousin die? The Indris I trained would never turn his back on family. Love was part of your problem in the first place."

"Perhaps some lessons have sunk in, neh? There're only so many times you can abuse trust before it runs out. And you've run out, old teacher."

"I could wring what I want out of you!"

"What?" Indris snorted. "How much success has that bought you so far? None! And it'll continue to bring you none, because you, like I, have no Ancestor's damned idea what happened to me, how to fix it, or even if it can be fixed!"

The two stared at each other, sparks flying, flames starting to spread, the air becoming stagnant. She could kill me. Indris felt the bubble of his newfound abilities swell in his head. Unbidden, plates and saucers began to rattle by themselves. Femensetri cast a surprised glance around the room. Within seconds, the furniture began to shake, and the *ilhen* lamps sang like fingertips around the lip of a wineglass. She stared at Indris, measuring, before she took a step back and shuttered her jhi-reflex. Indris maintained his for a second longer, trying to shut down the different parts of his mind that wanted to release pent-up frustration, anger . . . and sorrow.

Indris wrestled his mind and spirit back under control, until he was left trembling. He and Femensetri stared at each other across the short distance between them, the emptiness filled with words that, if said, could never be unsaid. It was Indris who stepped back, and Femensetri who broke the silence.

"What's the price for your help?"

"Before I do anything to help you, or the Suret, I want access to the Black Archives."

"How many different kinds of fool do you think I am?"

"Very few, truth be told. But that's my price."

"And who's to say you won't just piss off once you have what you're after?"

"I suppose that this time around, you'll need to trust me."

5

"WHAT WOULD YOU CHANGE IF I TOLD YOU THE INEVITABLE WAS NOT?"

—from *Counting the Sands of Time,* by Kobaqaru, Zienni Magnate to the Serpent Princes of Kaylish (490th Year of the Shrīanese Federation)

DAY 56 OF THE 496TH YEAR OF THE

SHRĪANESE FEDERATION

Waves pounded, the foam slinking away from the jagged rocks that bucktoothed through the churn. Across the circling arms of the black stone breakwater that fenced off the bay, ships rocked on the rolling tide. The sky, a torn mantle of cloud in shades of backlit iron, lead, and pewter, smelled of rain, and worse weather besides.

Mari finished her drink in a single gulp, then slammed the bowl onto the balcony rail, where it dislodged a layer of rime. The warmth of the alcohol settled pleasantly in her belly.

"Dhoury, we can help each other." Mari leaned forward and rested her hand on her cousin's shoulder. She cursed quietly when he flinched. "If you can get me my weapons, I can get us away from here. You said it yourself—our grandmother hates you."

"She hates you more." He looked up at her miserably, his unhealthy pallor marbled by bruises. He rubbed his soft hands together, fingers working like thick sausages. "Mari, you're a constant challenge to her authority. Nobody talks back to the Dowager-Asrahn, or Eladdin. You risk us all with your defiance."

"I'll take you with me, Dhoury. I promise. But unarmed I'll be brought down and end up in the surgery, or worse. I'm no expert on the South, but I figure once winter sets in, there're few ships of any kind willing to ply sea or air to get off this dump. Once the season turns, we're stuck here." She grabbed Dhoury's chins and lifted his head, but he would not look at her. Mari slapped him in the face to get his attention. It was not a hard blow, but it startled him. *Good! There was even a hint of anger there! Something I can fan into flame!* "You wanted to survive? Then help me to help you."

The doors to the balcony opened and two of the Dowager-Asrahn's Savadai, the elite guard of Tamerlan, with their shark-leather armor and short tridents, gestured for Mari and Dhoury to come inside. As Dhoury scampered back indoors, partly under threat of the guards and no doubt partly for the warmth of the hearths inside, Mari clamped a hand on his shoulder. She leaned in and said so that only he could hear, "Time isn't our friend. I can show you a better life than this."

Once inside they went their separate ways: Dhoury ambling down one of the torchlit corridors deeper into Tamerlan, while the two Savadai gestured for Mari to precede them down the glassed-in halls that led to the Dowager-Asrahn. Woolen rugs were strewn on the floor, islands of softness on a sea of grim stone. The four hearths in the room were lit, enough to take the edge off the cold but not enough to be comfortable. For a woman raised in the sun, every day in Tamerlan was a constant reminder of how mean the place was.

Musicians played in one corner: lute, theorbo, deep-voiced pipes, and drum playing a mournful dirge perfectly suited to

Tamerlan. At the far side of the room a colorful assembly of the Dowager-Asrahn's nieces, nephews, and grandchildren chatted and laughed over bowls of steaming wine. A few of them looked at Mari disinterestedly. Others whispered, pointed, or giggled. Servants in thin tunics plied the Dowager-Asrahn and her guests with food from seashell trays and wine from rough crystal decanters.

"Mari." Nadir rose from his seat, listing slightly. Mari noted the jug of wine on the table and the empty bowl. Nadir gestured to a seat on the opposite side of the table from Jhem, Nadir, Eladdin, and the Dowager-Asrahn. The Emissary was a bruise with folded arms in the shadows between two windows. A squad of the Savadai stood guard nearby. Mari remained standing. One of the Savadai approached her, hand extended to put her in the seat, until Mari's gaze stopped him in his tracks.

The Dowager-Asrahn grinned, her filed teeth spotted with brown stains, her skin folding like a fan. The old shark speared strips of raw flesh from a glazed seashell, her bony fingers tipped with pointed nails painted a deep blue. She popped the food into her mouth and chewed with obvious pleasure.

"What do you want?" Mari asked.

"You need to learn some manners, cousin," Eladdin the Sidewinder said from where he lounged nearby.

"You can try to school her if you'd like," Jhem lisped. He looked on Eladdin with dead eyes, a snake eyeing a rat. "But you know how well that's worked out for people in the past, and it wouldn't be much different for you."

"I'd just take my time, is all," Mari said as she slowly settled into the chair.

"Mother!" Eladdin whined. The Dowager-Asrahn's eyelids twitched in irritation. When he spoke, the words tumbled over each other. "Let me show our cousin how things are done here in the South."

"Be still, Ela." The Dowager-Asrahn waved her son down. "There will be time enough for demonstrations. The Emissary has asked to inspect Mariam and now is as good a time as any."

"Inspect?" Mari did not like the sound of the word at all. "I don't think so."

"You are in Tamerlan, girl. If I want to parade you like chattel in the Hearthall, then I will, and there is little you can do to prevent it."

"You'll do no such thing," Mari said. "My father would—"

"*Would what?*" The Dowager-Asrahn rose from her chair and prowled toward Mari, her sea-colored over-robe flowing behind her. As she approached, her long nails clacked together like scissors. "Corajidin is a fool. Was he the man I tried to raise, a man who embraced the old ways, you would never have turned your back on your duty, or shame yourself in the bed of our enemy! You will do whatever you are told. Be thankful I do not give you to the sea!"

Mari stood and looked down at the old woman. The Dowager-Asrahn bared her sharpened teeth and Mari winced at the reek. The old shark clawed at Mari, who slapped the woman's sharpened nails away. With a snarl, the Dowager-Asrahn slashed at Mari again. Mari gripped her grandmother's wrists and squeezed.

The old woman screamed, "Help me, you idiots!"

Movement in her periphery and Mari pushed her grandmother back. She fell across the table, limbs flailing. Eladdin and Nadir approached from the left, the Savadai from the right. Grabbing her chair by its leg, Mari spun and bashed it into the faces of the Savadai in a powerful stroke. The chair broke into kindling and the Savadai went down as Mari turned to face Eladdin and Nadir, the splintered end of the chair leg still in her hand.

Eladdin drew his long-knives, blades glittering. Mari allowed him to stab with one, angling her body so the blade missed. He changed the angle of his attack. Mari felt the acid sting of the blade as it opened the skin over her ribs. The attack brought Eladdin close. She smashed the chair leg hard across his face, breaking his nose and splitting his lips. As his fingers flexed with the pain, Mari caught the falling knife. Eladdin dropped his knee into her leg, hammering her knee without breaking it. Mari swore at the pain. Guiding Eladdin's weight, keeping him between her and Nadir, she punched Eladdin in the nose, sending him reeling as his hands went to his smashed face. He screamed a string of expletives as he fell.

Jhem, as still as a snake, stood watch over the Dowager-Asrahn. Mari wondered how capable he was, given how close to death he had come from the blood poisoning. His son attacked Mari. Though drunk, Nadir managed to dodge the falling Eladdin. Mari danced away from Nadir's cuts, making for the closest door. Nadir thrusted. Mari wrapped the chair leg down hard across his knuckles. He swore. Mari chuckled and blew an errant strand of hair from her eyes. She risked a glance around her, then skipped closer to the door.

"There's no escape, Mari." Nadir matched her closely, the two of them exchanging blows with weapons, feet and shins, knees and elbows. Nadir had learned some new tricks during his time in Tanis. His style was founded in warrior-poetry, yet there was a subtle dishonesty to it that Mari found disconcerting. Feints within feints, constant misdirection, and obvious flaws in his technique she learned to ignore at the first bleeding wound. She was reminded of one of the tenets of the daishäri: When we fight, we reveal our souls.

Nadir's technique betrayed him as a prince of liars. Mari and Nadir left precise wounds upon the other, each one painful, blood streaking their bodies. The Savadai moved in, tridents stabbing at her, trying to catch her limbs in their tines. Mari was forced to dance for her life, becoming more fatigued by the moment. Eladdin had risen and stumbled in their direction.

The Dowager-Asrahn leaned on her chair, rubbing her wrists, eyes intent on the fight. Jhem remained on guard, his expression hidden by his mask. Mari spun on her heel and dashed toward the doors only to pummel into the locked shields of the Savadai. She rained blows on them, trying to reach over the shields with her knife and the chair leg to no avail.

With a cry of rage, Eladdin hurtled at Mari, his single knife held with more forethought this time. But his approach was reckless. His blows easy to anticipate. Mari bludgeoned him across the jaw with the chair leg so hard that Eladdin stood for a moment, drooling blood and a tooth, before he toppled to the floor. Nadir used the chance to leap in, landing a powerful kick to Mari's stomach with the flat of his foot. Mari doubled over. Turned her fall into a roll. She avoided Nadir's foot where he stamped at her hand.

Mari came to her feet and backhanded Nadir's knives away. She swung overhand with the jagged chair leg. It bit into the flesh of Nadir's shoulder, then slid through and behind his collarbone. Nadir made the barest grunt. His eyes betrayed his agony as Mari wrenched on her weapon and snapped Nadir's collarbone. She stood over him, her heaving breaths turning into a relieved laugh.

The Savadai closed in, tridents raised as the Dowager-Asrahn cackled with glee—

"Stop!" The Emissary's voice cracked across the room. Mari felt the power of her, so like Indris, as the chains of sound wrapped themselves around her limbs. She crumpled to her knees, hands opening involuntarily to drop her weapons. The Savadai stopped dead in their tracks. The Emissary laid her hand in its moldy gauntlet on the hilt of her sword. "Mariam is not to be harmed."

"Did you not see what she did?" the Dowager-Asrahn cried in outrage. The crone came to where Eladdin lay, while Jhem went to his son. The Dowager-Asrahn spat on the floor and pointed a trembling finger at Mari. "You—"

"I've got plenty more if you want a taste," Mari shot back. *I could kill her now.* She moved forward.

"Be still." The Emissary crossed the room. Mari stood her ground, though she wanted to recoil from the menace and chittering whispers radiating from the Emissary's cloak. Mari swallowed her fear and stepped toward the Emissary, earning a dry chuckle in response.

Mari peered into the shadows of the Emissary's hood. Mottled skin, a square chin, and blackened teeth. Mari looked her up and down, refusing to be cowed.

"She suits my needs," the Emissary said. She swung back to the Dowager-Asrahn. "Do you understand me, crone? Mariam is not to be harmed."

"I rule here!" the Dowager-Asrahn snapped. "After what she has—"

"Not to be harmed," the Emissary repeated. She pointed to Eladdin. "He's flawed and not suited to the Feigning. But Mariam will be more than satisfactory."

The Dowager-Asrahn clutched at the Emissary's sleeve. She drew it back at the Emissary's sharp hiss. The old crone drew herself up and wrapped her over-robe around herself like the folds of her dignity. "Mari does not need to be whole for the Feigning. And she does need to be punished."

"Don't test me on this. My Masters have been kind to you and yours, and that can end with a word. Mariam will be whole, and unspoiled."

"Tamerlan is a dangerous place," the Dowager-Asrahn murmured.

"Then you'd best expend every possible resource to prevent her from harm. The Feigning will be punishment enough. Be content."

"But she is not fit!" The Dowager-Asrahn wrung her hands. "She is a disgrace!" She hawked and spat at Mari, though the phlegm caught on the old woman's quivering lip and drooped to her chin. She wiped it away angrily.

"Corajidin parented strong children, the best the Great House of Erebus has birthed in generations," the Emissary said as she turned to the door. "It was planned this way, long and long ago. When war comes, you'll see the strength of them. Should you live so long."

And with that the Emissary left a room gone silent. Mari felt eyes on her, but no expression was half so vicious as her grandmother's.

"What's the Feigning?" Mari asked. No one answered.

The crowd resumed their meal and the musicians began playing. She turned to Nadir, held up by Jhem, no doubt heading to the infirmary. Eladdin, carried by two of the Savadai, followed Nadir from the room. Mari went to follow them when a hand clutched her hair, pulling her head backward.

Mari relaxed and dropped as she spun. She grabbed her grandmother's bruised wrist and applied pressure until the old woman gasped, and let go. The Dowager-Asrahn swore as she massaged sensation back into her hand.

"I'm not to be harmed, remember?" Mari looked down at her grandmother. "I should make you bow as sende demands, you disgusting hag, if from nothing other than spite."

"You are a stain in the eyes of every Erebus, living and dead."

"Which you're not part of, are you?" Mari smiled at her grandmother's twisted face. "You're Savajiin—not Erebus. Family, not Great House. Yet you cling to a meaningless title, on this filthy rock in the middle of nowhere, as if it validates what you were. And you call me a disgrace, you wretched old leech."

"Empty words, girl. Everybody answers to the Shark of Tamerlan."

"Not anymore."

"Listen to you now! I may not be able to touch you, girl, but I can still do you harm. I do not need to lay a single hand on your pretty, sun-kissed skin to aggrieve you."

"And if you do, I'll make such an end of you that people in a hundred years' time will cringe when they learn of it."

❊ ❊ ❊

Word spread throughout Tamerlan. By the afternoon, bound-caste servants, some of the warrior-caste guests, and even a handful of her cousins openly smiled at Mari as they passed her in the corridors.

Mari lay in the hot water of the bath chamber long after her freshly cleaned skin had started to prune and scalp had prickled with sweat. The distant booming of the surf through the cavern wall and floor was relaxing. The vibrations reminded Mari of Indris's voice against her skin, a resonance she felt as much as heard. Not for the first time she wondered where he was. She yearned for his touch, yet could not resent his absence. They both knew the consequences of the lives they had chosen for themselves. If Indris was not in Tamerlan, he was somewhere people needed him. Besides, Mari was capable of saving herself.

The sooner she escaped the better. Doubtless this Feigning was something Mari wanted no part of.

The light scuff of a boot on wet stone caught her attention. Mari opened her eyes to see Dhoury and Qesha-rē approaching through lantern-lit clouds of steam. Mari relaxed again, allowing herself to sink deeper into the milky waters of the bath.

"Seems you're the talk of Tamerlan, Mari," Qesha-rē said. The surgeon carried her small wooden box of instruments and medicines, which she set down on a stone couch. Dhoury hovered close by, wringing his hands. Even had the baths not been steaming hot, Dhoury would have dripped sweat. Qesha-rē stood by the edge of the pool. "Do you think aggravating the old shark was the smartest thing in the world?"

"Probably not," Mari admitted. "But for the time being, the crone isn't able to lay a finger on me."

"Which gives you the freedom and time you need."

"I hope I'm not the only one to be leaving Tamerlan." Mari splashed water at Dhoury, then smiled as he scampered away.

"How do you plan on getting off the island?" Dhoury asked from a distance.

Provided I am right, Morne Hawkwood and his crew came here to find me, Mari thought. *But can you be trusted, Dhoury?* "I'm working on the details."

"Oh, by the sacred dead," Dhoury groaned into his hands. "You're going to get us killed!"

"Not if I can help it." Mari looked up at Qesha-rē. "What about you? I can think of almost every place in the world you'd find more fulfilling than here."

Qesha-rē nodded briskly. "And there are others who we should take with us, people who'll not survive on Tamerlan long after you, or I, are gone. Without a skilled surgeon, Tamerlan will soon become a charnel house unfit for anybody without a taste for blood."

"I'll need weapons," Mari said. My Sûnblade, my amenesqa, and anything else I can use. And armor. In fact, we'll want any armor we can get our hands on. Vahineh in particular will need help."

"You're going to need this." Dhoury reached into the folds of his coat and pulled out a heavy, irregularly shaped key on an iron chain. It swung ponderously as he held it out. "This is a skeleton key to Tamerlan." Dhoury placed it on her folded clothes.

Now Mari was surprised. "Where did you get it?"

"It was Nadir's," Dhoury said. Qesha-rē looked at Dhoury with some surprise and not a little admiration. "I stole it when Qesha was tending to his wounds."

"Very well, then," Mari said. "It looks like we're one step closer to leaving this cursed rock."

Dhoury and Qesha-rē smiled at each other, and Mari felt invigorated by a sense of purpose. *This is what I was trained for. To protect the many.* Mari gestured for Dhoury to turn around as she climbed out of the bath, dried herself, and got dressed.

Qesha saw to Mari's wounds, chanting her canto over them so that they sealed under Mari's eye, then became faint white lines on her skin. Mari murmured her thanks. As her friends prepared to leave, Mari stopped them with a question.

"What can either of you tell me about the Feigning?"

6

"THERE ARE GENERALLY TWO REASONS FOR DOING ANYTHING: THE REASON ONE TELLS OTHERS, AND THE REASON ONE KEEPS TO THEMSELVES."

—from *The Manifold Life*, by Teren-karem, Sēq Magnate
(991st Year of the Awakened Empire)

DAY 56 OF THE 496TH YEAR OF THE

SHRĪANESE FEDERATION

The wind was bitterly cold, Corajidin's face close to numb. The muscles of his thighs, stomach, and lower back burned in protest. He wanted to laugh with joy: This was no effeminate hart he was riding, no venison with a saddle. This was how a person should ride, on the back of a warhorse, man and beast as one. Beneath him Asha maintained a steady pace, snow churning from his hooves.

A morning mist had poured out of the Mar Jihara. It had pooled in the high plains, filled the valleys like watered milk, and flowed down to settle in the streets of Avānweh. Despite, or perhaps because of, the pressures of the past days, Corajidin had taken the opportunity to escape the city. At least for a little while. The Teshri went on without him as the political factions made and broke their alliances as a symptom of their indecision. Word had reached Corajidin that Ajo had petitioned the Arbiter-Marshall and the Kherife-Marshall to continue their investigation into the allegations against him. Those in the Teshri who had missing loved ones had agreed: once the abductees had been located and returned. For now the no-confidence motion was held in abeyance, though not for long.

The time would come when a witness was found, or somebody was careless, and Corajidin would be implicated in the abductions. He needed to make use of his captives before then. How would they be most effective in pushing his plans for unification, and war against Pashrea, forward?

It was a pure world through which he rode, with only the snow, trees, and mist for company. The surrounding wood was silent, stark against the gathered white. Corajidin risked a glance behind him. He had outdistanced his guard, who could be seen as ephemeral shapes racing behind him, outlines blurred, except for Wolfram, who flopped around in his saddle like a scarecrow.

Corajidin reined Asha in and dismounted. He took a long draft of the Emissary's potion, kept in a small flask in his over-robe. What had started as a few sips every other day had turned into a secret shame. He drank almost a liter of the potion each day just to function.

Slowly, the ache in his muscles dwindled away to be replaced by a pleasant tingling warmth. Within moments he saw individual clusters of frost and the bend of grass stalks beneath them. He heard the gentle hissing of the wind through the pines and the pro-test of branches abrading each other. The air was alive with the smell of pine needles and sap, horseflesh and oiled leather. Corajidin grasped for the insight his re-Awakening had granted him since the Communion Ritual. There was the fleeting touch of seeds that lay dormant beneath the soil. An elusive flash of hunger from an owl as it dropped from the sky to take a squirrel. Beside him the power of Asha's great heart and lungs. But nothing real, nothing lasting. The Emissary's potion and the Water of Life together had not been enough to grant Corajidin the strength he needed to undergo Unity. The depth of a connection to the land was denied him, and what little he could experience faded daily.

According to the laws of my own people, I am unfit to rule . . . In the long and lonely shallows of night, he sat huddled in his robes in front of the smoldering embers of his hearth, while Mēdēya trembled with unspoken fears in her sleep, and he wished he was not reminded of everything he had lost. *I must face the fact that what I have may no longer be what I want.*

"Then give up, but there's nothing more for you than this." The Emissary's rusted voice was loud at his side. *Is a thought all it takes for her to appear?* "Lie down here in the snow and die. It might be easier for you than the fall to come. Abdicate and let Kasraman, wise and gifted and powerful Kasraman, do what it's clear you can't."

Corajidin bristled at her tone. "Kasraman is not ready. For us to succeed, I need you to help Narseh survive, just as you helped me."

"Ah. You can delay all you like when it comes to your commitments, yet I'm supposed to carry ever more of your debt to my Masters?" Asha whickered nervously and Corajidin heard faint whispers from within the folds of the Emissary's cloak. "You're becoming a poor investment, Corajidin, which is stupendously unwise. You've war to make, and thrones to topple, and scholars to destroy."

"I do not take orders from you, Emissary!"

"Perhaps not. But you're already indebted to my Masters, and here you are asking for my help again. I've given you your son, your crown, and your wife. You've given me nothing. Your mother is much more responsive to our needs. Perhaps she would make a better Mahj?"

Corajidin wanted to spit. *My mother? What has she to do with this?* "I've banished my daughter at your request. Freed the witches of the Mahsojhin, financed—for no good reason I can see—those useless wastrels of the alchemists and the artificers. I have given! But I am unable to make war on Pashrea without the support of the Teshri! The Asrahn can be replaced, you know, and I have no doubt Roshana is looking for any opportunity to make it so. Narseh is my only Imperialist ally. I need her alive. If I do not have influence, I cannot pay my debts. I am worth more to you right where I am."

"Everybody can be replaced, Corajidin."

He forced a smile and hoped it looked stronger than it felt. "Is that a threat?"

"A promise. You, Narseh, your daughter . . . all will become history unless you make good what you owe. Change comes with need, Corajidin. And if you can't change the people, then change the people."

"What do you mean?"

"There are other allies I have that can help you maintain a, shall we say, firmer hold on your power, and make the headway you desperately need. These allies will ensure that none of your people ever betray you, nor will they argue. You'll be able to do as you like. All the powers of the Mahj, just lacking the title. For now."

"And these allies are . . . ?"

"I want you to accept the help of the Soul Traders," she said. The air about her blurred, and a gray-washed figure floated next to her, his legs ending in a boiling, ashen cloud. The man was a bag of sticks in the ghost of leathery skin pulled too tight across protruding bones, the remnants of centuries-old finery billowing about it. Corajidin wondered whether the ghastly Nomad had been dead for so long, he had forgotten what he used to look like. The creature smiled, exposing receding gums and chisel teeth. "The Soul Traders and I share a common journey," the Emissary said, "which means you now share their journey."

"I will do no such thing!"

"You will, and you'll shut your complaints behind your teeth. You are in no position to demand, or refuse, anything. I suggest you make use of what you quaintly refer to as the marsh-puppeteers, or malegangers. They are older than those names, and more powerful than you know."

"Next you will be telling me to recruit the Fenlings, or reedwives. Why not dholes, while we are talking about things that will never happen."

"As you wish." The Emissary held her hands up, causing Asha to flinch and take nervous steps away. The whispers from the dark folds of the Emissary's cloak grew louder for a few moments, words in a wet language Corajidin could not understand. The Emissary was silent for a moment longer before saying, "But your debts will be paid. My Masters are losing their patience, and Shrīan is only a thread in a much larger tapestry. All things must happen in their appointed time, and yours is expiring. You will make war on Pashrea, and you will hunt the last of the Sēq down. The Soul Traders will do what it is in their nature to do. They will follow you and your people, and take advantage of any . . . opportunities that arise. Use the witches, alchemists, and artificers. It's what they're for. If you don't do as you're told, you'll make way for somebody who will."

"What about Narseh? Without her, I cannot do half of what you ask."

"Then you'd best double your efforts, hadn't you?"

The Emissary turned and walked away. The Soul Trader faded from sight, a cloud torn apart by the wind, but Corajidin could feel it there, waiting, watching.

Kasraman and Wolfram approached after she had disappeared, their boots crunching on the frost.

"I neither like nor trust the Emissary, Father," Kasraman said as he watched her blend into the swirling white. "But will she help with Rahn-Narseh?"

"Our conversation did not have the desired outcome," Corajidin said, rubbing his hands together and trying to breathe warmth into them through his fur-lined gauntlets. "The Emissary did not say no, but neither did she agree."

"What does she want for her help?"

"Oh, what does anybody really want? The fall of Mediin, and the destruction of the Sēq. And that is only to bring me out of debt to her Masters."

"So Narseh will probably die of her illness?" Wolfram asked. "Her son, Anankil, is by no means a confirmed Imperialist. If Narseh dies—"

"I am well aware of the consequences, my friend. I need options."

"We could dose Narseh with the Emissary's potion," Kasraman said with a shrug. "It's not a perfect solution but it worked for you, and will buy us some time."

Use my stores? For Narseh? Corajidin shook his head. "I need all that I have." *More than I have.*

"Can you meet the Emissary halfway?" Kasraman asked patiently. "If refusal is not an option, then at least partial collaboration may be the answer."

Corajidin explained what the Emissary had said about changing the people, and using the marsh-puppeteers to enforce permanent cooperation. The two witches were stone-faced as they listened, though Corajidin could almost hear the wheels spinning in their minds. When Corajidin finished speaking, Kasraman and Wolfram shared a conspiratorial look.

"What?" Corajidin snapped. "What have you done?"

Kasraman spoke without apology. "I had Tahj-Shaheh bring some of the marsh-puppeteers back from her last foray into the

Rōmarq, so I could experiment on them. I thought they'd be an interesting way of infiltrating our enemies and possibly using some of our hostages as assassins . . . Father? Did you hear what I said?"

Corajidin gazed at Kasraman. He was plagued by something close to a memory of something once seen. As he grasped for the image—of a face tattooed with fire, the curving horns, the eyes like looking into the heart of a star—it shattered in a flare of pain behind his eyes.

"You were wrong to do so," Corajidin replied as he rubbed at the pain in his head. The marsh-puppeteers were grotesque perversions, parasites who brought nothing but mayhem. "Destroy them, son. We will find other ways." Saying the words was like a weight off his shoulders. *At least I have some moral compass left to me.*

"What other ways?" Kasraman snapped, hands held wide. "We should use our captives for our own purposes, before they are discovered, or can escape and talk. The malegangers give us an advantage we—"

"I said no!" Corajidin yelled, his voice cracking through the mist, spooking the horses. He calmed himself, laying a hand on each of the witch's shoulders. "We walk a narrow path, and I will not sell the future because we were rash today. After the liches, witches, and elemental daemons in Avānweh, have we not had our fill of monsters, at least for a little while?"

"The Emissary is a monster, Father. Yet you treat with her."

The Emissary is a monster . . . and I have indeed had my fill of her.

※ ※ ※

Corajidin did not enjoy the rest of his morning ride. Asha sensed his discomfort and was skittish. What should have been the smooth flow of muscle and sinew in an effortless gallop was jarring and painful.

As Corajidin reined Asha in at the stables, a palatial fortress of marble domes and patterned archways, he passed a squad of the powerful Iphyri shock troops. Satyrs were rumored to walk the woods of Erebus Prefecture, goat-headed and goat-legged primal lords of the wood. Corajidin had tried to find them in his youth, despite the rumors of their passions and perversions. Centuries before, one of his Ancestors must have had the same fascination, paying them homage in the form of the Iphyri. But where the satyrs were goatlike, the Iphyri resembled horses. They were men once, changed forever to reflect the totem spirit of the Erebus stallion: With the heads and manes of horses, their legs were replaced with the powerful haunches of destriers, with tails that swept the ground. An Iphyri had long arms and large hands, and could run on all fours for vast distances, then stand and fight like heavy infantry. They were strong, virtually fearless, and loyal, if not terribly bright. They were good at killing and dying, and there would be much of both once winter broke and spring brought warmth and war. Corajidin dismounted among his guard, seeing the Jhé-Erebon—the Wives of the Stallion—grooming their Iphyri, polishing the horse-folk's armor and sharpening their massive weapons. An all-female cadre, the Jhé-Erebon wore lighter armor and rode their Iphyri into battle, dismounting to fight side by side with them. They were an elite fighting force few soldiers wanted to face.

Mēdēya watched with fascination, bundled in a sable over-robe and thick gloves, a red-and-black–checked taloub around her dark hair. She came to Corajidin and took his hand, dragging him over to where the muscular Iphyri exercised.

"Who needs the other sayfs when we have warriors such as these?" she said, eyes bright, breathing heavily. "They are incredible! Such a perfect fusion of muscle, and power, and obedience. To ride one must be . . . exhilarating."

"The Iphyri have their place—"

"I was reading that they were originally made from a Darmatian zherba stallion, and Erebus fa Baibaron, the greatest warrior-poet of his time, who sacrificed himself for the future." She breathed. "Why don't we do the same, but use the greatest Erebus warrior-poet of our time?"

"Belamandris?" Corajidin choked. The idea made him nauseous. "No. It is not something I would ever countenance. Put it from your mind, and never speak of it again."

Mēdēya patted Corajidin on the arm as one would a stupid child. "Not Belam. Mariam!"

Corajidin's laugh exploded from him. "As much chance of me riding the Rahn-Roshana around like a pony." His humor left him. "Mariam is my daughter, and will not be used for such dire purpose. Besides, we do not have any Torque Spindles to make such paragons of violence. Otherwise I would make the armies I need and be done with it."

"What if we did have Torque Spindles?" Mēdēya asked, smiling conspiratorially as she drew Corajidin out of the palatial stables and into the cool afternoon air. "What if there was no such impediment?"

"Tell me!"

Mēdēya drew a rolled-up scroll from her sash and slapped it into Corajidin's palm. She wormed her way into his arms as he unrolled it. The scroll was from Baquio, a Master of the College of Artificers. He read the scroll once, then again, to ensure he had not misread the message. A smile dawned on his face, and it took all his self-control to not shout out loud with joy. Mēdēya hugged him and lifted her face so he could kiss her deeply. When they parted, she sighed contentedly. "All the artificers need are more Torque Spindles to work on and you can make your armies, Jidi! And fulfill your promises to the Emissary."

Corajidin's excitement waned at the thought of the agent from the Drear. He looked into Mēdēya's eyes, so dark that no light of

Yashamin's soul escaped them, though her mannerisms, memories, and appetites were those of the woman he had loved to distraction. Or so close in the vertiginous rush of passion as to be indistinguishable. *Who are you, really?* But he sculpted a smile from his doubts before the grimace set in. "We will see what we see, when the artificers prove that they can do what they say they can do."

"Mariam would make a perfect—"

"Mēdēya, no!" She stiffened in his arms and he softened his tone. "Please make no more suggestions about my children."

"But this is the ultimate service she can do for her House. Mariam and the great stallion totem of the Erebus. The Emissary says it hinges on Mariam. She who will be the mother of many in the great Feigning of our time."

The Emissary says . . . How far would the Emissary go to distance Mariam from Indris? Mariam was already the prisoner of the Dowager-Asrahn, a fate that Corajidin would never have inflicted on his wayward daughter were it not for his debts to the Masters of the Drear. But a Feigning? There had not been one in centuries, certainly not of the scale the Emissary had suggested to Mēdēya. He extricated himself from Mēdēya's embrace, slowly, so as not to alarm her. A simmering rage at the Emissary rose in him. It was bad enough she threatened him, but for her to fill Mēdēya's head with her suggestions was intolerable! Yashamin would never have been so blindly compliant. *What else did the Emissary bring back with you, when she gave you new life?* Mēdēya looked at Corajidin questioningly but said nothing as he kissed the top of her head. They walked together through the snow-dusted courtyard with its silent fountains, then into the qadir where Nix waited.

"Asrahn." Nix's next words tumbled out like pebbles clattering on the flagstones. "I trust your morning ride was pleasant? Feyd and Tahj-Shaheh are waiting on your indulgence."

"I will join you soon, Nix. Please find Kasraman, and Wolfram, and wait for me in the observatory. Mēdēya, would you please go with Nix?"

Corajidin waited for them to vanish from sight before he made his way to the suites that had been set aside for the witches and their work. He paused in the corridor overlooking the courtyard, where Kasraman and Wolfram remained, standing close to one another. Kasraman made angry, chopping gestures with his hands. *What bothers you, son, that you would speak to Wolfram, rather than coming to me? Can I not trust any of my children? Do you all share Mariam's rebellious heart?* The Angoth nodded, or shook his head, by turns, once while resting his hand on Kasraman's shoulder, or gesturing for calm. Nix joined them presently and the three headed off through the doors that led through the qadir, and to the distant observatory tower.

Knowing the others would wait on his pleasure, Corajidin headed directly to the witches' workrooms. At every turn guards, bound-caste servants, and those of the middle-castes—artisans, crafters, and their ilk—dropped to their knees in the Third Obeisance, palms and brows pressed against the floor. Such behavior had not been as overt when he was the Rahn-Erebus: As Asrahn it was a different world altogether; sende demanded the utmost respect for the highest office in Shrīan.

Corajidin soon arrived at the black-enameled doors of the witches' suites, the door latches shaped into red-gold horse heads. Two witches in ornate robes stood by the doors, armored in layers of quilted silk and clutching tall staves. They looked at Corajidin warily as he approached.

"Stand aside," Corajidin said.

There was a pause, before the shorter of the two witches replied. "We are at the orders of Pah-Kasraman, and Lore Master Wolfram, to bar—"

"And those two take their orders from me." Corajidin drew himself up and folded his hands in the sleeves of his over-robe. He was reminded for a moment of Brede, and her fanatical loyalty to Wolfram when they had been in Amnon.

"Asrahn, we—"

"You will make way." Corajidin was pleased with the iron in his voice, the faint resonance the result of the Emissary's potion. The two witches on guard fidgeted under his glare. "Now. And you will be thankful that I, my son, or the Lore Master do not boil the skin from your bones for defying me."

"Yes, Asrahn."

Corajidin entered and took stock of the place where the witches worked their secrets. The chambers were surprisingly light, the air scented with cinnamon and vanilla rather than the reek he had expected. Tables crowded with metal and glass apparatus lined the walls, while small crucibles and cauldrons bubbled over hand-sized braziers of firestones. The burbling sound was oddly cheerful, reminding him of winters as a child, spent reading near the kitchens of Erebesq.

He crossed the room to another door, and opened it. The air within was almost oppressive, thick with warmth and damp. It smelled of brine and rotting vegetation, as well as corrupt flesh. Corajidin placed his hand over his mouth and nose, but the stench was already in his nostrils. Several tall cages with dry bushes, rocks, and sand lined the walls. The first few Corajidin looked into showed corpses in various states of decay. Small tables near each cage had journals, outlining the observations of whatever witch had been present, including some in Kasraman's and Wolfram's handwriting. Small boxes of thick glass had marsh-puppeteers in them. Some were nailed down while others twitched, writhed, or threw themselves against the walls of their prison in an attempt to escape. The sight of them made Corajidin want to vomit. Their reek was worse. The marsh-puppeteers resembled two strangler's hands joined along the thumbs, covered in pliant turtle shell. The tails were short, flat, and segmented like a lobster. Their finger-thick limbs were encased in a moist-looking carapace, tipped with hard black points that twitched and flexed. Their abdomens were pocked with a multitude of large pores, all of which showed the tips of oily barbed tendrils.

"You are the one they call Corajidin," came a rasping voice from the shadows at the end of the room. Corajidin's hearts jumped. His head snapped around and he squinted into the gloom. There was a shape there, standing with its pale hands wrapped around the bars of its cage. Mouth dry, Corajidin prowled toward it, treading as lightly as he could. His caution was met by a humorless laugh, almost like a wheeze. "I see you, little king with blinded eyes, ears deaf to the voice of the world. I see you, the twice-Awakened, now slumbering and broken."

Closer now, Corajidin saw it was a woman, with hair hanging in a mat about her face. Her long, intricately buckled robe was stained with mud and dirty water. Her delicate hands were streaked with filth. The steel bars of her cage groaned as she throttled them.

Corajidin stopped well out of arm's reach. "Who are you?"

"My name is as long as the world I have known, made longer by the minds I have eaten, and longer again by the deeds I have done. For such is the way of names, where words have meaning." The hands pulled apart the tangled weave of her hair to reveal a face Corajidin knew. He took a step back. "But I was, and contain within the mirrors of my mind, the woman you knew as Delfineh fa Jhem fe Kimiya. That name will do as well as any."

Tempted as he was to step forward, he stayed rooted to the spot, almost wilting in the miasma of her breath. *She smells like a dead thing, dragged from a swamp! Are these the wages of witches, then? What would my son unleash on the world?*

Turning on his heels, he fled the room as fast as dignity would allow him. Kimiya's malignant laughter gave speed to his exit.

"EDUCATION TEACHES US HOW TO THINK, INTELLIGENCE HOW TO
QUESTION, AND OUR MORALITY WHAT TO DO WITH WHAT WE KNOW.
BE WARY THEN OF THE EDUCATED, INTELLIGENT, AND AMORAL PERSON,
FOR THEY WILL KNOW ONLY THAT THEY CAN DO A THING,
NOT WHETHER THEY SHOULD."

—from *The Foundation of Learning,* by Yattoweh, Sēq Magnate,
teacher, and houreh (2230th Year of the Petal Empire)

DAY 57 OF THE 496TH YEAR OF THE

SHRĪANESE FEDERATION

Indris perched on the balcony of his room, huddled in his
over-robe as he listened to the layered vocals, jangle of sonesettes,
and the throaty hum of kahi flutes that rose from the Black Quill at
the mouth of the valley. Amarqa-in-the-Snows huddled beneath a
freshly laid mantle of white. Overhead, the nebulous arm of the
Ancestor's Shroud stretched out as if to sweep them jealously into
its folds. The Ancestor's Eye blazed brightest of all, its brilliant

sapphire flickering as it looked upon Īa. Soon, the clouded blue-green marble of Eln would rise, brightening the night further.

Like all such moments, part of its beauty came from its transience. Indris's breathing stuttered at the memory of Hayden and Omen, now gone like so many others who had been in his life. It was Shar and Ekko who dominated his thoughts, and their journey southward to find Mari. Of his friends, Mari's was the face Indris craved the most. Mari, with the smile that made his head feel light. Of her, too, there was no sign. Too many people in his life were gone, leaving only silence in their place. There was only one who had returned. Anj's presence was as much a mystery as Mari's disappearance: his new love vanished, the former within arm's reach. Anj presented questions Indris did not want to ask. His instincts told him the answers were something he was unprepared for and could never forget. Yet his long-missing wife supposedly had answers that the Sēq had been unable to find. Was he prepared to pay Anj's price for her help? And what had Anj become? The impression that she was but a memory painted over an unpalatable present strengthened with each meeting.

The present was filled with many uncertainties. The Sēq, once so solid in their foundations of the past, were on unsteady ground, facing a difficult future. The Order had fallen back on its strengths: the power of its collective intellect, stored knowledge, and arcane wisdom. Indris gazed into the night. With a sky free of the effects of both sun and moon, the disentropic tides were smoother than at any other time. He gingerly opened himself to the ahmsah for a passive search. The star-freckled night was seared with a web of vivid colors, tumbling geometries, and formulae that undulated like flying carpets across the sky: roving metaphysical patrols to bolster the fixed positions of the multiple layers of wards. Analogies soared there: birds wreathed in flame, hollow-eyed specters, armored phantoms, and a flying hunt of fey knights in gem-bright armor on horses that galloped across the sky. Since the arrival of the rahns, the Sēq had called upon their best war formulists to ensure Amarqa was the safest place in the world. Indris closed himself to the ahmsah, blinking slowly until his eyes readjusted to the natural darkness of night.

Indris went into his rooms to get his weapons, then swore to himself. Old habits . . . Changeling was not there. She had not been there since the Sēq Masters had taken her away from him in Avānweh. Changeling was a prisoner, kept as insurance against his departure from Amarqa-in-the-Snows before the Sēq were done with him. Not for the first time his rage boiled. Fire played behind his eye, and even without using the ahmsah, Indris could see the swirling shadows of his Disentropic Stain flicker about his clenched fists. Energy flared, snapping like a lightning storm in the murky clouds around his hand. Changeling was his! A Sēq's psédari was as much a part of him as—

His own mind.

Indris breathed in heated air. His skin tightened as it dried. The rug at his feet, as well as the edges of the fur on his bed, started to smolder. Soon the heat would reach the point where everything in the room caught fire. Indris forced himself to calm down. He took deep, even breaths, each one slightly longer and cooler than the last, until the air once more had the bite of autumn's chill.

Indris wrapped his arms around his chest until his hearts slowed. Changeling had been a constant in his life for years, and to have her gone was more distressing than he expected. *I didn't intend to fight my way into, or out of, anywhere tonight. But I'll have you back, old friend.*

There came a knock at his door. Before he had the chance to draw breath to answer, Femensetri barged in amid a swirl of tattered black, like a crow sheltering from a storm. She stamped her booted feet, heedless of the mud and clumps of snow she left on the rugs. Indris's old teacher pulled her hood down and eyed him darkly.

"You've got what you want, boy," she said. "But don't feel too proud of holding the Sēq to ransom. It's something neither I nor the Suret are likely to forget."

"Ironic, given how many promises you make that are forgotten as soon as they become inconvenient."

"Watch your tone!"

Indris walked straight to the door Femensetri had left open. He gestured down the corridor. "After you."

Femensetri's jaw writhed as she clenched her teeth, then stamped out of the room as quickly as she had entered. Indris released a slow breath, glad she had not tested him on his resolve. Their confrontation at Rosha's suites had left him with a pounding headache and the sour taste of fear in his mouth for the better part of the following day. Seeing Femensetri, one of the most experienced—and most dangerous—scholars, in her wrath was something Indris could pretend to be unafraid of, but the reality was quite the opposite.

Until they had wrung what they wanted from him, the secrets of his missing years and any message or knowledge of hallowed Sedefke, Indris knew he was safe. Once that happened, he was expendable, if not an actual liability. Best he learned what he could now.

Femensetri led Indris along ancient paths, over bridges that crossed streams narrowed with ice, and up winding, wind-blasted stairs. All the while Indris's eyes were fixed on the cold glow shining through the windows of the Black Archives.

Taking a switchback path up the cliffs, Femensetri paused before a massive door made of hundreds of pieces of aged wood, like a huge puzzle box. Characters in square Maladhoring glyphs were etched there, flowing across some of the wooden pieces, only to appear elsewhere on the door in disjointed and nonsensical sentences. Blackened steel statues flanked the doors: baroque armored knights on the back of powerful reticulated steel horses, with long horns emerging from the horses' heads. Crouched amid the horses were massive wolves with ridges of steel fur running in a long trail of razor-sharp spikes from brow to tail tip. Metallic foxes, squirrels, and crows were hidden among the roots and trunks of the trees that flanked the doors to the Black Archives.

There came the squeal of tortured metal as the statues turned to face Indris and Femensetri. One of the armored horses stamped a hoof, striking sparks.

Merciful Ancestors! Indris thought. "I don't remember Nomads being here."

"There was never the need until recently," Femensetri said. "But now the Sēq are no longer sacrosanct, and we need to protect what is ours against any who'd foolishly try to take it." Femensetri pulled a large glass key from the folds of her over-robe. She inserted the key and started touching the wooden pieces of the door, freezing words in place, making sense of some of the sentence fragments. Indris watched, but Femensetri moved so that he could see little of the message itself.

With a final set of gestures, Femensetri finished the code and the door collapsed into the floor like so many toy blocks. Warm air rushed out and Femensetri pointed inside the Black Archives.

"You've been here before as a student, but always escorted," she said. "This time you're on your own. The Suret will meet the letter of your demand by giving you access. They'll not approve anybody giving you any help."

"Then how am I supposed to learn anything? I'm doing this for you!"

"Don't take me for the fool, Indris," she murmured. "The Suret accepts that you have questions and are willing to meet you half-way. This is a great honor. Don't make light of it. Crowns have fallen, alongside the heads they were perched on, for what's kept here. You may take nothing with you save that which you can remember, and that which is yours. Do you accept the terms?"

"I do," Indris said firmly. "For what it's worth, thank you."

She said nothing as she walked away.

❊ ❊ ❊

Indris passed through the Black Archives. The geometries of the place tried to direct him away from the center. He passed through levels of hexagonal libraries, the walls honeycombed with niches for scrolls, books, and relics. The faceted *ilhen* stalactites sprouted from the ceilings. The air was scented with lacquered wood, dry wool, and the leather and paper of thousands of ancient volumes. Doors led off to other libraries dedicated to cultures both living and dead. As much as he desired to stay, he passed wide-eyed through vast chambers where the Sēq had collected the lore of Afternoon People Races: the Avān, the Humans, the Tau-se, the Fenling, and the Y'arrow-te-yi. There were also volumes on the Bamboo People, animals raised to sentience by the Earth Masters: the Iku, the vulpine Katsé, the ursoid Asash, the lupine Marou, and others. Yet greater still were those libraries dedicated to the Dawn Races: the Seethe, the Dragons, the Herū, the Feyhe, and before them all, the Rōm.

Making his way along well-remembered paths, Indris paused at a keyhole door no different than dozens he had passed. The stained-glass panels glowed with an inner radiance. Crook-shaped handles gleamed. He inhaled the beeswax scent that clung to the wood and felt the warmth from the door on his face. Opening his dhyna, Indris saw the lettering that burned like liquid fire in the depths of the glass: a spiraling message that flowed from pane to pane. From each set of squared glyphs, filaments of power arced out to form changing shapes in a web that was anchored to knotted points of disentropy—another circuit of alarms and traps. The Sēq Masters guarded their secrets jealously.

The words were in Maladhoring, the high language of the Elemental Master mystics. He read the words aloud as they twisted in the glass.

"*Verisis aré on aula, ilé laryn on naō un sarastum on damanas.*" Learn from the past, to inform the present and define the future.

The words faded away and the doors opened silently. Indris stepped inside and the doors closed behind him. He stood in a hollow tower that extended twenty floors above and another twenty floors below where he stood. Each floor in the hexagonal tower was marked out by inward-facing balconies, linked by an elaborate network of staircases and walkways. The stairs and walkways moved in time with the sonorous metronome of a device he could not see, changing the paths to different parts of the tower every few minutes. He did not know whether to laugh, cry, or both. There were thousands, handfuls of thousands, of books, scrolls, boxes, and chests. Some of the niches on the honeycombed walls were taller than he was, and most were closed behind fretwork *serill* doors. There was a crackle of pent-up disentropy, so much so that his skin prickled with it.

How am I supposed to find anything in here? What was it Femensetri had said? Look, listen, and feel.

Indris stepped onto the moving stair and allowed it to ferry him around the tower. Conscious of time and the repercussions of failure, Indris jogged along the stairs, trying to gain his bearings from the names of those who had authored the many volumes. An indexing system slowly became apparent. As a test, he started to predict what types of material would be present as the stairs and walkways cycled around him: There were the dialectics of Kayet Al Tham and Robaddin of the Hoje. Farther around and up, various editions of the *Nilvedic Maxims*. A wall of volumes bound in black leather contained the works of the greatest minds of the Sēq.

At the seventh level moving upward, the stairs became fixed, leading up to the next tier. Indris stared awestruck at the ornate sculpture that hung from the ceiling—an inverted quartz tree with a canopy of glowing colored *ilhen* leaves. The walls on these levels were covered in tall hexagonal doors that reminded Indris of the vaults he had seen in Banker's House. These, however, were of swirling colored *serill*, not steel. Each vault had a nameplate in Maladhoring, including one for each of the Eight: Saroyyin and Taqrit. Majadis, Demandai, Lilay, and Ravashem. One for Anj-el-din, and one for himself. There were others, names he recognized and ones unknown to him. None of the vaults had locks, handles, or any obvious means of opening them. Under the ahmsah, Indris's senses were assailed by a complex set of formulae that fell like rain in long lines of fusing characters. Words appeared and disappeared every other second. He turned away, feeling the faint tug of vertigo.

Indris leaned out to inspect the tree more closely. Clusters of leaves were colored with tinted veins running along the branches, and down what he saw were twelve faceted trunks sprouted from innumerable roots that covered and vanished into the ceiling. It was all engraved with pictograms he could barely see, let alone decipher. Of the twelve trunks, six remained lit, the canopy bright with scores of shining leaves. Reaching out farther, Indris saw the leaves had names carved on them.

Thousands of names joined over the years by blood and the friendships and hatreds that came with it. This was the record of the twelve Great Houses of the Avān—though only six survived. The ruby and black trunk, with its polished blood leaves, showed him the long line of the Great House of Erebus. Beside it, the amethyst of the Selassin, the citrine of the Bey, and the milky quartz of the Sūn. The emerald of the Kadarin, and the colorless leaves of the

Great House of Alif that they had destroyed. The Chepherundi, the Damjah, the Aj-Tanēs, and the Ilmalan, all of whom had retreated to Tanis and lost their Unity with Ïa, their Awakened rahns a memory. And the Khal-alēt, who vanished into history along with the last remnants of the Time Masters.

But shining most brightly of all, its trunk and branches in glorious sapphire, was the First House: the Great House of Näsarat.

Other names were there, leaves blown from different trees to settle in the foliage. The names of the Hundred Families, the luminaries of the consortiums, and Exalted Names risen for a single generation, to fall back into obscurity on the death of a legend. Indris swore at the extent of it. Thousands of names from across history tied together to produce names he knew as well as his own. Some names and ancestral lines were connected by radiant filaments of gold, specific merging of bloodlines throughout the millennia . . .

It may have been a history of the greatest and most influential of the Avān, but it was far more specific. Indris had heard rumors of the Genealogy Tree and now could not refute them: This sculpture tracked the ancestry of the Eight, or as Femensetri had also referred to it, the Dionfar, or the Great Labor. Each name had the day the person was born and the day they died, if they had passed on to the Well of Souls. He found Ariskander, the tree already reflecting his life and death, and his sister, Indris's mother, Delaram. And her only child—

It was not Indris's name written there. He fought for breath. Etched in precise characters was the name Näsarat fa Kahrain. Born in Mediin in the summer of 461 . . . and dead before the season was out. He traced the line of the Näsarats back, then again. Yet nowhere in all the arranged marriages and selective breeding across Houses and Families and Exalted Names was Näsarat fa Amon-Indris to be found. Other names were there he did not expect. They were also the products of the Great Labor though not fostered by the Sēq: Erebus fa Kasraman and Nix of the Maladhi.

Other members of the Shrīanese upper-castes. Bensaharēn, Neva, and Yago. Mari's and Belamandris's names were there, as well as Nehrun, Roshana, and Tajaddin. The Näsarat and the Erebus, as ever living in each other's orbits. The other Houses had been pruned from the Great Labor generations ago.

Ariskander's words echoed in his head. *It is what your mother sent you to us for.*

"Sent?" Indris muttered. "But sent from where?"

"You are asking only part of the question."

Indris spun at the sound of the many-layered voice, his hand reaching for a weapon that was not there. Standing close by was the Herald in his cloak-like folded wings. His head was tilted to one side, the mirror mask shining with warped reflections.

"Who are you?" Indris asked as he backed away.

"They call me the Herald."

"That wasn't what I asked."

"But it is my answer, nonetheless. I mean you no harm, Amon-Indris."

Indris spoke carefully. "How do you know me?"

"Because I've been waiting for you."

"How long have you been there?"

The Herald paused for a long moment. "I have always been here."

Indris frowned, uncertain of whether he was being made sport of. He stepped away from the balcony toward the vault with his name on it. Extending his hand, he almost touched the *serill* door, but caught the quick movement of the Herald's masked head.

Why am I not on the Genealogy Tree? "Who am I?" Indris murmured.

"That, too, is only part of the question."

Indris clenched his fists in frustration and his teeth around what was going to be his flippant response. *The Herald does not say much, but when it talks, the Suret listens. Not a person to be on the* wrong side of in a place where Indris already doubted how many friends he had. "Will you answer my questions, or won't you?"

The Herald turned both his palms up in a version of a shrug, or to show they were empty and there was nothing to be had from him. "All things happen in their time, Indris, and not before. What value is there in knowledge given, when wisdom comes from the knowledge learned? But you have learned things. Learned things earlier than you should have. Sooner than you, or others, was safe to know. With knowledge comes expectation, and with expectation comes action, and action must only come when it can provide—"

"The most appropriate and beneficial reaction." Indris nodded. "That's from the sixth volume of *The Prescripts*."

The Herald clapped his thigh with a large hand. "There are few questions you can ask to which you do not already know the answers. As the number of possibilities diminishes, so, too, do the actions and reactions left to us. Sadly, some things have been writ in stone, when it would be better they were writ in sand."

"Like who I am?"

"In and of itself part of a question, the inertia of which remains to be seen. Yet such a derivative question, dependent as it is on when it is asked and under what circumstances. Rarely are we but one thing. There are also the more fascinating questions of what, when, or where you are. Or how and why." The Herald's voices echoed around the vaulted archive, becoming scores of voices laid one atop the other. "So few questions asked when there are really so many to ask. And in that many we find there are in fact few questions that have any material difference, dependent as they are on the limits of what a person can see in a single moment among millions."

"You're a frustrating man, you know that?"

"Both subjective terms, but ones I have heard on no few occasions."

Indris snorted as he looked around the trove of knowledge. "Femensetri told me none of the Sēq would help me. I don't even know where to start."

"Of course you do," the Herald replied. He was silent for a moment, as if considering his next words. "And I am not of the Sēq."

"Then you'll help me?"

"I will provide insight into some questions, yes."

Indris's mouth gaped for a moment, ready to argue, before he understood that he had the answer he was after. He looked into the mirrored surface of the mask, his reflection altered from true as if seen from under running water. *Because how I am depends on when I am, and where I am, and what I am doing, and when I am doing it* . . . Questions going back to the one question he had never thought to ask because he had been given answers to it his entire life.

"Though I'm here to learn what the Sēq know about me, I've also agreed to help find a cure for the rahns."

"Irrelevant."

"Not if the country is to be saved."

"Saved from what, for what, and for whom?" the Herald intoned darkly. "Have you not considered that the plight of the rahns—and their downfall—is part of a greater design?"

"You'll not help me understand Awakening?"

"You have already been Awakened twice, which is twice more than I. What help could I be, where I have no experience?"

"But you'll help me learn more about myself?"

"I am forbidden from talking on some subjects lest it begin a sequence of events for which the world is ill prepared. But I will not interfere when you discover facts for yourself."

Forbidden? "Very well." Indris's mind whirled. The Herald clearly served some force of which Indris was unaware, a force the

Sēq either respected or feared. Which was in and of itself something to give him pause. "Why am I?"

"You are to be both the cause and the effect of questions, promises, and actions from a time few still remember. You are, because we were promised a light to guide the way."

"I don't understand."

"Which is the perfect place to start," the Herald said. He then pointed to the *serill*-doored vault that had Indris's name on it. "But I might suggest that this is better."

8

"SENDE PROVIDES THE SOCIAL CODES THAT STRUCTURE OUR LIVES, BUT IT
IS FROM OUR FAMILIES THAT WE LEARN CONTEXT. WHEN SUCCESSIVE
GENERATIONS SET THE WRONG EXAMPLE, WE EXPERIENCE THE TURMOIL
OF SOCIAL DISORDER. THIS IS OFTEN THE BEGINNING OF THE END FOR A
BLOODLINE AS IT TURNS ITS BACK ON COMMUNITY AND FALLS TO THE
DISARRAY OF MISGUIDED AMBITION AND MISINFORMED SELF-INTEREST."

—from *Immortality of the Bloodlines,* by Tamari fa Saroush, philosopher of
the Awakened Empire

DAY 59 OF THE 496TH YEAR OF THE

SHRĪANESE FEDERATION

Mari stood tall in the freezing wind as her cousins made the
Second Obeisance to the Dowager-Asrahn, their eyes fixed on the
lichen growing between the wet marble tiles of the Sea Shrine.
Mari and the old shark glared at each other across hillocks of
bowed heads lightly dusted with snow. She dropped her gaze in
guilt and shame. Her fists were clenched and cold, clipped nails
digging into her palms, and the muscles in her hands and arms

ached from the strain. Tears pooled at the corners of her eyes, eas-ily explained by the biting wind, rather than as the wages of her obstinate pride.

It was my task to keep Dhoury safe. But it's my actions that have damned him. Mari flicked her glance left and right, and took in the deployment of the Savadai. It was possible she could move quickly enough to take one of their weapons, rescue Dhoury, and fight her way clear.

And then what, Mari? You'd still be trapped on an island in the middle of the freezing sea, and they would find you eventually, and Dhoury's life would still be forfeit. Learn from this. Absorb it. Make it part of you. A man will lose his life today because of you, and there's no amount of training, bravery, or defiance that can change it for the better.

Cold flurries stung Mari's brow and cheeks. The open-air Sea Shrine vibrated with every outraged boom of the surf against the rocks. She breathed in deeply, nose crinkling at the odors of low tide and the teeming sea beyond the distant rock wall. Once the tide rose, the entire shrine, its pitted stairs, and the surrounding rock shelves would sink beneath the waves.

Mari's cousins were arrayed in order of the Dowager-Asrahn's favor. Those who had succumbed to the Shark of Tamerlan's will were seated toward the front, closer to the coral and barnacle–sheathed arches that rose like entwined octopus tentacles from the rippled surface of the tidal pool. A waxy-skinned Eladdin grasped at splendor in his polished scale armor, his face swollen and mottled with bruising. Beside him, Nadir shivered, pale beneath his tan. He favored his recently wounded shoulder. The surgeon had done her job well, yet they were far from at their best. The cousins fanned out from their mistress's back, with Mari at the edge of recognition. She listened as the crone prattled on about the cold embrace of the ocean, and the beneficent horrors it contained. Beside her stood the Emissary, her face hidden in the shadows of her hood, and Jhem, whose disfigurement could only be guessed at behind the scaled half-mask he now wore.

Mari refused to give voice to the chanting rubbish the others gave themselves over to. When it came time to bow, Mari stood even taller. Her attitude caught the attention of the Emissary, who spent far too much time facing Mari for her comfort. *Whatever your Feigning is, which nobody knows a damned thing about, rest assured you'll do it without me.*

The tide splashed over the rock wall. From behind Mari there came the creak of leather and the wet slap of boots, as a squad of the Savadai dragged Dhoury, the fleshy man stripped naked, his body covered in welts and bruises.

Mari moved to intercept the Savadai, when her grandmother's voice cracked. "You'll not interfere with this, girl!"

"That's Pah-Mariam to—"

"I have had enough of your posturing," the Dowager-Asrahn growled. "If you try to interfere in our sacred practices, I will have you whipped—"

"No, you won't," Mari warned, rocking to the balls of her feet. "And beaten—"

"No, you won't," the Emissary croaked in her rusted voice. "No whipping. No beating." She faced Mari. "But that said, you'll not interfere. We'll have you removed if necessary, and confined until the Feigning. Is this what you want, Mariam, or would you retain the illusion of your freedom?"

Mari steadied her breathing, ready to take action. She met Dhoury's terrified gaze. He reached out for her, sobbing. Mari took a step forward and one of her cousins laid hands on her. Mari shrugged them off. Another rose and grabbed her shoulders, and Mari hammered him into the cold ground with her fists. She relented only when the Savadai in the Dowager-Asrahn's entourage leveled their tridents. Dhoury shrieked, a high-pitched keen filled with terror. The color drained from his face.

The Savadai dragged the struggling Dhoury to the edge of the Sea Shrine. One of the soldiers peered into the water, thrusting down with the butt of his trident before walking down several stairs and a few meters out onto a submerged shelf. He crouched down, eyes fixed on the surface of the water, until he found what he was looking for. The soldier heaved up a set of manacles affixed to thick chains and covered in seaweed and tiny shards of coral. He dragged the manacles back toward his comrades, who hauled Dhoury out onto the shelf. With speed born of practice, mixed with what Mari suspected was a healthy dose of fear, the Savadai shackled their prisoner's hands and feet, then dashed from the water.

Rising to her feet, the Dowager-Asrahn tottered down the stairs and out onto the shelf toward Dhoury, water lapping around her skinny shins. Her ceremonial over-robe fanned about her, its ragged blue-gray skirts blending with the sea. She drew a short club from the folds of her over-robe, an ugly thing of driftwood set with scores of shark's teeth. The flanged club rose and fell, scourging Dhoury's skin until ribbons of flesh hung from his crouched body. Blood flowed, swirling in the brine as he mewled.

"From the far east, across the Deep we came!" the Shark of Tamerlan shrieked into the easterly wind. "From the Deep we are nurtured and made strong. And to She Who Writhes in the Deep do we send this child of the Blood Royal, that she, too, may be nurtured, may remain strong, and may know our devotion to her."

Dhoury struggled to his feet, tugging on the chains as he screamed. The Dowager-Asrahn clubbed the man to his knees, her face lit with rapture. "For once show the strength of your bloodline! This is an honor for which you are not worthy, man-boy. But I give you grace nonetheless."

Dhoury tried to wrap his hands around the Dowager-Asrahn's throat. The crone stepped back, club swinging. Dhoury fell, stunned and silent, while the Dowager-Asrahn walked back to her family with head held high. The woman caught Mari's hateful stare and smiled as she returned to her place at the head of the gathering.

"Observe and testify!" the Dowager-Asrahn cried. She glared at Mari, teeth bared in a vicious smile. She stared down those about her. "Think on this in case any of you seek Pah-Mariam's company! The sea is always hungry."

They waited there as the waters rose, and the snow fell. Dhoury looked at Mari, eyes wide. She watched him tremble until he was blocked from sight when her cousins rose around the Dowager-Asrahn. They followed her as she made her way along the slick rock toward the stairs and safely from the quickly rising tide.

At the top of the stairs, Mari turned when she heard Dhoury scream. The water had reached his throat.

Mari swore, rooted to the spot. Thick, rubbery tentacles coiled out of the water. They undulated, causing small waves of their own. The wind carried the stench of the mottled appendages and Mari almost gagged. Dhoury's head whipped from side to side as the tentacles flexed against his skin. Those on the shore maintained their silence while Dhoury howled around mouthfuls of frigid brine. He was dragged beneath the water but rose, gasping. The manacles snapped and the man was dragged farther out to sea. When he submerged the third time he did not surface again.

Through it all Mari watched, blinking away her tears of frustration and rage. *Is this why my father is what he is, raised by such a woman? Is this what generations of the Erebus are doomed to be?*

Never again.

❊ ❊ ❊

The morning dragged on, and those in the fortress made no mention of Dhoury, or the sacrifice at the Sea Shrine. It was a common enough event that people kept their heads down and their voices low, none wishing to be singled out for the honor the next time.

Mari haunted the corridors listlessly, her guards in tow. Qesha-rē was not in the surgery, nor what passed for the library with its warped shelves and mold-dappled books. Dhoury's death. The enmity of her family. The Emissary. The Feigning. Mari's reasons for escaping grew, but there was also Vahineh to consider. Mari could not in conscience leave the woman here, not when it had been Mari's fault that Vahineh's father and brothers had been murdered by the Erebus. Or that Vahineh had been in Mari's care when they were forced into the Dead Flat, then captured and imprisoned in Tamerlan.

Flanked by six of the Savadai, Mari allowed herself to be taken back to her room. They all but shoved her inside, then slammed the door closed behind her. Bolts groaned in their rusted mountings. The sound of locks clicking shut was new. The footsteps of most of the guards vanished down the hall outside, but Mari guessed there were two, perhaps three, guards remaining stationed outside her door.

With quiet haste, Mari crossed her room. Among the meager clothing that had been given to her was an old over-robe, several sizes too large, stained, and lined with patchy fur. It was musty, with spots of mold staining the leather. Definitely not the kind of thing Mari would be seen wearing in public—but it would prove useful in not being seen. She changed into her oldest and most decrepit clothing, and dragged the over-robe on over the top. To all intents and purposes a local nahdi, down on her luck. Such stories were not uncommon on Tamerlan, and Mari hoped that people would see what they expected to see, rather than who she really was.

An icy east wind slammed into her face when she opened the mean little window, and it almost took her breath away. She gently slid two of the bars on her window out of place, their looseness the product of more than two score days of labor. Mari clambered onto the window ledge and swallowed at the vertigo that dizzied her. The ocean pounded into the cliffs more than one hundred meters below, jagged rocks like a mouth opening and closing in the swirling water.

A long, narrow ledge joined Mari's chambers with a disused balcony, built at once into Tamerlan and the mountainside. Part of the mountain had subsided, smashing walls and windows, and sheering away half the balcony. The area was overgrown with weeds and saplings, but there were the remains of a narrow stair that led down the mountain and into the village. It was one of several routes Mari had mapped out for her escape.

On careful feet, hands gripping the deep cracks between the stones, Mari made her way cautiously across the ledge. The wind became her ally, sweeping in from the east and pressing her against the wall like a huge, cold hand. Tamerlan vibrated under her fingers and toes, and her breath came in short, sharp sobs as her mind constantly told her to look down look down look down and anticipate the long, lonely fall that was to come. Mari stopped, and stared fixedly at the dark stone face before her. She controlled her breathing, slowed the hammering of her hearts, and concentrated only on the grip-step-slide of her progress.

Once both feet touched the wide safety of the ruined balcony, Mari dropped to a crouch and hugged her knees with relief, unsure whether to laugh or cry. So she did both.

Mari made good time down the snow-slick stairs to the town, obscured for the most part by jagged rocks and pines. The township knelt at Tamerlan's feet, slick granite and slate salted with white. Steam and smoke rose into the air, the tattered banners of domesticity and industry, ripped to nothing by the wind. Mari heard the distant clamor of the black rock salt mines, the foundries, and the forges, in counterpoint to the heartrending cries of gulls that seemed to float in the air. That same air reeked of fish, and tar, and the rotting piers that were home to more ships of war than merchant or fishing ships.

She turned at the sound of whips cracking. Overseers' arms rose and fell where they flailed at another boatload of workers unloaded from the galleys. The prisoners were downtrodden and filthy, though a few wore a defiance that told Mari they were captured soldiers. The majority appeared to be of the trade-castes: merchants, farmers, and artisans, the kind of people most often sold into the ranks of the bound-caste until they could pay off their debts. Mari doubted most would survive Tamerlan long enough to procure their freedom. The townsfolk of Tamerlan kept themselves to themselves: They set about their tasks, eyes downcast as prisoners were hurried along toward the mines.

The harbor was raucous. If Mari could find Morne Hawkwood there, she may have a chance of escaping the frigid rock to which she had been abandoned.

She strode toward the shale beach, set farther south than the piers, where ships huddled in the bay. As newcomers to Tamerlan, Morne and his crew would not have the influence to secure a place at a pier. The boats moored in the harbor were of different sizes and shapes, but all had the scarred look of reavers.

"Help you, miss?" a wind-burned merchant asked, keeping one eye on a barrel of a man in a stained apron. The two of them reeked of smoked and salted fish.

"Pardon?" she asked. Hearing her voice, the merchant stood straighter and tried to bow his head at the same time. It would have been comical were it not for the crowd around them. She cursed herself for her manners and her accent. "I'm looking for a company of nahdi who've made camp in Tamerlan."

"Plenty of them about, miss!" The man smiled, showing gaps where his teeth were not the color of burned ivory. He scratched at his salt-cured cheek with a dirty nail. "Have a name, do you? Or a ship?"

Mari pretended to give it some thought, chewing her lip for a second or two. "I'd heard that the company under Captain Hawkwood was hiring." She looked down, scuffing her feet on the ground. "And I'd rather have a contract while they're to be had, ahead of the winter, and out of here in the spring."

"I hear you. Reckon you'd be after *The Seeker*, at the far end of the bay." He pointed a thick finger toward a two-masted corsair with neither figurehead, nor colors of any allegiance. "Last in, last served. They'll have a rough time of it when winter falls and the weather gets rowdy. All the inns is double- and triple-booked, and the Dowager-Asrahn ain't known for letting mongrels she don't know in her kennel."

"Better any safe harbor than no harbor at all," the apron-wearing merchant said, his companion nodding in sage agreement. "But Hawkwood's crew mind their manners and pay for what they want, which is a nice change of pace from most of the stray dogs that descend on Tamerlan. There's music playing late at night, and singing."

"And lights. Always keeping the lights on aboard *The Seeker*."

"Lights?" Mari smiled, her hearts racing a little faster.

"All the day and all the long night," the weathered merchant said.

"Must have a lot of shadows to banish, that one," the man in the apron added. "Fellow like him, hard as an anvil but nice spoken for all that."

"Can you get me out there?" Mari asked.

"We've deliveries to make. If you're all right with perching among the cargo, we can take you."

Once the merchants had loaded their cargo, Mari walked up the bowing plank and boarded the felucca, making herself as comfortable as she could among the cargo. The merchants took up a deep-voiced dirge of the sea, of sunken ships, faraway lands, and lost loves, their voices accompanied by the hum of the wind through the ropes and the snap of the sails. From ship to ship they went until eventually they drew closer to *The Seeker*. The closer they got, the more excited Mari became.

Mari heard the metallic twang of a sonesette, and tears came unbidden to her eyes. Shar! And where there was Shar, there was Indris. She clasped her hands together, face flushed, feeling like a teenage girl and laughing at herself for the butterflies in her stomach.

As the felucca came alongside *The Seeker*, Mari came to stand by the gunwale. It felt like an eternity for the rope ladder to be lowered from *The Seeker*. Mari leaped from the felucca and scrambled up the ladder and over the rail, to be met by the cold and wary eyes of *The Seekers'* armored crew. It was then that Mari heard the words to Shar's song and noted the deep, angry sound of it. Many of the crew stamped their feet on the deck like scores of leather-soled drums.

Falling like a frozen stone

Sundered flesh and broken bone

Lives are lost, we're all alone

Now the laughs and light are gone

So

When passion burns and mercy's stilled

With vengeance high and sinners killed

By bitter hate our hearts be filled

We rend and end by iron will

When strength and love are not enough

Draw your steel and make the cut

Take your cup and hold it up

Taste their tears and never stop

Heads held high

We will never stop

The angry strumming of the sonesette continued as one of the men Mari recognized from the Hearthall of Tamerlan approached. Close up he was shorter than she imagined, stockier, with fine hair swept back from a high brow. His eyes were a vivid hazel against his tanned skin, his face scored here and there with old scars and wrinkles.

"I'm Pah-Erebus—"

"We know who you are, Pah-Mariam," the man said as he peered toward shore. He grabbed her elbow and escorted her through the wall of the crew. "We're here for you, and I take it you've not much time before your absence is discovered, so let's be quick about it." He gave quiet orders to those around him to recall the crew who were ashore, and to make ready to leave Tamerlan. "I'm hoping you weren't followed. We risk much by leaving unannounced, so close to the south becoming closed with the season."

"I heard Morne's invitation." Mari shrugged his hand off and stood her ground. "But I can't leave now."

"Then why risk us all by coming here?" the warrior snapped.

"That's enough, Kyril," Morne Hawkwood said as he approached. Unlike Kyril, Morne was even taller than Mari remembered, almost as tall as Ekko, carrying the weight of his leather hauberk easily. His basket-hilted knife hung within his easy reach. He wrapped an arm around Kyril's shoulders and kissed him. "I said the words, love, and Mariam answered. What did you expect?"

"We need to get gone, while the getting is good. If we're caught with her here, this could be the end of us."

"How?" Morne looked perplexed. He ran his fingers through Kyril's hair playfully, bringing a smile to the man's face. "You'd never let me die. Besides, we've faced more, and worse, than the yapping mongrels who've slunk here for the winter. We'll slip out on the evening tide, Mari hidden away and us long gone before anybody's the wiser."

"You don't understand. It's not just me going with you," Mari said. "The Rahn-Selassin fe Vahineh is also being held captive and I've sworn to help her escape, as well as her surgeon. I'm trying to plan how I can get us all out of the fortress, but wanted to speak with you myself first. I don't have much time, and I don't want to put anybody at further risk, but I have exhausted all my other options. I fear that if I don't get away from here soon, I'll not get away from here at all. My grandmother's taken something of a colossal dislike to me, and there are plans made for me that I dearly want to avoid."

"Can't imagine how you'd annoy anybody," came a breathy voice. Mari spun, and found herself in the circle of Shar's arms. The Seethe woman's orange eyes were bright with unshed tears, and the feathers braided into her fine quills fluttered in the wind. Behind her, Ekko loomed, a furred mountain, his eyes narrowed with joy. Shar hugged Mari close. "I never thought I'd see you again!"

"Nor I you!" She kissed Shar, hugged Ekko, then looked for the man she wanted above all others. Moments turned long and remained empty, until Mari faced Shar and Ekko, bewildered. "Where's Indris? I thought he'd be here."

Shar's face fell and tears made her eyes shine a brighter orange. Mari felt her own face tingle as the blood rushed there. Her breath caught. Shar tried to speak. The words were trapped in her throat. When they came, it was amid a strangled sob.

"Oh, Mari! You didn't know? I'm so sorry, but . . . Indris is—"

Don't say the word don't say the word don't say the word don't say the word. The roaring in her ears grew so loud that she did not hear what Shar said.

She saw her friend's lips form the word anyway.

Dead.

❋ ❋ ❋

Mari trudged up the mountain stair, back the way she had come, numb to the wind and the cold. Shar and Ekko were alive and a ship waited in the bay, ready to whisk her away to somewhere safe. Soon, Mari could start the rest of her life, but there was business to be concluded here first.

"So many died, Mari," Shar had said of the events at Avānweh. The pain of the reopened wound made her voice brittle. "Indris was taken by Femensetri to the battle and he never . . . he never came back. Then all the Sēq left and there was nobody to get any answers from, or to even make sure Indris was planted, like a mourner's rose in a field of ashes."

"And then Asrahn-Corajidin was crowned and the trouble started in earnest," Morne had added. "We heard about the strife in Amnon while we were defending the Conflicted Cities. The Catechism of Manté see Corajidin's Assession as a sign they should redouble their efforts to destroy the Avān. So I decided to pick up and bring the Immortal Companions to Narsis, hoping to take service with Rahn-Roshana in opposition to your father. That didn't work out very well. So when Shar and Ekko arrived, traveling with them was the logical choice. I left most of our strength in Narsis, and brought with us what we'd need."

"And with Indris gone," Shar had said, "we decided to do the one thing we know he would've wanted us to do. To find you."

What Indris would have wanted. Indris would tear this dung pile apart, stone by stone. It seemed like as good an idea as any. Mari looked up at the ancient fortress, its black stone clawing jaggedly at the sky. *It's past time I left.*

But only once she had made an end of those who ruled it.

Shoulders square, lips set in a mockery of a smile, Mari headed willingly to the darkness of Tamerlan.

9

"A CHARACTER STRONG ENOUGH TO RULE IS NOT FORGED IN PEACE,
QUIET, OR AN EASY LIFE. IT IS ONLY THROUGH THE RIGORS OF
EXPERIENCE, OF SUFFERING, OF MAKING DECISIONS, AND OF
ACCEPTING THE CONSEQUENCES OF ACTION, AND INACTION,
THAT ONE WHO WOULD WEAR A CROWN IS TEMPERED."

—from *The Intransigent Winter of Monarchy,* by King Voethe of Angoth,
thirteenth year of his reign (493rd Year of the Shrīanese Federation)

DAY 59 OF THE 496TH YEAR OF THE

SHRĪANESE FEDERATION

"How can we trust something we cannot understand?" Corajidin pointed to where Kimiya sat, strapped to a wheeled chair at neck, torso, and limbs, morning sun limning her as it streamed through the conservatory windows. When they had moved her from Kasraman's laboratory earlier that morning, Kimiya had broken free and killed four of the Anlūki before Wolfram, Elonie, and Ikedion had managed to subdue her with witchcraft. All the while, the thing that Kimiya had become, spattered with gore, had laughed.

117

Corajidin shook his head. "Kimiya is gone. All that remains is the marsh-puppeteer!"

"You need to do something, Corajidin." The Emissary lurked at the other side of the room. "Time marches you know, and the malegangers offer you a unique solution. Kimiya, and those we make like her, can be the instruments for your will."

"Instruments for your objectives?"

"Our objectives. And what of it? A debt paid is a debt paid."

"Isn't she a pretty, mad, little murdering thing?" Nix said, eye twitching as he crouched on his chair, a slender knife spinning between his fingers. "Can you imagine the carnage she'd cause? A Soul Trader could have given us malign souls to use, but the ones I've met are cracked as old cups, and I'd not trust them. But this little beauty? Oh, yes . . ."

"You've really no idea," the Emissary replied.

"With malegangers we'd still have an Ajamensût." Kasraman ran his fingers across Kimiya's matted hair. She looked up at him, expression wild and not far from insane. "It would be a War of the Long-Knife without the need to buy assassins, or nahdi, or risk the lives of our own people."

"It's not right," Belamandris said. Corajidin glanced at his golden son. Belam had returned to Erebesq last night with Sanojé, but without an explanation of where he had been. Belamandris's disgust was apparent on his face. "It's worse than the abductions."

Nix bounced in his chair enthusiastically. "Imagine one of these let loose in every Federationist Great House or suspect Family. Ancestors' names, we could unleash a maleganger against any enemy! They're perfect for our needs and they'd justify the arrests my ban-kherife have been making. We could actually make traitors out of the traitors we've made."

"Not to mention what damage we could do if we unleashed the puppeteers against the ambassadors," Mēdēya added. "Provided the puppeteers take instruction, they could well pave the road we've been trying to make all year."

"Puppeteers? The pullers of string. Such a little name for something so old," Kimiya rasped. Rivulets of drool shone on her cracked lips. "For we have seen empires rise and fall and remember the mad symphonies of our sleeping makers. You're vain things, lusting after hats and chairs of gold. Your belief that we could be used for anything other than our own purposes is the height of arrogance."

"You hear this? To what end would we even want to use such a creature?" Belamandris asked. "It'd be pure carnage, with innocents harmed in the process. What example are we setting if we can't follow sende ourselves? Did you buy Shrīan just to dismantle it, Father?" He stared at Kimiya, hand lingering on Tragedy's hilt. "It's a monster, and we should put it down."

"My Asrahn," Wolfram said as he leaned on his broken staff. The leather and old steel of his calipers protested. "Perhaps Belamandris is correct. We should reconsider such rash action."

"You see!" Belamandris gestured at Wolfram. "Rash. Action."

"Belam, please!" Kasraman said. Kimiya giggled, thrashing against her bonds, veins protruding from her neck, face red and eyes rolling. "We need to unite the country, one way or the other. This is the fastest way. The Golden Kingdom of Manté, and the rest of the Iron League—"

"And the Sky Lord suspects we engineered that, too," Sanojé added.

Corajidin raised his hands for peace. "Can we please focus on—"

"We lied to the nation about Manté!" Belamandris snapped. "The Humans and their Iron League were never attacking Avānweh. Are our memories so short, that we believe our own falsehoods now?"

"My liches are hidden away against reprisals, after all they did to help secure the city," Sanojé said. "You've sharpened hatreds against Humans and Nomads—"

"All the better to unify and make war on Pashrea, then the Iron League," Kasraman said.

"But not the best way." Belamandris shared a glance with Sanojé, who was chewing her finger in uncertainty. "Not the best by far. What have we become? Your regicide I understood . . . to a degree. Even buying the crown was something I could accept because I believed, then, that you had a compass that would guide us. But this? And releasing the witches? Raising Yashamin from the dead? Where does it end, Father? Erebus himself must be spitting on us from the Well of Souls."

"You dare say these things to me?" Corajidin thundered. He took Mēdēya under his arm. He felt the rage rise in him so mightily that words failed.

"Brother, the Erebus have been given the chance to rise once more," Kasraman said as Corajidin choked on his anger. The others all looked to Kasraman where he stood behind Kimiya. He rested both his hands on her shoulders, clearly unafraid. Tall, handsome, a hero of Avānweh and the heir to one of the Great Houses, his pale eyes blazed in the light. Corajidin wanted to spit the sourness from his mouth as the others hung on Kasraman's words. "We've been given this opportunity. History will remind future generations that it was we who forged Shrīan in a new, vital image. That it was we who made the Avān great again!"

"Enough!" Corajidin felt a painful twinge at his temple. His fingers trembled and he clenched them against the faint tingling there. *What was it the Emissary had said? Abdicate and let Kasraman, wise and gifted and powerful Kasraman, do what it's clear you can't.* "You have all said much more than enough. Mine is the voice that will be heard."

"And what would you have us hear, Corajidin?" the Emissary asked into the silence.

A good question that deserves a better answer than the one I do not have.

Corajidin summoned a smile and walked to the sideboard. He slowly, methodically, poured the water and whisked a bowl of green lotus tea. It was a calming ritual and one that would give him time to reflect, without appearing weak.

Since the beginning of the year, his plans to abduct and hold for ransom influential members of Avān society had netted few quantifiable results. True, it served as a lever to enforce unity among those who might oppose him, but the longer his prisoners were kept, the more likely those he tried to influence would act of their own accord. His guests were being treated with kindness and compassion, in a closely guarded villa in the mountains above Nix's ancestral seat of Maladhi. But they could not be held there forever. Mariam's plight at Tamerlan would be nothing compared to what his guests would face should they be exposed to marsh-puppeteers.

As Kasraman had explained it, the vile creatures would throttle their victims to near the point of death, affixing themselves to their victim's backs, merging with them until little more than ridges of scar tissue spoke of their presence. Knowing everything the victim knew, yet fueled with the puppeteer's malevolence, the creature would seek to sow discord wherever it went. Kasraman was correct: They were a brilliant weapon. A killing machine none would expect. Each one made at the cost of a person's life.

Corajidin was reminded of the ritual on Sycamore Hill, where the Weaver had somehow managed to place Yashamin's soul in Mēdēya's body. He glanced across the room at his wife and shuddered at his memories of what had happened to her. Another bargain with the Drear that came with a bitter twist. *And I want these people to help Narseh! What will they do to her? Erebus, deliver me! The sooner I am freed from the Drear and their Emissary, the better.*

"Kasraman? Wolfram? Can you and the other witches make this thing talk?" Corajidin pointed at Kimiya. "It hails from the Rōmarq, and by its own admission has the memories of its kind that have come before—"

"What one knows, all know," Kimiya said.

"Then you will know what I am looking for when I ask it of you." Corajidin wrapped the folds of his over-robe around him like armor as he approached her. She glared at him through the filthy length of her fringe, baring her teeth in a low hiss as he came within arm's reach. "There are secrets in the Rōmarq I would have. Knowledge and weapons. Power. Things locked in the sediment of ages, lost to the Avān."

"Yes."

"Things lost to the Avān," Corajidin said, leaning closer to Kimiya, "but not to you. The Sēq and their Black Archives are beyond me at the moment, but you . . . you are not."

"You would trade favors with me, oh drowsy rahn?" Kimiya's body seemed to thrum with excitement. She flicked a glance at the Emissary. "Have you not learned that we who are servants of the old ways can be capricious? Often demanding, even cruel?"

"If you give me what I want, then I will give you and your people what you need. But you will need to deal with me in good faith."

"And you presume to know—"

"Bodies," Corajidin said flatly. "I will give you bodies. Leaders of enterprise, merchant sayfs . . . people of influence. But we must work together for a time."

And Kimiya stopped fighting against her bonds. Her only movements were a nod and a grotesque smile.

❇ ❇ ❇

"You'll turn the nation against us when they learn what you've done." Belamandris's tone was condemning.

"We will survive as we have always survived," Corajidin replied. He kissed the top of Mēdēya's head where she leaned against his chest. She felt warm in the circle of his arms. The observatory at Erebesq was a cold and cheerless place, of dark veined marble, glossy black floor tiles. Of polished metal wheels, gears and levers for the telescope, and sliding panels of the roof dome. Corajidin looked up at the sky. There were no stars, only the blue-green patina of the moon streaked with white.

"So, Father. Are you really going to do it?" Kasraman poured thick coffee into silver cups and handed them to his family and those closest to them. Corajidin had gnawed on his displeasure when Sanojé had joined them, but it was worth it to have Belamandris's company, sour as it was. Wolfram stood alone in the middle of the floor, halfway between Corajidin and Kasraman. His big knuckled hands rested on the huge canted tube of the telescope. The old witch bent to peer into the eyepiece, though what revelations he expected to find in the cloudy sky were beyond Corajidin.

Am I really going to do it? Corajidin had been asking himself the same question in the hours since he had dismissed his counselors. He regretted speaking so hastily, but the Emissary's presence was a constant reminder of how far he had come using her treatment. There was no recovery from his illness, of that he was certain. The Emissary had loaned Corajidin every second of his life since the Battle of Amnon, and he had mortgaged his future to her without thought for the ramifications. *I am the servant of destiny, and I make my own fate. I am Asrahn. I am my people's keeper.* Yet having desire and destiny travel the same road did not make all decisions the right ones. As Wolfram was fond of saying, the future was a pond whose banks we can't see. When we start throwing stones, we've no idea where the ripples will go, how long they will take, or what they may swamp on their way to their destination.

Belamandris sat hip to hip with his Tanisian lover: she who had brought Nomads into Corajidin's life with her Chepherundi Box, and the liches inside them! Were it not for her, Corajidin would never have looked to the Nomads for answers. He would have left Yashamin as a memory, grieving her as was right and proper. And the Emissary! With her traveling show of gifts and temptations, so like the Seethe cirqs and carnivals that wandered the world, dazzling the unwary with things they should know better than to offer. Dealing with the Seethe—ageless, virtually death-less, and world weary—was like a child accepting rum from adults lost to drink. The elders should know better, yet were so steeped in their own misery, and oblivious to its consequences, that they simply did not care anymore. The Emissary's gifts had left Corajidin intoxicated at first. Now he was sobering. He suspected his sobri-ety may be too little, too late. The damage was done, however, the ripples spreading out, and only more, larger, ripples might set things right again.

Corajidin surveyed his extended family, including Sanojé, for Belamandris would have it no other way. Another thing Belamandris had in common with Mariam: loving unwisely. He took comfort in the knowledge that Indris was dead and gone, the Sēq retired from the field, and there were few who stood in the way now.

"Father?" Kasraman asked, waiting for an answer while Coraji-din's mind had wandered.

Am I going to do it? Corajidin thought again.

"I do not know," Corajidin answered. He hugged Mēdēya, pre-tending for a moment she was the original he adored and not the replacement he doubted. "There is much to be said for the use of the marsh-puppeteers and as much to be said against."

"More to be said against," Belamandris murmured.

"He speaks truly, Asrahn," Sanojé said. "We've seen malegangers in Tanis, and experienced firsthand the havoc they cause. They're unpredictable, uncontrollable, and untrustworthy."

"But have you ever made a bargain with them?" Kasraman asked. "Offered them something they want, to pique their enlightened self-interest?"

"No," the beautiful little Tanisian admitted. "We've not. Nor did it occur to us such a thing was possible. They and the Fenling are not creatures we'd deal with by choice."

"You traffic with Nomads, and your Ancestors turn themselves into liches." Kasraman smiled condescendingly. "Consider the irony."

"You revere your Ancestors," Sanojé replied. "Your rahns hold them in their minds and traffic with them daily. We both cling to the ones we've loved."

"We choose our own paths, it's true," Kasraman agreed. "And what if we've run out of choices? Or good choices at least. What then?"

"Do we need to act so quickly?" Wolfram asked. The old man stretched and rubbed his back. "Belamandris was correct in that we've fallen for our own story regarding Manté and the Iron League. There's nothing driving us to haste. My Asrahn, you've been in power for a short time and still have almost five years of your current term to unite the country. I counsel a more cautious path, less prone to unwitting disaster."

"But we are driven to haste," Corajidin said. "The College of Artificers has said that they can get the Torque Spindles working. This knowledge will not be kept secret for long. Once the Iron League discovers that we can make large armies in a short time frame, they will fix their attention, and their very large military force, on us . . ."

The others stayed silent, letting the thought sink in. Corajidin took advantage of their silence and continued, "The Iron League are aware the Imperialist faction will unify Shrīan for military and economic conquest. It has never been a secret. The Mercantile Guild, the Banker's House, and the other consortiums of the middle-castes will rally behind the chance to expand their interests, flooding foreign markets with Shrīanese goods and procuring inexpensive labor to make more. It will give their political agendas a practical focus. With the threat of both military and trade wars looming, we will find that time is something we do not have."

"You can control the merchants and bankers, Father," Belamandris said.

"Can I?" Corajidin mused. "The Upper House of the Teshri is run by the Great Houses, but the Lower House is controlled by the Hundred Families, most of whom have grown fat on the gold they earn from trade and taxes." *And my bribes, the bastards!* "The State and Crown are the tip of the tree. But the roots dig deep in dirty earth and are much harder to find, let alone remove."

As much as he hated to admit it, the marsh-puppeteers offered him an elegant solution, and one not easily traced back to the Great House of Erebus.

"But all this aside," Corajidin said gently, "the Emissary demands action. And I need to save Rahn-Narseh if I'm to have an Imperialist ally in the Upper House of the Teshri. Which means for now we must unite Shrīan under a common cause, to achieve our goals."

"And to leverage from what we've already started with the abductions," Kasraman added.

"And those goals would be what, Father?" Belamandris did not look up when he spoke.

"To take the next step in unifying the Avān." Corajidin spoke the words but felt like the Emissary lurked at the back of his tongue. "There cannot be two Mahjs over one people. We will use the marsh-puppeteers to silence dissent and to destroy our enemies. In return for bodies, they will locate the most powerful weapons in the Rōmarq for us.

"When the marsh-puppeteers have served their purpose, I will use the weapons they helped me find, and the witches we freed from the Mahsojhin, to destroy the puppeteers once and for all. Then we invade Pashrea and destroy the last of the Sēq power base."

"And that's all?" Belamandris mocked.

"Then I become the next Mahj, and lead the Avān across the world in conquest."

The words did not taste as sweet as he had thought they would.

✳ ✳ ✳

Corajidin swayed as he walked the empty corridors of his qadir. The skirts of his sleeping gown and over-robe swept the rugs behind him with a gentle shushing sound that soothed him. His slippered feet were silent, and the only other noises were the occasional footfalls of the guards and the faint crack of ice as it formed on the windows. He cradled a golden bowl in one hand. Dark wine sloshed over the brim with every step. The neck of a vintage bottle of ruby lotus wine was clutched in the other. Corajidin emptied his bowl and clumsily filled another.

"You don't need the other rahns, my love," Mēdēya had said as she had straddled him, his fingers lost in the masses of her hair as he drowned in her gaze and inhaled her panting breath. Riding him to crescendo, she had leaned in, urgent and remorseless in her passion. "No Mahj shares power! End them all, and rule alone as you were destined to."

In the shallow hours of the morning, her words echoed in his head yet. He could not look at his own reflection in the windows for fear he would tell himself, in the quiet, prideful places of his mind, that she was right.

Corajidin meandered in the near dark, a ghost among his own memories. Some good, most shaded with the darkness of his father, Basyrandin, and the powers he and Corajidin's mother had trafficked with when they thought Corajidin was asleep. What was it the Emissary had said? *My predecessors have had a long and mutually beneficial relationship with your house, Corajidin. Such as your mother, the Dowager-Asrahn . . . we know you of old. And have done well by you.*

He found himself in Mariam's old bedchamber. It was large and cold, the fires unlit. The big wooden bed with its ornate head, carved with the seahorse and stallion of her mother's Family, as well as his own, was made as if she would tumble into it at any time. He touched the empty weapon and armor racks. Ran his fingers across the gilt leather spines of her old books. On impulse he took one down from the shelf and flicked through pages of sketches she had done when but a teenager, before she had become willful like her mother.

Corajidin smiled at the memory. From wine came truth: Farha of the Dahrain had been a formidable woman, a woman who refused to tolerate Corajidin's antics. It was something he had treasured in her as much as it had frustrated him, and it was something that first Mariam, and now Belamandris, had inherited.

What have I done to you, my daughter? Of all the places in the world, how could I have sent you to Tamerlan?

"What are you doing, Father?" Belamandris asked from the doorway. Corajidin turned, almost tripping on his over-robe. Wine spilled on his clothes and spattered the rugs. Belamandris was fully dressed, armed and armored. A fur-clad Sanojé stood by his side.

"Where are you going at this time of night?" Corajidin articulated with inebriated pride. He carefully placed Mariam's book of sketches back on the shelf, happy it took only three attempts. "You should be in your beds. Your separate beds."

"Father, you long stopped commenting on whom I slept with, be it women, men, or any combination of the two. Might I suggest that your silence on this matter will be more appreciated than whatever drunken insult you're about to spew at me?"

Corajidin staggered forward, arms wide, but stopped at the chill in his son's posture. "What happened between us? We were close, you and I."

"That's a conversation for a later, more sober time. What are you doing in Mariam's room?"

"Regretting, mostly." He took a deep breath to steady himself. "I have done wrong by Mariam. So very wrong. Had I the chance to amend the past then, perhaps, I might have exercised the strength a father should on behalf of his children."

Belamandris and Sanojé shared a look. He whispered something to her. They kissed, and she dashed off. Belamandris looked his father up and down, eyes narrow with suspicion. "Do you mean that, Father? Would you try to undo some of the wrong you've done?"

"Of course!"

In a swift move, Belamandris took Corajidin in his arms and hugged him. Corajidin felt his face grow warm, and tears formed in his eyes. He buried his face in the fur lining of his son's over-robe, wiping the tears away, but others soon followed. Belamandris turned his head and whispered into Corajidin's ear.

"Then I'll tell her as much when I bring her back from Tamerlan, and our grandmother's idea of hospitality."

With those words he was gone, a fleet shape that flickered between pools of light and shadow down the corridor.

Corajidin staggered back to sit on Mariam's bed. His son had forgiven him! His daughter would be saved.

Because he had done what the Emissary, and destiny, demanded of him.

Finishing the bottle of wine in one draft, Corajidin lay back on the bed. He pulled a fur over himself against the chill. Curled into a ball around his empty wine bowl, he at last allowed sleep to take him.

"TRUTH, LIKE BEAUTY, CHANGES FROM PERSON TO PERSON."

—Karisa of the Ijalian, troubadour and poet to Rahn-Näsarat fe Roshana
(496th Year of the Shrīanese Federation)

DAY 60 OF THE 496TH YEAR OF THE

SHRĪANESE FEDERATION

At the end of another tiring day, Indris returned to the Black Archives.

Inside, the Herald waited, its mirrored mask showing Indris a distorted reflection of himself. The Herald followed Indris through the central archive, and along the changing route of stairs to the vaults. On his way up, Indris collected scrolls and some journals, bound in soft black leather, that had showed promise. The formal grimoires had proven to be a disappointment: Sedefke had covered his arcane tracks well, with few hints at Awakening in what remained of his work.

The biggest disappointment was the lack of any reference to the mental disciplines of the Mah-Psésahen. The high mental teachings were not even alluded to, let alone found, in any of the Master's collected works. It was as if the practice had never existed. Similarly, references to the Dream Key, something Taqrit had questioned Indris on at Avānweh, were scarce. Some historical works described it as a physical artifact, others a person, and two books discussed it as a thought process that accessed layers of dreams that could be used as weapons, or to alter the fabric of space and time. The reasons for the existence of the Dream Key had been heavily redacted, in some cases to the point where whole chapters had been excised from the books. The one thing all the sages agreed on was that the Dream Key was a legacy of the Dragons, a shared academic stance that gave Indris not the slightest bit of comfort.

"Is it safe for me to open this vault?" Indris asked the Herald as they returned to the uppermost floor.

"No harm will come to you."

Indris chuckled. "That wasn't what I asked."

"Yet it is my answer all the same."

"You said I learned things I wasn't supposed to know . . . or know yet. I don't need the Possibility Tree to figure that my memories were tampered with because of what I discovered. If somebody is going to stamp around in my head again because of what I'm doing here, I might just save myself the time."

The Herald shook its masked face, reflections swimming, sending myriad points of light dancing. "You were sent to the Spines because somebody else found a reference to you going, and acted precipitously. So rather than finding it for yourself when it was time for you to do so, you caused effects to happen sooner than they should. This is different. You are learning these things now, at this moment, because it is you that have chosen to do so."

"You're not talking about prophecy, are you?" Indris barely kept the derision from his voice.

"There is no such thing. There is only observation and extrap-olation."

"Like the Probability Tree."

"If you like." Indris caught the broad brush of condescension in the Herald's voice. The Herald picked up the glass jug of water Indris had brought with him, and the old silver drinking bowl. Holding the jug high, the Herald poured water into the bowl. "This is how you see the passage of time. A stream that flows from one point to the next."

"You sound like Cennoväl in his lectures on comparative phi-losophy and causality," Indris said. "He said much the same thing. I take it there is another way of perceiving time?"

The Herald plucked two buttons from Indris's over-robe, then dropped them into the jug of water. He held up the glass jug and swirled it around, faint rainbows glimmering, the buttons circling on invisible currents. The water continued to eddy for a few moments before becoming still. The buttons fell to the bottom in gentle curves, tapping the jug on their way down, landing in differ-ent places. "We can see a stream, or we can see that from a remove, all things happen at the same time. From that remove we see the direction of all things at all times. The water moves when agitated, but does not escape the container. Though the buttons entered the container together, and followed their own paths to their destina-tion, we saw it all from our vantage."

"That's observation without the need to extrapolate anything."

"What then if I placed my fingers in the water and diverted one, or both, of the buttons? Or removed one and replaced it with something different?"

Indris nodded. "Then you would need to understand the vari-ables in a constantly changing and often erratic universe, delivering infinite variation." *But who sees time this way?*

"It does not matter who, Indris," the Herald said. Indris's eyebrows shot up at having the thoughts plucked from his head. "It only matters that there are those that can, and do. There are those that observe and extrapolate, and they know when to take action to ensure the bouncing stone does not become an avalanche before it is ready to do so."

"My journey to the Spines caused you to reveal yourself, didn't it?" Indris moved to stand in front of the vault with his name on it. "Ojin-mar said you arrived unannounced to work with the Suret, guiding them. Would I be correct in saying you arrived eight years ago—about the same time I arrived on the Spines?"

"Yes. And just as we Heralds arrived to guide those we were chosen to work with, so, too, were others delivered to the hands of those who would oppose us. I am only one of a number of Heralds, just as the Emissary that advises Corajidin is only one of her kind, also."

"What is an Emissary, and why does one advise Corajidin?"

"For the same reason I, and those like me, support those who will one day need to gather for the greatest conflict of the age: because you were made, were sent, to the Spines too early, and learned what you did ahead of time."

Indris felt his face flush, and his head felt light. *What have I done? Maybe it's better off I don't know!* He looked past his name-plate on the vault at the pattern of the Maladhoring glyphs that dripped like rivulets through the tinted *serill*, changed from moment to moment, became gibberish.

See beneath the surface, Indris commanded himself.

He looked deeper, his eyes slightly unfocused so he could see the words behind the words, then words behind those words.

The tiered mess of Maladhoring glyphs became ordered questions. They ranged in complexity and topic from the theories of arcane formulae, to history, to advanced calculations for disentropy and entropy. The deeper he looked, the more questions were revealed, each more complex than the ones before. It was a Reason Lock.

Over the next several hours, Indris answered the questions as best he could. When he announced an answer in Maladhoring, the question shimmered, then solidified in the glass. Some became the spokes of a wheel. Others curved like parts of a tumbler. Each answered question etched the lock mechanism in the *serill* door. The Herald remained quiet and attentive. Indris did not ask him the answers to any questions: As the Herald had said, what value is there in knowledge given, when wisdom comes from the learning?

On several occasions, Indris had to leave the vault to find his answers in ancient volumes of lore. It became apparent that some of the questions were Master-level knowledge, if not higher. There were some topics with which Indris was completely unfamiliar. Each volume he opened, and each passage he read, helped further his understanding of the Esoteric Doctrines.

Eyes burning with fatigue, Indris grimaced at the vault door. It was not long until dawn, and there were few questions left: one on the nature of matter, transformation, and shape-shifting, another few on arcane engineering principles in different mediums, two on the histories of the Time Masters and the rise and subsequent disappearance of their Haiyt Empire, one on methods of translocation he had never heard of before . . . and one on Awakening he did not even begin to understand.

"Am I ready for this?" Indris asked the air, forgetting in his musings that the Herald was there.

"If you can open the door, there is no doubt you are ready."

"And if not?"

The Herald shrugged, cloak rustling against his frame. "You will not open the door."

"Helpful."

"You are quite welcome."

Indris shook his head as he trudged to the only place where there was anything of note on Awakening. It was a secluded part of the archive set aside for the works of scholars considered too dangerous to be part of the orthodox canon. Most forbidden of these were the volumes of Yattoweh the Apostate.

Among his works—from the time he had been Sedefke's most gifted student as well as the Arch-Scholar and Grand Master Magnate of the Sēq Order—were those that formed the foundations of learning for the earliest scholars of Isenandar. The Pillars of Sand was where Yattoweh had taught many hundreds of students before his Fall, then dragged some of the best and brightest with him in his descent into the Drear. Though he had traveled the darker paths of learning, his early work was considered brilliant, and it rivaled that of Sedefke himself. Yattoweh was the only other person reputed to have properly understood how Awakening worked. Indris had seen similar things in Jiom, Atrea, and Manté, where scholars, artificers, and witches had tried to understand and bring life back to the ancient relics of the Starborn. Some still worked, thousands of years after the Humans had descended on Īa, but once they failed there were none who could fix them.

The energy of Indris's Awakening, coiled through and about the energy centers of his body, shifted in something he suspected was anticipation.

On a small witchfire pedestal, its white leather covers turned ivory with age, were the eight volumes of Yattoweh's greatest literary work: *The Foundations*. Penned in the Pillars of Sand, *The Foundations* was part Yattoweh's journal, part text and part challenge, confounding most of those who read it. Indris, however, was only interested in one part of the book.

Flicking through the ancient writings, Indris found what he was after at the middle of volume one. He centered his mind, tracked the lines of precise calligraphy that were faded on the page, and opened his consciousness like a flower to absorb the work of one of the greatest minds in history.

The reading was difficult, as much allegory and metaphor as information. Indris was forced to read, then reread, whole sections where they cross-referenced each other. *The Foundations* was a literal title, for without comprehension of the early chapters, those that came after were useless. As the hours passed, Indris began to understand the fundamental changes Awakening made to a person, the way it rerouted the flow of energy not only in the body, but in the interchanges between physical, mental, and spiritual states. He tapped his finger on a brightly colored picture of a person with arms and legs outstretched, where a serpent was depicted as coiling about the spine. It passed through the five physical energy vortices, then upward to the vortex of the mind, and out through the vortex of the soul, where it connected with the vast consciousness outside the body.

There was one passage Indris read twice, then a third time, to ensure he understood it correctly:

> Awakening is an unnatural state for us at our current level of awareness of whom, and what, we are. Put simply, neither our bodies, nor minds, nor souls, are capable of sustaining the kind of energy that they channel once Awakened.
>
> To be Awakened is the beginning of a long road into eventual self-destruction and madness. Regular doses of the Water of Life can mitigate these effects, as can the sparing use of the abilities Awakening bestows. Even so, the entropic effects of Awakening are considerable over time. We need to find better ways to attune with such vast powers. But until we interbreed with races such as the Inoqua, the Rōm, or others of the Elemental Masters—or create a generation of superior beings as part of a great Feigning—any Avān not properly schooled in the Esoteric Doctrines is doomed to suffer effects such as ahm-stroke, or mindstorms, and advanced entropic decay . . .

He felt a sinking sensation in his stomach, followed by a rising anger that made him almost throw the precious book against the wall.

Faruqen Suret! All along they knew that Awakening was a death sentence, and yet still they did it! What else haven't they told us?

Indris slumped, dazed. Angry and betrayed, Yattoweh's revelations in his lap. While what he had read of the book had not given the answers to the question to open the vault, it had enlightened him in a different sense. Indris's muscles protesting, he stretched, and groaned as his joints popped. He carefully placed the book back on the stand.

At the top of the well of knowledge, the Genealogy Tree shimmered, flickers of light among smears of darkness. Like fact, among truth, among lies.

✳ ✳ ✳

Indris spent the morning at the Manufactory. But that morning the heat and fatigue bested him, as did his hurt at the findings in Yattoweh's ancient texts. Weary, he curled asleep on the warm tiles in front of the forges.

It was almost high sun, the first Hour of the Spider, when Indris made his way to the Black Quill. Mug of tea cradled on his belly, he sat slouched in an overstuffed chair in front of the fire. The din in the tavern was refreshing, far better than the stilted silence of the study chambers and libraries. Behind him a handful of Sēq novices were performing an impromptu concert.

The noise and bustle of the Black Quill filled the silence he had come to despise: the silence that reminded him of his missing friends. Worse, he heard Mari's voice or imagined she was sitting with him, or lying in bed, breathing gently. But it was always the wind, laden with secrets for those who knew how to listen, none of which could help him overcome the emptiness he felt.

The Black Quill exorcised his loneliness, packed to the rafters as the inn was with townsfolk, students, and scholars rubbing elbows. Avān, Humans, and Seethe, with a smattering of Iku and a few of the red-haired Katsé, the fox-people who ranged the nearby wooded valleys. Crowded as the Quill was, Indris was more aware of the distance around him: empty tables nearby, chairs moved to overcrowd cluttered tables farther away.

Indris went to take a sip from his tea and scowled when he saw he had already finished it. He raised himself in his seat to gesture toward one of the servers as Ojin-mar slipped nimbly through the crowd, a laden tray in his hands.

"Here you go." The Sēq Executioner placed a tray of meats, fried flatbread, and dips on the table. There was a cast-iron pot of tea and a small bottle of honey. Indris moved his journal, brush, and inkpot to make way for the bounty, and smiled his thanks as Ojin-mar perched himself on the only other chair that remained near Indris's table. With nimble fingers Ojin-mar wrapped himself a small parcel of food and popped it into his mouth.

"What news?" Indris asked around a mouthful.

"Corajidin has requested all the rahns and sayfs to attend the Winter Court in Avānweh," Ojin-mar said as he chewed. He poured tea for them both. "He's speaking of reconciliation between the factions, as well as a more unified approach to how he'll govern Shrīan. He's even invited all the foreign ambassadors, though they had fled the country before the throne had warmed under Corajidin's rump."

"He's up to something. I've grave doubts it'll work out well for anybody."

Ojin-mar's smile was wry. "Really? We'd not noticed. Half of his army is camped just outside Fandra. Siamak's eldest boy, Harish, and their Poet Master, Indera, arrived in Amarqa this morning by wind-galley to plan the defense. All the heirs of the rahns arrived overnight—those that weren't here already. As well as their advisers."

"Corajidin wants what's in the Rōmarq," Indris muttered. *Watch the Sēq once more become the facilitators of the nation's future. When they left Shrian's leaders, the panicked leaders came to them.* "We stopped him once, and even as Asrahn he needs permission from Siamak to enter Bey Prefecture, but he'll forge on regardless. There'll be violence, of that you can be sure."

Indris sipped his tea, feeling eyes on him from around the common room. When he glanced up, people hurriedly looked away. Ojin-mar noticed and gave a rueful laugh.

"What?" Indris asked sourly.

"You scare the wits out of people, Indris. The legendary Dragon-Eyed Indris, returned to the Order!" Ojin-mar's eyes were wide with mocking wonderment. "The only man to have traveled to the Hazhi-shok and returned—"

"I'm not the only one to have come back from the Spines. Cennoväl the Dragonlord has done it. Anj has done it. But the Hazhi-shok? The Dragon's Teeth? Really, is that what people are calling them now? Bit dramatic, neh?"

"Ha! Dragons aren't dramatic? Nobody here has seen one, other than you."

"Not that I remember."

"And let's not forget you also survived the slave pits of Sorochel. There's also what you did at Amnon, the stories of how you were Awakened, then refused it. And let's not forget Changeling." Ojin-mar went on as if Indris had not spoken, or as if he had not noticed Indris's angry expression at talk of his confiscated mind blade. The mention of Sorochel made Indris's stomach lurch in remembered fear. He sipped his tea to calm himself while Ojin-mar continued. "And to think we'd live to see the day when such a giant walked among us!"

Indris snorted. "I know all about me—"

"Do you?"

"Well, no, I suppose not. I know a lot about me, how's that? And I'd rather talk about what we're going to do next with the rahns. I'll be leaving Amarqa-in-the-Snows in the next few days. I've been here too long as it is, and there are things that need my attention."

Ojin-mar rested his elbows on the table. "Indris, we can't just let you go. There are too many things we don't know—"

"And let's face it: You'll continue not to know them!" Indris could not keep the exasperation from his voice. "You've no idea what was done to me or how to undo it. But I can do some real good out there, if you'll let me."

"Can you heal the rahns?"

"No," Indris replied honestly. Ojin-mar scowled. "Don't reproach me for something you can't do yourselves. But I do know—as well as you do—why the rahns are dying."

The executioner narrowed his eyes, all veneer of affability gone. The man who sat there, ahm scarred and fingers missing, was hard and intractable as any member of the Suret could be. Ojin-mar said, "I'd choose my next words very carefully were I you, General Indris. Almost as if my life depended on it."

"Threats? Really? How dull. Is it because you don't want the truth known"—Indris lowered his voice—"or because you were actually unaware that the moment the Sēq stopped giving the rahns regular doses of the Water of Life, their Awakening would begin to unravel, poisoning body, mind, and soul? How did the Sēq do it, over all those centuries?"

Ojin-mar did not so much as bat an eye. "Our agents in each Great House dosed the rahns with the Water in their food and wine. How did you—?"

"That's not the point." Indris then looked Ojin-mar in the eye. "The Sēq did the same thing to Corajidin, didn't they? He became inconvenient, so the Suret elected to murder him by inaction. But the other rahns were hurt purely out of spite. Is it any wonder I

141

don't want to come back to the Order if this is what the shepherds
of the people do to their flock?"

"Be realistic, Indris!" Ojin-mar slumped in his chair. "Shepherds. We've not had a flock since the Scholar Wars. People forget
what the Order has done for them—"

"Because you hide under mountains, or in valleys, and don't
involve yourselves other than to bluster and threaten!" Indris's shoulders bowed with disappointment. "The Sēq were a marvel . . . once.
They were the light that shone in the darkness, banishing ignorance,
bringing hope, and illuminating the way to the future. But now?
You'd kill our leaders because you had your feelings hurt."

"Watch your mouth, General," Ojin-mar warned.

"A bitter truth stings a little, doesn't it? But I don't care why
you did what you did, and I know it wasn't one person's decision.
Treating the rahns with the Water of Life won't be enough. But you
already know that. The damage from withdrawal can't be undone.
We need something more potent, an extract of fluid from the ahmtesh itself, but even that won't work forever. They'll need more and
more over time until they can't drink enough to sustain their own
lives. The only options are to Sever them, or to find a way to re-
Awaken them again and to reestablish their connection with Īa."

"Would the Communion Ritual help?"

"It's no better than drinking the Waters. It's Severance, re-
Awakening . . . or death."

"Can you re-Awaken them?"

Indris felt a weight settle across his shoulders.

"I can't, but I can try to learn how."

❋ ❋ ❋

Anj was waiting for Indris in his chambers. She had divested
herself of her over-robe and cassock, and wore only her vest,

breeches, and high boots. She had untied her quills so they formed a wild storm-colored mass around her head. Her skin flickered with the radiance of her desire, and light smoldered in her sapphire eyes. A bowl of wine was cradled in her hand: black lotus from the smell of it, pungent and faintly narcotic.

"Come in and make yourself comfortable," Indris said, gesturing to the door. "Oh, wait, you already did."

"I'm your wife." Anj reclined on the couch, legs sprawled, invitation clear. "We should be living together, not in separate chambers across the vale from each other."

"Hmmm." Indris went to his wardrobe and picked out a fresh tunic, trousers, and cassock. He stripped, washed, and dressed as quickly as he could. Anj's moue almost made him laugh but he did not want to encourage her. "Why are you here, Anj?"

"We're overdue our talk, husband. You know how annoying I can be when I'm made to wait."

"Where've you been?"

"As I said before, my business takes me here and there. Suffice to say I've spent time there. But I doubt you've spent much time seeking me out."

"I've been busy, Anj. You may have heard that the rahns are quite inconveniently dying?" Her bored expression spoke volumes. "I've been helping the Sēq find a cure."

"And?" Despite the petulance in her tone, her gaze sharpened with interest. "Have you found one? I've seen Femensetri walking you to the Eibon Hoje each night, and coming for you at dawn—"

"You following me now?"

"—And a wife is interested why her husband works mornings in the Manufactory, afternoons with the Suret, and nights in a library." She unlaced her vest. "Rather than warming his gorgeous wife in the bed they should be sharing."

"Anj . . . give me some time, please." Her expression turned, and Indris held up his hands in a placating gesture. "You're right, we do need to talk. Let's start by you telling me what happened to me on the Spines."

She rose from the couch, clothing in danger of sliding from her. She sauntered across to him, wrapped an arm around his shoulders, and stared him in the eye. "Let's make a deal. You want your past from me and I want your present from you." Her face came close to his, her blue lips parted, tongue a hint of pink against her white teeth. Desire welled up in him but was countered by his feelings for Mari, and the faint sense of oily nausea that proximity to Anj now gave him. For a moment she smelled of rotten seaweed and brine. "The future we can figure out together."

"What happened to me in the Spines, Anj? The Suret never approved of us being together, so why would they send you to find me?"

"Can you save the rahns and their Awakening, Indris?" she countered. "Or will you need to Sever them, because there's no way they can survive otherwise?"

Indris felt a chill. "How do you know that?"

"We both have questions we want answered, Indris." Anj drained her bowl of wine, and fell back on the bed. Her smile faded when Indris remained standing. "Get yourself down here, husband. You want answers. I want answers. Now seems the perfect time."

"I've work to do, Anj. My own curiosity needs to wait a little longer."

"Until lives don't depend on you?" Her tone was sharp. Anj's veneer of affability slipped to reveal a hint of the darkness beneath. Indris felt the greasy residue across his Disentropic Stain, and her form blurred for a second, before it became stable once more. *Do I want to ignore what you're hiding, more than I want to know what you know?* "And when will that day be, husband? Will there ever be a day when you're not rushing off to save somebody, when there are people much closer to you who need your help?"

"They need my help, Anj. Am I to turn my back on them?"

"Sometimes people need to be abandoned to their fate, Indris. To rise above, or drown below. It's the nature of things."

"And sometimes people need to be shown how to swim. That's what the Sēq are supposed to do. They learn, they teach, and they protect."

"It's not what they are anymore."

"Some of us, them, try to be."

"Weak?"

Indris held the door open for her, and gestured for her to leave. When she did not, he walked out, and closed the door behind him.

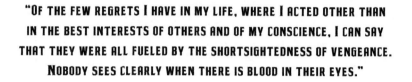

11

"OF THE FEW REGRETS I HAVE IN MY LIFE, WHERE I ACTED OTHER THAN IN THE BEST INTERESTS OF OTHERS AND OF MY CONSCIENCE, I CAN SAY THAT THEY WERE ALL FUELED BY THE SHORTSIGHTEDNESS OF VENGEANCE. NOBODY SEES CLEARLY WHEN THERE IS BLOOD IN THEIR EYES."

—from *In Service to the People,* by High Palatine Navaar of Oragon, second year of his reign (490th Year of the Shrīanese Federation)

DAY 60 OF THE 496TH YEAR OF THE

SHRĪANESE FEDERATION

Mari kicked the easel over, sending the precious paper and sticks of charcoal, skittering across the floor of the sunroom. *Not that there is any bloody sun in this place! All there is, is cursed rain, and snow.* The world beyond the grimy window was an unfinished and monochromatic watercolor where the artist's thumb had smeared the gray hints of morning smoke, mist, and rain across town and sea. The world looked small enough that she could open the windows and touch its edges. Abashed, she picked her paper and charcoal up, smoothing the corner of one sheet where it had bent. The supplies had been hard to come by, a present from somebody who saw new hope in Mari's resistance to the Dowager-Asrahn.

Tears formed in her eyes, angrily brushed away. The news of Indris's death felt like stones in her stomach. A heaviness deep in her bones, where love had once made her light. Love. The word echoed in her head, at once sweeter and more sour for never having been said. Mari strode to the small cabinet and poured herself a tumbler of whiskey, downing it in one gulp. She poured another. She clutched the glass tighter as her hands shook, and tears welled in her eyes again.

"Am I disturbing you?" Qesha-rē said from the door. The surgeon carried her box of instruments and unguents. Mari wiped her eyes and gestured the surgeon in. *Ancestors know I've nobody else who seeks my company.* Qesha-rē came across the room, her concern evident.

"It's a little thing; don't worry yourself." *The man I love is dead.* Mari took a quick, stuttering breath around what almost turned into a sob, but smiled anyway. "To what do I owe the pleasure?"

"I'm off to give some of your cousins their routine examinations, so don't have much time. We need to be careful how much time we spend together, Mari. But you asked whether I knew anything about the Feigning. This morning, I overheard Nadir and Eladdin discussing it. Apparently Eladdin is overjoyed that it won't be him, and was horrified that his mother would ever have considered it. To be frank, I don't think either man knows exactly what it is, save that the person used in the Feigning will not emerge the same . . . if they emerge at all. Apparently it relies upon a device your father has been trying to get working for some time, and now the College of Artificers in Avānweh has the answers he's after. The Emissary speaks with his voice, so they say."

"A device?" Mari wracked her brain. The description hardly narrowed the field: There were many devices of the old empires that her father coveted. She felt a chill. *Father. It's becoming little more than a word now. Certainly something less than the man who raised me.* With very great care she asked, "Was it a Torque Spindle?"

"They didn't say."

Mari swore to herself. "Is Vahineh healthy enough to travel?"

"Not fast and not far, but we're poor for choice," the surgeon said, nodding toward the white outside. "Mari, moving her may kill her—"

"These people will kill her, Qesha. One way or another, Vahineh will die at their hands. I appreciate your ethics and your oaths as a healer, but if she stays, she dies."

The surgeon raked fingers through her hair. "Very well. What about Nadir's soldiers, or the witches who guard her?"

"Let me take care of those, my friend. Please make sure both you and Vahineh are ready to travel tonight."

"How are we to escape?"

Mari looked out into the murk. The bowl of the bay was filled with gently swirling white, with no sign of *The Seeker*. "I need to make contact with some friends, but I expect that we'll need to be ready to leave very quickly. I doubt my grandmother will find it in the cold stone she has for a heart to forgive what I'm about to do."

"You've friends in Tamerlan?"

Mari allowed herself a quiet laugh, and for the first time in a long while, her smile was genuine. "The likes of which you can't imagine."

❄ ❄ ❄

"What did the surgeon want?" Nadir asked a few minutes after Qesha had left to treat other patients. Mari glared at Nadir from beneath lowered brows.

"She came to check on my wounds. Why else would she be here?"

"It was the why else that I asked." Nadir glided farther into the room. Two of his Exiles remained watchful at the door, hands on the hilts of their long-knives. Nadir gave Mari an admiring glance. "You look good. Much better than one could expect, given your time here."

"My time at yours and the Blacksnake's mercies, you mean?" Mari chuckled bitterly. "Or at the hands of the Dowager-Asrahn? You're all as bad as each other, and you'll all fall together. Trust me on that."

"You're not in the world that loves you, Mari." Nadir's tone was urgent. He extended a hand, but dropped at something savage in Mari's expression. "Not in that world at all. There's still time for you to be saved."

"From this Feigning you speak of? What is it, Nadir? What do my father and the Emissary have in mind for me, exactly?"

"The Emissary hates you, Mari. She threatened your father that he was not to harm Indris—"

"Why? I've done nothing to her! And what does Indris have to do with any of this?" *Indris is dead, Nadir. There's little my father can do to him anymore.*

"But there is much that can be done to you, Mari. Even you will break in the end. Everybody does. Accept it."

"We'll see about that." Mari's lip curled. "I may be imprisoned on this rock with you, Nadir. But you're also trapped here with me. Before my end comes, I swear I'll plant your corpse in the Garden of Stones and watch you burn."

"I'd listen to her, Nadir," came a familiar voice from the doorway. "My sister is not in the habit of making idle threats."

"Belam?" Mari's breath caught. Her brother stood in the doorway, his ruby-scale armor glittering beneath his black clothes, the hood of his over-robe thrown back from his golden head. Beside him stood a small Tanisian woman. To Mari's surprise, Nadir's Exiles looked at the Tanisian with something akin to terror, and backed away. Belam gave Mari a small, hesitant smile that remained fixed as he assessed Nadir.

"Belamandris!" Nadir choked, his face pale. His hands dropped toward the hilts of his curved knives, when Belam made a gentle shushing sound. Nadir froze.

"Would you leave us, Nadir?" Belam asked. "I'd appreciate some time with my sister. Alone."

"But my father and the Dowager-Asrahn—"

"Do not concern me in the slightest, Nadir." Belam adjusted the folds of his over-robe so that Tragedy's hilt became visible. "Go, while I allow it."

Nadir flushed with anger, but did not press his luck. The former Exile stormed from the room, taking great care to give the Widowmaker and his Tanisian companion a wide berth. When he had gone, Belam gestured to his companion to enter, and to close the door behind her.

Anger burst like a boil in Mari. She stepped forward and slammed her elbow into Belam's jaw. Her brother fell to his knees. Tears formed in Mari's eyes. When the Tanisian woman started to chant, Belam held up his hand for her to be still. He rose unsteadily to his feet, where Mari hammered her fist into his stomach. This time her tears flowed. Belam doubled over, but rose again. Mari struck him harder, and knocked her brother to his back. She sobbed as he rose again, wiping the blood from his lips. Her next blows were ineffectual things of grief, loneliness, and sorrow. Belam took all she gave, and did not try to defend himself. The witch woman looked on, eyes wide.

"What are you doing here?" Mari asked through her sobs. "You left me here, Belam! My own brother left me with these—"

"I'm sorry, Mari." Belam held his arms open, but Mari was not ready to take comfort from him. "There's nothing I can say to undo what's been done. I had no idea that Jhem and Nadir would bring you here. Father ordered me home, and left you in their care."

"Care!" Mari wanted to scream. She bared her fangs in a snarl, fists clenched. "Do you have any idea what they've done to me?"

"No." Belam's voice was as ice, his expression no warmer. There was a terrible poise about him that gave Mari a chill. "What did they do, Mari?"

She straightened. "Nothing I couldn't handle. Nothing like you might think, Belam—there are some lines they wouldn't dare cross. Are you here to execute Father's last request, this Feigning the Emissary is going to perform?"

The Tanisian woman choked back a bitter laugh, and said something in singsong Tanisian Avān that Mari did not understand. The woman repeated herself in Shrīanese Avān. "Your father has made one too many questionable choices, Pah-Mariam. Belam and I have decided it were best if we tried to find facts, before we formed truths."

"Who's your friend?" Mari pointedly asked her brother.

Belam gestured toward the woman with him. She appraised Mari, her chin tilted toward the much taller woman. Belam took the Tanisian by the hand and said, "Mari, this is Pahavān-Chepherundi op Sanojé, formerly of Tanis, now of wherever we happen to find ourselves."

"We can help you," Sanojé murmured. "We know your father's plans, and the dark twists his mind takes. We know about his dealings with the Emissary—"

"The Emissary?" Mari scowled. "Somebody needs to plant that woman in ashes."

"She was the one who saved Father, and continues to hold his life in her hand," Belam said. He opened his mouth as if he were about to say something else, then closed it again. "She demands more with every boon he asks—and she's the one who made him banish you to this forsaken place."

"I hear she's no friend to me. But what am I to her that she'd do that?" There came the sound of a horn from down the corridor, and the strident clash of metal. "If you're not here to end me, why are you here?"

"A mission of liberation," Belam said. "One long overdue. One that'll help me regain my honor, and your friendship. Eventually, perhaps even your love and respect."

"Belam," Mari said hesitantly. "I can't just forget what's happened to me here."

"I don't expect you to. I'm your brother, and by my inaction you've been wronged. By my actions, others have been wronged. Sanojé and I know it'll take a lot to redeem ourselves for what we've done, but can't our attempt at helping you be a start?"

Mari caught and held Belam's gaze. "I could use the help, and plans are in place for which you're ideally skilled to help. You're my brother, and you've never lied to me. But don't make a fool of me, Belam. You don't want me as your enemy."

"I don't, and I'll not."

"Then care to join me?"

"In what?" Belam asked.

"Leaving."

※ ※ ※

The high sun was hidden behind clouds, and the Hearthall of Tamerlan was filled to bursting. The fires burned so hot that most of the people had stripped to their tunics and trousers. The rough windows and tiled walls sweated, water dripping from the ceilings. A bound-caste servant sluiced blood from the floor with a bucket of water, while another used a rough broom to send the filthy mess toward the great Maw.

The Dowager-Asrahn's family flocked around her, faces etched as much with fear as pride. Eladdin stood bare-chested and bloody on the floor, arms held wide, knives dripping gore as his sycophants chanted his name.

Mari made her way to a table laden with platters of seafood, rice, and grilled seaweed, and jugs of beer and horns of mead kept cool in vats of melting snow. One look from her cousins was enough to tell her she was not welcome at the high table. Belam and Sanojé played their parts, nestled in among family members. Mari let her gaze slide to the empty chairs at one end of the table, where she and Dhoury had sat. Her fingers curled in anger, imagining they were wrapped around her grandmother's scrawny neck.

As long as I live, that old hag will give nobody else to the sea.

Cradling a mug of beer and a small plate of food, Mari sauntered through the crowd. Occasionally she checked to see whether anybody in authority paid her undue attention. Soldiers sworn to the Dowager-Asrahn kept their eyes on Mari; two followed at a distance, but did not get close. She swatted away the grabby hands of swaying, sweating drunkards. Eladdin glowered at her, face reddened by drink and bloodlust where it was not marbled with bruising from their last encounter. The Sidewinder turned to his crew and said something: They looked in Mari's direction and laughed. Mari smiled back, pointed to her own nose, and pantomimed crying. His clique prodded him, but Eladdin averted his eyes, and kept his distance.

"Waiting is a dangerous thing, Pah-Mariam," Kyril said as he wandered past. He stood to watch two oiled young men wrestle. "The weather's turning, and we're running out of time. We need to leave soon if we're ever going to." He sipped at his beer, grimaced, and let it dribble from his mouth, and back into the mug. "How can people drink this swill? The thought of wintering here with nothing but this piss to drink is, frankly, more than I can stand. So, darling princess, let's get you and your sick friend away from here, eh?"

Mari nodded. "Is tonight soon enough for you? There's one thing I need to do before we go."

The nahdi looked at her with raised eyebrows in a silent question.

"I need to end my grandmother, and her influence."

Kyril snorted, until he realized she was serious. "We don't have time for vengeance, Pah-Mariam! Your friends—and my husband—risked much by coming here to find you. Morne's an honorable man, sometimes to the detriment of common sense, which is why he has me: to remind him of when a job is no longer a wise investment. For the love Morne bears the late Indris, and the love your friends bear you, save retribution for another day."

Mari stepped aside to let the crowd gather around the wrestling men. She gestured for Kyril to join her, and the two slipped away as the crowd grew, eluding the soldiers that followed her in the press of bodies. The corridor outside was gloomy and chill, their breath steaming in the cold gray light as they walked away from passersby.

"We can leave quietly, Mari." Kyril spoke softly. "There's no need to poke a stick in the wasp's nest."

"Is Morne here?"

"No." Kyril looked at her suspiciously.

"I need to speak with him."

"You're being followed, or hadn't you noticed?"

"I noticed. Can you bring Morne here?"

"Not until tonight, no. And I'll not risk him for you unless I have to."

"Then I'll need to go to him. Now."

"That poses much the same problem," Kyril said dryly.

"I've a way of coming and going without being seen, though it's not without its risks."

Kyril muttered under his breath, but gestured for Mari to go. "I'll meet you at the old sundial in the smaller of the town squares in an hour. Will that be enough time?"

Mari nodded as she walked away. On her way she came face-to-face with her complement of guards.

"Who were you talking to?" one of them snarled.

Mari affected boredom. "I'm going to my room." She rolled her eyes. "The quality of what you call entertainment has quite underwhelmed me, and I need to rest from all the nail-biting excitement."

The Savadai put a hand out. "*Who was—*"

"Some bloody nahdi wanting an introduction to the old shark." She barked a laugh. "Calm yourselves, boys. I sent him on his way. Now I'll be on mine, if you please."

The guards gave Mari sour looks as she walked by them, chuckling. But they asked no more questions, and fell into step after her as she went back to her room. When the door closed behind her, and the locks sounded, Mari rapidly changed her clothes and steeled her hearts for another nervous traversal of the ledge.

❋ ❋ ❋

Kyril was waiting where he said he would be, amid a crowd of merchants and customers who milled between the storefronts on the square. He was rubbing gloved hands over a brazier when she approached.

"It seems, dear, that we are both children of the summer." The plume of his breath vanished in the gray. Buildings and people and wagons were little more than indistinct shapes. Street braziers painted the faces of those around them a ghastly orange. Sound was muted: the creak of ship timbers, the groan of wagon wheels, and the voices of people unlucky enough to be outside. He gestured for her to follow.

"Where are you from, Kyril?" Mari asked as he led her through the shadowy planes and angles of the town. "Originally, I mean."

"I was born in Darmatia," the warrior said wistfully. "It's beautiful country. Rolling fields of emerald grass, and a sky so big and broad you'd think you could just fall into it and never stop. And horses! Have you seen our horses, Pah-Mariam?"

"Just Mari," she said. "And no, I've never left Shrīan."

"You should come to Darmatia if for no other reason than to see the zherba. They are a natural wonder, Mari. Strong and intelligent, they choose their riders, not the other way around. Legend has it they are the very essence of the world, Īa's longing to run free and unfettered, made manifest."

They turned into the shadows that buttressed a narrow lane. Light shone between the slats of shutters, and lanterns hung like fireflies over doors. Leatherworkers, glass blowers, the pounding clang of a smithy, carpenters, and merchant stores: no tea or coffee houses, no galleries, or libraries. Kyril paused and held open an ill-fitting door, and unpegged the leather curtain behind it. They entered quickly, the sudden warmth a pleasure. Mari waited while Kyril pegged the curtain back in place.

The tavern was a claustrophobic place with smoke-darkened beams above a cobbled floor, low benches and tables scattered under dirty yellow lamplight. Indistinct shapes huddled over their meals and drinks. The air was thick with the smells of fish and seasoning, and decades of wine and beer that had been soaked up by the timber. It was a quiet place, filled with an equally quiet menace.

"And where did you meet Morne?" she asked softly.

Kyril's eyes crinkled in delight, his smile so infectious that Mari responded in kind. *He truly adores him*, Mari thought. "Morne

Hawkwood. We met in service in the Immortal Companions, fighting in the Conflicted Cities on the Tanis-Manté border. It was about ten years ago, I suppose. He was so beautiful before the world took its toll on him, chipping away the pieces to reveal an even more beautiful man beneath. Morne, his sisters and brothers, plus no small number of the Immortal Companions, are descended from the refugees of Ivoré. We—"

"Ivoré? I've never heard of it."

"Few have," Morne said as he loomed large out of the darkness between pools of lantern light. He kissed his husband, then leaned down to kiss Mari on the cheek. "Because it no longer exists, and few other than us remember the name. We are a people without a country, and our numbers dwindle with each generation. But we happy seekers look for better days to come."

Morne took Kyril's hand and led the way to the back of the tavern. Mari passed a few faces she recognized from the deck of *The Seeker*, nahdi tanned by the Tanisian sun, armed and armored in precious metals, stones glinting. She was reminded of the Exiles and the fortunes they had brought back with them from the Conflicted Cities, fortunes her father had used to buy the Asrahn's crown. Seated around a table were what Mari took to be Morne's officers, as well as two figures that pulled back their hoods to reveal themselves as Shar and Ekko.

"You weren't followed?" Morne asked as he sat down.

"In this soup?" Kyril replied. He took off his great cloak and folded it neatly. Morne poured wine into two chipped tumblers, and handed one each to his husband and to Mari. Kyril nodded to Mari. "There's a bit of attention on Mari, but she said she needed to speak with you, and we've no time for delays."

"May I talk freely?" Mari asked, gesturing to the others around the table.

"My officers can be trusted," Morne said.

Morne looked at Kyril, who shrugged before he spoke. "Mari apparently wants to kill everybody in Tamerlan."

"Not everybody, no," Mari said. "Just those who would follow the example the Dowager-Asrahn sets. The Avān need to be better than that. Getting Vahineh out will not be without its challenges, but I can't leave a rahn here that the Dowager-Asrahn, Jhem, Nadir, or this Emissary can use to strengthen their position. I've seen enough of the Dowager-Asrahn to know the world would spin a little more lightly without her walking on it."

"Mari speaks truth," Shar said. "Corajidin wants nothing more than to raise the Avān to an empire again, and he's proven he'll stop at nothing to get what he wants."

"This Emissary bothers me, also," Morne added. "I've seen her like in Eidelbon, the great City of Masks in Manté. That Emissary was masked in blackened jade, and was known to provide counsel to the Catechism who rule Manté—and where Manté points, the Iron League walks."

"Well, this one serves my father," Mari replied. "And if we can end her, I'd count it a fair day's work. But, Morne, what I need from you and the Companions is a distraction, so I can get Vahineh out in the confusion."

"Do you want big, bigger, or biggest?"

Mari reached out and patted Morne on the cheek, making the scarred man smile. She nodded at Kyril and said, "I see why you love this one. He's worth keeping." Mari returned to Morne. "How do you feel about biggest? Something whoever remains on Tamerlan won't forget in a hurry. I've an unexpected ally in my brother, recently arrived."

"The Widowmaker!" Shar spat. Ekko's eyes widened dangerously.

"We've spoken," Mari said. "Belam is here to help. So, Morne. Biggest?"

"We can do biggest," Morne said confidently.

"Then tonight, in the Hearthall, will see the end of the Dowager-Asrahn's reign." Kyril wrapped his long fingers around his tumbler of cheap wine and raised the glass high. Everybody finished their drinks to the last drop.

Mari placed her tumbler on the table, rim down.

"Tonight, we'll see the end of the Dowager-Asrahn's life."

And the others, too, slammed their glasses rim-down on the table.

"OUR FATE IS THE RESULT OF CHOICES, NOT CHANCE."

—Penoquin of Kaylish, Zienni Scholar and philosopher

DAY 60 OF THE 496TH YEAR OF THE

SHRĪANESE FEDERATION

Corajidin heard the burbling echoes of the voices from the deep places of the Drear, and felt their gaze, and the touch of their tentacles about his limbs, and saw the flashes of sea-green light behind his tightly shut eyelids. The cold of the depths seeped into his limbs, weighing them down. He opened his mouth to scream but no sound came. His feet pounded on an analogy of reality and the hands on his arms guided him through the murk until eventually there was giddiness and nausea and—

The contents of his stomach pooled in his mouth. It was more an act of pride than will that allowed him to walk with an infirm step to where he could privately spit the foul mess out. As much as he wanted to collapse to his knees, to heave and tremble and suck in great gasps of air, he stood straight and was glad of the shadows that hid his terror. The Anlūki, more experienced in traveling the Drear, took station around him.

The yellow-white glow of the sunlight lanterns softened the shadows, but did little to cheer the place. A recent gift of the alchemists, the globes burned with a warm radiance to reveal a spherical chamber that reeked of damp and mold. Curtains of fibrous roots hung from the ceiling, and lichen clung to stone walls that had been hidden away for Erebus knows how long. It was an oppressive place with people clustered cheek by jowl between its walls. Corajidin glanced over his shoulder at the ornate gazebo of the Weavegate, the end of the disturbing road that led them here from Avānweh. Every surface was carved in round glyphs, joined by arcs and lines in geometries only their long-vanished scribes understood. Try as they might, Kasraman, Wolfram, and the other witches had made little progress in translating the language of the Time Masters.

"This way, Father." Kasraman opened his fist and sent a will-o'-the-wisp down the corridor ahead of them. Corajidin lifted the skirts of his over-robe from out of the muddy water and followed. After several twists and turns he could see natural light ahead, and the walls eventually opened up into a round hall topped with the skeletal remains of a domed glass ceiling. He blinked against the gray glare of the afternoon sky and felt slight flurries of rain so cold they stung his face. The black stone walls were covered in creepers and vines that shone in vivid color from within, the detritus of the ages filling the thousands of characters carved into the glassy rock. A golden astrolabe hung from what remained of the ceiling, a stilled pendulum surrounded by characters that were spheres rather than circles: as if the Time Masters wrote in three dimensions, or possibly more.

Corajidin stood to the side, surrounded by his guards, as Wolfram, Elonie, and Ikedion escorted the manacled Kimiya out into the open. The puppeteer-possessed woman lifted her face and sniffed the air, making an inhuman rattling sound deep in her throat, part purr, part the clatter of chitin. Kimiya rolled her head in Corajidin's direction. "You stand in the ruins of cowards and traitors, Corajidin. Best you don't follow their example; my people aren't known for their tolerance."

"No," Wolfram said as he scuffed the ground with his staff. The old man leaned down to rub at his legs where his breeches were bunched under the leather straps of the calipers. The witch looked up at Kimiya through the ropes of his fringe. "Your people are murderers and anarchists who feed on the terror they bring."

"Yet you are helping us all the same."

"That we are, Kimiya." Kasraman stood close to her. He looked on her with a wonder that made Corajidin uneasy. "And you'll show us all the treasures of the Rōmarq and be our allies for so long as the Erebus live."

"As you say, Master. And not for the first time." Kimiya responded to Kasraman, but gave Wolfram a smile that would have been seductive once. Wolfram slammed the butt of his staff on the ground, splinters and a rusted old nail falling from it. Kimiya's eyes widened, and her lower lip trembled, momentarily granting her a disturbingly innocent air. Then she smiled and the effect was ruined by the insanity writ in the twist of her lips. Wolfram gestured sharply, and Kimiya was led away by Elonie and Ikedion.

Not for the first time? Corajidin suppressed a shudder. *First the Emissary, and now the marsh-puppeteers. What have my Ancestors done? But you will not answer me, will you? Now, when I need your guidance most, you are silent.*

Corajidin, Kasraman, and Wolfram walked cylindrical corridors and through spherical chambers sometimes completely enclosed, at other times open to the elements. They exited in a circular plaza, where weeds and the stumps of trees protruded from between paving stones. The smoke of wood fires and cooking fowl was familiar, and made Corajidin's mouth water. He heard none of the sounds of the Rōmarq, blanketed by the sounds of his army. Command tents dotted the plaza. He saw Feyd, Tahj-Shaheh, and Nix bent over maps that flapped in the wind. Part of their assembled fleet floated above, Torque Spindles flickering with mother-of-pearl radiance. There was Tahj-Shaheh's flagship, the *Skywolf,* lean and hungry beside her sister ship, the *Sea Witch.* Corajidin's massive *Art of Vengeance* and the destroyer, the *Wind Stallion,* loomed nearby. Martūm had ordered Selassin ships into the mix with the *Dawn King* and the *Sunspear,* their lion figureheads gleaming sullenly. Yet all paled in comparison next to the enormity of the *Manifest Destiny,* the dreadnought's hull near blazing with the multitude of spindles needed to keep her airborne, dotted with the protruding cylinders of storm cannons, and the spinning platters of her Tempest Wheels. Smaller skiffs and cutters soared out on patrol or stayed parked by their larger brethren like remora.

To the side of the fleet there lurked a shade-washed and rickety avian shape of split timbers and tarnished fittings, its figurehead two skeletal hands holding an hourglass on its side, the light from its spools and wheels tinted red. Corajidin grimaced with distaste at the Soul Trader's ship. He imagined the rag-garbed crew of Nomad and living merchants aboard peering hungrily at the world below, anticipating their harvest in the wake of such chaos as the Rōmarq would likely deliver.

Through a semicircular arch in one wall, Corajidin caught a glimpse of tents set in concentric circles around the higher ground that held the command pavilions. The black and red of the Erebus, a paltry showing of the green and gold of the Selassin—not surprising given the questions around the future of their leadership— and even a small number of the green and gray of the Kadarin.

With every passing moment, a noise grew in Corajidin's head. Soothing and sweetly familiar, it reminded him of waves against the sands of Erebesq. Colors were more vivid, his vision sharper, the world more clearly defined. He took in a deep breath, and the air tingled on his tongue and warmed his chest. He turned to Kasraman and Wolfram, who nodded their awareness of what Corajidin experienced.

Feyd and Tahj-Shaheh bowed as Corajidin and the two witches approached. "Have our forces gathered in full?" Corajidin asked.

"We'd enough to take Fandra. The rest are on their way. We'll maintain two camps, Asrahn: a command compound and set of soldier's precincts here, as well as a garrison at Fandra, about three kilometers away." Feyd's mahogany face was seamed by time and trouble, his iron hair and beard fitting accompaniments to his much-used armor and bloodstained tribal clothes. He looked tough as an old tree. Beside him, Tahj-Shaheh was windblown and rakish, her clothing, armor, and weapons a tatterdemalion collection from the nations that bordered the Marble Sea: Tanisian silks, Ygranian leather and plate armor with its curlicues and embossing, a Shrīanese shamshir and knives at her belt. Nix's bronze-shod steel, leather, and wool were the colors of the marshes. Knives were strapped to his thighs, and the pommel of a shamshir reared above his shoulder. Lean and dirty, nimble fingers never at rest, Nix surveyed all with a twitching eye beneath greasy hair dyed in greens and browns.

"My Asrahn!" Baquio tittered. Mud stained the hems of the damasks that Corajidin's investment in the College of Artificers had bought him. A baroque, many-lensed device graced his brow, and a wide belt contained a multitude of complex tools that Corajidin could not speculate on. "I was informing your Master of Arms and Sky Master about the miraculous engines I've brought you! Newly designed storm-cannon, incendiary devices, weapons and armor forged with new metallurgic techniques—"

"It sounds fascinating, Master Artificer," Corajidin interrupted. "However, as you can appreciate, there are many demands on my time. I am certain my commanders can accommodate you later in the day."

"Of course, of course!" Baquio's smile was as ingratiating as Corajidin's was insincere. "I'll return to my fellow artificers. I've no doubt Prahna and her alchemists will likewise be excited to demonstrate their creations! Salves, potions, fire water—"

"If you would be so kind as to excuse us?" Corajidin said. Baquio bowed as he backed away, uselessly lifting the hems of his too-long over-robe from the mud. The man turned with a nod and traversed the soupy ground, carefully avoiding anything likely to stain his clothes more. Corajidin scowled at his back. "At least the Sēq and the witches just did what they did, without needing a pat on the back."

"True enough, Asrahn," Nix said. "But Baquio's and Prahna's people have made a small fortune in new markets for their wares. The taxes on their revenue fill the Crown's coffers nicely. And at least the artificers and the alchemists want to please you. The scholars and witches? Well, not so much."

Corajidin grunted. "Feyd, you were discussing our progress?"

The Master of Arms pointed a whorled finger at the map. "We can hold Fandra for now. There wasn't a large force here, mainly townsfolk. They fight like daemons when pressed, and if this is the accounting the tradesfolk of the Rōmarq can give for themselves, we'll have a rough time of it here. When it became apparent they could not hold, the few marsh-knights and those townsfolk we'd not taken fled into the wetlands. I've no doubt we'll be harassed by the marsh-knights for so long as we remain here." The old tribesman shook his head. "Asrahn, by invading the Rōmarq, you've started an unsanctioned war against another Great House. And you've had us break faith with sende. The people won't take kindly to you bringing war to civilians."

"What?" Corajidin looked at Feyd with disdain. "I had not figured a man as ruthless as yourself to have qualms about such things. Besides, I am Asrahn. I will make what we do here legal."

"Legal?" Feyd raised his eyebrows. He gestured skyward with his head. "I know of the reputation of the Soul Traders: what they do, and why they're here. Can morals and ethics be changed as easily as laws?"

"As easily as you may be replaced as Master of Arms, Feyd." Kasraman's gaze was flinty. "The Soul Traders will prove their worth, or be dispensed with. They'll not interfere in anything we do. If you're not prepared to do what needs to be done for our undertaking, by all means let's find somebody who is."

"Whatever we do, it won't be all sunshine and parades, Asrahn." Tahj-Shaheh sipped a steaming cup of coffee, hands cupped around it for warmth. "Some of your soldiers were stupid enough to pursue the Rōmarqim, despite orders to hold their positions. We lost almost three hundred soldiers in that little debacle alone."

"Three hundred versus about forty, in a series of close-quarter skirmishes where our numbers counted for nothing." Feyd's tone was respectful. "We shouldn't underestimate the marsh-knights. They live in the harshest environment in Shrīan, even more so than my Jiharim. The Marmûn, led by Bey fa Harish, are all warrior-poets seasoned in the Rōmarq. Perhaps our forces will learn something from this cautionary tale."

"What other losses?" Kasraman asked. His eyes were fever bright, as were those of Wolfram. Both men's skin was flushed.

"We've lost another two hundred or so to Fenling attacks," Nix reported. "And some thirty or forty to malegangers, who in turn killed another hundred or so before we realized what was happening. Reedwives pick off our sentries at night, and there was a sighting of a great dhole about ten kilometers from here. Thankfully the wet ground here gives us some protection."

"Erebus's blood! A dhole?" Corajidin's curiosity warred with his fear. The tentacle-headed worms could measure almost one hundred meters from end to end, thick-bodied, and their maws, tentacles, and the gaps between their body segments discharged acid to make fighting and burrowing easier. "Anything else?"

"The witches," Feyd said darkly. He eyed Kasraman and Wolfram, then shot a glance at Elonie and Ikedion. Corajidin followed his gaze to where the two Mahsojhin witches looked about with something akin to rapture. The Master of Arms's tone was heavy with disapproval. "The witches go mad in this place. It starts off like it is with those that have come with you, with energy and excitement. Soon after, it's as if they're lust-drunk, passions inflamed and cruelty made manifest. Then? Well, they reveal their true faces, and must either be restrained or put down, before they drape themselves in their Aspects and vanish into the marshes."

"Put down?" Kasraman asked dangerously. Wolfram drew himself up to his considerable height, staring down at Feyd with hostility.

"Later." Corajidin waved Kasraman to silence. "How soon until we can proceed deeper into the Rōmarq?"

"There aren't many cities to take, Asrahn." Nix chewed on a mangled nail. "The Rōmarq has always been problematic that way: Why would you bother invading it, when everything that lives in it wants to tear your face off?"

"Because this feculent mire has the greatest collection of ancient relics in Shrīan, and the Sēq have not got their hands on everything. Besides, we have recently acquired a guide that will help us find the way to these places, hopefully reducing our losses."

"Hopefully?" Feyd scowled. "Losing warriors unnecessarily is—"

"My concern, Master of Arms." Corajidin looked at the map, then glanced out to scan the stained brown mirror of the wetlands. Once it had been a green and flowering lowland, dotted with ancient cities and places of learning and culture. Until the Näsarats and the Sēq had sunk the center of Seethe power beneath the waves, formed the Marble Sea, and flooded the Rōmarq. Now it was a place of ruins, of wonders and horrors, buried beneath the sediment of ages. If it took every second warrior in his army to take and hold this place to get what he wanted, then it would be worth it. Corajidin had been ousted once from the Rōmarq: He would not be dislodged again.

Sedefke's writings are hidden here! His research on Awakening, answers to the questions I need to rid myself of the Emissary, her threats, and her Masters of the Drear. Weapons, power, lost knowledge: the echoes of empire that will be heard more clearly, recited in my voice.

"It is time we had Kimiya show us her worth." Corajidin turned to Kasraman. "Bring me some of the captives from Fandra. Let us give the malegangers some bodies as a gesture of good faith. Then she can show us the treasures we have come for."

❋ ❋ ❋

Tahj-Shaheh piloted the wind-cutter herself, landing on a rock shelf surrounded by pools, streams, and flowering grasses. The Anlūki deployed and scouted the surrounding area before indicating that it was safe for the other passengers to disembark. Corajidin reached out to touch the grasses that sprouted from the water, so green and healthy they were as fronds of backlit emerald. The waters, too, were radiant. Everything he touched gave him a delicious tingling sensation, and despite the cool winds, he was warm. The weight of his armor and shamshir felt less than he remembered them from the battle in Avānweh. Voices echoed in his head, too soft to be understood, but more than the background hissing that had been his companion for so long.

Father? Grandfather? Can you hear me? A rise in volume, but no clarity. Corajidin looked about him at the wetlands of the Rōmarq—pools reflecting the sky, flora swaying in the breeze, a cacophony of beasts—but everything burned with vivid, unreal color. *What is this place, that I feel so restored? No! Made new and whole again . . .*

"You feel it, too, Asrahn?" Wolfram asked. Corajidin glanced at the Angothic Witch, who seemed enraptured. "When we came here before the Battle of Amnon, I felt the power of this place. Kasraman and Brede both commented on it, to the point where Brede did not want to leave."

"How is it possible?"

"This place is strong with the ahm," Kimiya said. Corajidin turned to see the woman. She had bathed, or been bathed, and was once more pretty and groomed, dressed as a soldier. "It is the source of many folds in space and time, and the ahmtesh penetrates our world here, much as it does in some other places of Īa."

"Like World Blood Mountain," Kasraman offered.

Kimiya nodded. "That is a strong place, and pure. This, too, is a strong place." She stopped talking and walked over to where ten of the townsfolk of Fandra were manacled together. Kimiya had helped select them: all fit, young, and attractive. She turned to Corajidin and said, "These will suffice for now. To do what you ask, to cause the wanton destruction you want, we need the bodies of those with influence."

"It will be done," Corajidin said. "But let us start our mutually beneficial arrangement with something smaller, neh? These ten, for the location of a ruin nearby that has not been sacked over the years. Something that I will find useful."

Kimiya's laugh was a wet rattle. Heedless of her clean clothes, she walked into the water until it reached her waist, her over-robe floating about her like lily petals. She cocked her head, listening, then crouched until her mouth was below the waterline. Corajidin heard the faint clicking noises she made, a rapid tattoo in the back of her throat. It stopped and started, paused, gained tempo, but was clearly repeated, and clearly a message. Or an invitation.

Rising from the water, she said, "Best if the rest of you stay well clear. My clan are coming and may not discriminate between one meatsack and another. You've been warned, should worse come to worst." Kimiya took the chain that linked the captives and tugged on it with surprising strength, dragging the now struggling towns-folk toward the water's edge.

And with that the Anlūki closed ranks around Corajidin and Wolfram, leading them back to the safety of the cutter. Kasraman refused to be cowed and instead walked closer to the water, his fascination clear. Tahj-Shaheh took her place at the controls, spinning up the Disentropy Spools and the Tempest Wheels against the need for escape.

The grasslands became preternaturally quiet. Light flared and faded as clouds skidded across the sun, reflections licking the surface of the water with flashes of silver. One of the captives screamed, "I felt something on my leg!" She tried to step away, then screamed again. Her body jerked with revulsion, and she tried to reach down and pull something off her. A marsh-puppeteer broke the surface. The captive flailed with her manacled hands, trying to dislodge the creature to no avail. The marsh-puppeteer climbed with the agility of a spider, reached the back of her neck, then wrapped its limbs around the woman's throat. Her screams were silenced as the marsh-puppeteer throttled her. The creature gave a moist, rattling purr as the woman's struggled slowed. She dropped to her knees, eyes rolled back in her head, skin colored by her asphyxia. There was little movement left in her when the marsh-puppeteer released its grip and scuttled down the inside of her shirt. The woman gasped feebly, but all Corajidin saw were the marsh-puppeteer's frenzied movements on the woman's back, beneath her clothes. Blood started to spread, and the lump that was the monster grew flatter, as the woman's struggles grew weaker, her voice gone hoarse.

One by one the other captives followed suit. Some collapsed into the water, limbs thrashing, cries and wails burbling as their mouths filled with water. Kimiya stood amid it all, her beautiful face contorted with a mad smile.

A handful of the puppeteers sped out of the water toward Kasraman. Before Corajidin would shout a warning, one of them leaped, limbs spread wide to claim Kasraman as its own—

Only for Kasraman to capture it in one hand. The creature thrashed and tried to escape. Another reared. Others edged forward. Kasraman pointed at them and they stood still or backed away. The one in his hands quieted as he looked at it, his glacial eyes luminous to the point of losing color. Other marsh-puppeteers came slowly out of the water.

They prostrated themselves. Kimiya, too, bowed her head.

"Kasraman . . . ?" Corajidin whispered. He turned to Wolfram. "What is he?"

"It's a question we probably should have asked before now," Wolfram muttered, hands white knuckled around his rickety staff. "But I'm more concerned with what he may become."

Kasraman lowered the marsh-puppeteer to the ground and gestured for them all to go. Some returned to the water, others to the long grass, but they all left at his command. Save Kimiya and the captives. Though the captives looked the same, there was something about their posture and facial expressions that was at once mad, and predatory.

"My people thank you, Corajidin," Kimiya said. "And Pah-Kasraman. You were true to your word. In honor of the gifts to come, we have agreed to take you to a place that will meet your needs perfectly."

Corajidin nodded briskly, barely able to contain his enthusiasm. "And what is this place?"

"In our language it would take too long to say. But in its time it was home to a hero of your people. His name was Sedefke, one of many names he had and not all spoken with adoration. This place of his was a small palace before it was lost to the memory of others."

"Sedefke?" Wolfram repeated. "We've searched so long for his refuges. To finally have access to one . . ."

Corajidin laughed, heady with excitement. "Take us there."

"Tomorrow," Kimiya said firmly. "My people need to adjust to their new bodies, and I need to ensure they do not unleash bloody murder among your ranks."

"But—"

"Tomorrow, Corajidin. We will not cheat you. What is one more day, against the centuries this place has been lost?"

One more day. A lot can happen in just one more day.

"Tomorrow, then." But the words tasted sour.

13

"TELLING A LIE OFTEN ENOUGH, EVEN BELIEVING IT, DOES NOT MAKE IT TRUE."

—Nimjé, Gnostic Assassin of the Ishahayans and Master of Spies for the
Great House of Näsarat (371st year of the Shrīanese Federation)

DAY 60 OF THE 496TH YEAR OF THE

SHRĪANESE FEDERATION

Bright streaks of afternoon sun crossed the valley, etching the shadows of trees, statues, and buildings into the snow. In Rosha's sitting room, Indris watched his breath flower in clouds on the glass. He did not need reflections to know Femensetri glared at him.

"What?" Indris turned to face her and the other members of the Suret present. "You thought nobody would ever find out how dependent the rahns are on the Sēq? That Awakening isn't something that just works forever?"

"What is it you think you know?" Femensetri asked. Ojin-mar stood near the door, while Aumh and He-Who-Watches were seated on either side of the Stormbringer, expressions stony. The rahns, their families, and their staff had been taken to the Thaumaturgeon's Hall, where the sick rahns were being treated with the Water of Life by the Sēq-trained mystic surgeons.

"The volumes in the Black Archives are spectacularly precise about it. The Awakening of those without the necessary mental discipline of the Ilhennim causes long-term damage to the body, mind, and soul. Regular doses of the Water of Life will prevent the acceleration of entropy, but once started must be maintained throughout the life of the person involved. To stop this treatment will result in the progressive and incurable degeneration of—"

"I think it's quite clear what he knows," Ojin-mar said.

"There's more," Indris offered. "Much more."

"Do you plan on revealing what you know to anybody else?" He-Who-Watches asked.

"To what end?" Indris asked. "I've no interest in the Sēq becoming pariahs. We know the Water of Life won't save the rahns. To save their lives, they need to be Severed from their Awakening, or re-Awakened."

"We can perform the Severances with mixed degrees of success," Ojin-mar offered. "It's a specialized skill, best done by healers. But to re-Awaken a person is something none of us know how to do. We can perform the rituals on a new rahn, and let the Awakening take its course. But to imprint new, unknown paths on the body, mind, and soul? There were few who could do it, and they're long gone from us."

"Can you do it, Indris?" It was clear that Aumh was not the only one interested in Indris's answer.

"I've only seen the barest hints of the rituals you've been using since Sedefke vanished, and those rituals require a person who's never been Awakened before."

"If you don't have an answer, then why are we here?" Femensetri said bitterly.

"Because we need to find out how to properly Awaken somebody, and to save the rahns. They need to survive and remain as the political presence in Shrīan able to stop—or delay—it from becoming a bloody war magnet."

"Thought you didn't care about the bigger picture, boy?" Femensetri sounded smug.

"I care about the friends and family who'll suffer, unless these things are changed." Indris tried to stare Femensetri down but she would not look away. His voice rose as he spoke, anger overcoming common sense. "The Sēq knew when they closed their doors that they would, in effect, murder the rahns of Shrīan. Nāsarat's bones, you were the ones who put Corajidin on this path of insanity when you stopped providing him the Water of Life. We'd not be where we are if it weren't for the Sēq!"

"*Faruq ayo, yaha an tehv vanha!*" Femensetri shook her head ruefully, even as the other Masters stared at her. She looked at them defensively. "What? He's what I trained him to be, more or less."

"Somewhat more, I think," Ojin-mar said.

"This is happening at the worst possible time," Aumh murmured. "As we feared, the Soul Traders are in Shrīan, and in numbers."

"Why?" Indris asked.

"If only we knew," Femensetri said. "They come at times of great strife, harvesting souls that they can torture, sell, or otherwise exploit. The more powerful the soul, the more they'll desire it. The dead don't forget anything they knew in life, so there are some souls the Traders would learn some invaluable things from."

"Would they be after the rahns, and their secrets of Awakening?"

"Possibly." She looked at Indris pointedly. "But there are other souls of power that would intrigue them more. The battle of the Mahsojhin would have been a feast for them. And what Corajidin has planned will see a lot of influential people planted in ashes. But I think they're looking for somebody specific."

"Then it's even more important I find a way to save the rahns."

Indris waited as the Masters began to speak in rapid Maladhoring, his understanding of the language not so advanced that he could gather the subtle nuance. He could tell they were not happy. "I'll go on a lore quest to find out how we can save the rahns. But I need to know how long you can keep them alive. My journey will be based on the time you give me." *And hopefully this lore quest will work out better than the one I undertook to the Spines.*

The Masters conferred, voices rising and falling, hands placating, crooks brandished or struck against the ground for emphasis. Indris went to the side table and poured himself a cup of tea, taking comfort in its warmth. He glanced outside, guessing it was only some three hours until sunset. *I need another night in the archives, and time to set things right with Rosha in case I don't get another chance.*

Then there was Anj. He needed to speak with her before he left, or else there would be no end of trouble the next time they met. There was much about her that still bothered him. It was one of the reasons he had made the Scholar's Lantern, to see the truth about her and to set his doubts either to rest, or in stone. *And yet I delay using it, for fear of learning another truth I can't forget, or ignore.*

"Indris?" Femensetri's angular voice broke his reverie. "We think we can keep the rahns alive for another few months . . . They weren't without the Water for very long, so the damage wasn't severe before they came here. But they will only get worse as time passes."

"Do you think you can find what we need?" He-Who-Watches asked urgently.

Indris replied, "All I can do is search for the answers—"

"Hope you do better than you did saving Ariskander," Femensetri said.

"—you've never had," Indris finished. He looked to the other Masters, his face warm with guilt over Ariskander's passing, in itself one of the reasons Rosha was unwell. In anger and disappointment at their millennia-long duplicity. "I'll spend tonight in the archives, and another few hours in the Manufactory to finish my projects before I go. I'll also need a couple of jars of the Water of Life. I'll also have Changeling and my other possessions back."

"And if we say no?" Aumh asked.

Indris smiled at the tiny, fern-haired Master. "You've already said yes."

※ ※ ※

Rosha returned to her suite almost an hour later looking fitter, but still nothing compared to her former vitality. She was supported by Taj, and surrounded by Mauntro and the Lion Guard. Rosha smiled at Indris and her brother as she entered her bedroom.

"How is she?" Indris asked his cousin. Taj went to the table, where he picked at a few morsels of food and poured himself a short, thick black coffee, offering Indris a cup, which he declined. Taj took a seat near him, fatigue apparent in every limb as he sank into the chair.

"She's stronger after the treatments," Taj admitted, what he did not say more telling than what he did. The pah sipped at his coffee. "But she needs to rest. As it is, she gets reports every other day on the state of the Federation, and it makes her both stressed and angry that she can't do anything to change it. Maselane, Danyūn, and Bensaharēn are running the day-to-day of Nāsarat Prefecture. Rahn-Nazarafine and Rahn-Siamak are likewise burdened with worry. Ziaire is doing what she can to influence the political parties to remain calm in the face of Asrahn-Corajidin's aggression, while Sayf-Ajomandyan challenges the Asrahn at every turn."

"Has it become so bad that the Great Houses and the Hundred Families are holding their long-knives so openly?" Ajamensût, a

War of the Long-Knife, was the classic way of fighting between the Houses and the Families. Rarely would a rahn or a sayf take to the field with an army unless they planned on conquest; otherwise they preferred a subtle and quiet victory over their enemies. Ajamensût solved many problems without the collateral damage and cost that came from an aj, or an ajam—military campaigns of increasing size.

"Yes. Some Imperialists doubt Corajidin as a leader, not surprising given his flagrant disrespect for sende, and the freedoms our laws try to protect."

"So, wars of assassins have become inevitable?"

Their conversation was interrupted as the door to Rosha's bedroom opened, and Rosha came out to join them.

Indris avoided the obvious questions, fully expecting that Rosha was tired of hearing them. Taj rose to get his sister some food and wine as Indris spoke. "Rosha, I need to—"

"Indris, wait. Before you start, let me apologize for the way I've treated you." Rosha played nervously with the pleats of her over-robe as she avoided eye contact. "It wasn't until Father's voice began to fade from my mind that I realized how much reason had abandoned me. In truth, I think I was becoming ever more him, but without any of his self-control, consumed by the anguish of my—of his—death. The things I said . . . that I did . . ."

"This was Nehrun's burden, not yours. You did the best you could for your House and the Federation."

Rosha laughed then, a bright sound. Tears flowed and she wiped them away with a firm hand. "I did poorly by you, and all you've ever done has been for the good of others. You did, you do, deserve better. And Mari? In the name of all the Näsarats that have come before me, I never thought I'd admit that there was an Erebus I actually liked."

"But . . . ?"

She shook her head. "No buts. You two are perfect for each other. Even Father thought so, but the anger, the betrayal, of seeing our country fall apart: I was filled with such blind, reckless, consuming rage—" Her words spat out like marbles clattering around her feet.

"I understand, Rosha." Indris took her hands in his. They were fever hot, the skin dry as old paper. "I take it that means you'll not stand in my way of being with Mari?"

"No. In fact, I'd be proud to call her cousin." Rosha leaned in to rest her forehead against Indris's. Taj came to join them. "I'm glad you're both here," she said. "And I've asked for Nehrun to return from the Shrine of the Vanities. He was a good brother, a good Näsarat, once. I'd have as many of my family here as I can. Now is the time to forgive, while we've the chance."

"My thanks for these words, Rosha." Indris felt guilt weigh heavily on him. *What has happened to me? I would have let you die . . .* "I thought unkindly of you, without ever stopping to consider your burden. There's nothing more I can do to help you, Rosha—or Siamak or Nazarafine—from here. This illness may kill you yet. What the thaumaturgeons are doing is a treatment, not a cure. There is no cure that we know of. But I've an idea that may work, and I'm leaving here tomorrow to find a way to save you and the others, if it's at all possible."

Rosha said nothing, only hugged Indris and Taj closer as she rocked, sobbing silently and whispering her apologies over and over.

❋ ❋ ❋

Indris did not wait for the setting of the sun to enter the Black Archives. This time Femensetri offered to join him, but Indris declined. His former teacher seemed more upset than angry, and it was clear there were things she wanted to say in private. Standing at the door, feeling her presence, he was taken back to his days as her student when she had always been there, helping him with the fear, and the pain, and the isolation.

Now is the time to forgive, while we've the chance, Rosha had said. But as he looked at Femensetri, her angular features predatory and beautiful and timeless, her old cassock held together by leather straps and lacing, the mindstone boring a hole in her brow like a third eye, he could not bring himself to do it.

So he nodded politely, then closed the door firmly on her as she turned away.

When Indris arrived at the central archive, the Herald was waiting for him. The masked figure watched as Indris made his way to the bottom level, and into those areas that contained the proscribed works.

Knowing it was fruitless, and feeling caught in a swirl of events he could not control—a nexus point where all his choices led to here, and from here in fewer directions than he hoped—Indris searched again for the information he needed to answer the question of his growing abilities. No matter where he looked, there was nothing of value written about the Mah-Psésahen. There were references. Hints that it had been studied here and there: that it was a relic of the Haiyt Empire of the Time Masters; that the Dragons practiced it along with their dreaming mysticism; that it had been the high watermark of the teachings of Khenempûr; that it had been a near sacred field of study by the Masters of Isenandar. But in all cases the message was clear: The scholars of the various orders had turned their backs on it for reasons nobody understood.

And the last place it had been taught was at Isenandar. The secrets of Awakening, the lost lore of the great mental teachings, the greatest school of the Sēq and all its secrets lost to time.

Everything pointed Indris toward the Pillars of Sand, and the man named Danger-Is-Calling, who may have the answers Indris sought.

Heavy-footed, Indris climbed the stairs back to the vault and the Genealogy Tree. Once more he scoured it for his name, even among the dulled leaves of the dead: He searched for some clue in the scratches around the heretical bloodlines that narrow-minded Masters had sought to remove from history. Indris touched a line abandoned, the ashen quartz leaves of Näsarat fe Malde-ran, her husbands, her children, all forsaken in her Great Heresy as the empire fell to ruin. It was a different Näsarat line that knew power now, rahns descended from Malde-ran's brother and cousins.

Indris turned to the vault with his name on it. Only a few of the hundreds of questions of its lock remained. The Maladhoring characters drifted there like blocks of rain on the glass. Of those questions, there was only one query he knew could not be answered here: What is Awakening, how does one prepare the mind for it to be effective, and how does one Awaken such a mind?

"There are times I wish I could reach back in time and slap some people," Indris mused.

"I doubt you are alone in that sentiment," the Herald replied.

"Hmmm. Well, it seems I'll need to search elsewhere if I'm going to answer this question." Indris flicked the vault door, with a fingernail.

"You are leaving Amarqa-in-the-Snows?" the Herald said without preamble.

"I'm going to try and find out how to re-Awaken the rahns." *And how to open this damned vault.*

"Awakened rahns are—"

"Irrelevant. Yes, I heard that before. Not to me they're not. One of those rahns is my cousin, and I've precious few anchors to family or friends left. I don't intend to lose another one if I can help it."

"Only the Mahj, and the mahjirahns, are relevant." The Herald intoned.

"How?" When Ariskander had tried to Awaken Indris in Amnon, he had said that Femensetri and the other rahns had all agreed that Indris was to be his heir, despite Ariskander having three of his own children to choose from. Indris recalled the yearning to embrace the connection to Ïa and all things on it. The sensation of a deep and abiding strength that would never fade for so long as the sun burned in the sky. With such power Indris could do a great many things, not all of which were good. His own Ancestors had proven that point: Näsarat fa Dionwē, the first Mahj of the Awakened Empire, had sunk the Seethe High Court beneath the Marble Sea. Malde-ran, the Empress-in-Shadows, had turned thousands of her people into Nomads, and commanded the dead to return from the Well of Souls to defend the empire. There were hundreds of stories with happier endings, of centuries of benign rule under Näsarat Dynasties, but in the extremity of their need, the Näsarats had proven they would abuse power. Indris stepped closer to the Herald as if he could see through his own warped reflection to the face of the person beneath.

Who are you? An obvious question, tainted by perspective and observation. But then so is why, how, what, where, and when. We are all of us different, depending on the circumstances we are in: we are kind and cruel by turn, sometimes tyrants or saviors, teachers and students, ardent lovers, or driven by anger and our darker emotions to cause harm in defense of a stance that may mean nothing in a week's time.

"Why are you and those like you so focused on giving the scholars power you know they can't be trusted with?" Indris asked.

The Herald reached out a gauntleted hand, the fingertips polished black and sharp as a talon, to tap Indris on the brow. "You know. You have seen."

And had it taken from me! "Enlighten me. Save me the trouble of learning again what I already know."

"You children of the Afternoon People do not have the patience to wait, and watch, for you do not live long enough to learn what patience means. Your lives are but a flicker in history."

"But they're everything to us."

"And rightly so!" the Herald said vehemently. "All life is precious, and the life you do not live is as lost as if it had never happened at all. But your passions, seen as just and true in your span of days, may be seen as reckless and wasteful from a different vantage."

The drowning of the Seethe under the Marble Sea . . . the gathering of the Nomads at the end of the empire . . . "I understand. But it's in our nature to act when we feel we must. What could be so terrible, so dramatic, that it had to be taken away from me?"

"What if you had found out that your entire life had been a lie?" the Herald asked. "What if the world was not ready to accept certain truths?"

"I don't . . ." Indris felt a terrible apprehension take root. *What would I do? What did I do?*

"This is why you had your memories hidden within the spirals of an Anamnesis Maze. You knew too soon some things that both you and the remainder of the world were unprepared for. You would have acted, and many would have died without purpose, when their deaths could be made to count at the right time and the right place."

"What about their lives?" Indris asked, aghast. "Their lives are what hold meaning. Dying is simple. Living for something is much harder."

"In their time, all things die. It starts from the moment we are given life, and accelerates from the moment we are aware of what death means. A good life means much, but a good death often inspires others more."

"Including mine?"

"When the time comes, most especially yours."

❋ ❋ ❋

Indris spent the next hour in the Manufactory, as he finished engraving the characters on his Scholar's Lantern, and anchored the final glyphs of his armor and shield to the disentropy streams of the world around him. Femensetri pushed the door to the Manufactory open just as Indris breathed the formulae to activate what he had made.

The characters etched along his lantern flared, then faded to a jade glow before becoming a faint blue-green shimmer. The *serill* head flickered with light at its heart, no brighter than a candle. Indris coaxed it to a brilliant white so bright that it drained the color from everything about it, banishing shadows to little more than razor cuts of darkness.

"Oh . . ." Femensetri breathed, her face lit with wonder. "It's been a long time since I've seen one of those. They were better times for all of us." She looked at her Scholar's Crook, lips turned downward with sour humor. The Stormbringer called out and two Sēq Librarians made their wide-eyed way into the room. They carried between them a long crate of polished ebony that they set down at Indris's feet before bowing and hastily departing. Once the door closed behind them, Femensetri leaned on her crook and nodded toward the chest at Indris's feet. "That's what you asked for."

Indris laid his lantern on the workbench beside his armored coat and shield. He opened the crate and breathed a sigh of relief as his fingers curled around Changeling's gentle curves. She crooned as he took her up, purred as he held her for a long moment. His satchel and journal, other personal effects, and storm-pistol were also there.

"Thank you," Indris said. With Changeling close by, his senses were sharper, and within seconds he felt stronger as she trickled disentropy into him. He had forgotten how much he had become used to the sensation, or how good it felt after its absence. He shrugged into his scaled hauberk, jumping a few times to even the weight. Femensetri came forward and helped him tighten the buckles and adjust the lacing so it did not hamper his movement. She helped him into a worn over-robe, brushing it smooth across his shoulders and back. Indris slung his weapons and shield, took up his staff and the bag containing the two jars of the Water of Life.

The two of them walked in a neutral silence down the valley, past the Black Quill with its steaming hot spring, and over the ancient stone bridge with its covered wards. They remained, the two of them, shoulder to shoulder and a footstep away from the border of the Sēq valley.

Femensetri looked at him for a long while, her expression wistful. "Indris . . ." She cleared her throat so when she spoke next her voice had none of the unaccustomed softness of that single word. She rested a hand on his shoulder. "Things here aren't as they seem. In time, you'll understand."

"Perhaps," Indris replied gently. He stepped into the outside world and cycled his breathing, raising his consciousness to the point where he could call out across the ahmtesh. *Chaiya? Are Shar and Ekko still in Tamerlan?*

It took a moment before his friend answered. Indris cycled his breathing once more, and his awareness dropped back to the cool valley and his old teacher.

"I've put life off for too long, sahai, and it's past time I was gone. If there's an answer for what ails the rahns, I'll find it. But you need to get the rahns back to Avānweh. There's nothing you can do for them here that you can't do there, and they need to return to governing the country."

"We've already made preparations," Femensetri replied. "We'll leave via the Weavegates tomorrow morning."

Indris took a mockingbird out of his bag and twisted the hemispheres. The clockwork mechanism began to tick, the characters he had inscribed slowly starting to form as the pieces aligned. "I need to speak with Anj before I go. Do you know where she is?"

"She's gone, and we don't know where." Femensetri's voice once more had its customary edges. "She's not what you think she is, Indris. But whatever she may be, you know she's no longer your wife. You can't see that woman anymore. You can't love that woman anymore."

"I'll always love her, until she does something to break it . . . but I'm not in love with her. I've not been for years. I don't know what she is, but like you I've suspicions I don't want to give voice to." *Who knows who's listening?* "She'll come after me when she knows I'm gone. No doubt we'll have words then."

Indris willed his staff into incandescence, and then he did something he had not done in many years, and only then when his need was great: He opened a portal into the Drear. The cold blue-green light washed the edges of his sight, and the deep basso groans, staccato chittering, and gibbering that came from its depths rolled up through the fluid space. Among the deeper shadows, in the sediment of lost dreams, forgotten hopes, and people's madness, Indris saw the slow ooze of gargantuan tentacles, and the opening of toothy maws, surrounded by clusters of sleepy eyes. The analogies of land formed around his feet, a marsh of sighing reeds, rank waters, and air that tasted like wet ash. He tossed the mockingbird in. It streaked away, chattering loudly, sacrificed for Indris's safety.

Indris's last sight was of Femensetri opening her mouth to speak. Her words were lost as the world splintered into fragments around him, and the Drear swallowed him whole.

14

"KNOWING ONLY WHAT YOU ARE TOLD IS A SMALL KIND OF LIFE."

—Nasri of the Elay-At, Shrīanese dramatist
(495th Year of the Shrīanese Federation)

DAY 60 OF THE 496TH YEAR OF THE

SHRĪANESE FEDERATION

The night mists and the drop in temperature had driven most of the nahdi in Tamerlan to the Hearthall. Mari avoided the frenetic press of sweating bodies, obscured by the shadows as the Dowager-Asrahn reveled in the heat, the clamor, and the rising temperature of people's blood. Nadir, Jhem, and the Emissary sat by her, heads bowed close in conference. Belam and Sanojé sat at places of honor, their smiles fixed.

Eladdin threw his arms skyward, spattered with gore, after gutting a man. Mari winced at the wet red tears in the young nahdi's stomach. Rather than finish him off, Eladdin watched, wide-eyed, his laughter manic. The man—no, the boy, barely past sixteen—tried to hold his entrails in. He staggered, slipped in his own blood.

The Dowager-Asrahn threw coins in a shower from her high table where they bounced and rolled in the blood.

Her cousin strutted around the Maw of Savajiin, stopping from time to time to hear the crowd shout his name. Mari folded her arms in disgust. *We fight not for ourselves,* Bensaharēn had told her during her training at the Lament. *The warrior-poet—the traditions of the daishāri—are rooted in our sacred calling to defend those who are unable to defend themselves. We are the ones who die, that others may live, our names remembered as those who gave themselves bravely for the greater good.* Had her teacher seen the likes of Eladdin, Mari had little doubt he would have cast her cousin down, broken his weapons before his eyes, and rescinded his Exalted Name for all time.

Spurred on by the crowd and the exhortations of his mother, Eladdin dashed in and punched the beleaguered boy in the face, driving him to the ground. The young man's wounds opened farther. Eladdin took a handful of his enemy's hair and dragged him toward the Maw. He pushed him in, the boy screaming all the way down. The crowd went wild, though there were a significant number whose cheers seemed more for form than enthusiasm.

Enjoy the spectacle, little rooster. Tonight it ends for you and the crone you call a mother.

Mari scanned the crowd until she found Morne, Kyril, and their crew of Immortal Companions through a haze of heat, smoke, and sweating bodies. The Companions were no more armed or armored than usual, so as not to raise an alarm. There were forty in all, each marked with a pin of a serpent made of ornate blocks, eating its own tail. It was the first time Mari had seen so many of the Immortal Companions in the Hearthall, and she was thankful for the general levels of inebriation. Had the other warriors in the hall been more sober, the presence of so many predators might have given them pause. But the night was cold, and the Hearthall packed.

"Hey there, pretty lady," came a breezy voice from her shoulder. "Can I buy you a drink, and talk you into doing something stupid?"

With a grin, Mari turned and gave Shar a kiss. The Seethe warchanter was hooded despite the heat. Other than her *serill* sword and knives, there was nothing to give away that she was Seethe. Ekko loomed behind her. Under the shadows of his cloak, she could see little else but his yellow eyes. One massive hand rested on the hilt of his *khopesh,* and he opened the flap of a bag to reveal a short bow and a quiver of arrows, each thick as Mari's finger. Mari drew Ekko into a hug, and the powerful Tau-se purred in response. "I'm glad you're both here." *There's nobody I'd rather do this with . . . No, that isn't true. Hayden . . . Omen . . . Indris. All gone.* She blinked rapidly against a stab of grief. *But never forgotten.*

"The Immortal Companions are ready to give you your diversion, Mariam," Ekko rumbled. "Shar and I will remain with you, to better your chances of success. We are not thrilled with the presence of the Widowmaker. We owe him a debt of blood for our dead."

"Now is not the time, and here is not the place," Mari cautioned. "Our objective is Vahineh."

"Ekko could carry Vahineh under one arm and still fight if it comes to it," Shar added with an impudent grin.

"Isn't your sonesette a little bulky for fighting?" Mari asked, eyeing the massive stringed instrument strapped to Shar's back.

"We'll need her before the night is done. I'll add a little music to a lot of wine, suggest a few things in song, help unpop some corks on the violence here, and let the Laughing Wind spirits have their way. I doubt many of these halfwits have dealt with a Seethe trouper before. I'd almost feel sorry for them, were they not in service with the evil old hag who governs this rock. They'll get what they deserve."

"You wanted a distraction," Ekko added.

"And you know how people say less is more?" Shar asked. Mari nodded in response, to which Shar grinned wickedly. "Morons. All of them. More is always more. Especially when it comes to distractions."

Mari could not help but laugh and hug both of her friends tightly. "I've missed you both so much. This may sound strange but I'm almost looking forward to what we're about to do."

"Ridding the world of villains is always something to be relished, Mariam." Ekko stood proud, an armored mountain of fur and muscle beneath his cloak.

"And it seems fitting we do this to remember the ones we've lost," Shar added.

"Shall we, then?" Mari asked.

"Oh, let's do!" Shar replied.

Mari turned her attention to the center of the room, where Eladdin was toying with another victim, cutting the man so he bled profusely without wounding him badly enough to kill. The guards who had been spying on Mari had their attention diverted to the bloodshed. The Dowager-Asrahn thumped her wine bowl, a gold-plated skull with sapphires for eyes, on the table. Wine, thick and dark as blood, sloshed over the side and down her hand. It stained the old crone's lips and turned her filed teeth red. Some of Mari's cousins joined the Dowager-Asrahn, though more had slid their chairs farther down the table.

Leaving Shar and Ekko where they were, Mari made a circuit of the room. She walked from small group to group, and smiled back to those gracious enough to look her in the eye, clasp her hand, or comment kindly. She marked those who preferred the sight of the ceiling, or the wine-soaked and bloody floor, taking their measure in turn. When Mari came to stand beside Morne and

Kyril, she subtly pointed out the ones who she thought would not interfere, versus those who were in the thrall of the Dowager-Asrahn. "Most of the nahdi are here because they've nowhere else to go. Down on their luck, or defeated in some campaign somewhere and forced to flee for the season. They're biding their time. But there are those who see a real future with my grandmother, and they're the animals that need to be put down."

"Starting with that one." Morne nodded at Eladdin where he preyed on a warrior much weaker than himself. "There'll be an uproar when he's history. Your grandmother will certainly attempt to have me killed on the spot."

"No doubt," Mari said. "I assume your people will be in position?"

"We'll seed them among those most likely to help the Dowager-Asrahn," Kyril affirmed. "Our warriors will put down the leaders of those groups first."

"And the witches?" Mari asked. "Can you drop them quickly?"

Morne chuckled, checking the buckles on his armored sleeve. "It's under control. I've three daimahjin in my crew, and some of my people learned some bitter truths fighting in the Conflicted Cities. They know the advantages of salt-forged steel."

Kyril spoke with those Immortal Companions nearby, who then took their squads with them and went out among the crowds, settling close to those Mari thought would rally to the Dowager-Asrahn. When they were in position, Mari turned to Morne.

"How are you going to do it?" Mari asked, gesturing with her chin at Eladdin. She winced as her cousin danced behind his opponent, pulled the man's head back by his long hair, and cut his throat. Blood gushed down the man's chest, and Eladdin dragged him to the Maw and shoved him in while the man was still alive. The applause was deafening as the crowd sloshily rapped their bowls and mugs against shields, tables, and chairs.

After stretching his arms, back, and legs, Morne leaned in to kiss Kyril. He smiled, his once handsome face wrinkling around the eyes. "You ask how? Like this."

Morne stepped into the combat round, each step more predatory than the last, palm resting on the hilt of his knife with its studded basket hilt. The other nahdi in the room nodded, and some cheered, for Morne was clearly a man not to be trifled with. Eladdin looked bored as he walked back to his sycophants, snorting, joking about how it was now up to the old-timers and has-beens to provide entertainment.

"Where do you think you're going, boy?" Morne said to Eladdin's back. Eladdin stopped, turned, and gave Morne an incredulous look. "Yes. You. Boy."

"Are you challenging me, old man?" Eladdin asked with a cruel smile. Mari quickly walked away from Kyril's side, using the crowd as cover as she made her way to where Shar and Ekko waited. Shar started to strum her sonesette—metallic, discordant notes that set Mari's nerves on edge.

"Sounds like it, *sau héj*." Eladdin's eyes bulged at the insult. Small man: weak, shallow, and unaccomplished. Morne swept his arm around the room. "Unless there are other opponents you'd feel safer fighting."

"Eladdin!" The Dowager-Asrahn's voice cracked over the swell of the crowd. She glared at Morne, the old shark recognizing a tiger among the dogs in her yard. "It is time to allow another to—"

The Sidewinder waved his mother down. He drew his knives and moved forward, gliding from one foot to the next. His blades made shining, weaving patterns in the air. Eladdin's face was dark with fury. "Stay out of this, Mother! The sharks are still hungry, and this fool seems eager to feed them."

The sound of Shar's sonesette jangled out across the Hearthall, woven with her breathy voice raised in song. Mari did not understand the words but felt her hearts rise at the sound. There were those around her who shrunk in on themselves. They looked about with uncertainty and fear. Mari remembered her sense of impending dread at the Battle of Amnon as the Seethe war-chanters sang, and their warriors enacted their battle as scripted by their dramatists. She had fought all her instincts to hold her blade in her hand, and not run for safety. Hearing Shar's song now, Mari felt invincible.

"Eladdin, no!" the Dowager-Asrahn shrieked. "My beautiful boy, do not—"

Morne drew his dagger and used his armored sleeve, and subtle foot and bodywork, to avoid the flurry of Eladdin's blows. Eladdin's expression was unchanged, apparently unaffected by the music. Flawed as his moral compass was, Eladdin had been trained as a warrior-poet, and the daishäri did not break, and did not run. Steel belled, clanged, shrieked, and chimed. Both men fought without speaking, intent on the play of muscle and metal. Red sprayed and both men leaped back, Eladdin aghast that his precious skin had been cut. Blood trickled down his abdomen. Morne reached up to wipe at the scratch on his neck.

Both men glided forward. There came a whirlwind of cuts, stabs, punches, and kicks. Eladdin seemed a font of energy, his movements explosive, impacts like adder stings. Morne's technique was an even burn, hot as a forge, intractable as an anvil, his strikes clinical, devastating. Feinting, Morne sunk his armored fist into Eladdin's stomach, and followed with a hammer blow from the studded hilt of his dagger. Eladdin went face-first onto the bloody floor, one of his knives skittering away. Mari's cousin rolled away to come to his feet, shaking his head. His lips were split, and he spit out blood and part of a tooth.

Morne gestured for Eladdin to retrieve his knife. The younger man cursed and held out his hand, calling for his sword. One of Eladdin's cronies dashed forward, to the grumbles of the crowd, and handed the Sidewinder a long-hilted shamshir, the blade sheathed in sharkskin. Eladdin kissed the serpent pommel of his weapon with a flourish. He stood, lean as his sword, renewed with greater confidence.

"You brought this on yourself, old man," Eladdin said.

"It was meant to be this way." Morne sheathed his knife and called over his shoulder to the smiling Kyril. "My love? Steel, if you'd be so kind." Kyril unfolded the cloth wrapping from around a long battle-axe with a chisel-shaped blade protruding from the back. Eladdin's face paled at the sight of it. Shar's song almost drowned out the Dowager-Asrahn's mournful wail. Morne hefted the axe. "Shall we?"

Mari's mouth went dry as both men savaged each other. The fight had changed, going from duelist's arena to the battlefield. Sword and axe glittered in the lantern light as the warriors traded blows. Sweat flew and ran down faces colored with effort. Yet it was the younger Eladdin who moved faster and faster, his cuts and footwork precise. Morne moved more slowly, deliberately, as he was driven back toward the Maw. The Dowager-Asrahn and her followers cheered loudly, and chanted Eladdin's name. The warrior-poet's grin grew wider.

Morne stumbled, his back to the Maw. He dropped to one knee, head bowed, hair drenched with sweat, his armored sleeve scratched and dented.

Eladdin slid from left foot to right, shamshir held crosswise in the fatal Penitent's End technique. It hovered for a moment, shining, before the blade swooped down toward the juncture of Morne's head and neck.

The crowd roared.

Mari swore.

Kyril smiled.

Morne was not where the blade landed. He rose, body spiraling, axe a blur as he twirled it over his head. It made a terrible and bloody crescent as Morne swung it down. The axe bit into the back of Eladdin's neck. Cut through flesh and bone. His body tumbled in two pieces into the Maw of Savajiin.

The Dowager-Asrahn shrieked, veins protruding from her sweaty neck and temples like worms. She hurled her wine bowl at Morne, though it fell well short of the mark, the gold skull clattering about uselessly on the bloody floor. Her screams were incoherent, inconsolable, and she raked at her face and chest with her sharp nails. Eventually her words took a hoarse form, birthed from mad grief.

"Kill him! A thousand golden rings to the one who brings me the head and manhood of this foul murderer. Kill him! Kill him! KILL HIM FOR ME, MY DOGS!"

The Savadai and those nahdi loyal to the Dowager-Asrahn took up arms. Belam drew Tragedy, and he and Sanojé took to wreaking red havoc among the Dowager-Asrahn's soldiery. Nadir, Jhem, and the Emissary scanned the crowd, most likely searching for Mari, who slipped behind a pillar. Shar and Ekko were at her side. Mari heard her name being screeched at the top of the Dowager-Asrahn's lungs.

Set amid the Dowager-Asrahn's forces, the Immortal Companions went to work with the ruthless efficiency born of years of service on hundreds of battlefields. From her vantage point, Mari could see the chaos they sowed. Belam was a bloody-handed menace, worse than anything the hounds of Tamerlan had seen, and warriors fled before him, or died. Sanojé pitted herself against the Sea Witches, flinging hexes while maintaining her arcane wards for herself and Belam. As far as distractions went, this served as biggest.

"It's time we went about our business," Mari said to Shar and Ekko. She gave the Dowager-Asrahn one last quick look as Mari and her friends left the Hearthall.

Grieve while you may, Grandmother. You'll join your son soon enough.

❋ ❋ ❋

Mari led her friends to the trophy room. Household staff saw them coming and made themselves scarce. Those few guards they met along the way were dispatched with ruthless efficiency, bodies left broken and bleeding. At last Mari, Shar, and Ekko came to the ironbound doors. Four guards stood there, leaning on their tridents, looking bored. It took them a moment to realize who it was that stood in front of them. They rapidly took a defensive stance but looked dubiously at each other, at Mari, Shar, and Ekko, then back at each other without much confidence.

"Way I see it," Mari said as she walked forward, unarmed and unarmored yet not slowing her pace, or giving them time to think, "you can move out of my way and let me take back what's mine. Or you can make the not terribly long-lived mistake of trying to stop me. You have until I reach the door."

With a final look at Mari, and Shar with her *serill* sword, and Ekko with his *khopesh*, the guards melted away like spring snow. Mari unlocked the doors with Dhoury's key and strode into the trophy room. Rather than one room, it was a series of interconnected chambers. The stolen relics of the centuries hung from the walls, gathering dust and growing rust in the damp air. In the center of the largest room, whose ceiling was lost to a cobwebbed darkness above, there were several couches and a small table with glasses, and bottles of wine and spirits. Weapons, armor, shields, crowns, jewelry, books, paintings: Shelves and cabinets and wall mountings groaned with the weight of it all. Mari dashed from room to room until she found her Sûnblade, and the heirloom amenesqa that had been lost in Amnon, restored to her by her father.

"Hello, ladies!" Mari felt a profound sense of relief as she slung the weapon across her back and buckled her weapon belt with the Sûnblade around her waist.

The sounds of combat rang down the corridor as Mari joined Shar and Ekko. "Now we can get Vahineh, meet up with Morne, and finish what we started."

There was more commotion in the corridors as they made their way to the surgery. More guards avoided them than engaged them in combat: The sight of an armed Mari with her two friends was more than they were willing to deal with. Battles, when they occurred, were brief and decisive, the bodies not even cooling before Mari and her comrades raced on. Shar sang dirges to the dead in backward-sounding Seethe as they moved, Ekko silent. When they arrived at the surgery, the doors were unguarded.

"Qesha-rē?" Mari called. Walls and floor shone under lantern light. Surgical tools gleamed on trays, rainbow patterns dancing on bottles of ointments, medicines, and raw ingredients. Alchemical instruments were burnished with loving care. Mari called out once more, and Qesha walked out of the convalescing rooms, wiping her hands.

"Time to go?" the Nilvedic surgeon asked. She looked at Shar and Ekko with interest, and Mari made introductions. Qesha called out Vahineh's name, and the young woman shyly poked her head out the door, eyes widening as she saw Mari and her friends. The Rahn-Selassin—if such a title still applied—raced out and threw her arms about Mari with desperate strength. Oddly touched, Mari allowed the hug to continue for a long moment before she extricated herself, nodding to Qesha that it was, indeed, time to go.

"Shar? Ekko?" Mari said as they entered a wide courtyard exposed to gentle flurries of snow. "Please make sure nothing happens to Vahineh."

"I need to kill him," Vahineh said with an almost childlike honesty. She looked at Mari sadly. "Your father, I mean. I killed his wife, and I mean to finish what I—"

Mari stopped short at Vahineh's words. The younger woman's face was without guile, her eyes those of an innocent. Mari caught the glances of her friends as she ordered her thoughts. "Vahineh, we can talk about what we do later. But we need you away from here, away from my family, so you can help the other rahns against my father."

"I can indeed help them against your father." Vahineh's voice was chilling.

"There's little left of the Federationist party, Mari," Shar said. "Since you've been gone, Shrīan's changed. Your father . . . the witches—"

"Let's worry more about what we can do, neh?"

Footsteps behind her caused Mari to turn. Ekko growled and Shar swore. Both took combative stances as Belam and Sanojé joined them. Her brother and the witch were panting, their clothes bloodstained. Mari doubted any of the blood was theirs. Belam gave Mari a cautious grin that dwindled as he assessed Shar and Ekko, who had closed ranks. The Widowmaker allowed Tragedy's tip to fall toward the ground, his other hand held out and open.

"We've cleared the corridor between here and the skydock," Belam said softly. Shar and Ekko stepped toward Belam, and Tragedy's tip rose from the ground. "I'm here to help, not hinder. Mari? Tell them, please."

"Mariam?" Ekko said. "Allow me to clear your brother from our path so we may continue our journey away from Tamerlan."

Belam looked bemused. "You could try that, yes. Or, you could put your sword down, and live a long and happy life. There is no vendetta between us, Tau-se, so why should I spill your blood?"

"No vendetta?" Ekko growled. "Hayden . . . Omen . . . There needs to be a reckoning!"

Mari rested her hand on Ekko's arm and shook her head. *I don't need to lose any more friends.* "I, we, hold you responsible for the deaths of my friends, Belam. That's not something we can forget."

"And I hold your dead lover to account over the death of my Ancestor!" Sanojé spat. "But we don't all get what we want."

"Peace, please!" Belam took a deep breath. "I'm not asking you to forget, Mari. Nor am I asking for your forgiveness. All I'm asking is for a chance to help undo some of what I've done."

Mari nodded to Shar and Ekko. The Tau-se drew himself to his full and impressive height. "I have my eye on you, Widowmaker. Any betrayal by you will be answered."

"Be my guest." Belam's tone was less flippant than Mari expected, and entirely without fear.

❄ ❄ ❄

A blood-spattered Morne, Kyril, and a squad of the Immortal Companions careened out of the gates at the far side of the courtyard, weapons drawn. They pulled up short when they saw Mari and her company. One of the Companions, a compact woman in russet armor, carrying a heavy rapier with a dented hilt, began to swear soundly. She finished off with "We've lost them," in a heavy Ygranian accent.

"What happened?" Mari asked.

"The Dowager-Asrahn escaped," Morne said bitterly. Mari began her own round of swearing, raising the eyebrows of those nearby. Morne gestured her to calm. "There's no pouring that wine back in the bottle, Mari. Tamerlan is ours, but the Dowager-Asrahn and her inner circle are gone. Nadir, his father—both of whom I'd love to see dead—and the Emissary, gone. Along with their witches and some soldiery."

"How did they escape?" Shar asked, though the war-chanter seemed relieved there would be no more fighting. "There aren't that many ways off the island."

"The witches," Sanojé suggested. "The ones from the Mahsojhin that the Asrahn has in service. They've no fear, and little restraint in opening portals through the Drear. They're a different vintage from the witches and scholars I know."

"Because they're missing the last three hundred years or so," Belamandris said. "But as General Hawkwood said, what's done is done. We need to press forward. Father's agendas won't wait on us."

"Not yet," Mari countered. "We've got some cleaning to do. The Dowager-Asrahn wouldn't abandon Tamerlan so easily. She's here, lurking somewhere. Advise your people to caution and make sure nobody is alone."

The sky above them cracked; a slit of brilliant lightning flared behind the clouds. The air growled, groaned, wailed as it was ripped open in brilliant ripples like a stone had been thrown into the pond of the clouds. A column of silver-white radiance speared down, striking the courtyard with a titanic boom. A shining figure streaked downward, trailing liquid light behind it.

The light faded, revealing a man crouched in the center of the courtyard, the hood of his over-robe covering his head. He carried a tall staff that glowed gently, and an amenesqa with a dragon-headed pommel was slung across his back, as well as a round shield that was black as night. Everybody froze as he stood. The head within the hood looked this way and that.

With a casual gesture the man swept his hood back to reveal handsome features and a mop of untamable hair. Mari felt light-headed. Her chest hurt and her breath hurt and her eyes burned as tears welled and her hands trembled and her knees felt weak.

Indris gave Mari and the others a brief smile. "Sorry I'm late." He looked around at the blood-covered warriors and witches. "What did I miss?"

15

"HATREDS AND PREJUDICES ARE LEARNED, BORN FROM THE FEAR OF THAT WHICH IS NEITHER COMFORTABLE, NOR FAMILIAR, NOR IN OUR CONTROL."

—From *The Nilvedic Maxims*

DAY 60 OF THE 496TH YEAR OF THE

SHRĪANESE FEDERATION

Corajidin lay in his pavilion, entranced by the sensations that washed over him. He felt individual strands of silk in his sleeping robe. He smelled cloves on his quilt from where it had been stored for the warmer months and not aired long enough, and the arid smell of dust. He observed the swell of light where it descended to the shadowy curves of his pavilion. The tempo of his hearts, the beetles that scuttled around the base of his pavilion, the forlorn cries of marsh devils, the burble of the river, and the nervous whispers of those sworn to his colors. When he closed his eyes, he could almost hear their individual words and see in his mind's eye the speakers where they huddled around campfires that seemed all too small in the seemingly infinite, and oppressive, darkness of the Rōmarq.

Īa was alive with energy that renewed and sustained him. He had felt neither hungry, nor thirsty, nor tired since his arrival earlier in the day.

Unity had been something like this. Being fully Awakened, and aware, and in touch with the world around me. I'd forgotten how beautiful, how peaceful, and how humbling it all was. But the Rōmarq was more intense, more giving, than Erebus Prefecture, overflowing with energy. No wonder there were so many echoes of empire here.

I have been Awakened for a third time. Am I the Thrice Awakened that will both do and undo everything I have planned? Is it because of my actions that I will have all, and my children nothing?

Corajidin rose from bed and slid into his over-robe. He was reminded of dramatists' tales where rahns went disguised among their soldiery, to hear and learn what the common folk thought. He found himself glad and saddened in equal measure that the opinions of others were no longer his compass. *Does that make me weaker, stronger, or just older and more set in my ways?* He exited his pavilion and walked into the camp, the Anlūki his black and scarlet shadows.

Outside, the sky dazzled with the light of thousands of stars that burned like jewels against the velvet night, so bright Corajidin thought he might go blind. The Ancestor's Shroud reached out a nebulous arm across the sky, painted with more colors, and more brightly lit, than Corajidin had ever remembered. He blinked a few times to adjust his sight, each opening of his eyes showing him more of the world around him. Everything shimmered with life. Coronas around the trees, grasses, and marsh flowers. Whorls of brightness in the water, and people! People shone, their souls limned in the radiance of hundreds of candles. It did not take long for Corajidin's eyes to pierce the darkness as easily as if it were dusk, rather than deep night. He was overwhelmed by the scents of people, and steel, and oil, and leather, and the smoke of campfires, the horse musk of the Iphyri—and beneath it all the foundation reek of brackish water, decaying vegetation, and carcasses rotting in the mud. About him, the horizon glowed as if the ghost of dawn was about to come from all directions.

Soldiers made their obeisance as he passed, which he only vaguely responded to, so transfixed was he by everything about him. He felt his lips part in what felt like the first unencumbered smile he had given in . . . far too long. At the edge of camp, Iphyri guards walked the perimeter, horse heads swinging this way and that, nostrils and eyes wide, massive frames burdened by layers of steel and leather so that their hooves sank into the mud. A squad of the Iphyri sheathed their weapons, and dropped to all fours, before trotting out along a dimly lit path on patrol.

Corajidin stood on the riverbank, unafraid of what he could now clearly see. Fish seemed to hover, glowing in the depths like the reflection of kites. On the far bank a few huge marsh rats, big as Corajidin's arm, were cracking snail shells open with small stones. Reedwives soared on leathery wings above, their auras bruised. He even heard Kimiya as she approached, though her tread was light as the breeze.

"You see it, do you not?" she asked.

"See what?"

"Everything." She stood beside him, her filthy blonde hair limned by star and moonlight, face beautiful and peaceful in repose. Her lips and chin were stained with blood, as were her hands. She closed her eyes and inhaled. "You see . . . no, you feel . . . why this place has been so important, to so many, for so long."

"Why here?"

"Because this is where the walls between worlds are thinnest. There are other places, but few such as this. The Water of Life bubbles from the ground here, renewed and renewing, pouring its vitality into everything that lives here in the"—and she recited a long string of guttural and atonal syllables. "This is why many of those who came before tarried here. It is why their servants remain, waiting."

"For?" The word was no sooner out of Corajidin's mouth, than he regretted saying it.

"The right time." Her smile was chilling. "We watch, and we wait, and hear them in our dreams, promising us a return to the days we long for. You have seen them. Heard them. I can see it in your eyes."

Corajidin tried his best to turn his grimace into a smile, and knew from her expression that she found his failure amusing.

"Fret not, great Corajidin!" Kimiya looked north across the great shimmering flat of the Rōmarq, torrents of energy rising here and there like spectral fountains, to fall like diamond points of rain. "Those who came before know who has been faithful. When the time comes, your part in their revival will be rewarded."

"I have no part in their revival!" The words flew from his mouth. Corajidin looked about conspiratorially. "I have no part. My only concerns are for my people to be all that they can be, and for me to lead them to the greatness they deserve."

"And who is to say that one does not enable the other? And you carry more concerns than those, Corajidin. I see writ on your soul the weight of the burdens you carry, the doubts and the fears, like a drowning man deciding which bag of gold to release and which to keep, though both, or one, would see him sink." Kimiya reached out a hand and absently touched Corajidin on the arm. He felt her warmth radiate through his sleeve. "And you are right to fear him. He is exactly what he was always intended to be, and for that, too, there is gratitude."

Fear whom? "I will rule the world, girl," Corajidin said with more bravado than he felt. "I am surrounded by mighty heroes and mystics, and am soon to have the power of the ages at my fingertips."

"You will not, and do not," Kimiya replied solemnly. "But you pave the way for one who might."

"And that is . . . ?" *A dead man walking.*

"Kasraman, of course." Kimiya crouched by the riverbank and ran her hands through the shining water. "Or another, whose visage is shrouded from us, blurred between then and now, and there and here. We have neither seen nor do we see all. It has been long and long since the Rōm gazed upon the length and breadth of the worlds, but we were never their friends.

"If you are wise, you would take what life has given you. Find a place to live out the span of your years, and forget the lofty heights from which you will, no doubt, fall." She looked at him as if he were an unruly child. "But you are not wise, are you, Corajidin? No, you are not wise at all. You have sacrificed wisdom for pride. Morality for satisfaction. And honor for expediency. But you have done what was needful, when it was needful, and the old powers are content."

"The old powers?"

Kimiya gave Corajidin a sidelong glance. "How little you know of your own world. Empire built upon empire, knowledge stolen, borrowed, and assumed. It is rare for you Afternoon People to build for yourself. You forget what you should not, allowing fact to become belief, then fade into legend, and become myth, to vanish like smoke in the breeze. Speak with Wolfram, who peeled away many of the comforts which Kimiya held dear, stripping her bare as he broke and remade her. Us. The scholars know. The witches know. But those who would sit on their thrones and bend beneath the weight of their crowns know nothing—things that were great, and powerful, and old, and gone, long before the Elemental Masters brought the Bamboo People, or you of the Afternoon, into existence. But it matters little, now."

Corajidin did not voice the words before Kimiya answered his unasked question.

"Because the shadows grow long, the afternoon wears on, and night is sure to come."

✳ ✳ ✳

Corajidin dismissed his guards at the entrance to Wolfram's pavilion. It was a large thing, plain and worn, redolent of musk and the residue of years of burned incense. A brass bell hung by a chain from a post of scorched wood set with goat horns at the top. With his newfound vision, Corajidin saw the hundreds of figures carved into the blackened post: squirrels and owls, spiders and scorpions, lions, wolves, horses, all interwoven among curled leaves. Toward the top were eagles and a phoenix, but at the top and the bottom were carved black goats, their eyes hard and angular.

He was about to open the pavilion flap, then thought better of it. Corajidin had learned from experience there were things about his Lore Master that he was better off not knowing. It was best he did not enter unannounced.

"Wolfram?" he called. *I will not ring the damned bell like some petitioner.* "Wolfram? Are you there?"

"Yes, my Asrahn," came the musical voice. "Please, come in."

Corajidin entered the pavilion and almost gagged on the thick, pungent air. Tapestries formed a labyrinth, and thick carpets cushioned the floor. Corajidin flapped his over-robe in the oppressive heat. Light flared from between two tapestries, themselves portraying goat-headed women and men, and fornicating three-legged trees with lashing branches. The witch wore only his stained and patched leather trousers and rusted calipers, his narrow chest covered in a pelt of his own brindle hair, where it was not covered by the ink of ancient tattoos.

It was the man himself Corajidin saw—perhaps truly saw—for the first time. The emaciated ranginess was there, the vivid wolf's eyes and tangled mat of his hair and beard. Yet his aura burned like a black sun, constantly wavering with small fountains of energy. They arced away, and splashed back against the man's skin. But it was the looming presence around him, a half-imagined image, that gave Corajidin pause: a giant goat-headed beast with horns that drank the light, and eyes darker yet. It filled the tent to bursting, dwarfing the Angoth. Corajidin turned away, and blinked rapidly. When he looked back, the shadow beast was still there, nostrils flaring, glowering, taloned hands resting on Wolfram like a jealous lover. Corajidin concentrated on Wolfram's physical presence, until the shadow of the daemon faded from sight.

Wolfram gestured for Corajidin to enter. There were camp-stools, and many boxes and chests. The open ones had vials and jars. On a small table there rested alchemical equipment, the remaining space covered in books and parchments. The witch poured wine and water into two earthenware bowls, and handed one to Corajidin as he nodded to one of the camp chairs.

Corajidin wasted no time telling Wolfram all that he had seen, recounting the changes in him since they had arrived in the Rōmarq. He told all, except for what he had seen of Wolfram's shadowy daemon Aspect. When Corajidin was finished, Wolfram set down his wine bowl and massaged his own legs, wincing with the pain.

"This didn't happen to you when we were here last?" Wolfram asked.

"No. I felt no better here than anywhere else. But now . . . I've neither eaten nor touched a drop of the Emissary's potion, and the things I can see!"

"The Rōmarq is known to be rich in disentropy, and you've been taking a lot of the Emissary's potion." Wolfram waved away Corajidin's objection. "I've seen how much is missing, my friend. But it's neither my place to judge nor comment. My service to the

Erebus has lasted long enough for me to know that you'll do all that is needful to persevere."

Corajidin finished his wine and indicated Wolfram should pour another, but without the water. After a long draft, Corajidin stared moodily into his reflection where it wavered in bloody liquid. Without looking up he asked, "And that includes serving Kasraman? In knowing that he, too, will do all that is needful to persevere?"

"It includes all your children." Wolfram sounded hesitant. "But Kasraman most of all. He is your heir, and the future of your Great House."

"Is he a danger to me?" The Emissary's, and Kimiya's, words rattled in this head, wasps trying to escape the hive.

Wolfram leaned back in his chair and exhaled slowly. A gust of wind pushed against the pavilion walls as ripples of fabric spread across the roof. It moaned faintly between cloth panels, and the tapestry maze shifted grudgingly. In the silence, Corajidin heard the sounds of worms turning in the earth, and the slow and steady hammer blows of Wolfram's heart. *This place is changing me . . . or is it reminding me of what I could have been? Or worse, what Kasraman already is? My third Awakening has made me more alive than ever before.*

"Do you remember the night Kasraman was conceived?" Wolfram asked, his chin resting in his chest as he slouched, legs spread out before him.

"Not precisely, no. The healers and the astrologers placed it sometime during the month of the Amentehv Festival. Laleh and I were on a royal progress with my father. Why?"

"Do you remember where he was conceived?"

"It was in the only habitable part of Memnon." Corajidin finished his wine in one draft, got up, and poured another. "It was deep winter and the towers and walls were awash with lantern light. They burned from dusk till dawn, for the longest nights of the year."

"I remember the storms on those nights . . ."

"And the Dark Loving," Corajidin added, taking another sip of his wine. The witches had crooned into the storm, exhorting the spirits to take them all, and taste of the pleasures of the flesh: masked faces and passions running high, eyes bright with drink and drugs, skin flushed, bodies writhing in flickering shadows as the world became an undulating, gyrating, grinding ocean of naked flesh. The Mordamren was an ancient festival, dating back to the lust-fueled excesses of the Avān, when civilization was little more than a tattered over-robe: easily lost, and just as easily replaced. Corajidin did not recall how many lovers he had that night. He had felt as if he were filled with all the vitality of his Ancestors, loving for himself and for all of them while the Asrahn-Basyrandin, Corajidin's own intractable father, had looked down on the revelers, eyes burning with lusts and perversions that were only ever rumored, and never spoken of by his family.

So many people, wearing masks both literal and figurative, had celebrated the heroes and villains, myths and legends of the Avān. There was no telling who had been who that night . . .

"Wolfram, are you telling me that Kasraman is not my son?" Corajidin held his breath, divided as to what he wanted the answer to be. Were Kasraman not of the Blood Royal, there was no way Corajidin would allow him to become rahn. It would all go to his golden son—

"No." Wolfram struggled to his feet and limped over to Corajidin. "I'm saying he's not only your son, but also the son of whatever spirit infused you that night. I saw you, my friend, and some others. That you were the vessel for an elemental spirit is not in doubt. Kasraman is Avān, Erebus, and more."

"Why did you not tell me this before?" *Sweet merciful Erebus! What kind of creature have I raised to assume power? And should I stop him, or allow Kasraman to be the next generation of the Erebus, the first in almost a millennium, after myself, to be a Mahj?* "Wolfram, how long have you known?"

"Known?" The witch threw up his hands in disgust. "I know nothing. But suspect much, and have had my misgivings since Avānweh." Wolfram pointed to the piles of books on the table, and more besides on the floor. "And there are more near my bed. Astrological charts, Ulreich's *Gray Grimoire*, as many volumes as I could find of Amradiin's *Jafir Morden*, even the proscribed works of Yattoweh—a Sēq, true, but a man who knew more than his fair share about the dark places of the world. But it's all supposition. For all I know, Kasra's immense power could come from his mother's blood. Her family has always bred powerful mystics."

"I sense a 'but' in there somewhere."

"A prodigy like Kasraman?" Wolfram shook his head. "I'd hazard a guess that a birth such as his was by careful design rather than chance. Which isn't unheard of. The Avān were made from a breeding program, and the Great Houses and the Families still select their partners to keep bloodlines strong. Though you'd sooner eat your own face than admit it, Mari chose one of the best living Avān males when she became involved with Dragon-Eyed Indris. Their offspring will shake the foundations of the world. Who's to say you weren't in Memnon on the night you were just so Kasraman, himself a marvel, could be born?"

Corajidin stumbled to a nearby chair and collapsed into it. The wine bowl fell from his slack fingers to roll across the worn carpet. Wolfram listed back to his own chair, legs creaking with every step, and settled into it stiffly. He was breathing hard with the effort. Corajidin stared across the distance at the man who had served the Erebus for centuries, wondering at the perspective such a life could give. The little things that seemed so immediate and so pressing to Corajidin, the things that needed to be done now, for lack of time, might be nothing more than an afterthought to one such as

Wolfram. And Wolfram was not old by the standards of the Ilhen-nim. Femensetri the Stormbringer was Avāndhim, one of the few surviving first generation of Avān to be created in the Torque Spindles of the lost east. How would such a one perceive the world around her? What would inspire her to action, or what experience would give her the perspective to wait?

Kasraman. Prodigy. Marvel. Firstborn of Corajidin and stern Laleh and . . . what? Some daemon from the far shores of the Well of Souls? A spirit of fire, or something cold from waters darker and deeper than Corajidin wanted to imagine? He trembled at the dreams of what lurked in such places, and their awareness of him. And his debts to them, if such things were what he suspected the Emissary served.

"Will he be a great man, do you think?" Corajidin murmured.

"Kasra?" Wolfram nodded. "He already is, thanks to your guidance and oversight. Your son has been trained to wield power, my friend. And even without your Awakening, or the contact of the long line of your Ancestors, Kasra has a surfeit of his own power. He will be a rahn, an Asrahn, and a Mahj to be reckoned with. Possibly the greatest since the early days of the Awakened Empire. That is what you wanted, isn't it?"

"It was."

16

"THERE IS NO FAILURE IN FALLING, ONLY IN NOT TRYING TO REGAIN ONE'S FEET AND TAKE ANOTHER STEP."

—Penoquin of Kaylish, Zienni Scholar and philosopher
(325th Year of the Awakened Empire)

DAY 61 OF THE 496TH YEAR OF THE

SHRĪANESE FEDERATION

"Sorry I'm late," said Indris to Mari, who caused his hearts to quicken, and face to warm. And for Shar, Ekko, Morne, and his husband, Kyril, Indris tried for a smile, but it was as if his lips were not sure what to do, and just twitched on his face. "What did I miss?"

You idiot . . . He closed his eyes at the banality of his words. Then snapped them open at footsteps drumming toward him in time to see Mari as she threw herself at him and covered his lips with her own, which now seemed to know exactly what to do. Shar and Ekko followed not far behind her. The Seethe war-chanter's eyes and skin shimmered with emotion. Indris closed his eyes and kissed Mari like she deserved to be kissed, saving his questions about why the Widowmaker and Sanojé, the Tyrant of Massadesai, were present. *A lot seems to have happened in my absence.*

Morne and Kyril snapped orders to the Companions, who in turn broke into four units of ten. The unit commanders divided Tamerlan between them, then began a systematic search of the fortress.

Indris stepped toward Morne and swayed, dizzy and fatigued from expending the energy necessary to plunge through the Drear without a Weavegate. He buckled at the knees, head swimming. Thankfully, Mari, Shar, and Ekko were there to stop him from falling. Were it not for the sudden rush of energy from Changeling, Indris doubted he would have had the strength to walk.

"Indris?" Mari's face was etched with concern.

"It's nothing a week of sleep won't fix," he mumbled. Morne looked at him with concern, but Indris waved him away. Hawkwood was a seasoned campaigner, and Indris trusted his ability to take and hold a backwater like Tamerlan without help.

"Then let's get you out of here. You can tell us where you've been, and why everybody thinks you're dead, tomorrow." Mari looked to Belamandris and Morne. "Find the Dowager-Asrahn. And, Morne, please have some of your Immortals secure the fortress, the port, and the skydock. I doubt my grandmother will retreat from Tamerlan, but let's not make any assumptions."

The Widowmaker and Sanojé glared at Indris. Belamandris's fingers curled around Tragedy's hilt, as if he were prepared to draw and strike. Sanojé's Disentropic Stain flickered; her many-armed skeletal Aspect phased in and out of sight. Mari glared at her brother, and repeated her order in such a tone that Indris would not have refused, had it been him. Belamandris and Sanojé muttered to each other, then joined a squad of the Immortal Companions and dashed off. Morne and his own commanders set their tasks.

Indris held her face in his hands, and rested his brow against hers. Her skin was warm and dry, though the air about them was cold and damp. He stared into her eyes, as blue as he remembered, and ran his hands through the mess of her blonde hair. "I'm sorrier than you know to have worried you, but—"

"Tomorrow. You're a mess, and there are plenty of veterans here who can secure Tamerlan." Mari silenced him with a gentle kiss that lingered long enough for Indris to forget, for a moment, the bone-crushing fatigue. Their kiss became more heated. She pulled away, her lips stretching in the smile that was so much a part of her. "And for that, there's also tomorrow."

Ekko took Indris's bag, and Mari led Indris into the depths of Tamerlan.

The sounds of sporadic fighting could be heard as they walked through Tamerlan. Indris could see how ancient the place was: not something built by Avān hands, unless they worked to somebody else's design. The dimensions were wrong, the architecture lacking true symmetry, built with curves and circles, as if formed from the scouring of the tide, currents, and waves. It was disturbing, of an older world with less restraint and mercy than the ancient Avān had known. He paused from time to time, the others looking at him strangely, as he touched the fused stone, feeling the way the ahm flowed through the place like blood through veins. There were similar places in the Golden Kingdom of Manté, though much of their original design had been changed over the years. The Seethe, the Avān, and the Humans had added to the places they had inherited from the original builders: Eidelbon . . . Damarsan . . . Sorochel, with its tall towers and deeper mines, and slave pits. But Tamerlan was closer to its original construction with its lofty walls of glassy stone.

Mari led Indris to her room, as Morne's warriors—and those nahdi they were sure of—took station in the corridors and junctions. The room was a cheerless place, the tall window slits providing little light. There were no hard angles anywhere, everything smoothed off to gentle curves, lacking symmetry, while adding a subtle discomfort. People would sleep in this room—Mari had slept in this room—no doubt troubled by lingering fears, and unsettling dreams.

Indris thanked his friends as they left, one by one. Shar was last, her skin and eyes radiant, smile broad, tears making her eyes an even more vivid citrine. She hugged him fiercely, and whispered into his ear. "*Hem ahn nahasé, thē inya.*" She slapped him in the face, harder than playful, less than angry. "But don't you ever do that to me again!"

"I've missed you, too, my friend," Indris said as Shar fled the room, leaving him alone with Mari.

She was leaner than he remembered, her eyes bright against the shadows around them. Her hair had lost some of its gloss, and her look was sharper, but her smile was the same. They shed their armor and weapons until they were both wearing only their tunics and trousers.

Mari crawled beneath the furs on the bed. Indris joined her, and took her in his arms. Exhaustion pulled down on his eyelids, and he cycled his breathing into longer breaths, slowing his hearts, calming his mind. He smiled, eyes closed, as Mari nestled her head in the crook of his neck and shoulder, her arms across his chest, her breathing light as a feather . . .

❈ ❈ ❈

Indris, his friends, and Morne's senior officers all with their many fresh wounds, were gathered in the Dowager-Asrahn's sunroom, the mists thick and white against the windows, the hearths blazing. Morne's junior nahdi had been assigned the task of preparing and serving food until the servants could be assessed for trustworthiness. Under the good-natured jibes of their more veteran comrades, the young nahdi carried in platters of food. Indris inhaled the scents of tea and coffee, of freshly baked bread and hearty porridge laced with honey. Belamandris and Sanojé were absent. According to Morne, the two of them had joined another crew in the early hours after dawn, the Widowmaker in particular wanting a reckoning with Nadir, for his treatment of Mari. Indris did not imagine it would end well for Nadir.

Indris's reverie was broken by Mari's request for an update on the occupation of Tamerlan. He smiled behind the lip of his bowl as she controlled the room.

"There's been no sign of the Dowager-Asrahn or her inner circle," Morne reported. "There've been some skirmishes with those nahdi who remain loyal, though a larger number have stayed neutral."

"Waiting to see who takes the day, to get their pay," Kyril muttered.

"There are still pockets of resistance," Tamiwa said in a clipped accent. The captain was a compact, muscular woman from Jiom, her skin so dark it was tinged blue. The sides of her head were shaved, temples and skull marked with intricate tribal scars. She sat so close to the fire in her brightly colored cloak that Indris wondered whether she might catch alight. A shotel, a sword so curved it was almost a sickle, leaned against her chair in a worn leather sheath. "The Dowager-Asrahn abused her people, but many of them fight on for fear of her retribution. And, as Kyril says, the nahdi will want their money."

"Make sure they keep their hands off the treasury, and that there's no violence against the townsfolk," Mari said. "There are those among the Dowager-Asrahn's ranks who only know sende as a word."

Carmenya, another of Morne's captains, nodded in agreement. She was as lean as the heavy rapier at her hip. Her russet leathers creaked as she shifted in her chair. "We're still rooting them out.

Many tried for the harbor, some for the skydock. As best we can tell, no vessels escaped. It's only a matter of time."

"Accept the surrenders of those who offer," Mari suggested. The officers of the Immortal Companions looked at her incredulously. "I'm serious. The Dowager-Asrahn was a mean, spiteful stain of a woman. Many served her out of fear, but there are still those hidden away, ready to fight back, who served her out of shared enthusiasms. The Dowager-Asrahn, Jhem, Nadir, and probably the Emissary will be with them. We'll need all the nahdi we can get if we're going to try to put an end to my father's plots and restore some grace to the Asrahn's office."

"Mari's right," Indris added. "Corajidin has the largest army of any of the rahns, and the great majority of the Imperialist sayfs follow him. Narseh is ever his ally, and her heavy infantry are the best in Shrīan. Martūm, Vahineh's cousin, has taken on the mantle of the rahn-elect Selassin, acting as regent in her absence. We can do something about that to start with, and take away some of Corajidin's support. How is Vahineh?"

"Qesha-rē, the surgeon here, has Vahineh in her care," Mari replied. "I've not seen much of her since my imprisonment, but Qesha says Vahineh seems well enough. Did you manage to actually Sever her from her Awakening, or is she still going to be plagued by it?"

"I don't know, to either question. That she's alive is a good sign. I'll need to take a look at her, to see what damage there is to her mind." *And her body, and her soul . . .*

"What about the Sēq?" Morne asked. He and Kyril sat together, sheafs of reports scattered on the table in front of them. Morne leaned forward and tapped strong fingers on the tabletop to emphasize his words. "Without them we're doomed before we start. We've fought witches in Tanis, in Manté, and other places besides—but that was always when we had scholars, or our own witches. Will the Sēq get involved?"

Indris let his silence answer the question, at which Kyril swore. Indris finished his tea, grabbed a quick bite to eat. He noticed the sideways glances Mari gave him, as well as those of Shar and Ekko. As people broke their fast, Indris related what had happened to him since the battle with the Mahsojhin witches.

"After what could only be called a cessation of hostilities at the Mahsojhin," Indris said, "the Sēq took me into custody." *But how do I tell them that Anj has returned? I can't shoulder those questions right now.* He told them the rest of his story, of the interrogations, the long days and longer nights at Amarqa-in-the-Snows. Of the appearance of the Herald, and the plight of the rahns. Mari in turn related her tale, which caused Indris's chest to constrict, for Shar to take Mari in her arms, and for Ekko's leonine face to go hard as stone. Shar and Ekko, Morne and Kyril, recited the events happening around Shrīan.

Indris settled into his chair, excluding the drone of voices, the clatter of plates and cutlery one by one as he sorted through the information given him. It was not all bad news, and nothing had gone so far that the Sēq, provided they stopped sulking, could not set to right. This was the type of threat the Order needed to bring itself out of the introspection Zadjinn had diagnosed, yet poorly sought to treat. The symptoms of the Sēq's disaffection with the modern world could not be removed unless the cause was healed: Give the Sēq a purpose in the modern world. The Sēq needed to learn from their past, correct their present, and have a course into the future that was not reliant on obedience to an indifferent Mahj, trapped between the realms of the living and the dead.

Corajidin was the key. The man's reckless ambition was one of the greatest threats Shrīan had ever seen. Yet for all his faults, Corajidin the statesman had rallied a disjoined nation behind his cause, false as it may have been. His falsehood about the Mantéans' attack on Avānweh during the New Year's Festivals, of their purported summoning of elemental daemons, and the presence of Human witches recently escaped from the Mahsojhin, had been a masterful stroke. The Teshri had almost begged Corajidin to take action, using Kasraman, Belamandris, the Exiles, and their witch allies to put down the threat they had themselves started. Indris knew from experience that the easiest war to end was the one you started. He had toppled thrones and put crowns on brows the same way, treating nations, their rulers, and their people like pieces on a tanj board until his disillusionment with the Sēq and their agendas had driven him to find a different way to live.

Those were the days when he had thought in terms of the thousands, or the tens of thousands. *Anj helped teach me that . . .* Indris chewed his lip, taking in each of his friends in turn: Brave, noble, and honorable, they were the reason to keep fighting, for they were the ones who cared about the individuals who comprised the tens of thousands, the nations. Now he knew the parts were greater than the sum of the whole.

One of those who had suffered more than her share was the Rahn-Selassin, a brave young woman who, unlike the rahns, had not been ready for any of what happened to her.

"Mari? Would you take me to see Vahineh? Let's see whether I was successful in Severing her or not."

And whether what I've done for her could be used to save Rosha's, Siamak's, and Nazarafine's lives.

❊ ❊ ❊

Vahineh had been moved to comfortable quarters near Mari, and was under the constant eye of the Immortal Companions.

Indris stepped lightly in Vahineh's mind, following the char where her Awakening had burned her at her core. Deep soul wounds cascaded down the ternary stack, taking parts of the mind and the body with them. Indris saw not only with the ahmsah, but with his continually growing psé talents also. Looking in both spectra gave Indris a wider, more complete view: He could see the ebb and flow of her soul, hear her thoughts, scrutinize the cindered paths to see what was lost. He compared them to his own mind where the serpentine coils of his Awakening remained, though he had thought them withered after he had denied Ariskander.

There were parts of Vahineh's mind that were irrevocably gone. Even the Sēq Differential Baths could not repair such wounds. Some of her memories, passions, likes and dislikes had been destroyed. But her soul and mind had found paths around the damage, influencing the way energy and vital fluids made their way through Vahineh's brain. She would never be as she was, but the young woman would live, and be different, and perhaps be better off as she grew stronger and found new roads to follow. Even her physical wounds had mostly healed, leaving the rahn with nothing but a faint gray mottling on the cheek and jaw on her right side.

"She's going to be fine," Indris said. Mari and Qesha-rē, the old Nilvedic surgeon, beamed with relief. "The Severance worked, and she's free from any further damage. I think, given time and treatment, she will also lose the scarring on her face."

"You can Sever the other rahns?" Qesha-rē asked.

"I think so, yes. But I need to find the secrets of Awakening before I go back. It's a Shrīanese custom and not one I'm prepared to interfere with. Our Awakened rahns are key to our strength, and given the looming threat of the Iron League—"

"Thanks to my father," Mari growled.

"Made immediate by Corajidin's plans, yes, the rahns will take any advantage they can get to defend the nation. The Sēq have Severed other rahns before; it's whether we can re-Awaken them that's the question. At least I know where to look, to see whether we can tailor Awakening around the damage that Severance brings. That's the tricky part, to see whether it can be done again to the same person."

Vahineh grabbed Indris's hand. "Thank you, for everything. There are things I don't remember, and some memories are like mist. But you've given me the chance to take my vengeance on Corajidin for what he did to my family. Perhaps I can let go, and rest."

Mari patted Vahineh's shoulder gingerly, sadness on her face, and gestured that she and Indris should leave Vahineh in Qesha-rē's care.

Indris sensed Mari's discomfort, unrelated to Vahineh's cool words of revenge, and something that had come through their fevered, desperate passion this morning. He had thought it simply the symptom of time, and stress, yet Mari almost thrummed with anxiety. The two of them continued in a companionable silence until they came to the stairs heading into the Hearthall, where the din of the fortress would drown out a softly spoken conversation. Indris took Mari by the hand, and led her to the cool shadows between sea-toned columns.

"What's wrong?" Indris asked.

"Hmmm?"

"You've been nervous all morning."

"Vahineh is going to—"

"No. Something was bothering you before that. Talk."

Mari raked her fingers through her hair, tugging lightly on the ends, as she looked Indris in the eye. He waited for her to speak. When she did, the words came out in a rush. "What's a Feigning?"

"Where did you hear that term?" Indris kept his voice calm despite the surge of rage and dismay.

"The Emissary mentioned it." Mari was not fooled by his attempt at composure. "What is it, Indris? What was she going to do to me?"

Indris led Mari through the Hearthall, where he took a jar of wine and two deep bowls. They walked to one of the smaller dining rooms that looked out over the town below. The mist had lifted somewhat, though snow fell listlessly, adding to growing drifts of trampled slush in the narrow streets. Plumes of black rose into the air only to be shredded by the wind. Boats rocked on the rough water, and the seabirds had taken shelter from the weather. Indris poured Mari a bowl of wine, then filled the second one for when he told her what needed to be said.

"Mari, the Feigning is an old term that hasn't been used in centuries. Certainly not since the Golden Age of the Awakened Empire, when the Mahj and the Sēq were far more influential, and we enjoyed what many perceive as the high watermark of Avān culture.

"The term came about because the scholars, and the members of the upper-castes, saw themselves as the inheritors of Īa. They sought to mimic the natural order, and improve on it using Torque Spindles. Some of the rahns even tried making their own children and heirs through Feigning, seeking to make the most powerful descendants they could. In short, a race of superbeings, but raised and trained by people as flawed as everybody else. Your Ancestors made the Iphyri during these times . . . as well as some other creations that weren't so successful.

"History tells us those were amoral times, when the Avān sought to surpass all those who'd come before. Thankfully it was internal conflict that saw the decline of the Golden Age, and a restoration of more practical arcane science."

Mari lifted the wine to her lips, finishing the bowl in a single draft. She reached for the second bowl, and took a swallow as Indris refilled the first. Mari put the bowl down and laid her hands flat on the table. She kept pressing with more and more pressure until the tremors stopped. Without looking at Indris she asked, "And what happened to the people who were put in the Torque Spindles?"

"It depends," Indris replied cautiously. But Mari now, as ever, deserved the truth. "We thought those days behind us, the scholars involved punished most seriously. Progenitors in a Feigning mostly die, totally consumed by the process of making something else. Others lived for a short while, particularly if they were dismantled over time to make many new beings. Others, where their Feigning was used to create a small number of offspring, lived quite normally."

"But that wouldn't have been me?"

"Probably not."

"I would've died to make an army of what . . . an army of me?"

"Think about it." Indris rested his hands on hers, but she dragged them away to clutch the wine bowl again. "Could you imagine facing an army of soldiers that were even half as good as you? Imagine your skills and perceptions, your reflexes and training and intuition, merged with a predatory beast? Or another soldier who excelled in different areas? It would be a force to be reckoned with, and one that came instantly into existence rather than taking a lifetime to raise and train."

"But I would've died," she whispered.

"Yes. And the world, particularly my world, made desolate for it."

Mari downed a second bowl of wine, then threw the bowl at the window. Glass smashed and cold air dusted with snow gusted in. For some time Mari cursed her family, their history, their present, their future, and all their ambitions.

Indris handed her a filled bowl. "Mari, I don't want there to be secrets between us." She nodded, expression guarded. He took her hands in his and she frowned, clearly apprehensive. "When Femensetri took me to help the Sēq, they'd pretty much emptied the Amer-Mahjin of every scholar who could hold their own in a fight . . . and a few who couldn't. We were marshaled around the Mahsojhin, the first wave of Masters and knights already engaged. There were fewer of us than there should've been, but it wouldn't have mattered how many of us there were; she would've found me."

"Femensetri?"

"No." Indris took a deep breath. "Anj."

Mari slowly took her hands away. She looked at him from under lowered brows, her face and voice dangerously bland.

"Tell me everything."

Mari neither interrupted nor complained. She listened to all that Indris had to say, then leaned forward to kiss him when he was done.

"We've been through a lot this year, you and I," she said. "Parts of us have been born, and parts of us have died. I trust us, Indris. More importantly, I trust me, with you. If Anj is something else we need to deal with, then we'll deal with her together."

Mari walked to the door, where she paused. She did not turn around when she spoke. "But if you decide to go back to her, don't make me wait. I can't take what you mean to me lightly, and I won't share you.

"I love you, Indris. I've loved you for longer than I wanted to admit, and the words can't be unsaid now. But the world won't wait on my say-so. I've started something here that needs finishing. I've left my work to others while you recovered, but now it's time for me to find my grandmother and put an end to her. Jhem, Nadir, and the Emissary, too, if I happen across them. If you want to come with me, armor up. It's likely to be dangerous, and I'd hate for that pretty skin of yours to get damaged."

Mari left him at the table, the door open behind her in invitation to follow.

I love you, too.

Before Avānweh it had been seven years since he had seen Anj, the last two of which he had thought she was dead. There was no going back, no breathing life into the cold coals of his marriage, not when his heart burned for another. But Indris knew Anj, and knew that Anj—or whatever Anj had become—would never see it that way.

Indris rose and made his way to Mari's room, where his armor and other kit were stored. After all this time apart it would not do to keep the woman he loved waiting any longer.

"IF NOT NOW, THEN WHEN?"

—High Palatine Navaar of Oragon in his address to the Ygranian
Parliament on racial harmony (494th Year of the Shrīanese Federation)

DAY 61 OF THE 496TH YEAR OF THE

SHRĪANESE FEDERATION

I love you. Mari had said the words now.

Indris's revelation about Anj made things more complicated. Did she feel entirely comfortable knowing that Anj was alive? No. The Seethe woman had been a significant part of Indris's life since they were children. They had been raised together by the Sēq, trained to wield powers Mari could barely comprehend. But their life journeys had taken them to different places, and on those journeys they had become very different people. *The past is done. It is my turn now.*

Mari laughed, then covered her mouth with her hand. *I love you.* It was not the first time she had fallen for someone. But it was the first time she had found a partner she thought she could grow with, to learn from, to teach, to share a life as equals. She made good time to her room, resisting the temptation to turn, to see if Indris followed. Their weapons still lay together on the table, the serpentine, recurved shapes of an empire centuries in the grave, yet still the symbol of the greatest warriors the Avān had ever known. There were few other than warrior-poets and the Sēq who carried an amenesqa in the modern age, and most of those weapons—such as the Awakened Empire relics used by the Feyassin—were centuries old, yet strong and sharp as if they had been forged yesterday.

Taking up her weapons, Mari made a quick stop at the armory. Given precedence over the other soldiers by Leonetto, Morne's lance-lean captain of infantry, Mari made a quick circuit of the armory and pieced together a leather gambeson, a scale hauberk that had seen better years, plated gauntlets, and a gladiator's sleeve made of bronze-shod steel. She was unsurprised to find a relic from the Avān blood theatre in Tamerlan, where the old ways held true. Leonetto helped Mari on with her armor, checking her movement as he fastened the straps and laces. When she told him where she was headed, Leonetto ordered one of his harangued lieutenants to take charge of the armory.

"It's a crap job," Leonetto muttered. "Glad to be out of there before somebody draws blood."

The two walked together to a small yard where a garden had tried to grow. Withered sticks for trees sprouted from the snow amid broken stones and tilted statues. Shar and Ekko, Morne and Kyril, and two squads of the Immortal Companions waited. Indris trotted from the doors behind her, armed and armored. He had a grin on his face, his attempts to remove it making him look boyish.

One of the mine supervisors joined them moments later, bowing his head so often Mari wondered whether it might fall off. The man had agreed to show them the tunnels beneath Tamerlan that led between the caverns below the fortress, to the mines, as well as those tunnels used as boltholes.

"What do you mine?" Morne asked as they headed out, his nahdi removing the hoods from *ilhen* torches. The supervisor unlocked a gate, and led them through as it opened on popping hinges. Pale radiance slid across the crudely fashioned, shadow-pocked stone.

"Black rock salt," the man said in his gravelly voice, rubbing a dirty hand over his bald pate. Indris muttered under his breath. "Some iron. There's silver in a mine further south. Even a witchfire vein, though that's almost played out . . ." His voice trailed off uncertainly and he looked around, expression fearful.

"The Dowager-Asrahn can't hurt you anymore," Mari said kindly. "Her commands no longer have meaning here."

"Begging your pardon—and don't get me wrong, as we's all thankful as can be you done what you done—but until I see the Sayf-Savajiin's head on a stick, I'm gonna fear she'll be back."

The supervisor led them deeper beneath Tamlerlan. Though the fortress itself was black as a traitor's heart on the outside, it was clear where the stone for the interior had been mined. They passed through massive chambers of blue and green stone where the walls were still scored. It was unpolished but doubtless the same material that formed the fused walls of the fortress above. Water thundered in the distance. On their way through damp and twisted corridors, often where Ekko and Morne had to stoop to pass through, the supervisor regaled them with stories of sea monsters that took shelter in the caverns, sometimes preying on mining crews who were never seen again.

There were places on their journey where Indris was visibly strained, the stone streaked with veins of the black rock salt. It was in one such place, a huge cyst beneath the mountain, that the supervisor stopped. There were a number of corridors leading away, the sounds of picks and hammers echoing from them. Faint light flickered from those tunnels, while there was one that was conspicuously dark.

"Let me guess . . . ," Shar murmured. Morne and Leonetto smiled, while Kyril snorted a laugh.

Indris smiled at the supervisor. "Thank you but we can find our way back, and I believe you're right—this really isn't a place you want to be." The supervisor needed no other motivation. He bowed hastily, then headed back the way they had come.

"What's this?" Shar looked anxious. "Why is this familiar to me?"

"Sorochel," Indris muttered. "It feels like the slave pits of Sorochel. We're in parts of the caverns that were bored long before the Avān were brought into existence, or the Humans fell from the stars."

"And I assume you're going to suggest we go yonder?" Kyril nodded toward the one dark tunnel. Indris looked over and smiled for his answer.

Mari and Indris led the way, weapons drawn. Indris held his Scholar's Lantern before him. The long hexagonal head, similar to a spear blade, shone with cool radiance. The cavern was striated like muscle, bands of stone arched overhead as if they walked through the rib cage of a giant serpent. All the while Mari's Sûnblade grew progressively warmer, so much so that at one point she looked down to see a line of brilliant light burning at its heart.

"Sûnblades were given to heroes for a reason, Mari." Indris nodded to her weapon. "In the early days of the great Sûnsmiths, they were the only ones other than the Sēq who made weapons that could defeat daemons, Nomads, and other supernatural creatures. Such beings always gained their power in the nighttime hours, or under moonlight. So the Sûnsmiths made weapons that harnessed the power of the sun."

Mari cocked a skeptical eyebrow. "My sword is made from the sun?"

"Well, not the sun, no," Indris said. "But the Sûnsmiths learned their techniques from the Elemental Masters, who in turn learned from older powers besides. The light in your blade mimics that of the sun, the lattices in the metal releasing the power stored there."

"Why is it burning now?" Ekko glared about, eyes wide, *khopesh* held at the ready.

"Because it, like Changeling, senses better than we what lingers here," Indris replied. "Everything about this place feels tainted. I think there's a rift beneath it, like under Īajen-mar. But it's energy from the Drear that pools here. Something about the way Tamerlan was built allows the Drear energy to filter up through the stone and into the fortress above. It would ruin anybody who dwelled here too long."

"That would explain the Dowager-Asrahn," Mari muttered. *And why I never felt at ease here.* "The things I've seen make more sense." Mari went on to tell her friends about the sacrifice at the Sea Shrine, and the thalassic horror that had taken her cousin, Dhoury.

"*Faruq ayo*, Mari," Shar breathed as she shook her head in disgust. "*Parho iotha a bae shahat haylo.*"

"I don't speak Seethe, but I assume you weren't saying anything nice then."

Shar smiled, and clapped Mari on the shoulder. "Not so much, no."

"Fair play," Mari said. She looked around. "Beauty may be skin deep, but the ugly of Tamerlan is like rot to the core. Indris, how do we destroy this place?"

Indris laughed sourly. "Destroy it? We don't. There're too many questions to be answered in places like this. All we can do is try to ensure it doesn't fall into the wrong hands again. But this creature you speak of, and the Sea Shrine. Both sound important to your grandmother."

"We checked the shrine twice," Leonetto replied. "Once at high tide and once at low. We never saw sign of anybody. That said, we never knew these tunnels existed either."

"My grandmother keeps dangerous company," Mari warned. "Be on your guard."

Together Mari, Indris, and their comrades marched onward. The floor and walls became damp, rivulets of seawater trickling down the center of the passageway. Light came from ahead, and Morne gave the order for the lamps to be hooded. Indris darkened the fire in his lantern, yet Mari's Sûnblade flared ever brighter. Mari caught Indris's glance, and shrugged. "I can't turn the damned thing off," she whispered. She sheathed the weapon with a mumbled curse, hand never leaving the hilt.

Mari rounded the bend to see a broad cavern. Pools of water were scattered across the uneven floor, the stone worn smooth by the passage of the sea. There were several arches that looked out across the bay, and Mari saw the pillars of the Sea Shrine through a stone screen covered in coral growth. Around the edges of the cavern were rock shelves, each higher than the tide line. Chairs and bedding were there, and the air retained the warmth of firestones.

"Somebody was here recently," Ekko said. The lion man bounded up the stairs to scout the shelves, Shar close behind. Mari watched as they sifted through blankets, bowls, and plates. Ekko crouched on the edge of the shelf to report. "I estimate there were perhaps sixty people hidden here."

"And not gone long," Shar said. "The water in the urn is still hot."

"We'd best get back to the fortress," Mari suggested. "My grandmother and her supporters can't be far from here, and I've no doubt she knows her way around Tamerlan better than anybody. She's cunning, and won't give Tamerlan up while she lives."

❋ ❋ ❋

The courtyard near the Sea Shrine was in turmoil. Light flashed from weapons and armor. The clamor of struck metal, creak of leather, hacking of flesh, and screams of the wounded and dying broke the air. Mari inhaled the smell of war: voided bladders, bowels, and veins, and opened bellies.

A throng of Tamerlan's soldiers and nahdi loyal to the Dowager-Asrahn were in the thick of it. They attacked the defenders on the stairs to the port and its nearby skydock. Others loyal to the Dowager-Asrahn held the gates between the yard and the Sea Shrine. Warriors of the Immortal Companions, and those nahdi who had abandoned the Dowager-Asrahn, fought to dig them out.

Mari scanned the crowd for the Dowager-Asrahn, Jhem, and Nadir. The flash of silks beyond the Sea Shrine gate revealed them. The Dowager-Asrahn stood knee-deep in the turbulent waters, screeching exhortations in a language Mari did not understand, surrounded by her grim-faced Sea Witches.

"We need to get to the Sea Shrine!" Mari shouted to Indris over the din. He nodded, and took position beside her.

Belam danced in the rain of blood, his ruby armor and shield glistening with thousands of *serill* ingots so red it was as if the blood never touched them. Sanojé was in his wake as she spun her witchery. Belam fused the movements of his body, shield, and Tragedy into an art form. Never still, he flowed effortlessly from technique to technique in combinations Mari had rarely seen before. *Adder Tongue* became *Gryphon Claw*, and his sword rising in the air turned and swooped down in *Falcon Strikes Low*, then across in the *Horse Cutter*, his sword devastating, shield used as weapon often as not. Everywhere he went, Sanojé followed in her dreadful Aspect of the six-armed mummy dressed in rags, her form held together by shredded light. She flung darts of mystic fire, and hurled concussive bolts of air at those who defied her.

Mari and Indris matched Belam's and Sanojé's movements. They sidled closer, Mari's swords humming as Indris served as her mystic support. Her Sûnblade flared like an edge of the dawn. Indris's shield was rimmed in sunlight; his Scholar's Lantern blazed, more spear than staff. Changeling howled with joy. Mari and Indris, Belam and Sanojé, worked together: attacking and defending, feinting, coming together and breaking apart like the sea over rocks.

The last defender fell before the Sea Shrine, and Indris smashed the gates off their hinges with a gesture of his hand. During a lull in the fighting, Mari paused to gauge their progress. Shar and Ekko, alongside Morne and Kyril, fought in tandem and scythed their enemies down. A trident took Ekko through the thigh, pinning him. The Tau-se roared in pain, even as Shar severed the trident to set him free. Ekko stood, towering over all but Morne, and bared his fangs in a terrifying snarl. Blood streaming from his leg, he took up his sword and set to the business at hand, not slowed in the slightest.

"I need you," Mari said to Indris as she launched forward, Belam and Sanojé close behind. The glowering clouds hung low over an ocean that rose up to meet them. The sea defied the tide, crashing over the sea wall. Jhem and Nadir watched over the Dowager-Asrahn as she yelled her exhortations, her personal guard and Sea Witches intractable. Over her shoulder she said, "Indris, Belam, and Sanojé with me. The rest of you, the guards."

Mari did not wait to see whether her orders had been followed. She lengthened her stride, feet light as they splashed across the soaked stone. Indris and Sanojé wove formulae and hexes as was their nature. A series of translucent panels and spinning fractals appeared around them, deflecting both arrows and the arcane effects of the Sea Witches' onslaught. Indris swore at the power of their concerted assault, and bolstered the defenses to fill the gaps where Sanojé's hexes failed.

Behind the Dowager-Asrahn the sea became more choppy. Gray-green tentacles flailed beneath the foamed surface. Mari gagged at the stench. Her stomach turned queasy at the memory of Dhoury being dragged into the depths. She sounded a battle cry, giving voice to her fear.

The two groups of warriors crashed together. Mari angled her body so that Jhem's cut skidded across the metal scales of her armor. She pivoted on one foot and elbowed the man in the face, following through with the backhand of her fist, wrapped tightly about the hilt of her amenesqa. Jhem's scaled mask caved in. A crunch as his nose broke. Mari felt Jhem's knife pierce her flank: a trickle of blood and a sharp burn of sliced skin. She spiraled around Jhem, deflecting his serpent-quick strikes as she struck back. Jhem's knives found their target as often as not. Mari slid back and sideways, in search of distance: Jhem's knives were better suited to close-quarters fighting than her swords. The two traded blows, came together and moved apart as each sought advantage.

Jhem wound inside Mari's defenses. Stabbed twice: shoulder and forearm. Her Sûnblade clattered to the ground, its light dimmed. Mari bludgeoned him in the face with the pommel of her amenesqa. Blood poured from within his mask, yet his dead eyes betrayed nothing.

The Blacksnake's blades bit again. Screeched off of armor to pierce her bicep, and between the scales to pierce her belly. Several passes later, Mari felt nauseous. Her reactions slowed. Vision blurred. Poison!

Side to side they came together. Mari slipped between Jhem's stabs. Used her leg to entrap his; her sword held in gauntleted hands became a lever. She pivoted, her sword cutting across Jhem's throat, then around. She threw him down, his limbs splayed, head half severed. Mari collapsed to her knees, strength failing.

"No!" Nadir bellowed from where he stood beside the Dowager-Asrahn. He raced forward—

Into Belam, who bludgeoned Nadir in the face with his shield. Nadir staggered backward and tripped over a fallen body. Belam strode forward, only to be denied as the Dowager-Asrahn's guard formed ranks, cold-eyed and relentless.

"You need to retire from the field," Indris said to Mari. He quickly inspected her as weapons and armor crashed around them. Her skin was clammy, throat tight. "I need to—"

"When it's done!" Mari snarled. She sheathed her sword, and picked up the Sûnblade. It flared into brilliance. "Help me finish it, Indris. Otherwise it's for nothing."

Indris rested his hands against her brow and crooned a gentle song. Mari's vision sharpened, and strength returned. She vomited blood and bile down her chest. "I've given you about five minutes. See it done, Mari."

The two raced toward the Dowager-Asrahn, her guard, and her witches.

Tentacles flailed from the water. Mari gagged on the reek of rotten flesh, and breathed through her mouth to lessen the nausea she felt. The leathery skin was mottled, barnacles affixed to it. She quailed as the tentacles moaned. One rose high, its suckers irregularly formed. Mari swore when she saw that each of the tentacles was a skewed face, each different, with puckered mouths lined with needle fangs and eyes pale and staring. Water poured from the mouths. It washed over her, burned her skin with the chill. Her jaw went slack, and she stood still, overcome by dislocation and the need to scream until her throat bled.

"Now you see, girl!" the Dowager-Asrahn cried. "Now you know that for everything I give to the sea, the sea gives back!"

The tentacle hammered down. Mari's Sûnblade rose to meet it. Severed it. Cauterized the wound, so the amputated length—as long as Ekko was tall—coiled uselessly. Water foamed as the monster writhed. The mouths on the tentacles wailed. More tentacles thrashed. They coiled about friend and foe alike as they dragged screaming victims into the sea.

The strength Indris had given Mari waned, yet there was vengeance to be had. The Dowager-Asrahn, and the remaining Sea Witches not killed by Indris or Sanojé, urged the monster on. Something dark crested the waves, its back covered in spines like leprous coral. Its dimensions boggled the mind, more like a hill rising from the ocean than a living thing.

"No, you don't!" Indris slammed the butt of his lantern hard into the ground. Stone split. The lantern flared in a sphere of brilliance. Shadows dwindled to fine scratches. Color bleached away. The monster gibbered and howled, its leathery skin seared.

Mari leaped forward. She crossed the distance between herself and the Dowager-Asrahn in heartbeats. The old woman sneered at Mari as the tentacles wavered about her. They whipped forward, as much as something the size of a sapling could whip, but Mari was never there when they smashed into the stone, or the water. The smile froze on the Dowager-Asrahn's face.

The Shark of Tamerlan had not drawn her flanged maul before Mari's first cut severed her arm at the elbow. Her grandmother took a sharp intake of breath that was silenced, as Mari's Sûnblade cauterized the new cut in her throat.

The Dowager-Asrahn's body fell limply into the foaming sea. The crone was alive as a tentacle wrapped itself around her, the fanged suckers adhering to her flesh. Though her mouth was open, her eyes wide with fear, the Dowager-Asrahn made no sound as she was dragged beneath the waves.

Mari swayed on her feet as her comrades turned their attention to the monstrosity before them.

Her vision dimmed. Her hearts slowed. And Mari slumped into the frigid water.

18

"SOMETIMES ONE WILL AWAKEN, AND REALIZE THEY HAVE TRAVELED TOO
FAR DOWN A ROAD FOR THEM TO EVER TURN FROM IT, DESPITE KNOWING
THAT OTHER DIRECTIONS MAY LEAD TO BETTER OUTCOMES."

—from *Honor and Loyalty,* by Erebus fa Mahador,
Knight-Lieutenant of the Petal Guard

DAY 61 OF THE 496TH YEAR OF THE

SHRĪANESE FEDERATION

Corajidin strode through the camp, squinting at the sun. He
had not slept well, his head filled with the esoteric whispers of his
Ancestors.

Feyd locked step with Corajidin and updated him on the latest
reports: patrols not returning, and snatch-and-grab attacks by the
wetlands Fenlings. Corajidin had heard the screams, and knew too
well the Fenlings' taste for living flesh. Soul Traders had been seen
wandering the camp, windswept and cadaverous in their ages-old
finery now turned to monochromatic rags. The skeletal ruin of their
wind-galley hung low in the sky, reminiscent of an aged vulture.

"The ground is treacherous, and pretty much every living thing out there is happy to kill us, and quite capable of it," Feyd said. "This is a sorry place to make war. The Soul Traders make everybody nervous. None of us understand who they may, or may not, steal at the moment of our death. We should send them on their way, Asrahn. They're an abomination."

"On the subject of the Soul Traders, I agree," Corajidin replied. *But the Emissary would take unkindly to me evicting them. Besides, are they any worse than the marsh-puppeteers, when all is said and done? Both are parasites who revel in death.* "But there are larger concerns at play, and the Traders may yet prove beneficial. But we are not making war, Feyd, as much as we are taking control of resources vital to Shrīan's survival. I will send a Letter of Intent to Siamak, registered with the Magistratum and the Arbiter's Tribunal. We are as transparent in our mission as can be expected, Feyd."

"Except for our breaking every tenet of sende by making war on the civilians of Fandra," Feyd replied. "And then giving prisoners to the marsh-puppeteers, which was tantamount to execution, for they had committed no crimes."

"They took up arms against their Asrahn, Feyd!" *I had never thought you to have a conscience, you wily old butcher. Perhaps your silence might best be bought by your eternal sleep, here in the mud.* Corajidin smiled, though, and looked the man in the eye. "We will register our intent with the authorities. What we do here will be made right."

Feyd looked unconvinced, yet remained silent as they arrived at the wind-skiff. Tahj-Shaheh was at the pilot's station, and had spun up the Disentropy Spools and the Tempest Wheels. Corajidin stared at the way the spools threaded energy from the air around them, spinning dumbbells that reeled in gossamer strands as light as spiders' silk. Nix waited there, skin and clothes the color of the marshlands, a stiletto spinning between his fingers. Kasraman,

Wolfram, and Kimiya waited nearby, Wolfram's former apprentice staring at Kasraman with what Corajidin took to be awe.

Corajidin gestured for his inner circle to follow him aboard the skiff, two squads of the best Anlūki in their heavy-layered armor marching behind. Corajidin gave orders for the boarding ramp to be pulled up and the skiff to take to the air. A faint blur detached itself from the Soul Trader's galley. It drew closer to the wind-skiff, and Corajidin saw the vaguely humanoid shape trailing rags and dust as it flew with them. Nomads were all but invisible under sunlight, and Corajidin wondered whether it was the power inherent in the Rōmarq, and his Awakening, that allowed him to see the things when others could not.

The Soul Traders were here, while the Emissary who represented them was absent—and had been for too long. Time he would have been grateful for, but the lack of her presence left him more concerned than her being in his orbit ever had. Her intimations of a long and fruitful association with the Erebus continued to leave a bad taste in Corajidin's mouth. Had his predecessors dealt with the Soul Traders, also? Nix had mentioned his relationship with them, and that of Nix's father, Rayz. Rayz had been a contemporary of Corajidin's parents. *Do I unknowingly walk the same paths as those who have come before me?* He was far from the first Erebus to give himself over to the pursuit of power, regardless of the cost to others, satisfied that he knew his road to be the right one for himself and those of similar mind. But he had reached the point where the cost of his ambitions outweighed the quality of the goods he had bought. How much further had others of his line gone? History spoke of the Erebus as a tidal force, washing in with heroism and idealism for generations, but dragging all the good they had done with them when the waters washed away from shore, drowning everything and leaving those that survived in their wake to swim, but more often to sink.

*I am the son of a line that has bred Mahji and Asrahni. How could
I do other than is in my nature to do, or be other than is in my blood to
be? I will strive for nothing less than that which my forebears knew.*

Corajidin leaned on the rail and looked out at the blemished
mirror of the Rōmarq where it rolled below. At this altitude he felt
the power of the place, its energy infusing his limbs, keeping his
illness at bay. Neither food nor drink had passed his lips, yet he
was neither hungry nor thirsty. Sleep had been more from habit
than any sense of fatigue. Life teemed down there among the reeds
and the grasses that rippled in the breeze. Ponds reflected the sky
and light like shards of glass, and streams flowed slow and lazy,
filled with circling fish and rainbow-colored serpents. Vivid but-
terfly drakes soared low over flowers, each drake as long as
Corajidin's arm, swooping to take up fat beetles, mice, and other
prey in their claws.

The ground changed as they came closer to the ruins Kimiya
guided them to. Cut stone made dappled shapes beneath creeks
that had long ago formed new banks. Columns draped in dark ivy
and tenacious creepers leaned, forming complex shadows below.
Closer they came until the fragments of walls stood out like broken
molars, and then ruined domes, tall walls, and canted towers were
the norm amid thick trees that had long ago asserted their domi-
nance. Tahj-Shaheh piloted the skiff in a smooth circle until she
found a wide courtyard, trees draped with ropy vines pushing up
between the flagging. Birdcalls, hisses, spits, and the yowls of marsh
devils echoed across the deserted town, with other deeper and more
guttural noises that turned Corajidin's spine cold. The air smelled
of wet leaves and mulch, of mold and mildewed stone. And there,
the coppery hint of freshly spilled blood.

People emerged from the shadows of the surrounding trees: the
villagers from Fandra who had been given to the marsh-puppeteers.
They stood silently, mud and blood streaked, clothes shredded

from their nocturnal forays. One, somewhere between an older boy and a young man, stepped forward. He opened his mouth and clattered something at Kimiya, who responded in kind with sounds no Avān throat was designed to make.

Kimiya turned to Corajidin and said, "My clan have cleared away the interlopers. Fenling and some harpies, and an old nāga warrior that had taken up residence in the tower. It was for the best you did not happen upon her unawares."

"We could've dealt with it," an Anlūki lieutenant asserted.

"If you like," Kimiya said with a tiny smile. "The way is clear, Corajidin. It is as safe as we can make it."

"Not exactly a ringing endorsement," Nix muttered.

Surrounded by the Anlūki, Corajidin and his inner circle followed Kimiya through the long shadows and blinding light of the ruin. The marble had lost its gleam, and the edges of the sandstone had turned to porous curves, grass sprouting in sparse, dry tufts like an old man's hair. There was water everywhere, though it seemed to not bother Kimiya or her clan in the slightest as they splashed through.

The place felt old: from the size of the trees and the overgrown gardens, to the ancient architecture that nature had overcome. Walls and towers remained, along with stairs that had at one point led to places the inhabitants had found pedestrian, places Corajidin ached to know more about. Kasraman, Wolfram, and Elonie wandered with their eyes wide, trying to see and hear everything about them. The Soul Trader's presence was seen in periphery, where it glided above, silent, watchful, and waiting. They sense death. Are drawn to it. Worship it. Corajidin's skin crawled with a lurking menace, something watchful that resented the presence of others in its territory.

A serpentine shape, topped with a man's armored torso, arms, and head, shot from a wide crack in a nearby wall. It rapidly looped its coils around a warrior, who could not bring his sword to bear. With small blades in each hand, the monster cut the warrior's throat, turning his screams to gargles.

Cobra quick, the nāga lunged forward to bite another Anlūki on the face. It took another warrior in its embrace, whipped its body back, and hurled the woman into the trees, where the sound of snapping branches and breaking bones were indistinguishable. The bitten warrior took a step forward and convulsed, spewing a torrent of blood and bile.

Bowstrings snapped. Arrows buzzed, chimed, clattered. The nāga's tail rattled as it drummed the wet stone. Splashes rose like diamonds, incongruously beautiful. The remaining Anlūki moved forward in pairs, leaving two archers behind. Kasraman, Wolfram, and Elonie spread out and began to chant their hexes, Elonie's Aspect taking form around her while Kasraman and Wolfram exercised more control. Kimiya snapped out a sharp warning against the use of witchcraft. The witches, wide-eyed and blood high, struggled with their instincts to unleash their powers. Corajidin snapped his own order, and though it took longer than he liked, the witches let their incantations fade.

The nāga's torso and tail were streaked with blood, much of which was its own. Two more of the Anlūki were down, twitching, exposed skin marked with inflamed bite marks. Nix dodged in and out of the fight, his knives almost as fast as the nāga's, and Tahj-Shaheh fought with the fluid, rocking motion of one who spent her time on heaving decks. There came the rattle of other nāga from left and right, and the moist rasp of scales against stone.

"What are you doing?" Corajidin glared at Kimiya and her clan.

"Watching your warriors 'deal with it,' " came her response.

"If I die, our agreement dies with me!"

A murderous look flashed over Kimiya's face. She opened her mouth and clattered something incomprehensible to Corajidin, but the others clearly understood it. As one they surged forward, lightly bouncing from foot to foot as they approached the nāga. When they drew close, they divided into three groups, one staying as the other two disappeared into the ruins.

A feeling of power surged through Corajidin, the unfettered disentropy of the world around him. It flowed through his boots and infused him. He felt warm, his skin tingled, and he felt the hair on his body vibrate. A vitality he had not felt in years infused him, mending some of the tatters of his flawed Awakening. He drew his heavy shamshir and leaped forward, mouth open in an incoherent battle cry, fired by the lusts of his cannibal Ancestors. Joining the fray, he hacked with more enthusiasm than skill, often in the way of his own guard. But it did not matter! Nothing mattered, save the savage joy of the strength that coursed through him. His weapon was used more like a cleaver than a sword, and he became a butcher, not a duelist.

Blood flowed, metal belled, voices screamed, sweat blossomed, and all the while he was carried above it all, filled with the power of the ages. He could not be killed. Kimiya and her clan tore at the nāga with tooth and nail. One of them, arm broken and dangling, but seemingly undaunted, continued to bite and rend. An Anlūki sidestepped into Corajidin's path, and Corajidin cut him down. He was only vaguely aware of the man's look of betrayal as the body spiraled away, fountaining blood. There was no way the nāga could defeat the man who would be Mahj!

Corajidin raised his blade to strike the head from the monster. Watched it come closer. Felt his blade fall, seemingly of its own volition.

But the nāga was not where it was supposed to be.

And his parry missed . . .

And he could not scramble away . . .

And the nāga latched on to his throat . . .

And as the fangs pierced his skin, it felt as if his veins were being filled with acid.

And he tumbled, howling at the indignity, into twilight. His last sight was of Kasraman, and the look of satisfaction in his glacial eyes.

Then the tremors started. His head collided with the stone over and over, his body arching like a bow, and twilight became night.

❋ ❋ ❋

Corajidin's head pounded. His neck hurt. It felt as if there were leather bands around his chest when he breathed.

He recalled the look in his son's eyes. *Kasraman would be happy if I died out here . . .* Feyd said that this place drove witches mad.

With a groan, Corajidin clawed his way to a sitting position. He opened his eyes carefully to find Wolfram leaning against a nearby wall, his staff clutched in his folded arms. Elonie came forward to help Corajidin sit. Kimiya crouched close by, her face, neck, chest, and hands spattered with gore. The mud and blood that caked her exposed skin was like a second layer of clothing, seemingly suiting her better than what she had worn.

"You survived," Kimiya said bluntly. "Rare. Your soldiers were less fortunate."

"How many survived?" Corajidin asked. His voice was a weak rasp, his throat burning.

"We've four from ten left alive," Wolfram said tiredly. "And of those, one probably won't survive the night. Nix and Tahj-Shaheh were wounded, but will survive. And two of the townsfolk . . . Dear Goat of the Wood, the marsh-puppeteers tore the nāga apart."

"They ate it," Elonie said quietly, placing a bowl of tea in Corajidin's hands. "Then when one of their own fell, the puppeteer inside burst out like the body it was in was just an overripe fruit. They ate that body, too, and the puppeteer swam away."

"A new host will be found," Kimiya said absently, licking at the caked blood on her hands. "Such is the way of things."

Corajidin sipped the tea. It tasted worse than it smelled, but soothed his throat and took some of the tightness from his chest so he could breathe easier. Wolfram gazed at Corajidin speculatively.

Motion from the corner of his eye, and Kasraman entered the clearing with two of the puppeteer-bonded townsfolk. He looked at Corajidin. His smile took moments longer than it should have to appear. "Father! You're awake. We wondered whether you'd return to us."

"Your concern is touching." Corajidin rose to his feet, shrugging off the ill effects of his poisoning. Pins and needles of energy trickled into his body, righting the wrongs. *My Unity with Erebus Prefecture was never like this!* Corajidin was reminded of Wolfram's comments about the volumes of the Emissary's potion he had been drinking, but this was a different sensation entirely. Something more natural, and sustaining, than the potion had ever been. Corajidin smiled at Kimiya, and took in the ruin in a gesture. "Show us what we came here for, if you would be so kind."

The gangrel woman bounded to her feet and trotted off. Silence fell as they moved through the ruins, the local inhabitants aware now that a greater predator had arrived. Kimiya wound her way through tumbled walls held together with vines, beneath arches that looked fit to crumble should the wind change, and across flagstones shattered by time. Corajidin spied a stubby tower ahead with its verdigris bronze dome almost hidden among the ivy's avarice. They made their way closer until Corajidin stood in a yard long gone to seed. Wasp nests bulged like boils on the mossy walls of the yard, the openings large enough for Corajidin to have fit his thumb into, and he was glad the insects were hibernating for the winter. The grass reached Corajidin's thighs, the stalks bent with their own weight. The tower was four stories tall, with plain windows and simple architecture. Walls were covered in tourmaline-colored tiles, either a bright blue, vivid green, or pink depending on where the light struck. There was a path of sorts leading to where a door long turned to rust hung skewed on broken hinges.

Too excited to wait, Corajidin crossed the threshold. The rusted doors snagged at his over-robe, and he tore the garment in his need to press on. Kasraman, Wolfram, and Elonie were close behind, while Nix and Tahj-Shaheh followed at a less-than-enthusiastic pace. Kimiya ambled along, face inclined to the sun, humming to herself, the Soul Trader an elongated smear at her side. The doors screeched as the Anlūki prized them open. There was muffled swearing, then a loud clang that caused everybody to jump as one of the doors fell to the stone floor. Corajidin tersely ordered the soldiers to guard the piece. The last thing he needed was for them to break something useful.

Nix took the lead, as he sought out myriad dangers that might surprise the unwary. On a few occasions he was forced to seek help from one or more of the witches to dismantle a trap.

Corajidin imagined what the place would have looked like when Sedefke lived here. Rotten pieces of wood and scraps of canvas were evidence of art. Other detritus may have been tables and chairs, ceramic pots and other ornaments on shelves that had collapsed with time. Each floor presented the riddles of history, yet there was nothing of value, and Corajidin soon found his jaw clenching with frustration. Kimiya remained silent, her lips quirking in a smile Corajidin was tempted to slap off.

"Where are these treasures you promised me?" Corajidin's voice was low and menacing. "All I see are scraps!"

"I told you I would bring you to where Sedefke worked," Kimiya replied without even a semblance of fear. "I did not promise you that others had not come here before."

"Sweet Erebus!" Corajidin shouted. "Have there been others? What was here?"

"There have been others, and what was here has always been here."

"Treasure hunters came, and failed?" Kasraman asked.

"They came and died."

Everybody stopped moving.

Kimiya picked her way up a rubble-strewn stair. Corajidin looked with a new perspective: The time-bleached wood could have been bone; the cracked bowl, a skull. Other debris: teeth, or decaying weapons, or clothes left to rot around their unfortunate owners.

"I've found all the traps thus far, Asrahn," Nix said quickly. "Any physical trap would be sprung only once, though mystic ones might be triggered more often. I feel confident we're safe as we can be."

Corajidin nodded toward the stairs, and both Nix and Elonie trod as best they could in Kimiya's footsteps. The others followed cautiously; Tahj-Shaheh grumbled profanities at every crack, snap, and clatter.

The exploration party searched all the floors to find nothing. At the top of the stair there was a door, bright and new, though the walls around it were melted to a glassy smoothness, and part of the wall opposite missing as if punched out by a giant fiery fist.

"No guesses for what this trap is," Nix said with a giggle. He looked about, carefully removing what debris remained around the door: blackened bones, most snapped off jaggedly from the force of what had hit them. Smelted ingots of metal that might have been weapons. But little else. He crouched, looking at the complex mosaic. There was a combination of colors, words, and geometric shapes. The Soul Trader floated by the little man, bent almost double in apparent interest. Or anticipation. "How long do you think this place has stood?"

The other witches and the ex-pirate glanced about, before Kasraman said, "At a guess, more than a thousand years. The architecture is certainly of a style that fits the period."

Nix nodded, and pointed to the remains he moved aside. "I think there are ten to fifteen different lots of remains here, best I can tell. Not to mention what we saw on the stairs, or what got blown out the wall."

"Fascinating," Tahj-Shaheh drawled. "But I think I speak for all of us when I say: So what?"

"The so what is that if this were an obvious trap, somebody would've worked it out by now. So we need to think less obviously, and more like the person who laid it in the first place."

"Sedefke?" Kasraman asked, his tone intrigued.

"Seems to be a safe enough bet," Nix replied. "But let's move back, to avoid doing something obvious like setting the trap off, and blowing ourselves to ashes."

Corajidin remained where he was as the others debated what they knew of Sedefke. Corajidin had studied the man's work his entire adult life, knowing the man to be at once scholar and soldier, explorer and inventor, teacher and student. A man of opposites, who sought the strength in the culmination of opposing forces, to make a balanced and stronger whole: a man who had forged and tempered himself through everything he could experience. When all was said and done, Sedefke was a man who made history. Who handcrafted the future. Who shaped the ways of monarchs for time immemorial.

He would only want the worthy to inherit his legacy.

And the most worthy were those Sedefke had trained and illuminated: scholars, the Mahjs, and the rahns of the Avān people. Only those whom Ía had accepted would be fit enough to use such legacies as Sedefke had provided. Only those who had been Awakened to mysteries greater than themselves, as Sedefke had. His weapons were meant to defend, as well as attack, and what was a rahn if not the defender of his land and people?

If I am the agent of destiny, the Thrice Awakened, surely I cannot die here, or now?

Corajidin took a step forward. The Soul Trader flowed to his side like anthropomorphic steam. Elonie saw Corajidin, and rushed to stop him. In that infinitesimal moment, Kasraman threw up a defensive ward around himself and screamed for the others to get down.

It was not so much fire as it was incredible heat that boiled around him. It was invisible at first, then flared with brilliant white, tinged with palest blue. Elonie did not have the time to scream before she puffed into ash. The Soul Trader became visible for a bare moment, a negative thing where pallor was black and shadow white. It was a skeletal old man in rotting cloth with long gray hair, ruined nails, and lips pulled back from receding gums. It held an ornate annulus in its bony hands, a cat's cradle of light like a spinning funnel at its center. What remained of Elonie, the mnemonic analogy of her soul, saw the annulus and opened her mouth in a shriek as she was sucked into the rotating vortex. The Soul Trader bared its chipped teeth at Corajidin, annulus held in his direction, and Corajidin trembled in fear.

Sweet Erebus, no!

The heat licked at the walls, cracked them, caused them to expand outward as if taking a deep breath. Kasraman's hasty wards flared through the spectrum as layer after layer burned away.

Corajidin felt the heat. Knew the pain: indeed, almost passed out from it. Yet it flowed into him, and through him, and was grounded by him. Screaming with the agony, he expected to see his skin peel back and his bones blacken—

He remained unharmed. He slapped his hand against the door.

It opened with a gentle click.

The heat stopped.

The Soul Trader faded to a blur and drifted back, indistinguishable from the walls around it.

Ilhen lanterns in the room glowed softly and illuminated the mosaic on the inside of the dome: the story of how the Avān were created on Castavān, the semimythical isle of their beginnings, far across the Eastron Divide. Under the reflected light of the dome, Corajidin saw myriad books in age-defying crystal, mechanisms, schematics in hanging sheets of glass, and devices that he could barely comprehend.

Save one. It was an ornate, throne-like chair of fused witchfire and jade, *kirion* and *serill*. Its complex designs and round glyphs were made in silver, and gold as bright as if it had been minted this morning. The chair sat within a fretwork gazebo that flickered with a tracery of light, a baroque crown suspended from its apex. Corajidin staggered forward, eyes wide. Breath refused to enter his lungs save through conscious effort.

"Father?" Kasraman asked uncertainly. Corajidin heard his son's footsteps as he approached. He smiled at Wolfram's sudden intake of breath.

"Sedefke left his work in many places." Corajidin wanted to sit on the chair now, but restrained his ardor, difficult as it was. He turned to Kimiya, who looked about the room with indifference. *What wonders your people must have seen, disgusting and malformed as you are, now washed up on the shores of a time that does not want you. I do not want you. But you have proven your worth, and I will wring from you all that you are before I destroy you and yours.* He stood, giddy with excitement, and said, "Kimiya and her marshpuppeteers led us here in good faith. My son, my friends, let us look back when we have unified our nation under one voice, and remember that it started here. With us. With the power of a vanished empire we will see restored to glory.

"And with this. The Havoc Chair, with which I will exterminate any who stand in my way."

19

"BECAUSE I DO NOT TRAVEL THE SAME ROAD AS YOU DOES NOT MEAN I AM LOST."

—from *The Dark Roads of Enlightenment*, by Yattoweh, Sēq Magnate, teacher, and houreh (231st Year of the Awakened Empire)

DAY 61 OF THE 496TH YEAR OF THE

SHRĪANESE FEDERATION

Indris's left eye blazed, and the glyphs on his Scholar's Lantern shimmered with disentropy. His protective wards changed color through the spectrum as they were burned away, fractal prisms and planes of force fading under the repetitive impact of the Sea Witches' hexes. He spared a glance for Mari as she hurtled toward the Dowager-Asrahn, but could not join her lest the witches change their focus and level their arcane attentions on Mari.

He burned one witch to ash, leaving nothing but a smoking cloud that roiled on the water. The remaining two witches panicked, tried to join their hexes in concert, only to have their own wards race through the rainbow, and fail. Startled, they looked beyond Indris. The witches wore expressions of betrayal as they were sliced down by a rapid-fire series of superheated spinning disks that cut them to pieces.

Indris spun to see a hooded Sēq stride through the melee, her wards battered into the red. Anj pulled her hood back and grinned. Her octopus-pommeled sword dripped blood, which stained the brine at her feet. The other combatants kept their distance, leaving the two in the eye of the storm.

"What are you doing here, Anj?" Indris asked. Suspicion rose in him. *How did you know where I was?*

"Zadjinn and the Dhar Gsenni sent me," she replied, flicking the mess from her blade with a twist of her wrist. "Fancy meeting you here in Tamerlan."

"Fancy that indeed," he murmured. The *serill* blade of his Scholar's Lantern burned carnelian with her falsehood. He decided to test her. To know, rather than suspect. "So is you being here Dhar Gsenni mischief, or did you come here to find me?"

"If I'd known you were here, I'd have joined you earlier."

The lantern shone pale amber. She was being partially honest.

"I'm glad you're here, though. Our talk is long overdue."

"Have you been here long? And now isn't a great time to talk."

"Just arrived." Again, the carnelian fire of her lie.

Anj frowned at Indris's lantern, her smile faltering. "I've not seen that before. What is it?"

Months of uncertainty rose in Indris. The oily tint to Anj's Disentropic Stain. Her dealings with the Dhar Gsenni. Her absences. The little things that were so like somebody playing the role of Anj, rather than Anj herself. *It was time I faced the truth of her . . .*

He fanned the lantern into brightness. The light from his Scholar's Lantern laved her, revealing what she had become, from behind what she was.

"No!" Anj yelled. Sapphire eyes, storm-cloud hair, and the face of the woman he had adored vanished. Her cassock shredded in the glare, to reveal the ruin of the Seethe woman beneath: her blackened lips, shadow-vein skin, and the festered carbuncle on her brow.

"Oh . . ." Indris could not say her name. His tears flowed. He relinquished control, and her illusion surrounded her like clouds obscuring moon. Though resistance rose in Indris, Changeling was resolute: The blade thrummed with the need to kill. The weapon burst the banks of Indris's self-control, swamping him with both fury and power. "No!" Indris reined himself in after two steps forward. His legs trembled as he fought a compulsion much stronger than Rosha's Jahirojin against the Erebus. Changeling was a psédari: To fight her was, for Indris, to fight part of his own mind.

"It wasn't meant to be this way," Anj said. She walked forward, palms at her sides, oblivious to the din of combat around her. "I was going to tell you . . . going to show you—"

"Don't," Indris sobbed. He pointed Changeling at her heart. "Just stay away. For the love you once bore me, don't come closer."

"I still love you, Indris," she replied. She halved the distance. A figure detached itself from the melee, and bounded forward. Ekko swung his *khopesh* at her, and Anj backhanded the giant Tau-se into the ground. He hit the stone hard and lay very still, bleeding from his mouth, eyes rolled back. "I'll always love you. And my Masters want to meet you. They've plans for you, husband. Plans for us both."

"Your Masters in the Drear? I've seen them. What was it that made you abandon your self for whatever it is you've become?"

"My search for you!" She pounded her chest with her fist. "Always, and everything, for you! The beautiful champion who held the secrets of my heart. And when my strength failed, when I was almost dead, the Drear came to my aid like no others. Not even Zadjinn and the Dhar Gsenni realized what they'd done when they sent me into that world, though they, too, desired contact with the Drear. But they had no true concept of them.

"And those powers want you, love." She rested one hand on the hilt of her sword; the other was held out in invitation. "They've watched you for a long time. They've the answers the Sēq won't give you. I'm but one of their Emissaries, sent to speak their word."

Indris spared a glance to where Morne, Kyril, Belam, Sanojé, and the other warriors set upon the sea monster. Mari had sagged into the water, barely floating in the churn. Indris stepped toward Mari, but the Emissary interposed herself.

"I'm your wife, Indris. Not her. If your little Human needs to die for you to learn this lesson, then so be it. The poison I gave Jhem to use will take care of her soon enough."

Indris looked at the Emissary, and his hearts broke all over again. Though the Emissary wore his lost wife's face, she and he no longer shared a world. Inoqua had been an empire of madness and whim, of enlightenment through the suffering of oneself, and others. Of stripping away layers of sanity, flesh, and soul to discover the elusive meaning of existence. These were the beings that slumbered in the Drear. These were the things that had made the Drear what it was, when the Weavegates had stirred their eons-old slumber.

"Better dead," Indris whispered, "than the servant of such things."

"Truly?" the Emissary asked. "We were trained to be objective. My Masters aren't evil. Their motivations may be incomprehensible to you, but that does not make them evil. Any more than you are evil for destroying an insect that walks across your food. It is just that your motivations and perceptions happen to be different, your remove higher."

"I'll not go with you."

"You will, one way or another."

She drew her sword and struck at Indris. Changeling parried with a growl. Back and forth, Indris and the Emissary fought. Indris tried to circle toward Mari, who barely had her head above water. The Emissary countered. Nadir had come to his senses and drew closer, his face stony with hatred.

Husband and wife cut into each other, though neither took the killing blow when it was offered. When Nadir joined the fray, Indris was hard-pressed to fight them both. His wounds took their toll, slowing his responses, and he was wounded more in turn. Changeling flooded him with power, and Indris saw his wounds fade, felt his muscles revived.

Belam came to Mari's side and dragged her from the water. Nadir, furious, ran to intercept.

"Let me go!" Indris pleaded as their blades slammed together. "Mari needs my help!"

"She needs to die!" The Emissary's voice was chill. "You'll forget her soon enough."

"No. I won't."

The Emissary cried in anger and brought the flat of her blade down in a powerful overhand swing.

Indris parried. Changeling shrieked, a sound unlike anything Indris had ever heard. The sound of fracturing metal filled Indris's ears. Lightning crashed in his mind, and thunder rolled through his body. Changeling shattered into slivers. The force it released lifted Indris from his feet and flung him backward. Dumbfounded, Indris lay on his back.

He groaned, tried to control his weak and trembling limbs, as the Emissary teetered forward on unsteady feet. Her own blade was shorn off at the hilt. She leaned down and grabbed Indris by the ankle, crooning something discordant, a canto within the cadence and phrasing of a hex. The air bubbled as the Emissary opened a passage into the Drear.

Changeling's cry of pain reverberated through Indris's body. His limbs were palsied. Through a twitching eye he watched Belam try to drag his armored sister through the water. The energy Indris had given her would be all but gone. On the verge of an ahm-stroke, as one side of his body faded to numbness, Indris held on to his last coherent thought: *Mari needs me!*

Conscious thought aside, Indris reached out with the part of his mind that had been sheltered from the backlash of Changeling's destruction. He grasped one of Changeling's broken shards. With what strength was left in him, Indris hurled the shard at the Emissary with his mind.

It pierced her chest deeply. Red flowered and spread. The Emissary staggered. Coughed blood. Drew the long metal shard from her chest as she crashed to the ground.

Her illusion vanished, and there was only the Fallen Seethe woman. No part of the Anj he remembered remained to be seen. She smiled, lips bloody, her arm outstretched to take his hand.

A tentacle curled around her, lifted her high, and drew her to the water as the monster fled beneath the waves.

Indris's eyes closed as he fell into the tumult of his mind.

✳ ✳ ✳

He rode the whirlwind through brilliant blue skies that spiraled around him. Fragments of a broken mirror spun around him: some he was able to catch, and he placed them back where he thought they belonged. He saw himself and his missing pieces: His left eye burned like the sun, the skin about it scaled. His head was crowned by clouds and sunlight, while his feet stood firm and deep as the mountains. Oceans washed against him, and rivers poured down him, but there were so many pieces missing, and some of the pieces of the mirror showed no reflection at all, and all the while there was the ticking metronome of the world's passing . . .

A voice at the edge of hearing, sibilant and draconic, gently cried his name, and soothed the pain and the fear, and helped with gentle hands to turn Indris away from the mirror so that he could see—

Indris shot bolt upright, and regretted it. It felt as if his brain sloshed around inside his skull. The world spun around him, and he clutched the sheets for traction.

"You're awake," Shar exclaimed.

"If you say so. Mari? I need to see—"

"She's fine." Shar set her sonesette down and came to Indris's side. After checking his temperature, and listening to the clamor of his hearts, Shar went to a side table and carefully poured some tea. She handed it to Indris and stared him down until he drank the foul brew. "The surgeon has been hard at work since you've been absent from us. Mari was touch and go there for a while, but she's up and about now. She's only been away from your side long enough to grab a few hours' rest here and there. You just missed her."

"How long?"

"Three days."

"That long? Balls!" Memories of the battle asserted themselves. "How's Ekko?" *And how many other lives were lost for this rock in the middle of nowhere?* "How are you?"

"Awww, you care." Shar grinned. "I'm well, scratches and bruises mostly. Nothing time and what passes for lotus wine in this place won't fix. Ekko's wounds were more serious than he made out. The Emissary almost made an end of him, but the surgeon said he'll recover."

"I'm glad. I'd not expected this to be our reunion."

Shar leaned in to kiss him. "Better this than all the worse things it could have been. I can't begin to understand what you've been through, Indris, but I'm glad you're here. My next question is, where to next?"

"Does there have to be a where to?"

"There's always a where to." Shar gently butted Indris's shoulder with her head. "There are worse people to be a rolling stone with. We Seethe are performers, people of the winds and the open spaces. The sedentary life doesn't suit us."

"Well, you're going to love what's next."

Shar clapped her hands in delight, skin and eyes lit with humor. "Do tell!"

"Let's go get Mari and Ekko first. This is best said once."

Indris took up his armor and stopped when he saw Changeling's hilt, a broken sliver of blade all that remained of her graceful form. There was a bag beside the hilt, at which Indris raised an eyebrow. Shar explained they were the shards of Changeling that they found and collected. She hugged Indris, resting her chin on his shoulder. "In case you can remake her."

"I don't know how, Shar." Indris swallowed against the loss. Changeling's hilt crooned, almost too softly to be heard, her need for comfort a finger that stirred the waters of Indris's mind. He took the dragon-headed hilt and slipped it through his sash. Even this much of the weapon gave him comfort. Indris took up his Scholar's Lantern, and felt a diminished yet familiar sensation as energy was channeled into him. *It's not the same, but it will have to do for now.* Indris kissed Shar on the brow. "Thank you. Let's find our friends."

After a short walk, they found Ekko where he limped along on his way to the Hearthall. Indris hugged his friend, and laughed at Ekko's blank-faced refusal of Indris's offer of support. An Avān or a Human with such a wound would be bedridden for the better part of a week. The Tau-se were tempered of sterner stuff. Mari they found as she came down the stairs. Her eyes were red from crying.

"What do you need me to do?" Indris asked kindly as Mari joined them.

Mari sniffed, gave a brittle laugh, and wiped the remainder of her tears away with her thumbs. She leaned into Indris and wrapped her arms around him. "For now? Hold me. What's done is done, and now Belam needs to decide for himself what to do."

"What happened?"

"We talked frankly about Father, Kasra, ourselves." Mari's breath felt warm against Indris's neck, and there came the dampness of fresh tears. But her voice was steady, a comforting vibration against his skin. "I told him some facts that he didn't want to hear. About how Nadir and Ravenet ambushed us. About how I tried not to kill her, but she gave me little choice. Even about some of what Nadir did, here in Tamerlan."

Indris stiffened, and Mari looked up with a genuine smile. She touched his lips with her finger. She said, "No! Nothing like that, though he tried to rekindle emotions only he felt. Truth is, I caused him more hurt than he ever caused me."

"You'll not be alone." Indris tilted her chin up to kiss her. "Belam knows the truth?"

Mari nodded. "About Amnon. About Avānweh, and how I feel about you."

"How we feel about each other, you mean," Indris said. "You're the only adventure I care about, Mari. We've only one life, and I intend on living it with you."

Mari grabbed Indris's head in both her hands and kissed him soundly. When she released his lips, she rested her brow on his and said, "That's exactly what I need."

"I hate to intrude on your moment," Shar said, her grin wicked, "but Indris, weren't you going to reveal to us something of such stupendous importance, I'm likely to bed the first person I see in my excitement?"

Indris opened his mouth to retort but saw Shar's smile, and thought better of it. "Let's find somewhere quiet."

As they passed through the Hearthall, they piled platters high with steaming slivers of seafood, spiced vegetables, dips, rice, and warm flatbread. A couple of jugs of water and wine were added. They were greeted warmly by the warriors there, many who were bandaged and taking their ease in front of the roaring fires, most well into their drink. Morne and Kyril danced to a lively reel on the fiddle, pipes, and drum, while the captains clapped and stamped their feet.

Indris and his friends found a quiet dining room and sat down to a meal interspersed with inane chatter, bawdy jokes, and shared song. It seemed to Indris the first time in too long that he had laughed, or that he inhabited a moment without the Sēq looking on. The company of people he loved helped fill the awkward void that was not quite an emptiness of Changeling: He still felt her, in the roots of his mind. As the food disappeared, and the drink was replenished, Indris related to his friends what he knew of the rahns' plight, and what he had agreed to do to help them.

"So it all comes back to the Pillars of Sand?" Mari asked. She stretched her long legs out atop Indris's, and crossed them at the ankle. He held one of her hands, taking comfort from the warmth. "Not just the rahns, but even your own ancestry. And these new talents of yours." She leaned forward and tapped him on the brow.

"Apparently," Indris replied.

"Indris"—Shar's expression was serious—"are you sure this is a good idea? You said the rahns are being treated using the Water of Life. Can't you leave this with the Sēq to handle?"

"Particularly after all they have done to abuse you, and your trust," Ekko added.

"No," Indris replied. "This is as much about answering my own questions as it is about helping the rahns. Probably more so. I

saw something, did something, or heard something that some bastard felt was dangerous enough to hide from the world. The Sēq
have tried to open that box, and failed spectacularly. I need to do it
my way. And I think the time has come."

Mari finished her wine, then looked up at Shar and Ekko.
Both the Seethe and the Tau-se nodded to her unasked question.
She leaned across and tugged lightly on Indris's hair, her face lit by
the smile he adored.

"When do we leave?"

✳ ✳ ✳

"We'll come with you," Morne said. He fumbled for his axe, as
if meaning to travel then and there. Kyril laughed, and slid the axe
farther away.

"Thanks," Indris replied. "But you and the Immortal Companions can be more effective in service to the rahns. Corajidin has
sent some of his force into the Rōmarq to finish what he started in
Amnon. Even as Asrahn, he can't simply send an army to occupy
another prefecture. It's clear he has long-term ambitions that need
to be stopped."

"It will take us bloody ages to get to Beyjan from here," Kyril
said. "Even hugging the coast of the Spectral Strand along Pashrea,
navigating the Maw in winter won't be a picnic. And heading to
Selashan and going by river across Shrīan will take too long."

"There are wind-ships at the skydock here, enough to carry the
Immortal Companions with room to spare," Indris said. "Nobody
will prevent you taking them. Leave The Seeker here for the winter.
Head straight to Avānweh." Both men nodded in response, old
habits of taking orders from Indris ingrained. "I'll mindspeak
Femensetri to let her know you're on the way, and that you'll have
Rahn-Vahineh with you."

"We will?" Morne asked.

"Vahineh needs to get back so the Federationists can form some kind of cohesive leadership in the Teshri. With the Companions back to full strength in Avānweh, you'll be a force to be reckoned with."

"By air it's about a week's travel," Kyril said. He frowned. "Unless we are diverted by storms."

"Unless you get blown off the map, you'll arrive in plenty of time. Armies don't move that quickly, and I doubt Corajidin has even the slightest control over the Rōmarq." Indris recalled what he knew of the marsh-knights, their skill and ferocity. "I can't imagine he's having too great a time of it. Besides, he needs the time to learn how to use anything he finds there."

Indris kissed the two men and wished them fortune, then made his way back to the room he shared with Mari. He was surprised to see Belamandris waiting for him. The two men looked at each other apprehensively, neither certain of who would defeat whom in a conflict. With the adrenaline of battle gone, Indris sensed the greasy stain on nearby disentropy that only came from salt-forged steel. Indris's glance flicked to the long-knife thrust through Belamandris's sash, and Tragedy's elegant curves—while the Widowmaker cocked an eyebrow at Changeling's dragon-headed hilt.

Belamandris smiled tentatively, and held his hand out.

"Mari said we have to stop the hatred somewhere," Belamandris said. "She told me everything, and she's no reason to lie."

"And your response to everything would be . . . ?"

"That I don't like most of what I heard," Belamandris admitted honestly. "But what's done is done. I've seen that you're an honorable man, and if I ignore the poison of my upbringing, I have to admit I've no grievance with you. It's old anger best left in the grave."

"I hear you," Indris muttered. He looked at Belamandris's hand, extended if not in total friendship, at least not in war. "Are you here to see Mari?"

"I'm here to offer my hand." Belamandris shook the appendage. "And the sword that comes with it. My sister has been gone for months, part of something our father is doing that may lead us all to ruin. Mari thinks you're about the only person who can stop it."

"And you?"

"I'm inclined to agree."

Indris came forward and took Belamandris's hand. The grip was hesitant to start, but both men relaxed into the unfamiliar contact. Indris was glad the Widowmaker was coming along—no doubt with Sanojé, though her reputation was dappled at best. With the two Erebus siblings by his side, Indris felt better about facing the unknown.

The door opened and Mari poked her head into the corridor. Her smile was hesitant as she took in the two men. Indris smiled at her, then rested his hand on Belamandris's shoulder.

"Best get your things together, and say what farewells need to be said. We leave for the Pillars of Sand tonight."

20

"THOSE WHO WERE NEVER THERE WHEN EVENTS UNFOLDED PERHAPS
SEE HISTORY THROUGH A DIMMER LENS, FLATTENING THE HIGHS AND
LOWS INTO A MORE ACCOMMODATING MIDDLE GROUND. HISTORY IS
THERE TO TEACH US NOT WHAT WE WANT TO LEARN,
BUT WHAT WE NEED TO LEARN."

—Kemenchromis, Sēq Magnate and Arch-Scholar
(1st Year of the Shrīanese Federation)

DAY 64 OF THE 496TH YEAR OF THE

SHRĪANESE FEDERATION

One step out of the Drear, and Mari fell to her knees and
vomited. She looked down into the pool of bile in the sand in
front of her face and wiped her lips with a shaky hand. It was
warmer in the Dead Flat than Tamerlan, but far from hot. Sand as
fine as silt streamed across the dunes in currents of pale gold.
Sunlight deep-etched her shadow in stark contrast.

Indris came to her side and helped Mari to her feet. He held
her face between his hands. She wanted to back away from the

fire that guttered in his Dragon Eye, and felt that Indris was inside her head, checking that the house of her mind was still on stable ground. The sensation passed quickly. He handed her a flask and she rinsed her mouth, then spat the water into the thirsty desert.

"What was that about?" Mari pointed to her head for emphasis.

"Sorry," he said. "We need to check to make sure none of you brought any passengers out of the Drear with you."

"That can happen?"

"Often enough. If not riding the back of somebody, they find ways through naturally forming rifts. Devices like the mocking-birds help, but we need to be careful."

Mari watched as Indris and Sanojé moved among their small group, checking everybody. The two shared a quiet conversation, and Indris reached into his satchel and gave the Tanisian witch two clockwork spheres, brothers of the one he had activated before taking them all through the Drear. Sanojé looked surprised, then grateful as Indris showed her how to work the mechanism.

Sorrow washed over Mari as she noticed where they were. The sand-cloaked ziggurat nearby was where she had been betrayed by Roshana—to Hayden's death, and Omen's destruction. Mari snuck a glance at Belam, who seemed lost in his own memories. He caught her eye but did not cheapen the moment by smiling at her. This was not a place to be remembered with fondness, or pride.

"There she is!" Indris trotted through the sand toward the half-buried shape of the *Wanderer*. After so long in the desert, the sands were piled high over it. It would take them days to dig her out. Indris and Shar clambered aboard. The two of them inspected the downed galley while Mari sat with Belam, Sanojé, and Ekko.

"The Drear," Belam said by way of greeting. He looked haunted. "I hate that damned place."

"Why would you have reason to spend time in a place like that?" Mari asked.

"Father's ambitions know few bounds, Mari." Belam let sand run through his fingers. "We found part of the old Weavegate network in a hall of the Qadir am Amaranjin, in Avānweh. Father hasn't taken the place as his own, given it's the Mahj's palace, but he's not been shy about using it when he needs to."

Mari was appalled. "Why use the Weavegates?"

"We warned the Asrahn it was unwise." Sanojé shook her head. "The Weaveway was abandoned for a reason, and we—the witches—told him that to use it would arouse unwanted attention from what dwelled in those depths. Things best left undisturbed."

"That doesn't tell me why you used them."

"Once Father ran out of people to hold as parole against good behavior in Avānweh," Belam said, "he decided to harvest his hostages from further afield. Where there was a Weavegate, and more of them have survived the ages than I'd ever have thought, we'd use it to stage raids. Each raiding party would take a witch to guide us through, and get us home again in case there was no gate on the other end."

"Father is taking hostages now?" Mari could not hide her disgust. It went against everything sende stood for, a repudiation of the social codes that held Avān society back from the unbridled savagery and violence that had once defined it. "Why didn't you stop him?"

"There's no telling him anything." Belam related to Mari everything that had transpired: Yashamin's reincarnation, their father's use of the witches to spy on Narseh and the sayfs, the Sky Lord's and the Arbiter-Marshall's open questioning of the events at Avānweh, and how their father managed to get witches into power. "Kasraman is Father's conscience in these things now, and I fear our half-brother is playing a game of his own."

"And is several moves ahead," Sanojé murmured.

Mari listened to the barrage of misdeeds that would stain her family for years, if not generations. Her hearts sank with the dreadful litany, until all she wanted was to ask Belam to stop speaking. She was grateful for the distraction when there came a groaning and hissing from the *Wanderer*.

Sanojé stared in wonder as Indris stood before his buried sky ship. Clouds of sand were blown from it, much faster than the paltry breeze could manage. The *Wanderer* rose into the air, sand pouring from one angled wing like a cataract. "How is he doing that?" she whispered.

"He's a scholar," Belam shrugged.

"But there's no disentropy here!" Sanojé scrambled to her feet and dashed across the sand to linger in Indris's shadow, her face lit with a manic grin. Mari, Belam, and Ekko joined her. "He should be like a mute, trying to sing! This isn't possible!"

Indris stood with his legs planted wide, sunk into the sand past his ankles. Sweat poured down his brow, veins thick as ropes on his neck. His gaze was focused on the *Wanderer*, his face in a rictus. He raised his palms upward and the *Wanderer* rose higher. Shar pirouetted in the sand for joy, and clapped her hands.

The last of the fine sand that covered the *Wanderer* slid away in a cloud, and the galley shuddered in midair. Indris gasped, frowning as the vessel dropped three feet toward the ground, only to stabilize again. He grunted with the effort, body quivering, and the *Wanderer* dropped slowly toward the ground. At just over a foot, the strain became too much. Indris swore, and fell to his knees as the *Wanderer* came down on her damaged landing gear. The ship listed somewhat, but seemed whole.

Mari gave Indris some water, where he reclined red-faced and panting in the sand. Shar and Ekko wasted no time in moving their bags aboard. Belam and Sanojé joined them, the witch eyeing Indris all the while.

"What happened to you?" Mari asked quietly. *What else can he do that I don't know about?*

"She's heavier than she looks." Indris grinned as he fell back into the sand, sucking in deep gulps of air. "I couldn't hold her and the weight of all the sand any longer."

"No, I mean to you." She nudged him with the toe of her boot. "You shouldn't have been able to do that, Sanojé says. If I understand it correctly, there's no natural energy here. Do you have so much that you don't need any from elsewhere?"

"Ha! If only. Even with Changeling's help I'd have struggled to lift the *Wanderer* in this place." His face contorted with loss, and he rested his palm against the broken mind blade. Mari heard the faintest purr. Indris squinted up at her. "I've gotten stronger over the months, and learned more about what's growing in my head."

What are you becoming, love? "But not strong enough, I take it?"

"Nowhere near it," Indris muttered. "There had to have been a reason the Sēq stopped teaching the mentalist disciplines. I hope I've not opened doors in my head that were best left shut. But for now, we need to get into the air and head east."

"Do you intend to carry us all the way with your brain?"

Indris rolled to his feet and boarded the *Wanderer*. In his pack were two jars, filled with radiant water. Where beams of light touched her skin she felt a faint tingling sensation, warm and pleasant. Indris took one of the jars and jumped back to the sand, then made his way beneath the ship. Mari joined him. With deft movements Indris removed a scorched golden rod and replaced it with the jar. He flicked it with a fingernail. "This is the Water of Life, Mari. This jar will power the spools for a few days of flight. When we get off the flat, the spools will recharge normally, with no need for me to burn my brain out." He called out for Shar to start the Tempest Wheels. They jerked, and stopped. Trembled. Stuttered. Then started to spin, the platters gaining speed.

❋ ❋ ❋

For a day and a half the *Wanderer* flew along the Orjini Road that followed the Mar Ejir, Indris looking intently at the rock formations they passed. On several occasions they landed, and he searched the rock face and surrounding desert, only to climb aboard once more and ask Shar to resume their flight.

There was little for Mari to do on the flight save talk, eat, drink, sleep, and get reacquainted with Indris. Or mend fences with Belam. It had been a long time since they had talked as brother and sister. Sanojé came and went, though when she stayed with them she slowly revealed a softer side than Mari had first imagined. She and Belam were solicitous toward each other, taking turns to lay out bedding, to cook, or to make tea.

"You love her," Mari said on their third morning together. Belam smiled and glanced at Sanojé where she stood by Indris, patiently listening to what he had to say about their search. Whatever it was, it was the province of mystics.

"And you love him," Belam said. "Father would be so proud of us right now. His golden warrior-poet children, besotted with an Exiled witch and a Näsarat scholar."

Mari chewed on some bread and cheese, enjoying the simplicity of it all. "I'd rather a lifetime of days like this, than one more minute of the agendas of our family."

"Even though it was the agendas of our family that sent us here?"

"Well, maybe some agendas aren't so bad."

"Do you include Indris's agendas?" Belam asked. "What's he looking for?"

"A place, a man, and answers." Mari kept the rest of what Indris had revealed to herself. *I fear all three, Mari,* he had said, *and fear more what I'm leading you into. It's why I fixed the Wanderer first, so you and the others could escape, should something happen to me. It wouldn't be the first time I've been imprisoned for what I know. Or what I don't.* "Indris is a good man, Belam. He knows what he's doing."

Belam shrugged, and took Sanojé in his arms when she returned with watered wine and a bowl of sliced cheese, dried apricots, and apple.

Mari gave her brother and his lover some privacy. Indris leaned precariously out over the *Wanderer*'s phoenix-shaped figurehead and stared downward. There on the sand was a lone man in tattered blacks being stalked by his shadow. He walked with long and seemingly effortless strides across the flats. He did not look up as the *Wanderer* passed above him.

"Now what kind of man doesn't look up when a ship flies overhead?" Indris asked.

"A man bored by the sight?"

"We've passed him, and other orjini travelers, a few times as we've been searching," Indris said. "The other orjini look up and wave, or shout, wanting to trade. But him? He just walks along, always in this area, and always from nowhere, to nowhere, as best I can tell. The only thing that marks this place from any other is what remains of that megalith."

"How can you walk from nowhere to nowhere?"

"Exactly my point. There's something out here that we don't see."

Indris had Shar land the *Wanderer* farther westward, far enough away from the man's course so as not to seem a threat. This time he paid attention, for he stopped, and he waited, and leaned on his staff. Indris glanced at his weapon belt and armor, but left them where they were. He took up his Scholar's Lantern, slid Changeling's pommel—now bereft of any blade—through his sash, and turned to his comrades.

"I've no idea what waits out there. I've been warned that this man—if he's who I see—is ancient, and has had many names. It's likely he's profoundly dangerous. I won't think any less of you, should you want to stay aboard the *Wanderer*, but I doubt that's an option left to me."

"You're not taking weapons?" Shar asked pointedly.

"Don't know that they'll help much," Indris said. "I'm here to learn, not fight."

"We don't have that qualm." Mari stepped to Indris's side and buckled on her armor and weapons. Shar and Ekko did the same. Belam and Sanojé whispered urgently to each other, her hand gestures short and sharp. Belam eventually shrugged, and said, "Looks like we're with you, too."

Mari walked at Indris's side as they crossed the intervening distance to where the man waited patiently, his weathered black robes flapping in the wind. Mari stayed close by Indris, her hand never far from the hilt of her Sûnblade. The others had fanned out, veterans of many wars, taking a wide approach against an uncertain enemy.

Their shadows were long on the ground as they approached. The man stood between two tall standing stones of the megalith, stones canted over time to become a triangular lattice, while some few stood straight and tall. The edges of the stones were worn smooth, and Mari's attention was diverted by the random shapes of glyphs that formed in the play of light, shadow, empty space, and eroded stone. Whatever had been carved on the stones had worn away, leaving only faint bumps and lines. There was nothing else to mark the place: no walls, no remnants of a city, town, or village. No trees, or wells. It was an arbitrary place to build anything, and as good or bad a place as any for a lone wanderer to wait for strangers.

Warning bells rang in Mari's head as they approached. *We should not be here . . .*

The traveler unwrapped the frayed taloub from about his head and face. His long flaxen hair and unkempt beard looked dry and brittle. His sun-darkened temples and cheeks were inked with colorful orjini tribal tattoos, but Mari did not know enough about the orjini to tell what tribe they were from. The stranger carried a sickle through his sash, and a long staff, which on closer inspection was a smoothed-off branch. He had no other weapons and no armor that Mari could see.

And what kind of man wanders the dangers of the Dead Flat so blithely? The city of Ar Orjini was more than a day's walk to the south. The mountains were home to Fenling packs and bandits that raided along the road and across the sands. Even the orjini, at home in the Dead Flat like no other, traveled in numbers. Yet the stranger seemed to have no fear. His wide smile was welcoming and without concern. It bothered Mari very much.

"Indris?" Mari grabbed his arm before they came any closer. "This man feels . . ."

"Odd?" Indris murmured. The stranger cocked an eyebrow, smile widening slightly. "I've the sense he's somebody to be reckoned with, and has stories aplenty. But I have to know, Mari."

"And what if things turn out for the worse?" *As they seem to do,* Mari thought.

"Then don't wait for me," Indris said. "I've come here for answers, but I don't know how long those answers may take to find."

"I'll not leave you, love."

"If it comes to it, you may have to. The others will need your strength. People will rally to you, and that's what our people need now: something to oppose the darkness your father brings with him."

"Indris, I can't—"

"Promise me, Mari." Indris leaned close and murmured in her ear. "Promise me you'll take the others and do what needs to be done to stop your father. You know it's the right thing to do, and we both swore to do our duty till this was done."

Mari was reminded of their conversation outside of Nanjidasé. She had told him she wanted to be remembered as something other than what history expects an Erebus to be. *The clock is ticking for us, one way or another. But I have to believe that while I'm here, I can make a difference. Otherwise, what point is there to any of it?* She nodded her promise to him.

Indris thanked her, and gestured for the others to remain where they were. Mari sidled forward on light feet and stopped by Indris's side, weight in the balls of her feet, close enough to protect him and far enough away to initiate hostilities if it came to it.

"You'll not need your *Deer Stance* here, young woman," the stranger said. His voice was rough, as if it were not used often. "Nor will your *Humming Wind* draw serve you any better. Am I friend or enemy, you wonder? A pointless exercise. Only you bring with you such distinctions, give these nothings substance, and believe them to be true. I was nothing before you came, I am nothing now, and will be nothing when you leave. So please, be at peace."

Mari tensed. The stranger was too calm. His poise reminded her of Bensaharēn, but put her old teacher to shame. Indris studied the man intently, brow furrowed. Changeling murmured to herself, and the stranger gave the dragon hilt a tender look.

"May I ask your name?" Indris said.

"There is never harm in asking questions—"

"There is only harm in answers," Indris replied. The stranger maintained his silence for a long while before Indris continued. "Will you answer?"

"In time. There is power in names, even when one has many. But you know this, neh?"

"Time is something I don't have, I'm afraid."

"On the contrary, Amon-Indris," the man countered. "Time is something of which we all have exactly as much as we need."

"Erebus's bones!" Mari whispered for Indris alone. "Can't I just slap an answer out of him? I mean, really, who talks like this?"

"Pretty much every teacher I've ever had," Indris murmured. Mari thought about her years with Bensaharēn and was forced to agree. Indris gave her a sideways smile. "Besides, I doubt this man has anything at all to fear from any of us."

"I could prove him wrong." But Mari put her trust in Indris and let her thoughts go. The stranger stood lightly, an extension of the desert and the winds. Be like water, Bensaharēn had said. Let your form flow in the need of the moment. Be water. Be fire. But be mindful that we are, at our core, bound to the earth. The stranger seemed part of everything around him, as if it were what he was meant to be. Mari had to admit that Indris was right: There was little this stranger had to fear from her, or her sword. She allowed herself to relax.

The stranger nodded. "You, Amon-Indris, need to think about why you've come. I will give you the opportunity to prepare yourself. We will speak again when I return. Until then, please, take your ease and enjoy the silence."

"When will you be back?" Mari asked.

"What is when?" the stranger asked. "The world does not track time, so why should you? Suffice to say I will return when Amon-Indris is ready for me to return."

Turning his back, the stranger walked into the megalith, and was gone. He did not come out the other side. Mari entered the little course, searching for the stranger's prints, but he had left nothing that the faint winds had not already blown away. Nor was he hiding among the rocks.

"He's gone," she said. "I've no idea how, but there's no sign of him."

"What are you going to do, Indris?" Shar asked.

"What he asked." Indris sounded somewhat bemused. He sat down in the sand and faced the megalith. He rested his lantern across his lap. To Mari, he said, "I'm going to meditate on why I've come. I get the impression this isn't going to be as straightforward as I'd hoped."

Mari ruffled his hair, and leaned down to kiss him. "Did you think it would be?"

"Not so much, no. See you soon." Indris closed his eyes, deepened his breathing, and became still as the stones in front of him.

"What now?" Belam asked.

"Looks like we wait," Mari said. "And watch."

21

"THERE ARE FEW IN POWER WHO UNDERSTAND THAT IT IS THEIR DESTINY AND PURPOSE TO SERVE, NOT TO RULE."

—Cennoväl the Dragonlord, Sēq Master, explorer, and teacher
(115th Year of the Shrīanese Federation)

DAY 65 OF THE 496TH YEAR OF THE

SHRĪANESE FEDERATION

"Is that all of it?" Corajidin asked, looking with come disappointment on the extent of what they had pillaged from the ruins. Other than the Havoc Chair, which Kasraman and Wolfram had failed to activate, there had been little of significant military value.

A makeshift camp had been set up, pavilions used to house the workforce while those buildings that could be occupied became command stations. The clamor of picks and hammers rang sharply. Smoke from the cook fires hung in a greasy pall, black against a morose sky. The delays nagged him like an infected fingernail. Two days of rain made soup of the ground. Nix reported their losses each day. Several walls had collapsed, destabilized by the ongoing work, killing scores of his captive workforce, as well as some soldiers. Near a hundred more had died as the result of traps, but Nix could only be in so many places at once. Often enough it was greed on the part of the people that died, digging in areas that Nix had not cleared, hoping they could find something of value to squirrel away. Other times it was because Nix missed something, mistakes the little man made no apology for. Beyond the issues of the ruins, there was the Rōmarq itself, which was inimical to outsiders—though Corajidin doubted it showed any mercy to its own. Workers and soldiers died from spider bites, scorpion stings, and snakes—creatures that should have been hibernating, but did not either because such was not their nature here or because they were angered by the presence of interlopers in their habitat. Another thirty or so had been killed by nāga who had not relinquished their claim on the ruins. At night it was Fenlings and reedwives carrying people away for food, or worse. And the marsh-puppeteers were an ever-present threat. When Kimiya had been confronted about the attacks, her bland response had simply been "*They're not of my clan.*"

Corajidin smiled as the filthy woman walked into his presence. She looked like a doll that had been passed down from mother to daughter for generations, a favorite that should have been thrown away long ago. She walked to within arm's length of him, smiling. He neither flinched nor retreated.

"Thank you for all that you and your clan have done, Kimiya," Corajidin said. "Though we have not unearthed as much as I would have liked—and only what we have at great cost—you have upheld your part of our arrangement."

"And now it's time for you to do the same."

"Let us not be so hasty on that score just—"

Kimiya opened her mouth and made an insectile clattering at the back of her throat. Corajidin saw the fine, chitinous appendages that moved at the back of her tongue. He recoiled with disgust as she stepped in. The stench of mud, blood, and excrement on her was overwhelming. Kimiya looked left, and right, and Corajidin followed her gaze to where marsh-puppeteers skittered through cracks in the walls, floor, and ceiling.

"We have given," she said. "Now it is for you to fulfill your promise."

"Who do you want?" he asked, cursing himself for the fear in his voice.

"The bodies of those with influence. The ones that can cause the most damage. The ones that can still ally with your cause, whether the host would have it or not." Kimiya stepped back, but the other marsh-puppeteers remained as they were, all within jumping distance. "The Soul Traders want to establish a foothold in your new world order, but we would look disfavorably on that arrangement. Indeed, a lesson may have to be made should you decide to follow such a course. Am I clear, Corajidin?"

"Yes," he muttered. "You will have them."

"When?"

"I return to Avānweh today, to prepare for the Winter Court."

"Then we will come with you," Kimiya asserted. "We are an honorable people, Corajidin. Unlike the Soul Traders, who cast off their agreements like decayed strips of flesh. We both are faceless, but my people relish the world of the living and all it offers. Our tastes are not so cold as those of the dead. And unlike you, Corajidin, we do not so easily put aside our bonds of loyalty, or our word given in good faith. We will take those you gave to us, and those you will give to us, the ones you see as inconvenient and inconstant nemeses. This we will do. And in return, we will continue to show your people the things hidden here."

She turned and left, the other puppeteers skittering away the ways they had come. When he was alone, Corajidin allowed himself to collapse into a chair, uncomfortably aware of how closely he had brushed against his own end.

※ ※ ※

As soon as Corajidin stepped from the Weavegate, he felt twice as heavy and less than a quarter as strong as he had in the Rōmarq. He grunted at the near-instant fatigue, and again at the pain that shot through his knees as they crunched onto the marble floor.

"Get him to the Qadir Erebus!" Wolfram shouted.

He slept badly, dreams and reality blending into a sweating, stench-laden whole. A frigid wind howled across sodden grasses of Ast am'a Jehour, as biting and fierce as the wolves the plain was named for. Corajidin's banners—their black and red rearing stallions shredded against a mustard-tinted overcast—streamed like tattered plumes of smoke. His forces had their backs to Fandra, and the lure of the Rōmarq was strong: to run, to hide, to live out his life as an Exile with the greatest of all powers at his fingertips, rather than die an ignominious death. The weight of his armor, dented and drenched in blood, bore him down. His arm ached from fingertips to wrist, his hand numb where it held his notched sword. He was surrounded by the war-lean figures of his warriors, while wild-eyed witches in their flapping robes circled the sky above, stentorian voices calling out to the powers that dwelled in the shadows between worlds; mad-eyed sayfs cackled, bonded forever to marsh-puppeteers, and led their forces in chaotic formations that made little sense, other than to confuse, disrupt, and dismay.

Across the rain-flattened grasses, the banners of his enemies ignited as the sun streamed through a rent in the clouds: lotus blossoms of silver and white, orange and brown, and blue and gold. In the uncertain light a mist boiled over the nearby hills, etched with the spectral forms of warriors long dead. At their front was a figure armored in scales forged of stars, his shield shining like the dawn and his sword a brilliant recurved shard of moonlight. Belamandris and Mariam fought at his side, as did the hosts of nations, and overhead Seethe skyjammers descended gracefully through the clouds, storm-cannon coughing destruction.

The figure raised his face, eye blazing with dragon fire.

Corajidin fought with the sheets that coiled serpentine around his limbs. He cracked open an eye and squinted against the brightness of alchemical lamps set around his room like moons in his orbit. He rubbed the perspiration from his face. Was his dream vision, or metaphor? Was Indris alive? Had his children betrayed him?

He extricated himself from the sheets, fished for his over-robe, and came face-to-face with Mēdēya, who had stood in the shadows all along.

"Your dreams again, Jidi?" she asked. Light played on the edge of her cheek, nose, and jaw, leaving the rest of her in darkness.

"As always."

Mēdēya held out a vial of the Emissary's potion. "Perhaps if you did as you were supposed to do, you would know some relief?"

"Why is it that I hear your voice, but the Emissary's words dance on your tongue? I am destiny's agent, and was before that curse of a woman came into our lives. That the road may have changed on the way to me being the father of empire is a trifling thing: It is the end that concerns me."

"So you say," Mēdēya challenged.

"I will prove I am destined for greatness."

"And how will this miraculous proof, that defies all your previous failure, present itself?" Mēdēya jibed. Corajidin clenched his fists in rage, for he could hear the Emissary's words again. Even the cadence was the same. "The Emissary will not wait forever. She has given and given. Provided you with allies you've yet to use well—"

"I will not traffic with the Soul Traders!" Corajidin snarled. *Can you hear me in there, Emissary, as you somehow hide behind my wife's face?* "The marsh-puppeteers are one thing, but Nomads lead us down dangerous roads from which there is little chance to turn back."

"What about your promises to me, Jidi?" Mēdēya asked. "An end to Vahineh at my hand? You agreed to give her to me."

"Give me peace, Mēdēya!" he shouted. The sound stabbed in his head. Corajidin rubbed his temples with his fingertips, moving aside when Mēdēya tried to touch him. "I give Martūm to the marsh-puppeteers today. Once that is done, Vahineh will be yours."

Corajidin stormed away to his bath. He shook off Mēdēya's offer to help, closing the door in her face. He bathed quickly, and dressed in the most regal clothing he had: black and red damask, studded with rubies and red-gold stallion-head ingots. Layered silks, and sable fur on the hood and cuffs of his over-robe. His weapons and armor he had lost in the fire at Sedefke's tower, so he marched to his private armory and selected a shamshir more for show than battle. Tempted as he was to don armor, the Emissary's potion gave him strength enough to walk, and to talk, but little else.

Corajidin hastened through the qadir, Mēdēya behind him. He startled servants and caused guards to snap to attention with a clamor of arms as he passed. At his office, he took brush to parchment and wrote a missive that summoned all the rahns and the sayfs to the Tyr-Jahavān at the Hour of the Fox tomorrow morning. It was a civilized hour, giving the upper-caste members time to see to their morning business, and have little suspicion that Corajidin meant them harm, as would be the case of an early-morning engagement. Under sende, an impolite hour showed Corajidin's displeasure, his want to unsettle, or inconvenience. Late in the afternoon, or early in the evening, spoke of his disregard for their family, or social lives, for such were the hours of dining, the theatre, concerts, and assignations kept quiet for the benefit of those both involved and those who would be wronged as their result. Traditionally, the morning Hour of the Fox was the hour of intellect, of planning, and of guidance. And to a degree it would be, just not as any of them suspected.

He inked a second letter to a more select group. Recalcitrants mostly, who followed him for gold and personal influence above any shared commitment or ideology. This was a personal invitation to attend the Qadir Erebus for a private meeting to discuss the immediate future. For those who swore themselves to Corajidin and the Imperialist cause, without the need to bargain more concessions or boons, it would be the end of it. For those who proved unreliable, Corajidin would make good on his commitment to Kimiya and her clan.

"Nix?" Corajidin said. "Speak with Kimiya. I want a marsh-puppeteer made ready for every person who receives that letter. Make her understand that not all will be bound, but this will go a long way to honoring my commitment to her."

"Your will, Asrahn," the little man replied. He scanned the list, one eye twitching. "And what of the Soul Traders? Will you extend them the same offer?"

"Forget the Soul Traders. Any potential alliance with them is severed."

"They'll not be pleased, Asrahn." Nix's voice was colder than was polite. "I know them well. They can be intractable when defied, and have a subtle influence."

"My decision is final. Go now." Corajidin waved the man away. Nix bowed, and took the missive away. Mēdēa sat in the chair opposite Corajidin.

"What rahns and sayfs remain in the city?" Corajidin asked Mēdēa.

She sorted though a sheaf of reports on his desk. "Nearly all the sayfs, save those from the most remote cities. Rahn-Narseh is in her qadir, her condition limiting what she can do. Her son is here and your lack of assistance in the matter of his mother's illness has soured him against you. You can't trust the Kadarins after Narseh dies."

"The Federationist rahns?"

"Rahn-Nazarafine arrived early this afternoon, as did Rahn-Siamak."

"But not Näsarat?"

"It's reported that she'll arrive this evening, or tomorrow at some point."

"You wanted proof, Mēdēya? By tomorrow almost every member of the Teshri I do not trust will be bound with a marsh-puppeteer. They will be used for different purposes, as time and opportunity provide. But the factions that have tried to split power in the Teshri will end."

"And those who escape this plan of yours?" Mēdēya asked. "You can't bind every person in the Teshri to a marsh-puppeteer. What happens when word of your betrayal of your own nobles spreads like wildfire across Shrīan?"

"It will not," Corajidin said flatly. "On the surface it will seem as if the counselors have aligned their vision with mine. Some may suspect something is amiss, but what can they do? Unlike a Nomad, a marsh-puppeteer cannot be so easily dislodged from its host, nor can one be readily spotted. Eventually their natures will give them away, and they will revert to their insane barbarism. That barbarism will be given a nudge in the direction of quite openly murdering the Federationists. When that happens, I will declare them traitors, and an end will be made of them, as is just. But I will have none defy me, Mēdēya. And that includes you."

"And then?"

"Then I will be Mahj in all but name. My policies will be assured of passing through the Teshri. From here it is a short step across the mountains to Pashrea, and to Mediin, where I will see to it that the Empress-in-Shadows qadir of Ishuajan is tumbled from the mountainside."

※ ※ ※

Martūm begged off attending the Qadir Erebus, despite repeated and pointed demands to the contrary. With barely contained fury, Corajidin ordered Wolfram and four squads of the Anlūki to join him on his short journey to the Qadir Selassin. Corajidin rested his hand on the ornate alabaster jar that contained the marsh-puppeteer, trying to imagine the look on the dissolute Martūm's face when he opened it.

Corajidin was surprised to see warrior-poets of the Vayensūk—the daishäri of the Selassin Lotus School—at the qadir gates, as well as hard-eyed soldiers of the Selassin Lotus Guard, their helms and shields embossed with the lion and lotus totem of the House. Martūm had not been a popular choice as rahn-elect, yet apparently there were some who held loyalty to the role and not to the man who held it. The guards at the gate ushered the carriage inside the qadir, and closed the heavy steel gates behind them as they entered a long, dark defile to the inner yard of the qadir. Once inside, Corajidin waited for Martūm to appear. After ten infuriating minutes where the Selassin guards remained silent and attentive, Corajidin snapped orders to his people to join him as they climbed the sweeping stairs to the top of the qadir.

Without invitation, Corajidin threw the doors to the Lilly Hall open. The lofty room was dim, clouds occluding the sun through the quartz-paneled ceiling. Few of the *ilhen* lamps were lit, infrequent and distant pools of radiance in the long room. His boot heels clicked across the marble floor, softened when they hit a large rug, and became a squelch as he stepped in something wet. Clouds released the sun, and the darkness lifted.

"What in Erebus's name . . . ?" he breathed.

Blood spray littered the surrounds, and Martūm lay on his back, his throat cut from ear to ear, blood coating his chest like a bib.

Bowstrings twanged. Soldiers emerged from cover, and the Anlūki set to defending themselves and those they served. Bodies surged and Corajidin found himself swept away, separated from Wolfram. He quickly lost sight of the Angothic Witch, who chanted protective hexes around himself.

Almost deafened by the racket, Corajidin took his chance to use his Anlūki as a shield. He dashed toward the nearest exit. Screams rose from behind him as the alabaster jar was knocked over and the marsh-puppeteer released to cause the havoc that was in its nature.

Two squads of the dwindling Anlūki surrounded Corajidin in a fighting, frenetic cage of metal and leather, hustling him toward the nearest door. Corajidin yelled in pain as a Selassin warrior-poet opened his cheek with her lotus-headed hammer. He broke, and left his guard and Wolfram to fend for themselves. Corajidin sprinted through the door, slammed it behind him, and barred it so nobody could follow.

Face stinging, the taste of his own blood in his mouth, Corajidin dashed up the stairs. There was the sound of pursuit from down corridors. Shouts. Pipes and whistles. Slamming doors. He fled the terrible noise behind him, desperately hoping the qadir had a path that led through the mountains and back into the city, where he could make for a place of strength.

Corajidin stumbled into a secluded stone garden. It was a lacy thing of carved fretwork screens and marble domes, encompassing slender platforms of red stone that radiated out from the mountainside. A wind-skiff waited at the end of a long, slender finger of stone. Sobbing with relief, he trotted toward it, already out of breath and weak from his exertions.

He reached out to open the gate when he heard a mad giggle. Corajidin drew his sword, and shrieked as sudden pain flared in his wrist. He swung his sword in a shallow cut, only to see a fountain of blood where his hand used to be. The hand still gripped the sword as both hit the ground. The pain was incredible. Every exhalation an incoherent mewling, more like the sound of an animal than a rahn of the Avān.

"Surprise," came a hard voice from beside him. Corajidin flinched, curled around his pain. He craned his neck to see who addressed him. At first it was a silhouette, stark and dark and anonymous, against a sky, pale and carefree blue, all around. Then his watering eyes focused, and the features of Näsarat fe Roshana came into focus. A man stood by her, blond and unassuming, his innocent appearance belied by the weight in his eyes. *I know a dyed-in-the-wool killer when I see one.*

"This does not need to end in my death!" Corajidin said from between clenched teeth. Blood poured from the stump of his wrist, the pain incredible.

"It really does," Roshana replied. She flicked the blood from the blade of her well-used shamshir. "But I'll not be the one to kill you, as much as you deserve it."

"Then who?" Corajidin spat. "If you lack the courage, then who? Your assassin, hiding there in your shadow?"

Roshana smiled.

"That would be me."

Corajidin flinched and turned to the voice from behind him. Vahineh's dagger took him in the eye. The blade continued across his cheek, gouging part of his ear as he flung his head back. Half blind, terrified, Corajidin shouldered the smaller woman out of the way and ran for his life back the way he had come.

Vahineh pursued him. She stabbed him in the back and tore

clumps of hair from his head. Her screams curdled his blood. Tears streamed, mixing with the saltiness of the blood on his lips.

Corajidin tripped on the fur lining of his over-robe. He skidded, and slipped in the blood he had already walked through. Blinded in one eye, the world around him blurred with tears and blood.

He staggered to the edge of the skydock ramp. Teetered on its edge, arms windmilling for balance.

Vahineh caught up to him and stabbed and stabbed and stabbed with her slender knife. He screamed incoherently and grabbed Vahineh by the hair. And pulled her close as they both tumbled, out of control, into the cold and empty air.

"Knowledge is in the knowing that we know nothing."

—From *Principles of Thought*, fourth volume of the Zienni Doctrines

DAY ? OF THE 496TH YEAR OF THE

SHRĪANESE FEDERATION

Indris measured the passage of time through observations: thirst was first and foremost, its creeping demands interspersed with the waving and waning of dune shadows, the mineral sting of sand hurled by the wind, periods of heat and light, and obdurate blocks of dark and cold. The sky was sometimes a marbled blue that seemed an eternity away, then in its turn spangled with tiny points of fire that seemed close enough to touch. And always there was the wind through the stones, rising and falling in pitch, quickening and slowing, like and yet removed from speech.

Mari, Shar, or Ekko watered and fed him, his body reacting like an automaton to its most basic needs. Indris was aware of all that transpired around him, and reviewed events with clinical detachment. Arguments, singing, reproaches, reconciliations—and more than once, combat. Flashes of battle in the dark with mountain Fenlings, frozen moments of faces illuminated by orange firelight. Daytime struggles with bandits, or the orjini expelled from their tribes, to wander the trackless sands without tribe, or family, or the grounding of the familiar. None of these things roused Indris from his meditations. None of them alarmed him to the point of climbing down from the mountain of his mind. At all times he knew he was protected, for where was a man more safe, more secure, than surrounded by some of the most dangerous people in the world?

"Why are you here?" The stranger's voice was as gentle as the breeze, without the inflection of curiosity. Indris had watched as the man emerged from the megalith, even though Mari and the others did not react to him. He folded his robes about him as he sat, bleached sapling staff balanced across his thighs. Indris queried a part of his mind and decided that he had been sitting in the sand for six days. Indris looked about, but his friends were nowhere to be seen.

"Because I need to be here."

"No." And with that the stranger rose from the sands and walked among the stones, vanishing in plays of bent light and straight shadow. Indris thought about the question, and planted it as the root of the Possibility Tree, his answer dangling like fruit. Indris examined permutation, inflection, meaning, and metaphor, but there were no answers more fitting than the honest one he had given.

Another day passed. Indris glimpsed Mari for a long moment, her eyes staring, her lips moving, her hands on his face and in his hair. Then she, too, was gone.

"Why are you here?" the stranger asked when he returned.

"Because I choose to be here."

"No." The stranger rose to his feet and once more vanished among the stones. Once more Indris planted the question, and hung the answer, and sought insight among the branches, leaves, and twigs that joined the two.

After another day, the stranger took his place on the sand, legs folded, staff across his lap. Again he asked the question.

"Because I want to be here."

"No."

The next day, rather than answer the obvious with the obvious, Indris invoked the three Possibility Trees in his mind. He inspected them side by side, the one atop the other in a confusion of branches, leaves, and alternatives. None were wrong, but the whole was so discordant it was devoid of meaning, like trying to hear one voice in hundreds, or instantly see one word on a page. Only the trunk and the roots were clear and consistent. It was thought and speculation and expectation that made the question complex. There was little a person needed. Much a person chose, and more that a person wanted. When such things were unimportant, what remained?

"I am here, because I am."

"Yes." The man smiled peacefully, eyes clear amid the wrinkles at their corners. "Who are you?"

The Herald's words echoed in Indris's head. "That is not as important as how I am, or what I am." Indris lingered on the rest of what the Herald said, and added, "Or why I am."

The man's smile widened, and he nodded almost imperceptibly. "And why are you?"

The words had been laid out in his head in the Black Archives, almost as if the Herald had known the question was going to be asked. "I am the cause, and the effect, of questions, promises, and actions from a time few living can still remember. I am, because you were promised a light to guide the way."

"But do you know what it means?"

"I don't." Indris bowed his head in humility, letting the frustration pour from his limbs and into the sand beneath him. The admission felt good. Indris was about to deconstruct his mental frameworks and prisms.

"Yes," the stranger spoke softly. The word was almost a sob. He stood, and extended his hand to Indris. "Welcome, Näsarat fa Amon-Indris, to Isenandar, the Great Scholastic Library of Shrīan. I have been so very long waiting for you, and am glad you are come."

"And you are?"

"Who you expect me to be."

"You're Danger-Is-Calling, though it's one of many names given to you down the ages. Perhaps you'll share your other names with me, as I learn what I came here for."

"Only if you are unfortunate."

Indris paused for a moment, then followed Danger-Is-Calling through the ancient stones in the sand, circling and backtracking. Each stone was like a corner: When Indris rounded it, the world had changed, as if Isenandar were being built around them, or the illusions that had hidden it were being stripped away.

He stopped dead in his tracks. The dome of the heavens was brighter than he had ever seen it, the stars and the colored clouds of the Ancestor's Shroud more vivid. Eln hung low and glorious in the sky, a brilliant orb of sapphire blue, emerald green, and pearl white. The white swirled slowly, like clouds, with flashes of light blossoming here and there. And the mirrored floor reflected the wonder above, providing enough light that lanterns were unnecessary.

"Curiosity and the honest thirst for knowledge burn brighter than any lantern." The echoes of Danger-Is-Calling's voice rolled over the silence like a fog. "What need have we for such things, when here we light our own way?"

Columns marched in all directions, holding up the sky, or holding back the floor, depending on perception. Indris touched one, and his hand passed into it. Light shimmered around his fingers. It felt like dragging his hand through—

"Sand!" Light touched the silicate grains, tiny stars in their own right, cascading the light upward, downward, and outward.

With each double beat of his hearts, the illumination grew. Words flowed in the columns, then sentences, then whole pages of text in High Avān, Seethe, Maladhoring, and even the circular—no, the spherical—glyphs of the Time Masters' language, like orbs of spun toffee. There were other characters that Indris could only guess at.

He turned to Danger-Is-Calling, who spread his hands and lifted his face to stare lovingly at the testimony to knowledge that stretched around them.

"The Pillars of Sand, Indris. For all things we make, all the things we dream, and all the things we learn are based upon foundations that can shift and disappear from under our feet." Danger-Is-Calling looked melancholy. "Remember, my friend, that of all things that move through the world, we—seeking to change it for reasons that seem good and proper to ourselves—are the most imperfect, the weakest things of all. Nothing, no form, no substance, no shape, no opinion—neither love, nor friendship, nor hatred—is forever."

❈ ❈ ❈

"Will my friends be safe?" Indris asked. He knew it had been many days that they had waited outside, and it was likely to be many days that Indris would remain in Isenandar.

"I have brought them in here," the man said, his staff clacking on the floor as they walked. "Once you had become the way, and the door, it would have been inhospitable to leave them outside. They sleep, and dream, and take much-needed rest from the woes and turmoil they carry. You can see them at your leisure."

Indris nodded his thanks. "Do you know why I've come?"

"For music."

Indris opened his mouth to speak, then closed it again, thinking about the man's response. In *Climbing from the Top of the Mountain*, the Zienni Magnate Kobaqaru had said that knowledge is music, speaking to the heart and the head at once, persuading rather than forcing a reaction. Every piece of knowledge was its own composition, and would draw in, or send away, those who listened to it. There was no right or wrong: There was only music, and what a person took from it.

"Old music," Indris said.

"Then perhaps you will find your moment of perfect beauty."

"How do I find anything here?"

"There is nothing to be done, and nothing to do. What comes, comes, when you are ready to receive it."

"That doesn't help much."

The man shrugged. "Goals are sometimes only targets for us to aim at, while we learn more on our journey to missing."

"No better."

"Teachers give neither fact nor truth. But a teacher will point to facts, while the student learns truths for his or her self."

"You're not going to answer my question, are you?"

"I already have." And he smiled, and walked away.

Indris drew in a breath to dampen his frustration. All about him the Pillars of Sand glittered with the light of knowledge, glyphs making smooth progress from left to right, right to left, or up and down depending on the language. He looked down at his boots, where it seemed as if he were being held in the embrace of the Ancestor's Shroud. *All this while I've been striding among the stars, unknowing.* Indris lifted a boot, and the absence of his foot was filled with brilliant color reflected from the sky above. It was difficult not to smile in the presence of such beauty. Tension faded, releasing knots in his shoulders and stones in his mind. Form and thought moved more freely.

Alone again, Indris stretched, observing the seemingly unending procession of pillars around him. *"Take what you need, leave what you don't."* Femensetri had said that to him so many times as he was learning from her. *Would you say that here, sahai?*

Looking up at the pillar beside him, Indris absently tracked the rows of square Maladhoring glyphs. The sentence structure was archaic, and it took Indris a few attempts to think in the language he was reading . . .

> The mortal mind can grasp concepts to a degree, and can channel energy safely within the context of its own experiences and imagination. Generally, it is the fear of going beyond the familiar that causes failure in the use of the arcane science, for the mystics find themselves in an undiscovered territory for which they have no basis for understanding.
>
> The use of analogy and metaphor provides a framework within the abstraction, yet it is the abstraction that is the ultimate goal: the concept of manipulating energy without the constraints of what a person should do. There is only what a person can do. Let each person judge the right of their application of power according to mortality and ethics, but remember that Ĩa does not do so.
>
> Ĩa itself has a depth of understanding and a complexity of mental process—if one accepts the hypothesis that the mind and soul are inextricably linked, as demonstrated by the ability of spirits in the ahm to retain memories of their lives, and to learn and retain knowledge—that those who dwell on Ĩa do not. The only way for us to gain true insight, and to harness the breadth of our true capability, is to expand our context and our consciousness.
>
> To be more than we are, we must forget what we can do, and awaken what slumbers within: to go beyond our limitations and realize what can be done if we lose our need to exist only as we are, and not as we could be . . .

Indris read the last passage again, to ensure he had translated it correctly. He swore to himself, then swore more loudly at the man who had led him here. Like the teacher he was.

Here, in the encircling arms of the Ancestor's Shroud, in what seemed to be the center of the Pillars of Sand, was part of what Indris had come to find.

"Awakening," he breathed. The energy serpent within him shifted. Vortices opened like flowers facing the sun, and filled Indris with a sense of warm expectation.

✾ ✾ ✾

Indris read the works of brilliant minds until his own could take no more and his eyes burned from fatigue. He patted his stomach as it grumbled. There was no passage of time other than what his body observed by its needs, and Indris knew he could go for long periods with neither food, drink, nor rest. He had no idea how long he had tracked the knowledge he was after, moving from pillar to pillar and back again, the story growing more complete each time.

He admitted he would learn no more after the fifth reading of the same paragraph of Seethe characters. Part of his fatigue came from the constant changing of thought processes, from language to language. There were whole columns written in the imagery-laden and dreamy Hazhi'shi, something he struggled with, where one word could mean different things in the context of the words around it.

The library was filled with secrets, and haunted by its past. There were times when Indris felt eyes upon him. Heard whispers among the stars, or saw shadows moving between the columns. He called out, but nobody answered. Now there was a light in the distance, and Indris moved toward it. Set amid gentle hillocks of clover and violets was a towering ziggurat, bedecked with hanging gardens and water features. The fountains and waterfalls played a delicate melody that Indris found relaxing. He explored the ziggurat, moved from lighted room to darkened room, to scriptorium, to dining hall, to laboratory, to observatory, to rooms for the teachers and students. Most of the rooms were empty, but some still held the possessions of their former inhabitants. Indris wandered from room to room, idly flicking through sketchbooks, journals, and half-finished scrolls. Inkpots were stained and flaky next to dried brushes, the bristles falling free when Indris touched them. Musical instruments. The tools of carpenters, blacksmiths, and jewelers. Clothes millennia out of date from when the Avān had ruled an empire and a world.

Isenandar had been a city of learning, now hidden between folds of space and time. Now empty, except perhaps for the Nomads that abided in the corner of Indris's eye, or in their age-old whispers. Indris felt the presence of the students everywhere about him, the concentrated presence of vast intellects and growing power. Unlike in the Dead Flat beyond and about the library, Indris felt eddies of the ahm as it flowed through him. Changeling was quiet, lost in her own ruminations, her shape warm and comforting.

Indris felt for the bag of shards of Changeling's ruined blade. One of them felt different from the others; he drew it out, the metal oily, tinted with dark blood that would not wash off. Indris ran his finger along the raised pattern of the Emissary's blood and felt more keenly the disentropic taint, days after she had been killed. He coughed away the onset of tears, lost for a moment in grief for what his wife—for he could still not think of her by name—had become. Safer, and saner, to believe his wife had died years ago, when he thought she had, than associate her with the agent of the Drear that he had killed at Tamerlan. Changeling crooned in question; the faintest trickle of comforting energy flowed into Indris, helping assuage the guilt he should not feel. He had lost his wife years ago. He loved another now.

The messages in the pillars swam before his eyes. Indris stretched, and yawned. He was hungry, and he was tired, and he desired the company of friends. There was no absolute direction to anything in Isenandar, so Indris pictured Mari in his head and walked. Isenandar orientated around Indris until he was at the place he was. He knew his legs moved, the same way he knew his hearts beat and that he drew breath, yet the sense of movement without him going anywhere was unnerving.

The *Wanderer* was canted on her damaged landing gear by a wide pond. The star-shot sky was pale, hued by a fake dawn by *ilhen* lanterns shedding light where none was needful. His companions sat in an oasis, on spongy clover, surrounded by a ground covering of native violets, palm trees, and trees laden with figs, apples, and persimmons. Mari caught sight of him, yelled a greeting, and dashed across the grass to throw herself into his embrace. They kissed, and walked together back to the makeshift camp.

"I don't remember how we got here," Mari said nervously. She looked up at the unwavering sky. "And I've no idea how long we've been here either."

"What do you remember?"

"You, sitting in the sand, still as a bloody stone," Mari grumbled with real anger in her tone. She elbowed him in the ribs, almost hard enough to hurt. "I fed and watered you for days. We were attacked by the Fenlings, and some of the orjini. Belam and Sanojé wanted to drag you aboard the *Wanderer* and leave, but the rest of us decided to give it time."

"How long?"

"Nine days or so. Then we were here, wherever here is."

"Where have you been?" Sanojé asked petulantly as Indris and Mari arrived. "Is this the Pillars of Sand? There's nothing here! How can I learn if there's nothing here?"

Indris remained silent. Though the *Wanderer's ilhen* lanterns paled the stars above and below, he could see the long line of columns that marched away beyond the oasis, all equidistant from each other, as the trees were. Everywhere is its own center. But Mari, Shar, Ekko, and Belamandris nodded at Sanojé's sentiment. Curious, Indris went to one of the trees and touched it, to find that it, too, was made of sand and the knowledge of trees, rather than wood. The oasis was exactly that for his friends, a place of respite, something their assembled minds had built and felt at ease in. Indris focused his mind, and to his eyes the trees lengthened, straightened, and became the columns he had become familiar with.

"I'm sorry I can't explain more, but I don't have many answers about this place," Indris said. "Have you tried exploring?"

"We've not been here all that long, I don't think," Belamandris said. "Long enough to set up camp and dress our wounds—"

"And get hungry," Ekko said. "Thankfully there are fish in the pond."

Shar playfully ran her fingers through Ekko's mane, something he tolerated with a wide-eyed stillness. "Poor baby. When he saw all the fruit trees, Ekko thought he was going to starve!"

"There's what seems to be plenty of food and water," Mari said. "But how long are we going to be here? Morne and the Immortal Companions will have reached the Sēq long before now."

"We're useless here," Belamandris added. "We need to get to where my father is, and help stop him before he goes too far. Kasra won't scruple to fuel Father's ambitions, and the Emissary . . ." He looked apologetically at Indris, who had felt his expression harden with the memories of what his wife had become. "Sorry. I didn't think."

"It's not your fault. She was what she was, and there's no changing that."

"Even so," Sanojé said, "we can't wait here. It's been nine days already. The Asrahn can cause a lot of damage in nine days."

Shar suggested they eat, and talk later. They parceled out what remained of the food they brought with them, supplemented by fish and fruit from the oasis. Though the conversation was kept light, it was clear to Indris that his friends—including Mari—were not keen on staying. Sanojé was the worst, the tiny witch anxious at her lack of connection with the ahm, and the temporary loss of her abilities. After their meal, Indris took Mari by the hand and led her away, where they could talk in private.

"We don't want to stay," Mari said. "But neither can you leave. What are we to do?"

"What do you think is happening out there?" Indris asked.

"Very bad things, most likely."

"Things you can stop?"

"Most likely."

Indris chewed his lip, staring at the woman he loved. *I am so close to the answers we need . . .*

"There's more happening in the world than what I'm doing here," he admitted.

"True enough." Mari took his hand and massaged it, her thumbs working the skin, relaxing him. "But what you're doing here is important. For all of us."

"Anything we can do to stop your father is important, Mari. And this isn't a fight anybody can win on their own."

"Not even the great and powerful Indris?" Mari smiled, and he relaxed. She stepped closer to him, placing his hands around her waist in an enforced hug. She nuzzled his neck, her breath warm. When she spoke, her voice resonated on Indris's skin. "Not even the Dragon Eye? The Tamer of Ghosts? The Prince of Tides?"

"You forgot the Knight of Diamonds," Indris murmured. He kissed her deeply, which turned into hungrily, his fatigue forgotten. They parted, breathing deeply.

"We have to go, Indris." Mari's voice was hoarse with desire. She felt good in his arms—strong, and warm, and soft in the places he liked.

"Do you have to go now?"

"I think I've some time to spare . . ."

✻ ✻ ✻

The two of them sorted through the pile of discarded clothes, and dressed. They shared lopsided grins and few words.

As they returned to the others, Indris asked Mari, "Where will you go?"

"Depends. With the Water of Life we can lift off and get the *Wanderer* east, out of the Dead Flat. There, Sanojé will be able to mindspeak the other witches to find out what's been happening. If we're lucky, Father doesn't know about Belam's defection yet. It'll kill him, Indris. Father loves Belam so much . . ."

Indris held her hand as they walked, and discussed options.

"If the Sēq have decided to join the party," Indris said, "then there's a good chance we can stop your father."

"Let's hope so, love." Mari gave a sorrowful smile. "I don't want my father dead, but he can't be allowed to cause any more harm to our nation, or its people. I'll do what needs to be done, should it come to it."

They said their good-byes, in words, gestures, and caresses that would have to last them until they saw each other next. Saying farewell to his other friends was just as heart wrenching, but the tears were ones of love, and nothing to be ashamed of. Belamandris hugged Indris, and whispered a promise that he would die before allowing any harm to befall Mari. The two men nodded to each other, and Indris wondered at the friendship they might enjoy.

Indris stood by the side of the pond as the *Wanderer* took to the air, *ilhen* light clinging to her lines. She circled upward, set a course, and then vanished into a curtain of wavering light. No sooner were they gone than the oasis disappeared, the trees transformed into columns of lore, and the sky and the ground mirrored each other.

A deeper understanding and awareness of Awakening had started to unfold in Indris's mind, the paths that Ariskander had opened in Amnon widening with the new knowledge.

But there was more.

Fatigue tugged at Indris's limbs. He emptied himself of thought and the need for action, and allowed Isenandar to flow around him until he arrived at the dormitory. There were hundreds of balconies on a sweeping ziggurat backdropped by a sea of stars. The scent of lavender and vanilla was soothing. Indris entered the first room he found, and collapsed on the bed. He doubted the previous occupant, millennia dead, would mind very much.

As Indris dozed, there came the sound of a plaintive, mournful song: one of profound loneliness and regret. The song plucked at the strings of loneliness Indris had known in Amarqa, the sense of deep isolation and stillness that he had hated. He lay there, letting the sadness wash over him, feeling part of it, as he drifted away to sleep.

"WE ARE, AND WE DO, OR WE DO NOT. LIFE IS AS SIMPLE AS THAT."

—From the Nilvedic Maxims

The *Wanderer* soared through clear, cold skies, eastward over a high plain in the Mar Ejir. The snowline stretched thick fingers down the mountainside, touching mountain ponds and rivers. Giant mountain harts, goats, and ponies grazed below, and the smoke from a lonely homestead plumed from a lopsided chimney. A trapper, shaggy in her furs, looked skyward and waved as the ship flew by.

"We've been gone how long?" Mari asked Sanojé with disbelief.

"It's been sixteen days since we arrived in the desert," Sanojé affirmed. "Asking me a third time isn't going to change the fact."

"I count three days searching, then nine days waiting in the desert for the stranger to arrive," Belam said. "I don't remember us waiting another four days in Isenandar."

"None of us do, Belamandris," Ekko said. "But the world has spun on, regardless of whether we were aware of it or not."

The witches had been nearly hysterical when Sanojé made contact. It took a couple of hours, with Sanojé mindspeaking different witches, to get a comprehensive, if manic, account of what had happened since she and Belam left Avānweh.

"The nation is in an uproar," the Tanisian witch said. "Elonie, who was the closest thing we had to a leader, is dead. Best I can understand, the Asrahn's made good on his pact with the male-gangers for access to the treasures in the Rōmarq. There was a massacre at the Qadir Selassin—"

"Massacre?" Mari snapped. "What happened? Is Vahineh safe?"

"If you'll let me finish?" Sanojé replied. "Apparently there was a fight between the Asrahn's forces and some elements of the Federationists. There are also a number of people gone missing in the subsequent violence in the capital. One thing that is confirmed is that the last of the Selassins, Vahineh and Martūm, are dead."

Mari sat, deflated as the witch related the rest of what she knew: How there had been some sudden and dramatic reversals in those who had not enthusiastically endorsed the Asrahn's policies. Of how some of those who were once loyal to Corajidin had crossed the political floor, their faith lost. That other factions were walking away from their self-serving neutrality and choosing sides away from the center of the floor. The Arbiter-Marshall and the Secretary-Marshall have officially declared this to be a time of change, but neither of the predominant factions could even agree on that.

None of it changed the fact that Vahineh was dead. After everything she had endured, and their escape from Tamerlan, she had died in her own qadir! "How did Vahineh die, Sano?" Mari asked.

Sanojé's grin was wicked. "Trying to kill the Asrahn. Don't shake your head; that's the story! Vahineh was found dead, with a knife clutched in her hand, covered in your father's blood. Apparently

Wolfram, as well as a couple of the Anlūki, were chased away from Vahineh's body as they were retrieving the Asrahn's. Nobody knows if the Asrahn's alive or dead. There's talk among the witches that he was critically injured, and taken back to the Rōmarq."

Mari settled back against the rail, the hammerblows of grief painful in her chest. Vahineh dead, and her father's fate unknown. *It was always going to come to this, wasn't it?* But knowing it, versus feeling it, was quite different. *Are you truly dead, Father, or will you rise once more to plague the nation?*

"Sayf-Näsaré fa Ajomandyan, the Sky Lord, has been appointed the Arbiter of the Change," Sanojé reported. "But the opposing faction is refusing to recognize his authority, as he has known Federationist sympathies. The Imperialists are calling for a vote on who should be Arbiter of the Change."

"That's a decision for the Magistratum to make," Belam said. "They'll ratify old Ajo in the role. Avānweh's his city and he'll keep the peace."

"Where do we go now?" Shar asked into the depressing silence. In lieu of Indris, both Shar and Ekko turned to Mari for a decision. Belam and Sanojé kept their opinions to themselves, but Belam had sworn himself to Mari, and Sanojé to Belam.

"We've no armies of our own," Mari said. "Individually we'd not make much of a difference. So let's go somewhere where we can. We go to Avānweh, and pledge ourselves to the Arbiter of the Change."

✳ ✳ ✳

Shar circled the *Wanderer* around Avānweh, the galley buffeted by the howling mountain winds. Smoke rose from many buildings, and there was a thick layer of pale ash in the Bone Gardens, where the powdered remains of the dead were planted. The streets were dotted with color where banners had been ripped from homes and trampled underfoot.

The harbor was virtually empty, and the skies patrolled by armored gryphons and wind-ships flying the colors of the Näsaré. Two squads of gryhon riders intercepted the *Wanderer* on approach, their shadows wavering on the deck as the great beasts hovered above, sunlight glinting from spear points and armor. The gryphons moved into tight formation, the closest of the armored riders pointing in the direction they wanted the *Wanderer* to go. They had not traveled far before another squad of gryphons dropped from high above, wings snapping as they slowed their descent to fly alongside and above.

Mari bit back a yell as two of the riders swung their legs over their saddles, and dropped almost three meters to the deck of the *Wanderer*. The two landed with the clash and creak of armor. They were tall and lean, dressed in cropped coats, with leggings buckled over their trousers. Both carried shamshirs, short recurved bows, and heavy spears with disconcertingly long blades. The two Sky Knights lifted the eagle visors on their helmets to reveal Neva and Yago. Without their riders, the gryphons dropped out of sight.

"They'll be fine!" Yago gave them a casual wave. "No doubt happy they don't have to carry us around the sky all bloody day. Truth be told, those damned saddles could be more comfortable."

"Whine, whine, whine," Neva said, mimicking a flapping jaw with her hand. Though their smiles were warm, the siblings looked tired. Neva clasped Shar's and Ekko's hands in her own, as did Yago. Their appraisal of Mari, Belam, and Sanojé, however, was forbidding. "Have you come here to turn yourself in?"

"Pardon?" Belam asked. His hand drifted to Tragedy's hilt. The Widowmaker smiled at Neva, whose expression closed down. "We come in peace, if that's what you mean."

"Why, thanks ever so much for that!" Neva replied. "But no. I meant what I said, and I mean what I say. A warrant has been issued by the Arbiter-General for the arrest of any members of the Great House of Erebus . . . and others. I thought you'd come to make my life easy. You are going to make my life easy, neh?"

"Neva, Yago," Shar said. "Neither Mari, Belam, nor Sanojé are here as prisoners. We've come to pledge our support to your father."

"Little. Late," Yago retorted. His spear dropped fractionally into something not quite a fighting stance. "You know how it is."

Ekko glided forward to stand with Mari, enormous and lethal. Shar remained at the pilot's station, but Mari had no doubt where the war-chanter's attention lay. Mari flicked a glance at the other gryphons that hemmed them in, as well as the two wind-skiffs with their complement of archers that had joined the procession.

With a surprising calm, Mari unbuckled her weapons harness and laid her two swords on the deck, then stepped away. Belam almost choked in outrage, no doubt believing that they could kill Neva and Yago, then outrun the Sky Lord's forces. But what would be the point? *We came here to help the nation, not what our father intended the nation to be. We're far from in a prison cell yet, and there's much we can say to prove our cause.*

Ekko followed Mari's lead, placing his *khopesh*, bow, and quiver on the deck. Shar gestured to Yago to come and take her weapons.

"Seriously?" Yago asked. "You're going to make us arrest all of you?"

"We're not making you do anything, other than that you feel you have to do," Mari said. "We're not criminals. Trust me when I say that we can help."

"You may not have helped the former Asrahn in his most recent crimes." Neva lanced Belam and Sanojé with a glare. "But your brother and that bitch, among others, most certainly can't make that claim."

"Then that's something we need to discuss with the authorities," Mari said. "But we all came together, and we'll all go free together."

"Or not," Yago countered.

Mari hoped for the alternative.

✳ ✳ ✳

Hours passed in the relentless glide of a bar of light from the narrow cell window. There was little sound that filtered to them, for the gaols were in a remote part of the city, accessed by a warren of tunnels and ravines. From time to time the racket of strife reached them. Each time the guards tensed, ready for action, yet were never called to battle. When the sounds dwindled, they returned to their vigil.

"If somebody comes to take vengeance on us," Belam murmured to Mari, "we're not in the greatest position to defend ourselves. Good plan, little sister."

"Next time we're flying into the capital after our father tries to destroy the nation, you can decide what we do. Sound fair?"

"Sounds fair."

Stars had long since appeared through the window, with the first colored haze of the Ancestor's Shroud glimpsed at its edge, when Mari heard approaching footsteps. She nudged the others awake, so that they were all standing when Ajo, Neva, and Yago entered the gaol at the head of grim-faced Sky Knights. Ajo's face was dark with rage. He paced before the bars of their cell. Mari stood quietly before the fury that emanated from the Sky Lord, and hoped her brother knew better than to crack wise.

"Do you think for a moment," Ajo said, "that I have the time to worry about the likes of you?" He jutted his chin at Shar, and Ekko. "I've no grievance with the two of you, and you're free to go . . . No! No arguments. I want you out of this cell.

"As for the Erebus siblings and the witch, you will face charges for your crimes against the Shrīanese Federation."

"Would you care to enlighten me, Sayf-Näsaré?" Mari schooled herself to calm. "Surely I've proven I've nothing to do with my father's schemes?"

"How do we know what you're capable of?" Neva came close to the bars, and the two women appraised each other. "You've not been seen since you left the city with the rahns, and they were forced to march out of the Dead Flat by themselves! We were told that you left with the Widowmaker, the Blacksnake, and his son."

"I did leave with them," Mari admitted. She paused for a moment, memories of her incarceration painful. "Jhem and Nadir took me to Tamerlan, where I've been the prisoner of the Dowager-Asrahn since the beginning of the year."

"Convenient," Yago said from where he leaned against the opposite wall.

"Not as much as you'd think," Mari shot back.

"And we are supposed to take all this on your word?" Ajo asked.

Mari pressed her face to the bars, and spat at the old Sky Lord's feet. "When I was here last, I helped save your life. And Vahineh's. Before then, I defied my father at Amnon, and helped the Federationists thwart his plans. In the Dead Flat, I once more put my life on the line to protect Vahineh. I think I've nothing more to prove to the likes of you, Sky Lord. Believe me or not, but your prejudices have no place in determining my innocence."

"We should hand them over to the Arbiter's Tribunal for judgment and execution," Neva said.

"What Mariam says is true, Sayf-Näsaré," Ekko rumbled. "Every word of it. I fought at Mariam's side, watched her sacrifice. We lost . . . we lost close friends, yet never did Mariam's resolve to do right waver."

"We were there," Shar said, "when Morne Hawkwood and the Immortal Companions helped Mari end the Dowager-Asrahn's reign in Tamerlan. She'd been there since the beginning of the year, her grandmother's prisoner. You're wrong to accuse her when she's given so much, and asked nothing in return from a nation that should be forever grateful."

Ajo stepped away to confer with Neva and Yago. They spoke for several minutes, while Belam and Sanojé paced the cell nervously. While Mari had not been involved in her father's recent crimes, neither her brother nor his lover could say the same. Though they had come to Tamerlan to help Mari, and had offered their service to stand against the Asrahn, the truth was they were guilty of Ajo's accusations. One look at Belam's tense smile, and Sanojé's huddled carriage, told Mari that they knew things would most likely not go well for them.

Mari tracked the movement of the guard as he approached the cell door. He gestured for Mari, Shar, and Ekko to move forward. Belam gave a soft and unsurprised snort, and Sanojé glared like a cornered cat, but neither moved from where they were. Mari dashed back to her brother and hugged him.

"Don't give up, Belam," she whispered. "I'll find out what I can do to save you. Is there anything you can tell me that will help me plead your case?"

"None of the people we abducted are dead, Mari," Belam said in her ear. "I told Father that we'd hidden them away in some abandoned villas in Maladhi, that some had been killed on his orders. He had long abandoned a path I could follow. We hid those hostages away on a homestead in the mountains behind the Eliom-dei, safe from his impulses and hopefully far from his reach. They're under cousin Nima's protection. If the people in his care listened to what I told them, they'll all be safe and sound, right where we left them."

Mari's breath rushed out in a swell of relief. "Once we find the prisoners, it'll go a long way to establishing your innocence. Or part of it, anyway. Wish me fortune."

"Self-serving, perhaps, but sure."

The cell door closed behind her with a clanging finality.

Ajo led the way out of the cells. As they approached the threshold, Mari stopped. The soldiers around her clattered to an undisciplined halt, one of them bumping into her. He apologized profusely, and flinched as Mari patted him lightly on the cheek.

"You're free." Neva's sour tone made her opinion clear. "What are you waiting for?"

"My weapons, and those of my friends, if you'd be so kind."

"I really don't think—"

"Am I a prisoner?"

"No, but—"

"Am I being charged with any crime?"

Neva clenched her jaw. "No."

"Then my request stands on its merits. Weapons. Now. If. You. Please." Mari smiled insincerely. "Or if you don't please. I'll still have what's mine."

Ajo gestured and the weapons were returned. Mari buckled her weapons harness on, and bowed her head to Ajo as he gestured for Mari to leave the gaol. The Sky Lord led the way back to the roads and the rippled bowl of Avānweh below.

It was cold and dark outside, the wind sending litter rolling down the streets. Most of the city lights were out, whole sections that had once belonged to factional loyalists so dark it was as if a person had daubed the city in thumb strokes of black paint. The procession made its way down deserted streets, occasionally meeting squads of green-coated kherife, or nahdi flying the colors of the allied political factions that remained in Avānweh. Screams, shrill horns, and the sounds of conflict echoed from around corners, and up stairs, and from the terraces below.

"How long has this been going on?" Mari asked.

"Since the tragedy at the Tyr-Jahavān." Yago's tone was dejected.

"And what's my father to say about it all?"

"Nothing." Neva's ire was palpable. "Your father hasn't been seen since. We've been betrayed by so many of those we counted as friends of late . . ." Neva's smile was grim. "But at least your brother can atone for his crimes."

"What had Belam to do with any of this? He was in Tamerlan when we deposed our grandmother, and we've been at each other's side since."

"Be that as it may, Mari," the Sky Lord said, "Belamandris and the witch, Sanojé, abducted and murdered dozens of people on your father's orders. They must stand trial."

Mari placed her hand on the Sky Lord's shoulder. He stopped, scowling, but allowed his features to relax before he gazed at her with open curiosity. "My brother hasn't murdered anybody."

Neva shook her head in disbelief. "You're loyal, Mari. And please, despite what you may think, I don't dislike you. Your House, on the other hand, is a different matter. The Erebus can't be trusted, and your beautiful brother is a murderer. He makes a mockery of the finest traditions of the daishäri. Why do you defend him, when as a warrior-poet yourself, you should be more outraged than I?"

"Thank you, Neva. Any rudeness I've extended to you has been poor of me." *I thought Roshana was trying to marry you off to Indris . . .* "But tell me. Is there a homestead, or villa, in the mountains behind the Qadir am Amaranjin? Somewhere secluded?"

Neva and Yago conferred for a moment, even calling in others of the Sky Knights. After a few minutes it was Yago who said, "Yes.

It sounds like there are several in the high plains and valleys behind the city. Why? They're generally the retreats of middle-caste folk."

"They're places you might safely hide people, neh? I take it these villas have access to water, and perhaps places to hunt, or even orchards, rivers, and ponds for forage?"

"Of course," Neva agreed. "There are also a few hunting lodges and the like, scattered on the far side of the range."

"Sayf-Näsaré?" Mari could not hold on to her zeal. "May we take a couple of wind-skiffs, or perhaps even a merchant ship, and investigate these places?"

"What are you playing at?"

"Please, indulge me. If I'm wrong, all I've done is been a fool, and wasted some time. But if I'm right, you'll rethink your opinion of my brother."

※ ※ ※

It was just after dawn when Ekko and Shar pointed to the homestead perched on the edge of a cliff, almost obscured by a thick copse of snow-laden trees, and the spume from a nearby waterfall. The mountains swept up and away behind it, and a long sloping plain led to a wide valley, dominated by a secluded lake and packed with bare trees. The curtained windows were backlit, casting pools of radiance onto the snow.

Neva guided the merchant ship down for a smooth landing, the Disentropy Spools and Tempest Wheels crackling, sending flashes of pale light all around. Mari inhaled the scent of pine on the cold air, and the wind moaned gently through the trees. A solid bar of gold appeared in the wall of the house as the door was opened. Nima and a squad of his Anlūki, though, not wearing their colors. People milled behind them, young and old and afraid, each of them armed.

The boarding ramp was lowered, and Neva and Yago led the landing party to the house. They carried their torches high, their colors and gryphon sigils plain for all to see. Nima came forward alone, weapon sheathed. He spoke with Neva and Yago for a few minutes, and then gestured for the Sky Knights to follow him.

Ajomandyan joined Mari, his large knuckled hands curled around the gryphon head of his walking stick. The old sayf contemplated Mari for some time before he turned his attention back to Neva and Yago, who were returning from the homestead.

The smiles on their faces told Mari all she needed to know.

Neva and Yago waited silently as the Sky Knights helped those Belam and Nima had saved from Corajidin's wrath. The people who passed by were in good spirits, well fed and cared for. They bowed their heads to Ajomandyan, who did a head count as they passed. When all of the freed captives were aboard, Ajomandyan and Neva compared their tallies of the freed. True to Belam's word, none were missing.

"My brother was telling the truth, Sayf-Näsaré," Mari said.

"Seems to be the day for it," Yago said.

"He will still need to be punished for the abductions," Ajomandyan said. "But given the risks your brother took in saving these people from your father's agenda, I'm inclined to show leniency."

"Perhaps there are Erebus that can be trusted after all?" Neva said, clapping her hand on Mari's shoulder as they boarded the flying ship.

Mari took Ajomandyan by the hand as he turned to follow his granddaughter. "Thank you, Sayf-Näsaré. I've little family left. I love my brother, and he is a good man . . . if misguided from time to time."

"At this point, Mari, we can use all the good people we can get." He walked up the ramp, cane rapping on the polished wood. "And call me Ajo, my dear."

"COURAGE AND COWARDICE ARE PRODUCTS OF NECESSITY."

—from *Truths* by Cennoväl the Dragonlord, Sēq Master,
explorer, and strategist

DAY 79 OF THE 496TH YEAR OF THE

SHRĪANESE FEDERATION

Agony came and went in step with consciousness. Comfort eluded Corajidin in those rare moments he was able to shift in his bed, pain inhabiting his face, arm, and back like the unexpected guest who refused to leave. Day blurred to night, then shredded into day, his world one of sweet oblivion and unwelcome awareness, punctuated by glimpses of those who loomed over him. Corajidin's mouth was thick with the aftertaste of lotus milk. The Emissary's potion fired his nerves as if nails were being forced along his veins. Spectral images hovered over him, monochrome shapes with coffin lids for teeth who wore ragged finery and clutched rotting wooden hoops around swirling vortices in their hands. The Soul Traders were ever at Corajidin's side, sculpted from shadows and the memories of their living years, patient, silent, and watchful. Invisible to all but him.

"What happened?" Corajidin mumbled through numb lips. Half the room was dark, the other etched with shadow. He shivered as he perspired. The reek of putrefaction and old sweat was cloying. There was little to be heard beyond the creak of tent ropes and the faint hum of wind across silk.

"Rest, my Asrahn," Wolfram said. He tucked the blanket under Corajidin's chin. His fingers were certain where they examined Corajidin's face, then down his arm. When Wolfram reached the forearm, Corajidin hissed with pain.

"My arm feels hot." Corajidin's arms were too heavy to lift. "My face is itchy and my back feels like it has been branded."

"You sustained some serious wounds and a worse infection, but you are beyond the worst of it." Wolfram's voice was little louder than a whisper. He held a drinking tube to Corajidin's lips and bade him drink more lotus milk. "Now all that remains is for you to rest, and to heal."

"Where are we?"

Mēdēya placed Corajidin's palm against her warm cheek. "After Wolfram found you, we brought you to the Rōmarq."

"I do not remember." The lotus milk filled his head with cotton wool, making his limbs feel deliciously warm and heavy. Corajidin caught faint movement about him, yet it was too difficult to keep his eyes open. "What happened?"

"Avānweh was no longer safe for us, Jidi. Your plan worked for the most part. The marsh-puppeteers were bound to those you doubted. But we were ambushed at the Qadir Selassin."

"He'll live?" It sounded as if Kasraman spoke from the bottom of a well.

"He'll live," Wolfram replied. "I'll fit the prosthetics tonight while he sleeps."

"There was nothing to be done about . . . ?" Mēdēya's voice was colored with concern.

"Had we a Nilvedic healer, access to a Sēq Differential Bath, or a Rejuvenation Frame, then perhaps yes." Wolfram sounded frustrated. "I've done what I can for him."

"Thank you, Wolfram," Mēdēya said. "You have saved the Asrahn's life."

"Just as I saved Thufan's," the old witch said bitterly.

"For how long?" Kasraman's tone was bitter. "We may have lost everything this time."

"Your father has united many under his colors," Mēdēya shot back. "The others don't matter. Let them squawk and threaten. The Asrahn has destiny on his side."

"If he remains Asrahn," Kasraman muttered. "There'll be a vote of no confidence in Father's leadership, followed by an investigation on events so public we couldn't bury them in gold if we tried."

"This is destiny," Mēdēya spat. "It has been foretold!"

"Has it? Personally, I've always hoped for more," Wolfram said. "The Asrahn has ever interpreted the Weaver's predictions to his own liking. I fear that we're seeing the truth of it now."

"What did they say?" Kasraman asked. "Father has never spoken of it in detail."

"I was there and heard the words. You will know power, though for the children there will be naught, for you are the harbinger of the Thrice Awakened, who will both do and undo all you strive for. There was more, much of which has come to pass. I fear we are on a slide downward from which there will be no return, if the remainder of the oracle's words are also true."

"Hardly the grand destiny he painted it to be," Kasraman said bitterly. "There is no mention of this Thrice Awakened? Nothing we can act against?"

"No."

"Why are you talking about me? What happened to me?" Corajidin asked, yet the words were a mumble in his ears as he drifted into darkness.

❋ ❋ ❋

Corajidin woke to a pavilion saturated by daylight. He blinked against the glare. The right side of his face felt strange, as if it belonged to somebody else. Right arm in a sling, wrapped in bandages from elbow to the swaddled club where his fingers would be. The skin itched abominably around a lingering numbness.

Mēdēya woke beside him. She brushed his hair away from his face with her fingers, then tiptoed across the rugs to the tent flap, and said to persons unseen that Corajidin was awake. Mēdēya returned to Corajidin's side with Kasraman, Wolfram, Feyd, and Tahj-Shaheh following. Corajidin's inner circle wore grim expressions as they stood in a loose semicircle around his bed.

"Are you in pain, Jidi?" Mēdēya asked solicitously. "Do you need more lotus milk?"

"I am well for now," Corajidin replied. He gestured to the bandage on his face and to his arm. "What happened to me and how long have I been confined to my bed?"

"What do you remember?" Wolfram asked.

"We had gone to the Tyr-Jahavān . . ." Recollection flashed in his mind, disjointed pieces of a puzzle whose edges did not fit together properly: Faces rose and fell, arms waved madly. Screams, shouts, wails, curses, and condemnations. The smell of blood. The flash of weapons the need to escape. Fight or flight meant flight. The wind-skiff bobbing in the free air the flash of a blade—

Corajidin choked on his own sob. He looked at the bandage club of his arm. From the elbow down his arm felt like . . . "Where is my hand, Wolfram?" Corajidin's voice rose to a shriek. "Where, by all the names of the dead, is my damned hand?"

"Asrahn, please—"

"No!" Memory sizzled again. Martūm dead and good riddance, but his sister . . . that cursed woman who thrust her blade into Corajidin's eye and dogged him stabbed him sliced him as he tried to run and she tumbled with him—"Where is Vahineh?" he yelled.

"Vahineh is dead, Jidi!" Mēdēya gloated. "Shame it was not done at my hands, but the result is the same. She who ended my first life has run the course of her own."

"Small comfort to me, Mēdēya!" Corajidin trembled with anger. Pain lengthened in him as his temper shortened. "Get out. All of you. Out. Now."

Corajidin struggled from bed. He took a knife and cut the bandages loose from his right arm. When the knife twisted on what was underneath, Corajidin tore at it with his left hand, with his teeth, shredding the bandages till they hung in tatters. He sat down hard. Jaw slack.

From a handspan below his right elbow, his arm was encased in blackened *kirion*. Were it not a grotesque prosthetic, Corajidin would have admired the artistry in the delicate arabesque engraving and the bands of galloping horses. Where his fist would have been was a horsehead chased in red gold and blackened gold. In dim light one could be forgiven for thinking it was a closed fist—a fist Corajidin would never open, the horse's carved mouth never capable of gripping anything. He lifted the mockery of a limb, noted it was not as heavy as it looked, until he slammed it down on the table and dented the wood. With care born of near hysteria, he removed the bandages from his face to reveal the angry red scarring, missing eyelid, and the orb of polished *kirion* that shone red, blue, green, or purple as he turned his head.

Corajidin was reminded of Thufan, his former Master of Assassins, who had died a traitor, driven mad by the death of his son and the wounds inflicted on him by Indris. Roshana had taken Corajidin's hand. Vahineh his eye. Retribution for the fathers Corajidin had taken from them. Yet unlike Ariskander and Vashne, Corajidin had survived.

Such was a good thing, for dead men rarely took any meaningful vengeance.

With gritted teeth, he struggled into a tunic and formal robe, after the abject failure of trying to buckle his trousers. He was tempted to call for Mēdēya to help him dress, but his face burned with shame at his infirmity. A sash was out of the question, so Corajidin cinched his robe with a belt before he donned his over-robe. The mirror told no lies: He was a hideous mockery of the man he had been. The sleeve of his over-robe went some way to masking his amputated hand, though there was nothing to be done about his eye. An eye patch would mask the damage, though it would also admit Corajidin was ashamed—something he was too proud to do. The ruination of his body, first with his illness, now with his disfigurement, marked him as a survivor. It was how he would have the world see him, despite the tears he wiped away from his one good eye.

Corajidin strode from his pavilion with as much pride as he could muster. Mēdēya waited outside, and stood straighter as he emerged into the light of day. To her credit she did not flinch when he glared at her. Corajidin strode past her as he made his way to the command pavilion. It was the largest pavilion in camp, bustling with senior officers, their adjutants, and couriers. Iphyri patrolled the camp with their Jhé-Erebon, armed and armored. Wind-ships hovered low in the sky, hulls lit by flashes of arcane lightning.

Corajidin noted those among his officers who reacted to his injuries, mostly junior officers, relatives of the sayfs seeking advancement. Feyd rested his eyes on Corajidin for a few seconds, but his face betrayed nothing. Tahj-Shaheh gave his wounds barely a glance, so intent was she on a thumb-high sheaf of reports. Feyd pointed a well-used long-knife to places on the map.

"The Wives of the Stallion were on a long patrol to the south, and noted a force coming through the woods that run along the northern foothills of the Mar Silin. They did not engage. As best they could tell it is a small force, mounted warriors, and some animals of war, keeping to the woods to mask their passage. The Wives estimate somewhere between fifty and one hundred all told."

"Pashreans?" The memory of a dream flashed in Corajidin's mind, of Nomads in the phantom armor of the Awakened Empire, boiling like mist.

"We don't know enough about Pashrean forces to make a judgment."

"Send the Jhé-Erebon back," Corajidin muttered. "They are to take a witch with them so we can learn instantly what they know. An attack from the south is not something we had planned for."

"There's more. I've a witch in Beyjan and another in Amnon, spies hidden among the staff of Teymoud's merchants. The Rōmarqim are on the move. Heavier units are traveling the Southern Trade Road, and by ship up the Anqorat. Lighter units are using the Fandra Road, from Beyjan. They'll doubtless collect other Rōmarqim units as they progress, from Ifqe and the smaller towns. I'd expect to face armies approaching from the river, the roads, and out of the wetlands itself."

"Your recommendation?"

"Asrahn, we're not experts in wetlands fighting. Our troops are more heavily armored, and we've a sizable force of cavalry, and the Iphyri. I suggest we withdraw from the wetlands and prepare on solid ground that is more to our advantage. Fortify Fandra and leave a mobile force here at the compound. We can install the siege weapons the College of Artificers has provided, and use the storm-cannon on the wind-ships as mobile artillery."

"Very well. However, I will not abandon the Rōmarq and its treasures lightly." Corajidin calculated speeds and distances in his head. An army could only effectively move at the speed of its slowest units. "How long until the enemy arrives?"

"Twenty days?" Feyd surmised. "Perhaps less. Were I them, I'd send light infantry on ahead to harass us as much as possible. I'd also try and stop our work in the ruins, and claim anything I could for my own war effort. They may even be in the vicinity."

"Who are we likely to face?" Mēdēya scrutinized the map.

"The Great House of Bey for a certainty," Tahj-Shaheh said. The corsair took a sip of her coffee and grimaced. She tossed the dregs into the tramped earth. "Reports have confirmed that Siamak and his son, Harish, are in now Avānweh. They've some quick flyers there that will get them here in time for the ruckus. Indera, the Poet Master of the Marmûn-sûk, has command of the armies, but Knight-General Maselane—Roshana's Master of Arms—is on his way to join her, along with the Lion Guard, Roshana's Whitehorse Cataphracts, and Bensaharēn's warrior-poets. I'd not be surprised to see more of the Nāsarat's colors join in. The Sûn are too far away to add value, and we've all the Selassin colors we're likely to get, now that there's nobody left to lead them. Indeed, we lose what we have."

"Have our own people take command of the Selassin windships, and other units," Corajidin ordered. "I'll not lose them to any qualms of conscience now."

"How accurate is our intelligence from Avānweh?" Mēdēya asked.

"It's reliable. Nix remained behind," Kasraman said, arriving with Wolfram and Ikedion, the walrus-like Atrean now in command of the witches, in tow. "He's using the ban-kherife to nullify as many of your influential opponents as possible, and the huqdi, Erebus forces, and the Soul Traders to—"

"I thought I was clear that we'd not assist the Soul Traders!" Cora-jidin snapped. "We'll not hinder them, but we're not to engage them."

"Nix has a relationship with them, through his father, Rayz." Kasraman's lips quirked in a smile at Corajidin's expression. "The longer our enemies are embattled, confused, and busy with the chaos we create, the less time they have to act against us."

"Tell Nix to cease all engagements with them, or he'll soon find himself without colors to fly!" Corajidin went to point at the map, saw the blunt head of his prosthetic, and rather than change hands, thumped the thing on the map near the Lakes of the Sky. "Do we still have Erebus forces in Avānweh?"

"We do," Feyd said. "They've gone to ground for now, to avoid capture, and await orders. There are also another thousand or so of my Jiharim in the mountains to the north of Avānweh. We're expecting Rahn-Narseh's heavy infantry to arrive within days."

"Those forces can be used to take and hold Avānweh." Corajidin saw doubt in the glances his inner circle gave him, and each other. "Our objective remains the same: a Shrīan united for war, under one leader. This conflict was always going to happen, and now we can control when it does."

"If there's the need, the Mahsojhin witches, Wolfram, and I can ferry troops through the Drear," Kasraman offered.

Wolfram shook his head. "It's folly. We've used the Drear too much as it is and the things that dwell in it—things that have slumbered long, and by the grace of the spirits I hold dear, should have slumbered until after I'm rotting in the ground—are aware of us. Belamandris and Sanojé spoke out—"

"Both of whom are missing," Kasraman interjected.

"Who knows how far Belamandris's discontent has spread?" Mēdēya asked. "These, witch, are the voices you hold up as reason-able arguments to not use the Drear?"

"Mēdēya speaks true," Corajidin said. "There has been no word of Belamandris, or Mariam. Tamerlan has gone silent, and there has been no word of the Emissary. There is much we do not know, but much we need to do. Wolfram, we will use the Drear if we need to, and that is an end to it. Am I understood?"

"Of course, Asrahn."

"Very well," Corajidin said. "Wolfram and Ikedion, you will take what witches you need to get the Havoc Chair moved here and get it working. The same applies to any other weapons you have found. I also want everything you can take catalogued, crated, and shipped out. Sedefke's writings are in those ruins, I know it! Find them, no matter the cost. Go now. I will be more comfortable knowing our new weapons are in place and working well before the battle lines are drawn."

"Asrahn." Wolfram limped away, his staff sinking into the sodden earth with every other step. Ikedion waddled after, his sumptuous silk robes dragging in the mud. Corajidin pointed to Tahj-Shaheh.

"Crew the faster, smaller wind-ships with your better corsairs. And have a witch aboard each one. They are to keep an eye on the enemy advance both by river and by road. Send squads to patrol the marshlands and the rivers, also. The Rōmarqim do not have the same fear of the marshlands we do. They will also travel it faster. Let us not be surprised by their early arrival. Report back every four hours, no exceptions."

Corajidin scowled at the map. Fandra was good ground to defend, surrounded by the wetlands on three sides with access by river and two relatively narrow roads. Not enough solid ground for the Federationists, and whatever allies they had with them, to mount an effective siege. Their siege weapons would be airborne, and Tahj-Shaheh could take the fight to them long before they reached Fandra. Siamak's Rōmarqim would make good time regardless of how they approached, and Corajidin doubted they would make much use of the roads or river once they came close. Knight-General Maselane would likely use the marsh-knights in small squads, to cause as much damage as possible before the main force arrived. They would need to be stopped by those who knew the marshlands as well as they did.

"Kasraman? Speak with Kimiya. I want her people to harass the Rōmarqim at every turn. Slow them down, cull their numbers, whatever her people can do."

"Of course, Father." Kasraman chewed his lip in thought. "We could go further. The Malegangers hold sway across other races in the Rōmarq. The Fenlings, reedwives—"

"I have allowed myself to come to terms with Kimiya's folk, son. I will not have us treat with the other animals that live in this festering hole. Alliances now may prove inconvenient for us later on."

"As you wish. I'll speak with her."

Kasraman strolled from the tent. Corajidin wondered at the casual indifference with which his heir dealt with such monsters. *What alliances will you make after I am gone, Kasraman?* It was the kind of thing Corajidin's father, and the Dowager-Asrahn, would have done: They had not scrupled against using whoever, or whatever, was at their disposal to achieve their ends. Corajidin admitted to a level of ruthlessness: His soul was not without stain; the crimes in his closet made it hard to close the doors. Yet there were limits to the alliances he and Thufan had made in their time. No less red-handed, nor prone to acts of cruelty should the moment call for it, yet . . . cleaner. More comprehensible than the creatures Kasraman consorted with. Feyd and Tahj-Shaheh were people Corajidin could relate to, people of exoteric action, and thought that could be clearly understood.

"Feyd?" Corajidin said to his Master of Arms. "Have one of the witches try to communicate with Tamerlan again. If they get no response, order as many squads of soldiers as you think best through the Drear, and find out what happened. I would have Jhem and Nadir at my side for what we're about to face, as well as Belamandris. Advice from those of a more secular bent would be advantageous to me."

"Your will, Asrahn." Feyd remained at Corajidin's side, delegating the mission to one of his Jiharim captains.

"Once you start this fight, Jidi, the options for trade conquest the merchants have advocated will be harder to achieve." Mēdēya held up her hands to forestall Corajidin's protest. "I'm not disagreeing with you, my love. Once we're at war, trade will effectively grind to a halt. We've marched together on this road and I believe that the Avān should return to conquest by steel, not conquest by gold. But the point needs to be made that Teymoud and his political allies will be harder to deal with after this."

"Feyd? Tahj-Shaheh?" The two commanders glanced at Corajidin as he called them by name. "Tell me honestly. Can you defeat our enemies when they come for us here?"

"From everything we know about the forces against us, yes," Feyd said. Tahj-Shaheh nodded her agreement.

"Then I care little for what Teymoud and his peddlers think, say, or do. We will crush our enemies in the open, and the people of Shrīan will fall in line behind us when we continue south to destroy Pashrea." Corajidin gazed at the map and smiled. "The Emissary was right about one thing. There can be only one Mahj."

25

"KNOWLEDGE IS NOTHING WITHOUT THE INTELLECT
AND THE IMAGINATION TO USE IT, AS WELL AS THE
RESTRAINT TO KNOW WHEN NOT TO."

—From *The Polemics*, by Sedefke, inventor, explorer, and philosopher
(264th Year of the Awakened Empire)

DAY ? OF THE 496TH YEAR OF THE

SHRĪANESE FEDERATION

Indris lay amid a sea of stars. The pillars of knowledge rose about him, both canted and straight, a bizarre sculpture of intersecting lines of architecture and thought.

"Do you have time to rest?" Danger-Is-Calling asked.

Indris yawned. There was no sense of time for him, other than the visitations of hunger and fatigue. "I think I understand the concepts of Awakening well enough, though only because I've gone through it. It's reasonably simple to map what I've learned here to what I've experienced."

"Then why do you wait?" Danger-Is-Calling leaned over Indris, blotting out the stars above. "Go to the House of Induction and test what you have learned! Awaken yourself."

Indris chuckled ruefully. *That horse has already bolted, and I'm hanging on as best I can.* "Not so fast. An Awakened scholar isn't something to be taken lightly. I'm here to learn so that I can save the rahns—"

"Awakened rahns are irrelevant," the man said flatly. "Awakened scholars are relevant. The pathways of Awakening make a scholar significantly more powerful than they would otherwise be. More powerful than any rahn."

"You sound like somebody I know," Indris mused. "The lives of people I care about, rahns who will at least try and do the right thing by Shrīan and the Avān, are relevant to me. Too many rahns have been lost, and more to follow unless I find the answer." Indris sat up. He ran his fingers through his tangled hair, rubbed his face to fight lethargy. "What I can't find here are the parts of the Esoteric Doctrines I need for myself."

"The Mah-Psésahen was abandoned," the man said. "It is dangerous. Reckless. It opens gaping doors in the mind best left closed. All who practiced it Fell, without exception. It is the gateway to madness."

"Sedefke said that power is never evil, or wrong, in and of itself. It is our application and motivation that makes it so. There are many things I've learned here that are no longer taught by the Sēq. Formulae for translocation without using the Drear, the specifications on how to build Torque Spindles, and the theory behind Destiny Engines. Healing techniques we thought lost to all save the Nilvedic scholars. Combat wards, battle formulae, Ancestor's teeth . . . There was a complete school of study on mapping and remapping the energy flows up the ternary stack. What happened for the Mah-Psésahen—for all of this knowledge—to be lost?"

"Not all scholars have the capacity to learn all things, Amon-Indris." Danger-Is-Calling leaned on his bent old branch. "Or to control them. For some it is a constant struggle, where every revelation is an epiphany. For others, it all comes too easily, the labor not recognized for what it is, respect for their powers in short supply. Those who grasped for the Mah-Psésahen were flawed, seeking only the power itself, without considering the consequences. Nature is a thing of balances, and nothing is given for free."

"But Sedefke—"

"Ah, Sedefke!" Danger-Is-Calling's voice was bitter. He throttled the staff in his hands, wood creaking. A frenzied expression overcame him. Memories of his other faces blurred over the one he wore. "The great and wise Sedefke, who unlocked all the secrets! He who had access to all the power in the world, yet never asked for anything in return. What kind of person does that? Has it not occurred to anybody to ask the simple questions about the man?"

Indris rose to his feet and ignited his Scholar's Lantern. The stars faded around them in the harsh sphere of its radiance, the shadows of the pillars casting all beyond them into darkness. Danger-Is-Calling stared wide-eyed at Indris. The other man's color was high, the whites around his irises vivid. Dipping into the ahmsah, Indris was blinded for a moment by the man's Disentropic Stain. It was a chaotic mess of energy flares, spirals, and frenetic, bobbing geometric shapes like paper boats cast in rapids. There was power there, insane power: a pent up dam that should have burst its walls long ago. Indris saw the shimmering formulae as they confined the man's stain, layer upon layer of binding. In that moment Indris saw the true faces the man had worn over the years, each face with a different name, anchored to the one mighty soul.

"It was the search for the truth of him that drove me mad, you know." The words shot out of Danger-Is-Calling's mouth. "The first of the Avān say they saw him when they awoke. But how, if they were the first? What came before the first? The last of something else? The reminder of a memory? A morality play in flesh?"

"Wait, I—"

"It was always Sedefke. The one who knew everything. The one who did everything, and led everybody. In the early years, we took for granted the wonders he led us to. Our minds opened like flowers and we drank knowledge like sunlight and rain. We loved him as much as we feared to lose him, to lose all he could show us. But to scratch the surface? Oh, to scratch the surface showed the cracks in the story. But by then we had traveled too far, and seen much, and heard the voices in our dreams and listened to their promises and—"

"Who are you?" Indris breathed.

"I am the danger that calls," the other man whispered as his color faded. It left his skin as a bleached expanse of white under the glare of Indris's lantern. "The danger that has always been and always will be. I am the error, the lesson, the warning, and the watcher. The captive and the gaoler. The ternary of disaster made manifest—"

"Who are you?" Indris yelled. He stepped forward and thrust his lantern closer to the man's face. Hundreds of faces flickered, cards in a deck being flung into the air. There was no order Indris could determine, only a procession of identities throughout history. He reached out to touch the man.

Indris's lantern went out. The stars above and below faded. The pillars of knowledge diminished, became black, then nothing as the last of the light died.

Danger-Is-Calling's voice, saner than it had been, echoed from everywhere. "We all of us wear masks, Amon-Indris. For some it is a thing of choice. For us, it is forced upon us by the will of others, for the world may not be ready to look beyond the swaddling of their prejudices to accept the hard truths.

"With knowledge comes expectation, and with expectation comes action, and action must only come when it can provide the most appropriate and beneficial reaction. Are you certain the reaction to what you find here will be beneficial? How can you be certain all that has come to pass is as it was meant to? But most importantly, how can you be certain that you can learn what you want to learn, and still remain who you are?"

"I do what I do because I must."

"You do what you do because it was how you were made."

Indris's lantern flared back to life as the stars ignited in the sky. The Pillars of Sand shone with glowing, flowing wisdom. Yet of Danger-Is-Calling there was no sign.

✳ ✳ ✳

Indris worked to the end of his endurance. He absorbed knowledge like a sponge, discarded old ways of thinking for better, more effective ones. Stored scores of new formulae in his head, and wrote copious notes of what he had learned. Awakening was only the beginning, like the dawn that illuminated a world much larger than night gave it credit for. When exhaustion overcame him, he slept where he lay, unprepared to spend a moment longer than was necessary in Isenandar. Indris hoped he imagined the upswell of whispered voices around him. The barely seen tricks of light and shadow in the semblance of people. Were they the tragic recollections of those who had studied here? Or were they the manifestations of Danger-Is-Calling's broken mind?

Navigating the pillars had become easier, and with it the access to the knowledge he sought. Sedefke's work on Awakening was written as a framework, the specifics submerged within other work. Indris surmised it was to ensure the person attempting the process understood the foundations of the power they were going to access, as well as the options, price, and consequences of it. As soon as the framework had become apparent—based on theories on reality and substance, filled with further theories on how Ïa existed in a physical, mental, and spiritual form—Indris found his understanding progressed rapidly. He had not misled Danger-Is-Calling when he admitted his learning came from having had the seeds of Awakening planted in him. Those routes between body, mind, and soul allowed Indris to map his learning of Awakening to his own experience: the elements of him that were the minerals of earth, the energy of fire, water as the conduit for vital resources, and the breath of life. The intellect sat around this construct, while the soul permeated everything and joined the one with the many.

There were a number of bloodlines that had been designed in the Torque Spindles to have a greater affinity with the ahm, and the consciousness of the world. Fifteen clans had been made before all others in the Torque Spindles of Avānis, on the isle of Castavān, a land where the Water of Life sprung from a small rock pool underground. Fifteen clans, not twelve as Indris had been taught. Sedefke spoke of the work to align each of the great clans with the totem spirits that were each a facet of Ïa's consciousness, and how he and his kin had guided the Seethe on how such a feat was done. Of them all, the greatest spirit was that of the phoenix, which comprised the concepts of renewal, time, resurrection, and immortality. The totem of the Näsarat.

Danger-Is-Calling's words about Sedefke were writ in sand: *We watched the Wind Masters come, my kin and I, though there were few of us not in communion with the mind of the world in those days . . .*

Whoever Sedefke was, it was the leaders of the twelve most influential clans of the Avān he led to their Awakening. Trained mystics, their bodies were already fueled by the ahm. Drinking the Water of Life was a communion, not a catalyst. Were mystics never to drink the waters again, their Awakening would never fade, for the flow of the ahm would sustain them. It was not until after the fall of the Awakened Empire, and the subsequent Scholar Wars, that rahns were no longer mystic-trained: the era of the mahjirahns over. The Suret had the framework of Sedefke's knowledge, but lacked the key pieces to fully understand it. Awakenings under their guidance were effective, yet disintegrated. They did not understand the way the energy coiled, causing the vortices to bloom in a specific order, strengthened by them, as they rose upward through the ternary stack. When the first rahns grew ill, doses of the Water of Life kept them alive. Indris supposed it had never occurred to the Suret that they did not completely understand the Awakening process, until it was too late. By then Sedefke was gone, Isenandar was gone, the great mahjirahns were gone, and the last Mahj was an uncommunicative spirit.

"Can you save them?" Danger-Is-Calling asked. Indris swore, his hand going to Changeling's hilt. He drew . . . to see once again the blade splintered to less than a hand length from the hilt. Danger-Is-Calling cocked his head at the dragon-headed sword hilt and said, "You have been past needing her for some time. Your soul is your weapon now."

Indris slid Changeling's hilt back into his sash. "Where've you been?"

"Here."

"Not helpful."

"Watching."

"Strange, and unsettling."

"You are the first to enter here since the witches and scholars both tried to batter their way in during the Scholar Wars." Danger-Is-Calling cradled his staff in his folded arms. "It was on that day that I locked the ahm tides inside Isenandar, hid her from the sight of petty minds, and the Dead Flat came to be what it is. I swore that no scholar or witch would ever again be able to force their way into what I had built.

"Though I have long awaited your coming, it was not until you bested the warrior of the Drear that I decided to allow you access. You have vast power, Amon-Indris, though your fear—"

"Why do you call me that?" *He saw my fight with the Emissary?*

"Because it is your name."

"My name is Indris."

"If you like." The other man shrugged. "Though it is like Ia only admitting she is alive when her face is touched by the sun. You have immense power, but your fear of it gives me a hope that I need to confirm."

"Hope for what?"

It felt like fingers were poking around Indris's head as they moved facades aside to expose the truth behind. Indris slammed layers of mental shields down, yet the sensation persisted. The pain of the examination grew until it felt like his brain was being squeezed against his skull. Pressure built, the bubble of his metapsychic abilities out of his control. Indris dropped to his knees. Heat started to build behind his eye and he welcomed it, yet it was extinguished by Danger-Is-Calling as soon as it started. He vomited from the pain. Watched as long streamers of drool escaped his lips to become blurred trails of silver gray that stretched to the star-dusted floor.

"Hope that you won't destroy us all with it," Danger-Is-Calling said. "Not like those who have come before. In the end your power will kill you before you allow it to harm the ones you love."

Indris groaned, rolling onto his side as the pain receded. He wiped the tears from his eyes, then washed his mouth out with water from his flask. "Was that necessary?"

"I needed to know the truth."

"You could've asked."

"You could have lied."

"Surely you knew before now?" Indris asked. "Why else let me in here?"

"I did not know. I allowed you entry out of curiosity, mostly."

"Now you know why I won't allow myself to become Awakened." Indris got to his feet and swept his arms out to encompass the Pillars of Sand. "Knowledge. Grain upon grain of it. It can be shaped, but any shape it holds is fragile. Each grain will last forever, will be used to different ends, but it's rare for exactly the same shape to be made twice.

"This is what I hope for! I hope to see the Sēq remember they were formed to light the way, not be the way. That Shrīan's leaders will see how delicate civilization truly is, and nurture it rather than destroy it. And I hope that the day never comes when I must choose to do a very great wrong for what was a very great right at a single moment in time. Because history tells us over and over that moments are fleeting, that change always comes, and that when all is said and done, our very great wrong is always a very great wrong."

"I know of wrong," Danger-Is-Calling said. "Such wrongs that you would never sleep again for fear of the nightmares. Guilt is something we share. It is why we are here in this place, in this time."

"Yes. I am driven by it. And thus I cannot ignore the possible consequences of my actions."

"And while you are driven by it you will always second-guess yourself."

"Better than having one guess and getting it wrong."

Danger-Is-Calling laughed. It was hesitant at first; then, as the floodgates opened, it became a deeper, richer sound that rang around the pillars. Indris smiled to hear it, for in the moment he saw the madness desert the other man's eyes, to be replaced by something if not peaceful, then closer than the alternative. The man walked to Indris and hugged him. "Thank you. It has been long and long since I have had reason to laugh. Or to hope."

"I think my time here is almost done." Indris gazed at the stars around him, at the pillars of knowledge where he would otherwise while away a lifetime. *Others are depending on me.*

"Yes," the man said, sadly. Indris cocked an eyebrow, wondering if the man was answering his question, reading his mind, or both. "Indris, I am trained in the Mah-Psésahen. There are few places it was ever taught, and every place is now condemned to history. I beg of you, do not look further. I have seen what is unfolding in your mind. Rather than seek the wisdom of others in this, hold to your own counsel. If you must allow these gifts to grow in you, I know you will use them wisely—but seek not the wisdom of others. Forge your own path.

"Perhaps then you will not make the same mistakes I did, nor cause the kind of suffering I did, nor become the apostate I once was. Sedefke did well when he trusted you."

"I remember nothing of it," Indris muttered. "My memories from the Spines were taken from me."

"I know not what the two of you shared, but I do recognize what he has done to your mind. The same techniques were taught to me to guard the worst of myself from myself—let alone others. But beware. The Sēq are playing a long game. They have known the agents of the Drear were coming for some time, and while they appear to lose some pieces along the way, they see the board clearly, and know what they want to achieve."

"I'm familiar, yes."

"Then know that you may have little choice in how much power you allow yourself," Danger-Is-Calling said. "When all is said and done, your life—like mine—was planned without your consent."

Danger-Is-Calling walked away, his staff rapping on the stars at his feet. Indris called out to his retreating back, "Will we meet again?"

"Before the end of everything."

Indris watched him vanish into shadows and distance. With a last fond glance at the greatest store of knowledge in the world, Indris gathered his meager belongings and walked in the direction of the gates of Isenandar. With each turn around a pillar, the library became less substantial. The stars in the floor and ceiling vanished first. Followed by the massive pillars, which shrank into the sand below. The hard floor became pliant, then sandy. Striding past a pair of canted stones, Indris stood on the windy expanse of the Dead Flat.

He turned. The entrance to Isenandar was still there, visible to him now he knew where to look. An open invitation, should Indris ever need to return. He was not sure whether it boded well or ill.

Indris stretched his thoughts to Femensetri, and found her in Amarqa along with Mari and their friends. Rather than risk traveling the Drear, Indris called up the ancient formulae he had recently learned, a cleaner way to cross the vast distances of Ia. Complex formulae unfolded in Indris's mind, informing him of the force required to warp the distance between what he had always previously thought of as here and there. He flexed the ahm, and a corner in the fabric of the world opened as here and there became one.

With a smile, Indris stepped through to Avānweh, where those he loved were waiting.

"WE DO NOT CHOOSE FAMILY. WE CHOOSE WHAT WE ACCEPT FROM THEM, HOPE THEY ACCEPT US, AND DO WHAT WE CAN FOR THEM WHEN THEY NEED US MOST."

—from *By Ship from the Shrine of the Vanities* by Pah-Näsarat fa Nehrun (496th Year of the Awakened Empire)

DAY 79 OF THE 496TH YEAR OF THE

SHRĪANESE FEDERATION

Mari leaned against the wall of the sunroom in the Qadir Näsarat. The glass doors and fretwork shutters had been closed against the wind, panels backlit. Small pedestals of firestones made the room almost uncomfortably hot. They were perched so high over the bowl of Avānweh below that no sound rose from the streets. The room smelled of warm wool and furniture wax.

All eyes were on the rahns, huddled in their over-robes beneath opulent silk blankets. They had wasted away since Mari had seen them last. She was reminded of her father, and the way he had seemed less of himself as the weeks of his illness passed. Yet to see the cumulative effects of the sickness displayed between one day and the next was horrific. Roshana and Siamak were frighteningly lean, honed down to the bare essentials of bone, muscle, and ashen skin stretched too taut. Nazarafine was the worst, her skin loose where opulent curves had been. Her jowls sagged, her eyes sunken in wrinkled orbits. She could barely stand without the assistance of her nephew and heir, Osman. Mari hoped the man was harder than he appeared.

The other heirs stood at the shoulders of their rahns: Siamak's daughter, Umna, who had her father's height and imposing presence, with her mother's delicate features; and Roshana's brother, Tajaddin, who wore the garb of a scholar and the demeanor of an ascetic.

"Our spies in Corajidin's camp report Vahineh was unsuccessful in her brave attempt to kill him." Ziaire swatted her palm with her steel-veined war fan. "Apologies, Mari, but I only give voice to what we all feel."

Mari waved Ziaire's apology away. Her father had skated perilously close to the rim of the Well of Souls so often, Mari wondered whether he could be killed. It was entirely possible he was an instrument of destiny, kept alive until his role in the drama was complete.

"What's done is done," Ajo said.

"Has Indris spoken to you, Mari?" Rosha said.

"Briefly. Femensetri and the other Sēq Masters took him away as soon as he arrived. We'd not the chance to say much."

"He wouldn't have returned without a solution," Rosha said hopefully.

"But whether it is the solution we want is a different matter." Nazarafine's voice was weak. She peered around the room, her eyes unfocused. Nazarafine patted Osman on the hand. "I have lived a full life, and my family is with me. If this is the end, I am content."

"Aunt, stop it!" Osman's eyes were large and damp. "We need you yet."

"Is it true that Anj-el-din had been helping Corajidin?" Ziaire diverted attention away from the sniffling Osman. "That she Fell, and became a servant of the Drear?"

"That's what Belam tells me." Mari related what Belam had told her of the Emissary's involvement with the Erebus. "We were there when Indris made an end of her."

"That must have been hard for him," Ziaire mused. "To have searched for so long—"

"It's not something we spoke of." Mari's voice, and the look she gave Ziaire, were steely. "No doubt when he wants to speak of it, he'll let us know."

"Indris did what was needful, no matter the personal cost, and there is honor in that." Bensaharēn presented an elegant figure as he crossed his legs, and sipped at his tea. He looked more a banker or wealthy merchant than the greatest warrior-poet in Shrīan. Mari smiled, for when she had met Bensaharēn's husband she had thought him a merchant with the mannerisms of a soldier.

Indris entered, Femensetri in tow. He came to stand beside Mari, his smile warm, kiss lingering. His mouth tasted of mint. She nuzzled into the circle of his arm. Femensetri rolled her eyes, yet kept any words she had to herself. The Stormbringer fixed herself a cup of black tea and laced it with wine, before taking her place in the middle of the room.

"The good news is we can save your lives," Femensetri said without preamble. "We can Sever you from your Awakening, and Indris can re-Awaken you—"

"If you decide that's what you want," Indris put in.

"Yes, if you decide that's what you want." Femensetri's tone was sour. "The process is not without its risks. None of you are in the best of health and Severance is difficult under ideal circumstances. We can't re-Awaken you until you regain much of your fitness."

"Why could not the Sēq do this before?" Ajo said. "You have been Awakening rahns for centuries. What has changed?"

"If I may?" Indris offered. Femensetri nodded for him to continue. "Awakening has always been a thing of rote and ritual. Most of the time, an Awakened rahn will select an heir and pass into that person on their death. Understand that when this happens, there are usually years, if not decades, of familiarity between the rahn and their heir. Almost always it's a family member who becomes Awakened, so there are many similarities. The predecessor guides the heir through the change, and remains with them for life as a constant source of knowledge.

"When a new rahn—such as Siamak—is Awakened, the Sēq follow an established process that has been repeated over and over. It's the difference between a painter creating original art, versus a person who traces artwork to make a copy. The tracer doesn't have the skill to create something new, but is adept at forging. When the rahns stopped taking the Water of Life, the original painting—the complex interconnections between body, mind, and soul in the rahns—was damaged. The Sēq do not know how to trace around what was damaged and make a painting similar, if a little different, from the original."

"And you can?" Rosha coughed.

"I can, and will," Indris said. The sense of relief in the room was palpable. Mari found herself smiling as the others smiled, laughed, or sobbed with relief. She felt the agitation in Indris. He waited for the noise to abate, before he continued in a gentle voice. "Understand that Awakening was never intended for those without mystic training. In the days of the Awakened Empire, every Mahj and rahn was a product of the Sēq, and spent much of their lives learning how to understand, harness, and channel power. You don't have this training, and without a lifetime of study, you never will."

"What are you saying?" Umna asked.

"I'm saying that an Awakened rahn, not trained as a mystic, will be reliant on the Water of Life for so long as they live. It must be taken regularly to prevent the kind of illness the rahns now suffer. And even then, their re-Awakening is not without risk."

"Which means we'll be reliant on the Sēq forever," Rosha finished. "Who've proven they're willing to keep such things secret, and withhold certain truths for their own purposes."

"Yes." Indris's one word fell to the ground, where nobody touched it.

"So we lose our power," Siamak said, "or we keep it, our health held hostage by the Sēq?"

"Yes," Indris replied frankly.

The silence that followed became aggressive. Femensetri stood unabashed amid the sullen anger. She offered no argument, explanation, or apology. Clad in her weathered cassock, she was the obdurate nature of the Sēq made flesh: something eternal, partially familiar, yet never truly understood.

"Indris, you've given us much to think on, and I thank you for your candor." Quiet as it was, Nazarafine's voice startled Mari. "If you can make me feel well again, I will take that as about the greatest blessing you can give. I will heal, and decide whether or not I want to be re-Awakened when the time comes. To be both dog and master at the same time for the rest of my life is something I need to reflect on. But I can rule my prefecture almost as well without my Awakening, should I need to. Indeed, perhaps only living with my own memories would be good for me, rather than having generations of experience in my head."

"Where nothing is ever new . . . ," Rosha added quietly. She looked to Siamak, who gave a brief nod.

Mari kissed Indris on the cheek. He turned into her and they held each other close. "I know," Mari said. "They need you."

"I need you."

"Later." She patted him on the chest, flattened the folds of his brown over-robe so he looked, if not respectable, less like a vagabond. "Come to me when you're done. There's much to be discussed with Shrīan's leaders, and other than our friends, nobody in the Teshri knows that you, or the Sēq, are in Avānweh."

Indris kissed her. Their embrace was not long enough. Mari let him go and he gestured for the rahns to follow him to the royal suites, where they could undergo their Severance in comfort. Her hearts swelled with pride at what he had done, what he continued to do, for the people he was sworn to protect.

Do this thing, love. Save the rahns, so that I know there is even the faintest hope that we can recover from my father's malcontent.

* * *

Two hours passed without word from Indris. More of those allied to the Federationist cause had arrived over the past half hour, until the high sunroom of the Qadir Näsarat was filled to bursting. Tajaddin opened the folding doors, adding the space of the larger salon so people were not cramped. The senior voices of the Federationist faction had come, as had the leaders of those parties who believed a safer future lay in their shared direction. Dozens of people milled about in a riot of color, the cacophony of their voices making it so people needed to lean in close to be heard. It lent the gathering a misleading intimacy.

Chairs and couches had been set in a semicircle that faced inward toward the heirs of the rahns, and the nominated heads of the political parties. Ziaire's presence as head of the Peace Faction was no surprise, her drive for harmony sometimes financed by the wealth of secrets and scandal at her disposal. Ironically the Unity Circle had no leadership to speak of, and was represented by four people who argued more than they agreed. Mari was most surprised by the presence of a sumptuously garbed Teymoud. When questioned why the

Trade Consortium was present, the gray-skinned merchant sayf had replied that he saw no future with an Asrahn who would kill markets, rather than win them.

"My brother and Poet Master Indera are marching on Corajidin," Umna said. "Though we know the Rōmarq better than any others, we're still hopelessly outnumbered! The Asrahn has invaded our prefecture with soldiers, witches, and the alchemists and artificers have made weapons for him we can't match."

"We're a number of days away from any conflict, but must be careful what we do and say," Danyūn, the Näsarat Master of Spies, replied. "Nix and his ban-kherife are active in the city. To be safe, I assume he's a witch with him, and in regular communication with the main force in Fandra."

"Nix is a ruthless little psychopath," Ziaire said. "He'll have gone to ground, but will have his contacts among Chanq's criminal organization. My houreh will find him."

"It'll need to be soon," Belam said. "Nix can cause a great deal of carnage for one mad little man. He did it at New Year's with his daemon elementals, and he'll do it again. We'll need to time his capture carefully, so as not to alert my father."

"I can help," Sanojé offered. "I know Nix, and can cast a seeker hex to locate and track him."

"You find it so easy to betray the man you once served with?" Umna jibed. "You change masters faster than many change their sheets."

Sanojé narrowed her eyes dangerously, though it was Belam's deadly poise, the way he tapped Tragedy's hilt, that alarmed Mari more. Umna smirked.

"I'm only saying what we all think." She shrugged. "But it seems you've managed to trick the others into—"

Ajo rapped his walking stick on the floor. "Enough, Umna! Are you the Asrahn, to have abandoned sende? Pah-Belamandris and Pah-Sanojé are of the royal-caste, which in and of itself demands your respect; that you are a rahn-elect does not give you the right to disrespect them.

"It was the Widowmaker and Sanojé who saved the prisoners from whatever fate Corajidin had planned," Morne added. Beside him, Kyril voiced his agreement. "They led the rescue party to where the detainees were being kept for their own safety. The hostages were well cared for, and able to defend themselves if the need arose. I've come to respect these two, just as I respect Mariam."

"Don't judge them by their father's actions," Ziaire said. The smile she bestowed on Belam was radiant enough to cause Sanojé's hackles to rise. "Belamandris, Mari, and Sanojé stand to lose everything by siding with us. Give them the credit they're due."

Umna looked sullen. "I will leave it be for now, if such is the collective will. But I'm not convinced of these newfound loyalties to our cause. So instead let's address our inferiority in the field. It's my brother who marches on the Asrahn. My lands that are threatened. The Teshri has done nothing to censure Corajidin over his gross misconduct, and now we are on the brink of war!"

"We have an advantage Corajidin does not expect." Kembe's voice was a deep velvet rumble, the High Patriarch of the Tau-se prides massive in his armor of layered leather, felt, and bronze. "The Sēq have come to aid us, and will prove a valuable asset against Corajidin's mystics. Morne Hawkwood and the Immortal Companions are our allies, and Indris has returned from the dead. I'm sure that last will unsettle Corajidin somewhat."

"But do we have the Sēq?" Neva asked. "Or is it only Indris?"

Voices raised in debate. News had spread of the Sēq's duplicity in the rahn's current state. Faith in the exiled order was low on the ground. Though some might trust Indris and his reputation, there were those among the Teshri who remembered recent events, would rather have naught to do with mystics, and were quite happy to share their opinion.

There were few points of solidity. The heirs were ignored for the most part, considered too young and inexperienced to add any value. Tajaddin was given some deference for his lineage, and his Zienni training. Ziaire and Ajo were the mountains about which the clouds gathered, with Teymoud rising in their shadow. Maps were unrolled. Distances, supply lines, and travel times were calculated. Military strengths and weaknesses were compared: The caliber of the Masters of Arms was debated, Maselane's military genius over Feyd's unorthodox tactics and Tahj-Shaheh's style of raid and run that had served her well as a Marble Sea corsair. Rahn-Narseh was discussed and discounted: the Knight-Marshall had been absent so long with her illness it was assumed she was bedridden, or dead.

Belam and Sanojé came to Mari's side. Her brother shook his head. "They're afraid, but don't seem to know what to be afraid of most."

"So they're afraid of everything," Sanojé said.

"They need somebody to lead them, Mari." Belam glanced at Ajo and Ziaire. "Those two are extraordinary and that's no lie, but neither are rahns. They can't instill the same kind of cohesion that Roshana, Siamak, or Nazarafine would."

"What about Indris?" Sanojé asked.

"He'd never do it," Mari replied. "He'll advise, suggest, and put himself in harm's way, but he won't put himself in power."

"I wonder whether it matters?" Belam sounded melancholy. "The Erebus has the largest army in Shrïan. Half of it is at Fandra; the other half is within and around Avānweh. Father has called on those who fly his colors, plus the witches, plus whatever alliances Kasra has made with those monsters that dwell in the Rōmarq. We're outnumbered pretty much every which way."

"Come with me," Mari said. She asked directions of the first

Näsarat soldier she saw, who curtly directed them to the royal suites. It was a short walk down the corridor, through doors guarded by hostile—though silent—soldiers, to an ornate round solarium with a stained-glass dome overhead. There were more than a dozen doors enameled in blue and trimmed in gold, each marked with the Näsarat phoenix. Only one of them had Tau-se guarding the door, with Knight-Colonel Mauntro giving orders to his warriors. The lion-man saw Mari and smiled.

"How may I be of assistance, Pah-Mariam?" His deep voice was almost a purr.

"We're looking for Indris. Is he here?"

Mauntro barely hesitated before asking Mari and the others to follow. He led them through the guarded door, into a suite of rooms. In a large bedroom where Rosha slept peacefully, Indris curled bonelessly in a chair, his chin resting on his arm, breathing deep and even. Shar and Ekko stood by him with Femensetri, her tender expression hardening when Mari entered the room.

"What do you want, girl?" the Stormbringer whispered sharply.

"We need you in there," Mari said, jerking her thumb toward the solarium. "It's like cats trying to herd themselves. Ajo and Ziaire are doing what they can, but—"

"They're circling the drain," Belam finished.

Mari crossed to Indris's side. He was pale, his eyes shadowed. There was a faint frown line on his brow, the one he sometimes wore when he slept and was thinking of things he feared to show the light of day. They had spoken of it, once or twice. One long-fingered hand was curled around Changeling's hilt, bringing him comfort. Mari looked up at Femensetri in a silent question.

"He's done what was needed," Femensetri said. "The strength and control needed to Sever three dying rahns, to heal them and set them on a course of recovery . . . I've never seen it done. He finished with Siamak, came in here to check Rosha, and fell asleep."

"Indris did it all himself? Couldn't you help?"

Femensetri gazed down at Indris with naked admiration, and no small degree of love. "Truth is, Mari, I couldn't. I don't have the compassion he does. I could have Severed them, but it would've been a clinical thing, and I'd have taken more than their Awakening in the process, like a surgeon who needed to cut out rotten flesh. Indris cares. I've often berated him for it, because it held him back, but—"

"Now you're not so sure?"

"No." Femensetri's expression hardened. "I'm quite sure it stopped him being the Sēq we wanted him to be. But it let him be the Sēq others needed him to be. What was better? Only time will tell. And by Sedefke's will, we'll all survive to know the answer."

"What about the re-Awakening? Did he at least show you how to do it?"

Femensetri snorted. "If only. I badgered him until he showed me a rendition of the interconnectivity between the body, mind, and soul. He wove an illusion that showed me how it worked, where the power sources were derived, routed, anchored, and shunted up the ladder of existence. He showed me the formulae of how the disparate elements are annealed, at what directions they apply force, and where they are leveraged from each other to make the whole greater than the sum of the parts. Indris showed it all to me."

"Then why do you sound so disappointed?"

"Because I didn't understand it." Her laugh was self-deprecating. "I realized today how far my greatest student has come without me."

"It happens," Mari said. "It's what every teacher wants of their student, and every parent of their child: for them to be better than the one who came before. But there are those in the qadir who won't come any further without your, and Indris's, help."

Femensetri gazed at Mari, her lips quirked in what was almost a smile. "I think I know what he sees in you, girl."

"Then perhaps you'll stop trying to stand in the way of our happiness?" Mari said with false sweetness. "For now, we need you to be the abrasive martinet that people have come to loathe and fear."

"I can manage that."

Together they got Indris to his feet. Mari and Shar lent their shoulders, half guiding, half carrying Indris along the corridor. He was awake, if bleary, when they came to the solarium. Femensetri was what Mari expected of her: a force of nature. She strode to the center of the room, crook planted firmly on the floor. Her presence, with Indris at her side, demanded silence without the need for words. Mari, Belam, Shar, Ekko, and Sanojé stood at Femensetri's back. The message was clear.

"Ajo? Ziaire? Do you mind if I take over for a bit?" Femensetri asked.

"Not at all." The Sky Lord smiled. Ziaire nodded her agreement, her expression relieved.

"What if we do mind?" Osman said. "The Sēq have been—"

"Poor timing to grow some stones, boy." Femensetri eyed the man until he reddened. She cocked an eyebrow at Umna. "You have anything to say . . . ? No, I thought not. Listen, all of you. Much has changed of late. Little of it for the better. But we're here, and willing to help, if you're willing to put aside your differences."

"But the rahns . . . ," came a voice from the crowd.

"Are alive and will recover. But you can't rely on them for the moment. You need to take action for yourselves. Corajidin would have you blindly follow one leader. Himself. But the Shrīanese Federation was formed to heed the voices of many, and give no one person absolute authority over the destiny of all. It's your sworn duty to act!"

"Corajidin's army is formidable, Stormbringer," Teymoud said fearfully. "And our forces are outnumbered and far from where they need to be."

"We've no generals," another voice called.

"You've got Knight-General Maselane in the field," Femensetri countered. "One of the finest military minds alive. With him is Indera, the Poet Master of the Marmûn-sûk, and Harish, the Master of Arms of the Rōmarq.

"You've got me, who commanded armies before Shrīan existed, before the Awakened Empire existed." She spread her arms to include Mari. "You've got Mari, the Queen of Swords, commander of the Feyassin, the hero of Amnon and dozens of other battles besides. Her brother, Belamandris the Widowmaker, and commander of the Anlūki. They've both defied their father. With them is Pah-Sanojé, a witch of fearsome reputation. Shar. Ekko. Champions of the people who fight because it is the right thing to do, not because they follow a rahn!

"Morne Hawkwood and his Immortal Companions are here, in Avānweh, ready to help you. Warrior-poets of the allied schools, elite guards. And Sēq Knights wait in the woods to the south of Fandra, ready to act if needed." She jutted a finger at Indris, whose head snapped up like an old man battling sleep. "And you have him. Do you really need anything else?"

The tone of conversations changed. There was less debate, more agreement. Ideas were fielded and changed, rather than brought down before they could be grown. Mari saw smiles on people's faces, and gestures that were definitive, not defensive.

Femensetri came to Mari's side. "Is that what you were after?"

"It's a start." Mari gestured for Shar and Ekko to take Indris to bed, the exhausted man almost asleep on his feet. "But we need more if we're to survive all this."

"You'll have it."

"Then show me why the Sēq have led our leaders for so long. Make me believe in you, and make me believe that we can win."

27

"HOPE AND EXPECTATION ARE NOT THE SAME THING, THOUGH BOTH WILL
LEAD TO DISAPPOINTMENT. EXIST IN THE MOMENT, ACCEPTING ALL
THINGS AS THEY ARE, NOT AS YOU WOULD HAVE THEM BE."

—from the Nilvedic Maxims

DAY 80 OF THE 496TH YEAR OF THE

SHRĪANESE FEDERATION

Corajidin held Mēdēya in his arms and watched the industry
of war. Below him, the outlying precincts of the Erebus camp were
broken down with clockwork efficiency. Tents were standing one
moment, sagged upon themselves the next, to vanish into packs
and wagons. More than three-quarters of the remaining infantry
had been mobilized to occupy Fandra, as well as a third of the
Iphyri shock troops. The Erebus cavalry remained at the command
camp, the elegantly dressed military elite sipping from bowls of
warmed wine as the infantry pounded the ground beneath nailed
boots. The crews of the wind-ships looked down upon all, safe and
clean. Wagons groaned southward along rutted trails, toward the

line of the Fandra Road. Teamsters yelled. Soldiers grunted and swore by turns. The crisp wind shredded the smoke of camp and cook fires alike, adding to the wintry pall.

"Smells like snow." Mēdēya's nose crinkled, cheeks and brow wind-burned. She stamped her feet in their long sheepskin boots. "Three kilometers is a long distance on a flat field, Jidi, but the marshland will make the journey take longer. Our reinforcements will be a long way away."

"We'll know well before our enemies arrive what their disposition is," Feyd said from the entrance to the command pavilion. The man eyed a fistful of reports, gave orders to his officers, then stretched. "Mēdēya is correct in that the journey for the cavalry will take longer than usual. I've had them doing practice runs for days, planning the best route, timing their approach. We're prepared for the difference. Another two hundred of the heavy cavalry will be positioned closer, in a small gully to the east where they'll not be seen until they emerge."

"I want a decisive victory to show the doubters we are ready for the next step, Feyd." Corajidin accepted a steaming bowl of wine-laced tea. "Though the Rōmarq has its treasures, its strategic value comes from its proximity to the Ash Field Pass, and the Moon Gate that will lead us across the Mar Silin. From Fandra we will march south, cross the Mountains of the Moon at their lowest point, and come upon Mediin from the west."

Feyd took a string of Ancestor beads and kissed the small medallion to ward off misfortune. "Pashrea isn't a place we know enough about, save from legends, and those are dark enough."

Mēdēya took Corajidin's tea and drank from the bowl. He leaned in to kiss her head. Her hair smelled different. Not the aloe vera and henna Yashamin loved: This was something more cloying, and sweetly floral. The kind of scent one used to mask putrefaction. Corajidin gestured for another bowl of tea to be brought him.

"We'll need to wait for spring," Mēdēya said. She gazed south thoughtfully, though the tallest peak this far west, Tehvari—the Nightblade—was just a smudge on the horizon. Mēdēya eyed Corajidin challengingly. "Unless you plan on going to war in the south in winter? It can be done, of course, and the Emissary wants us to assault Pashrea—"

"Our soldiers will not fight well in the snow, whereas the Nomads are unlikely to care," Feyd countered. "Perhaps we can notch our belts with this battle, before we start planning the next?"

"Feyd's right," Tahj-Shaheh added as she arrived. She was blowing into her hands, her hair disheveled from the wind. "I've sailed the Spectral Strand in winter, both by air and sea. I've even made a drunken pass over the forests between Jafir and the mountains. There'll be precious little forage as the nights lengthen and the temperature drops. You'll have added more to the ranks of the Nomads than you'd planned, before you even arrive in Mediin."

Corajidin accepted their truths. The battle at Fandra would unite the disparate political parties under his colors: because either they agreed with his direction or were too frightened to resist. He would need the winter months to solidify his authority, as well as to stack the Teshri more in his favor. Fandra was a large enough city to house the infantry and cavalry he had in the south until spring. The other Houses and Families would muster here before the weather warmed and the snows in the mountains receded. Regardless of what the Emissary may or may not want, or her constant pressure on him to repay his debts, the war on Pashrea would have to wait until the season turned.

Corajidin would have preferred to strike north and bring Tanis into the fold of an Avān nation, but the Emissary had been clear: She wanted the Empress-in-Shadows removed, and the Sēq a thing of the past. Taking the war to Pashrea made Corajidin uneasy. He admitted that it was necessary, but to fight Nomads and scholars was a different war altogether, one for which most would be unprepared. To that end, the artificers and the alchemists would add value, as would the witches. Enchanted weapons, hexes to summon daemons and to bind and banish Nomads, salt-forged steel from Tamerlan stockpiled since the new year.

But how high would the body count be? Who would be left in Shrīan for the Avān to take their rightful place as leaders of the world? Who would Corajidin rule as Mahj, if the majority of a generation were lost in raising him up? And how long would the Iron League wait, were Shrīan to be seen as an easy conquest?

Everything was a risk, but adherence to destiny's road was not supposed to be a challenge easily overcome. Here at the crossroads, Corajidin sipped at his tea and took what comfort he could from his success. He gazed out across the Rōmarq, seeing the life where it shone in plant and water, soldier and animal alike. His own Communion Ritual had been a re-Awakening—making him twice Awakened. Had not his mortal wounding in Avānweh, and his resurrection here in the Rōmarq, made Corajidin the Thrice Awakened?

So far all had happened as the oracles had foretold, though they had said nothing of his near death, or maiming. It was hard to swallow the price he had to pay, but there was light to be seen: This was his escape from the Emissary's clutches. No doubt she suspected as much, and had deliberately brought back Yashamin as a spy, and an anchor around Corajidin's heart and mind.

Beautiful Mēdēya, a prison in which Yashamin languished, or a palace given to her by the Emissary with a different view of the world? At every turn, Mēdēya spoke the Emissary's message, an echo of her demands in sweeter tones. There were times when Mēdēya looked at Corajidin and he wondered whether there was a trace of the Emissary lurking in there, spinning the words on Mēdēya's tongue. A spy secreted in a house he still loved, though its architecture was not quite right anymore.

"Will you do as the Emissary suggests, Jidi?" Mēdēya asked as if on cue. "Will you wage war on Pashrea sooner, rather than later?"

Corajidin took her in his arms. He rested his chin on her head and struggled with the temptation to strangle her then and there. What would the others do? He was Asrahn. He would make his every act, no matter how heinous, legal. He rubbed her back with his prosthetic hand, as he clenched his natural one. "The Emissary has made no mention to me of a winter assault. Though she has alluded to a schedule. Have you spoken with her about it?"

Mēdēya paused for a long moment. Corajidin was not sure whether her breathing had stilled. She sounded confused when she spoke. "No, she has said nothing to me. Perhaps it was something I overheard?"

"Perhaps."

❋ ❋ ❋

As snow drifted down outside, Corajidin warmed himself before a small ahm-fueled heater the artificers had recently invented, the ornate metallic pillar a gift from Baquio. Kasraman reclined, muddied and exhausted, on a couch nearby, his hand curled around a bowl of spiced coffee. Mēdēya sat cross-legged on the bed, idly chewing the end of an ink brush as she read, then annotated, or swore at, the reports from the various departments of the Erebus war machine. A witch in a neat robe of red wool kneeled on a cushion, her eyes rolled back into her head, privy to vistas only she could see.

"What progress on removing the Havoc Chair?" Corajidin asked the witch, the intermediary between himself and Wolfram.

"Removing it is proving more difficult than anticipated, my Asrahn." The witch spoke in her own voice, but with Wolfram's cadence. "Our work is not without disruption. We encounter resistance from Fenlings, reedwives, and marsh-puppeteers daily. We've lost another handful of witches, and a score or more of soldiers to nāga attacks. The natural energies of this place are a magnet to the monsters of the Rōmarq."

"How do you fare? And Ikedion?"

There was a pause before the witch replied. "It's not without its challenges. There's a sense of mania if we spend too long here. I've little doubt the mystics who dwelled here in ages past had a solution better than to remain on the edges of narcotic stupor, but this is what Ikedion and I are reduced to. Asrahn, the longer we stay, the less effective we become."

Corajidin tapped his foot impatiently. "Mēdēya? What weapons have been ferried from the ruins to Fandra thus far?"

Mēdēya did not need to refer to a report to answer. "Nothing remotely close to what we'd hoped for, and nothing we'd call a siege weapon. Less than fifty suits of witchfire ingot armor in reasonable repair. Some one hundred witchfire and *kirion* swords, spears, and long-knives. Twenty or so storm-rifles, only half of which work. And thirty Salamander Lances the artificers and alchemists are trying to make operational, their power sources drained, or parts damaged.

"We've also retrieved some black rock salt, and a stock of salt-forged steel that we can work over the winter into weapons."

"This was supposed to be Sedefke's great laboratory!" Corajidin snarled. "Where is everything I expected—everything I was promised—that would be here?"

"And it may well have been." The intermediary related Wolfram's message. "This is what we could expect of a well-armed garrison at an isolated qadir. The wealth here was not in manufactured weapons, or industry. The riches are in knowledge."

"Have you discovered much of that?"

"The qadir and its surrounding buildings cover a lot of ground, Asrahn. We find new sources of interest every day. Most of these are trapped, and we've not the witches left—and those who are here suffer more the ahm-mania than Ikedion or myself—to progress faster than we are doing. For all I know there's an armory hidden in a cellar, somewhere in the ruins. Or if not here, elsewhere. We're excavating five different ruins as we speak. Please don't despair, Asrahn."

"These traps you speak of. Do the traps destroy the contents?"

"Not as far as we can tell, no."

"Then I'll send more of the captives from Fandra so you can use them to expedite matters." Corajidin felt Kasraman's and Mēdēya's gazes on him. They kept their thoughts to themselves. "Once the traps have been triggered, use the time wisely to retrieve all you can."

There was another pause, longer this time, before Wolfram's reply. "As you will, my Asrahn." No need for Wolfram to be in the room for Corajidin to hear the reproach.

"I will have the fodder sent to you in the next couple of hours," Corajidin said. "Work faster, Wolfram. I want that place, and others like it, cleared of anything useful as soon as possible. End communication."

The witch slumped, her eyes rolling back down. She was pale, her brow dewed. Corajidin ordered her to make communication with the witches in the field with Tahj-Shaheh's corsairs. Their reports were bland by comparison, with the enemy forces moving in textbook order, at optimum pace. There was no communication from Nix, though his last had reported the counselors that had been bonded with the marsh-puppeteers were in place, and behaving themselves for now.

"Kasraman, why are we suffering at the hands of these puppeteers?" Corajidin asked. "I was assured they would comply with my wishes."

"Like the Great Houses and the Hundred Families, there is more than one voice among the malegangers." Kasraman sounded as limp as he looked. "That which is merged with Kimiya will do as agreed, as will her clan. The ones we've not dealt with act according to their nature, which is homicidally territorial."

"And the Fenlings? The reedwives?"

"We've made no overturns to them, so they're quite hostile." Kasraman finished his coffee and poured another. He brightened some at the infusion. "There are a number of different societies in the Rōmarq, of which we're only peripherally aware. The nāga, for example. Added to the native inhabitants, we've the Rōmarqim—who'll kill anybody wearing Erebus colors on sight. There are renegade Seethe who remained after Far-ad-din was deposed, bandits, freebooters, road rangers, and tomb raiders. We're beset on all sides by those who want us dead, or at least gone."

"And how are you coping with the mania of being in the Rōmarq?"

"Well enough, Father." Kasraman smiled. "You can rely on me to do whatever is needful. What we do here ensures the future of our House. Kimiya will do as I command her, and Ikedion is sworn to our cause. He follows my instructions to the letter."

And there is the rub, my ambitious son. Kimiya does as you say. And the witches, through Ikedion, are your creatures. Your purpose is revealed more than you know. But remember it is I who have to Awaken you to power. Betrayal will profit you nothing.

Aloud, Corajidin said, "Are there any more places we can excavate? Any that are less problematic?"

"We've discovered another handful within easy distance. But the Emissary warned me there are parts of the Rōmarq best avoided," Mēdēya added. "Places even the native inhabitants avoid."

"And when did she tell you of this?" Corajidin's voice was neutral. Kasraman looked at Mēdēya speculatively.

"I . . . it was . . . shortly after we arrived?" Once more Mēdēya sounded uncertain as to when she had spoken with the Emissary. "Or perhaps in Avānweh, when she spoke of the Feigning and using Mariam as the—"

"That will be enough on that topic, love." Corajidin felt his chest tighten. Mēdēya's expression was closed, her attention focused elsewhere. *Is it only you there, Yashamin? Is it her who shares our bed? Is it her darker passions we also explore?* The thought of them sharing each other's bodies while the Emissary looked on from behind Mēdēya's eyes sent a chill down his spine.

When Mēdēya gazed upon him, there was only love, but Corajidin knew too well how easy it was to hide away the lies. Kasraman's loyalties were also a riddle, the witch's pupil who may or may not be more than Corajidin's son.

Corajidin wondered at what point the loyalties of his son and wife would break.

And what he would need to do to them when they did.

28

"WAR IS BASED UPON DECEPTION, SHROUDED IN ACCEPTABLE TRUTHS."

—from *The Nature of Conflict,* by Kohar san Ankher,
Field Marshall of Manté, Third Dynasty of the Ebon Masks
(3rd Year of the Shrīanese Federation)

DAY 83 OF THE 496TH YEAR OF THE

SHRĪANESE FEDERATION

The allies met at the mist-shrouded Lotus House of Avānweh. Their meetings were held in different places around Avānweh. But only after each place had been thoroughly scouted by Indris, Mari, Shar, and Ekko. Prior to the gatherings, Sanojé cast her seeker hex on Nix, an added precaution to ensure he was not nearby when the allied members of the Teshri met.

The Lotus House, a tiered fretwork building of alabaster and red stone, was as much carved into as built from the curving walls of a steep ravine between Star Crown and World Blood mountains. Dark grass bobbed in the rain, the memorial pillars of the Garden of Stones slick. Water collected in streams that carried handfuls of snow down the long stair, to the terraced city streets. The chill downpour made travel precarious and casual visitors nonexistent.

Indris leaned against a wall between two windows, listening to the counselors debate. Hazy bars of wan light shone dully on silver bowls and cutlery, bleaching the crockery. The air was rich with the aroma of porridge and honey, hotcakes and freshly baked flatbread. Tea and coffee added to the comforting scents of a family kitchen. Meeting over meals had given the alliance less formality, with less stress on political agendas, and more focus on the people who comprised the Federation.

He divided his attention between the words coming to his ears and the words flowing across his mind. The counselors' thoughts shot with rapid intensity, but were not as distracting as the siren call from the World Blood Mountain, Īajen-mar. The mountain, one of Shrīan's richest sources of the Water of Life, strummed his soul. The Awakening that Indris had paused, but failed to stop, desperately wanted to answer the call, and tried to grow beyond the layers of the mental and spiritual wards he had erected. Indris wanted to succumb. His paused Awakening knew the paths in Indris's body previously traveled: In Isenandar he had surrendered his physical form in order to learn enough about Awakening to save the rahns. The channels of power in him were changing, and growing. But Awakening did not stop with the body. Like water through the cracks in a wall, it seeped, and pooled. Tried to spread upward through his mind, and from there to his soul. Indris clenched his fist around Changeling's hilt, drawing what resolve he could from her. There was a faint croon from the weapon, a hint of what she once had been.

Counselor Teymoud huddled in his layers of patterned silks. The many rings on his fingers flashed as he drummed the table. "We're still outnumbered, no matter what decisions we try to push through the Teshri. Now even more so, since several counselors suddenly changed from supporting our reforms to sharing Corajidin's worldview. Our former allies now obstruct both State and Crown from any action."

"Now we've returned," Rosha said, "we'll ensure the Upper House of the Teshri makes some decisions. There are some actions we can take that the Lower House may not veto."

"The no-confidence motion won't get passed." Ajo smiled acceptance to Neva, who brought him a bowl of coffee, returned from her patrol over the city and its surrounds. She leaned forward to whisper in Ajo's ear, who stiffened. He whispered back, and she rejoined her brother at the rear of the room. Indris was not comforted by the tension in their postures. Ajo cleared his throat. "Might I suggest that the Upper House call for the motion, second it, but hold off on the vote until we are better represented?"

"You need to focus your attention on what your former allies have become," Belamandris suggested. "And remove them. That would tip the odds in our favor."

"What do you mean?" Siamak asked. The huge man had regained much of his former vigor. Osman, Nazarafine's heir, sat beside him. Nazarafine was still confined to her bed, her health worsening. Osman was proving to be next to useless: The man lacked the common sense the Ancestors gave a stone. But his voice, as Nazarafine's heir, still purchased decisions in the Teshri—provided he was guided where to vote.

"The Asrahn dealt with the malegangers." Sanojé did not sugarcoat her words. "I heard Pah-Kasraman negotiate with the woman who had once been Kimiya. And I witnessed his early experiments, in order to blend malegangers with members of the Teshri. They planned to force their capitulation, and drive through the changes Corajidin wanted. I'm uncertain whether he followed through with his plan."

"It would explain some of the changes in direction we've seen," Ajo said. "And the way in which the Teshri has been recently dead-locked in every vote that doesn't progress Imperialist policy."

"Sedefke's balls!" Femensetri croaked, and her mindstone flared. "Malegangers? Here? *Faruq ayo!* How did you people let this happen?"

Belamandris frowned. "We're talking about a man who used Nomads to fake attacks by the Iron League. Who used Nix of the Maladhi to release daemon elementals in the city. My father under-stands the price of power, and its rewards. My half-brother Kasraman is even smarter, and more ambitious."

"Belam is right," Mari admitted grudgingly. "Dealing with my father won't be enough. We need to cut the heads from all his ser-pents at the same time, and leave such a vacuum of power that those who fly his colors won't know what to do."

"They'll fall over each other to lead," Belamandris agreed. "It's the kind of people Father surrounds himself with. Nix. Tahj-Shaheh. Feyd . . . the late Jhem, and Nadir, who we have captive. They're deadly, but deadlier, and more ruthless, when focused on their own interests."

"We can use all of this to our advantage," Indris said. He cursed himself for speaking, as the others in the room adopted a respectful silence. It had been this way since he had saved the rahns, all of them turning to him as the leader he had no intention of being. "People—generally—see what they expect to see, which informs thought, cause, and effect. Things that are normal are comforting. We need to ensure Corajidin's inner circle do our work for us, by making them see what we want them to see."

"How do you propose that?" Neva asked.

"Why don't you tell us what you told Ajo; then I'll answer your question."

Neva and Yago glanced at their grandfather, who bade them speak with a wave of his cane. Neva stepped forward, to find herself standing by herself. She looked over her shoulder to see that Yago had remained where he was, shrugging an apology with his eyebrows.

"We've been patrolling further afield," she said. "There are significant numbers of the Jiharim bivouacked in the mountain passes to the north and east of Avānweh. They're just off the trade roads north, huddled around small paths and tracks, close to water sources and game. This morning, we saw wind-frigates flying the Kadarin colors unloading heavy infantry, and archers."

"An invasion?" Osman quavered.

"For the love your Ancestors hold you, relax your scrotum, boy." Femensetri gave the man a withering glance. "You may live longer, or at least enjoy the time you have more."

"Father has the largest army in Shrīan," Mari offered. "Plus the forces he's wrangled from Martūm, Narseh, and the sayfs. Let alone the nahdi he can afford: Both the Freelancers and the War Party support him. He could split his forces and still have more warriors in the field than we."

"Let's deal with one threat at a time, neh?" Indris said. "Neva, what kind of numbers are we looking at?"

Neva and Yago conferred for a few seconds before she said, "Some four hundred of the Jiharim. Perhaps two hundred Kadarin heavy infantry, and another two hundred archers."

"Not big enough for an invasion," Femensetri said. "They must be expecting help from inside Avānweh."

"The ban-kherife?" Padishin guessed. "We believe they're under Nix's command, on behalf of Corajidin. There are also Erebus soldiers who went to ground when Corajidin fled, plus the huqdi, and other criminals, that infest the city. Karim and his friends in the Malefacti have a firm hold on the lower-castes, as well as those of the struggling middle-castes."

"Good chance to rid ourselves of another problem," Kiraj added. "The criminal element has flourished under Corajidin. The Whisperer Under the Bridge has united many of the street gangs and petty criminals, and made the Malefacti a threat we should deal with sooner rather than later."

"What forces do we have in the city?" Mari asked.

"As of this morning?" Morne had become their general in Avānweh. "We've the seventy Feyassin we could call back to duty; they report to Mari. There are almost fifty Anlūki brought in by Nima, under Belam's command. Kembe has four hundred of his Tau-se who'll serve the Näsarat as nahdi, much as they did at Amnon: It gets them around being considered a hostile foreign force. The Sûn have one hundred Sûnguard, and another fifty of the Saidani-sûk warrior-poets. And last but by no means least, there are one hundred and fifteen of the Immortal Companions, all veterans."

"I have fifty of my Lamenti here," Bensaharēn added with a smile. "They came aboard my husband's merchant ships yesterday. Poet Master Tarhin of the Vayen-sûk will join us, and brings a further fifty of his daishäri."

"My houreh are placed in the city with key clients," Ziaire said. "They're not soldiers as such, though they are trained to hold their own when necessary. They also have other means at their disposal for ensuring people are where they should be, or elsewhere if needed. Most importantly we're confident we know the places the ban-kherife frequent, as well as those who aid them. I can have this information to you before sundown."

"There are also my Sky Knights, and the local kherife," Ajo finished. "Another two hundred or so."

"In excess of one thousand of Shrīan's most dangerous warriors," Mari said. "Smart people could do a lot with that."

It was not a huge force, but the counselors all visibly relaxed as they heard the roll. Most of the warriors in their service were elite, and commanded by Exalted Names. Talk turned to the disposition and numbers of the forces headed south, voices toned with more optimism. No longer the center of attention, Indris strolled to where Shar and Ekko sat. Mari, Belamandris, and Sanojé came to join them.

"When are you going to suggest it?" Indris whispered to Mari.

"Soon. They need to have confidence in what they're doing. Give them a little time to appreciate what they can work with."

"Are you sure about this, Mari?" Belamandris asked.

"Of course she's sure." Shar nudged Belamandris with her hip. The Widowmaker looked surprised, then smiled at the Seethe warchanter. Even Sanojé hazarded a grin, her tiny hand creeping into Belamandris's larger one.

"Mari knows what she's doing," Indris said. "I wish I'd have thought of it myself. I intend to follow her lead."

"And I trust Amonindris with my life, Widowmaker," Ekko rumbled. "He does not idly allow lives to fall, where there is a chance they can be saved."

"We're waiting on one more voice . . ." Indris locked eyes with Femensetri. She stood among the counselors, who debated the merits of different courses of action. The newly formed political factions worked together. But still they held back from an agreed course of action. Indris, Femensetri, and Ojin-mar had suspected something else would be needed to bring the counselors together. "And here it comes," Indris said.

"There's more." The Stormbringer's voice cut through the conversation. She put on a contrite expression, almost humble but falling short enough of the mark not to be disingenuous. She was, after all, who she was. "I've conferred with the Suret. Though the Sēq and the Teshri are not officially aligned, we're willing to bring a small number of our Masters, Inquisitors, and Executioners to your aid. We'll not be serving as Sēq: We will, for all intents and purposes, be daimahjin in the service of the Great Houses, and those of the

Hundred Families who offer us contracts." The room went silent for an extended breath. Counselors looked at Femensetri, then at each other, incredulously. Then their voices filled the space with questions, offers, demands, and denials. Trust was thin on the ground for the Sēq. Femensetri added that there were also soldiers the Sēq could field, ones that would give even the Mahsojhin witches pause.

"Now?" Indris asked.

"Now," Mari said. He kissed her deeply, took her by the hand, and walked side by side with Mari and their friends to stand before the counselors of the Teshri.

❈ ❈ ❈

Conversations stopped as Indris waited patiently for silence.

"I agree: We could potentially win a conventional war against Corajidin and his colors," Mari began. The excitement of the counselors pressed against Indris's mental shields. It felt like somebody held his brain and squeezed. He centered himself, mustering firmer control. "But we shouldn't fight on my father's terms," she continued.

"What do you suggest?" Siamak asked. "With respect, it is my people who are suffering."

"And I'm sorrier than you know, rahn. We need to show the people of Shrīan that they are not pieces on a board to be played with, or sacrificed, at the whim of Corajidin. We can win this war quickly, and quietly, with minimal lives lost."

"How do you propose that?" Ajo raised his brows. "We've armies in the field, approaching Fandra as we speak."

"But days away," Belamandris countered.

"We're not committed to a course of action," Mari said. "We can change direction and save lives."

"And what direction would you have us take?" Rosha asked tensely. "Corajidin needs to be stopped."

"He will be," Mari said. "Through the most expedient legal means at our disposal. A small group of people, who make targeted attacks that isolate and remove his center of authority."

"We can focus our efforts behind Rosha's Jahirojin," Ziaire suggested. It peaked interest around the room. "She declared Jahirojin against the Great House of Erebus, back in Amnon. It makes her direct action against Corajidin legal. It's targeted, and wouldn't require the armies to be involved unless it failed."

"And yet again, it comes down to a conflict between our two Houses," Indris said in Mari's ear. "Promise me that we'll never be the cause of this kind of hatred?"

"Legally, Jahirojin is strongly linked with Ajamensût," Kiraj replied. "I think the circumstances are clear enough for the Secretary-Marshall, Kherife-Marshall, and myself to expedite a War of the Long-Knife between the Näsarat and the Erebus. I can see no need for us to undergo a process of application and approval. Provided Rahn-Roshana is willing to—"

"How soon can it start?" Rosha's voice bordered on the manic.

Mari whispered to Indris, "Were it up to me, there'd be no conflict between us at all."

"Then change their minds. They'll listen."

Indris chewed his lip, listening as the counselors discussed the mechanics of how they might best abide by tradition, and limit the conflict to come. Mari's plan was bold, but sound. History would not remember this conflict as it had been: That Corajidin had invaded the Rōmarq, those who flew his colors at his side. The Bey rising to their own defense, assisted by an alliance of the Houses and Families. The Kadarins and the Jiharim descending on Avānweh, to be met by the allied forces of the Teshri. It would be remembered as history had so often recorded it: Näsarat versus Erebus.

"History needs to remember that many stood together," Mari said. "Not behind the colors of two Houses who've been at each other's throats for millennia. No Jahirojin. No Ajamensût. This needs to be something Shrīan settles as a nation. And those who have their eyes fixed on us need to see it that way."

"You said that we needed a solution that does not endanger the many." Rosha sounded deflated. "Are you now proposing we go to war, with the loss of life it entails?"

"Rosha is correct, Mari." Ajo rested his chin on his walking cane, expression sorrowful. "There are only so many ways to end this."

"There are, but not the way you think. We assemble a small force, comprised of warriors from the Houses and Families. With the support of the Sēq, they infiltrate Corajidin's position, capture him and as many of his senior officers as they can. They then bring their prisoners back for trial and the let the Arbiter's Tribunal and the Teshri—that which remains—judge them according to the law."

"That which remains?" Siamak asked.

"Belam has already told us our father trafficked with the male-gangers." Mari's disgust was evident in her clipped speech. "And Sanojé said that he wanted to subvert the Teshri with them. It's pretty damned clear we need to find out who has been compromised, and get the Teshri under control."

"Our father did it," Belam added. He curled his fingers around Tragedy's sheath. "It should be Mari and I who fix it."

"No," Indris said. "You need to be there, seen to be there, but everybody needs to fix it."

There was no debate, rather a spiraling chain of agreements that saw plans seeded, grown, and harvested. Mari's plan took form. The allies from among the Teshri assessed their strengths and weaknesses, commitments and loyalties. Together they looked at the defense of Avānweh, how they would neuter the ban-kherife, and quietly oppose those forces allied with the Asrahn. How they would deal with the infiltration of the Teshri by the malegangers. Ziaire coordinated the flow of information, questioning and countering.

The counselors fell into informal groups, one centered around Rosha and Ajo for the defense of Avānweh, another around Siamak for the efforts to remove Corajidin from where he was burrowed in the Rōmarq. Osman wandered listlessly between the groups, wringing his hands more often than he spoke.

Confident the counselors were headed in the right direction, Indris distanced himself from the whirlwind, and found calm at the edges of conversation. The sun had risen high over the mountains, and the old clocks chimed the eleven bells of the Hour of Wasp, the totem spirit of the Great House of Bey. It seemed somehow fitting, given how the events of the Rōmarq had helped bring the counselors together in common cause. Indris poured himself a bowl of tea. Food had been laid out, strips of grilled fish, rice, and steamed vegetables. He prepared himself a small meal and sat in the sun, his head resting against the wall. His hand dropped to Changeling's hilt. She purred gently, a pleasant vibration against his palm. Indris delved into his own mind, his mental shields assailed from without by the thoughts of those in the room, as well as the sweet, powerful song of Īa, and from within by the power of his Awakening, that heard the world call to it.

Indris's body, mind, and soul pleaded for Unity, the ultimate fusion of a person and the world around them. The energy in him coiled, and flexed, impatient to grow.

29

"SELF-DOUBT CAN BE A POISON NOT ONLY TO YOURSELF, BUT OTHERS."

—from *Principles of Thought,* fourth volume of the Zienni Doctrines

DAY 83 OF THE 496TH YEAR OF THE

SHRĪANESE FEDERATION

The clocks chimed the twelve bells of the Hour of the Spider, the morning over. Mari stood shoulder to shoulder with Roshana, Ajo, and Ziaire. The three of them had worked with the counselors to agree on how they would proceed, each counselor taking an equal burden of the responsibility. At the other end of the table, Siamak held sway. Those who planned the action in the Rōmarq spoke quietly, their gestures decisive, expressions serious. Mari was impressed despite herself, and saw in the Teshri something that she wished was the rule rather than the exception.

She glanced about the room, to find Indris on a thickly cushioned chair, an empty tea bowl held precariously in the palm of his hand. His Scholar's Lantern pulsed in a steady tattoo, limning his messy head. His brow was furrowed, lips a pallid line on his face.

Mari excused herself and went to him, gesturing for Shar and Ekko to join her.

"What can I do to help?" she asked without preamble.

"Nothing, but thanks." Indris's voice was flat. "Overtired, I think. Have the counselors agreed on a course of action?"

"So it would appear," Ekko rumbled. "It seems the mission to extract Corajidin from his base of operations is going to be . . . eventful."

"So of course we volunteered," Shar said cheerfully. She smoothed Indris's hair. "You can never have too much eventful, can you?"

"Most assuredly not," Ekko replied.

"I couldn't agree more." Shar nodded briskly. "And the best part is, Indris gets to play with us, too!"

"How wonderful," Indris replied. "I didn't see that coming."

Mari frowned at Indris's listless tone. Saw the way his hand was curled tight around Changeling's hilt, in an almost panicked grip. Ekko took the bowl from Indris's hand and poured more tea. Indris took it with a grateful smile.

"So, who's doing what?" Indris asked.

"For your part I'm not completely certain," Mari said. "Something frightfully clever, improbably dangerous, and a little on the insane side? For me, couldn't be safer. Belam, Sanojé, Ajo, and other warriors from the allies are going to expose the marsh-puppeteers, try and kill them without killing the friendly sayfs, then stop the occupation of the city before it starts."

"So, not much then?" Shar's grin was bright.

"What could go wrong?" Mari asked lightly. "When?"

"Ajo is calling a session of the Teshri to vote on the no-confidence motion against my father. That'll bring all of those dedicated to Father's cause, so we can have them all in the same place at the same time. It will be the Hour of the Horse."

"Seems fitting."

"Indris's job is much easier," Shar said blandly. "The Sēq will translocate small squads of elite fighters to targets in the Rōmarq, pop pop, pop pop pop." She flicked her fingers with each sound for emphasis. "It'll drive Corajidin insane, wondering how we moved so quickly and undetected. The squads will hit key targets, and damage as much as they can, before taking refuge in the wetlands. Meanwhile, Indris, Morne, and some others will command crews to take Fandra, and capture Corajidin. It'll be fun!"

"I'll be teaching some of the Sēq the translocation formula I learned at the Pillars of Sand, so they can move around without using the Drear," Indris said. "I expect that my target will be Corajidin's command post?" Shar nodded. Indris seemed resigned as he said, "I'll get Sanojé to teach me her seeker hex this afternoon, so I can find where he is. I'll speak with Siamak, and see what else he needs me to do."

Indris was worn, and unfocused. Mari took his chin in her hand and stared into his eyes. They were almost fever bright, his Dragon Eye flooded an orange-brown with yellow flecks. His other eye had also lightened, as if a fire burned behind it. He was feverish, skin clammy.

"You're far from well, Indris." Mari kept her voice low. "I ask you again. What can I do to help?"

"Mari, there is nothing you can do to help, except not worry." Indris did not bother to smile to take the flatness out of his tone. "This is the price I'm paying for everything that's happened of late. Amnon, my abortive Awakening, the battle at new year, my time in Amarqa-in-the-Snows, the Pillars of Sand . . ."

"I know you well enough to hear when you're telling me parts of the truth."

"I'm telling you the—"

"No, you're not." She crouched next to him. "Indris, lives are at risk. Our friends included."

"What do you want to hear, Mari?"

"The truth. All of it."

Indris clenched his fists in his hair, his expression stricken. The radiance behind his eyes smoldered, extending in flashes across his skin. Shar and Ekko loomed, though what they thought they could do was anybody's guess.

"Very well," Indris said. "To study Awakening, one must be open to it. I used what had happened to me as a map, to understand how Awakening fused the elements of physical existence with the mind and soul. For something as vast as Ĩa, it's a natural thing. For a mortal, even one who is scholar trained, it's difficult. Ĩa doesn't recognize boundaries, or limits: It's as uncompromising as nature. Long ago, the Sēq planted the foundations of Awakening in my mind—a common thing that makes us aware of the ahm, and trains us how to think in different ways in order to use it. Later, years of study—and of use—strengthened what was there. When Ariskander tried to Awaken me fully, he allowed what had been given me, and nourished over the years, to see sunlight, and know what it could've been. But I stopped it, or so I thought.

"In the Pillars of Sand, I woke what slumbered." He looked at his friends with horrified wonder. "I think I'm being fully Awakened, like the first generation of rahns, whether I want it or not. It's happening as my nature intends, and it scares me half to death."

"*Ahni sayhe fae enka!*" Shar breathed, her hand resting on his. "Can you stop it again?"

"I've been trying. And slowly losing. Being so close to Ĩajen-mar and the source of the Water of Life isn't helping."

"It'll be worse in the Rōmarq, won't it?" Shar asked. The Seethe woman explained to Mari how the Rōmarq was rich in natural springs of disentropy, itself what made the Water of Life so potent.

"Then you can't go," Mari said. "What happens if you fall apart

in the middle of all this? You'll doom everybody. I'm going to tell
Femensetri—"

"No!" Indris said. "The Sēq would abandon you without a
qualm if they knew a scholar was being fully Awakened. They'd let
you kill each other off, then install me as . . . No. I'm not in significant danger. Were Changeling not broken—"

"Thanks, Anj," Mari muttered.

"Had I Changeling, it would be easier to control myself. As it
is, the shards and pommel are helping. I can put stronger barriers
around my mind, enough to get the job done tonight. But we'll
need to decide what I'm going to do in the long term, and quickly."

"We?"

"I can hardly make a choice like this without you, could I?"

Mari was going to say more, but Femensetri's approach silenced
her. The Stormbringer rapped her crook on the ground, and spat.
She gestured for Indris to follow her: The Sēq had arrived, and
there was scholarly business to discuss.

Mari took him in her arms and kissed him. When they parted,
she said, "Do I need to say it?" *I love you.*

He grinned at her and held her close once more. "I know. But
I don't tire of hearing it, and the words taste good. I love you, too."

"Promise?"

"Always."

Torn, Mari watched Indris walk away. Shar's arms around her
did not help assuage her anxiety that Indris may have met a challenge he could not master. *He's chosen his course, as I've chosen mine.
And I, like he, have a role to play before this drama is done.*

❋ ❋ ❋

The Hour of the Horse approached, and the Tyr-Jahavān was
filled with counselors and townspeople. The allies took their usual

places, some together, others apart, with no sign of their common goal. Now that Mari knew what to look for, it was apparent which counselors maintained an awkward, almost hostile, silence. They spoke when spoken to, yet offered nothing by way of social niceties, as if they had forgotten how to react to people properly.

Femensetri, dressed in the faded earth tones of a daimahjin, sat at the opposite side of the chamber. Mari recognized some of Bensaharēn's Lamenti, as well as warriors of the Saidani-sûk and the Anlūki, above and beyond the ceremonial guards who protected the counselors. Knight-Major Qamran of the disbanded Feyassin stood beside Nima of the Anlūki, relaxed and deadly. Mari felt the giddy rush of excitement at what they were about to do, so at odds with how she had felt at Amnon, where she had been prepared to die.

Rosha, Siamak, and Ajo were the last of the counselors to arrive, a hooded Belam walking in Neva and Yago's wake. Belam and the siblings made their way around the room, walking unhurriedly between the smaller groups of the allies, until they came to sit by Mari and Sanojé.

"Quite the little party we've got here," Belam said. "Our forces are in position, both here and staged in the city. The Tau-se and the Sûnguard watch the roads from the mountains. The kherife have the secret police marked and cordoned off. My Anlūki and the Lamenti have taken their places close to those counselors we suspect have been compromised. Most of the Immortal Companions and the Sky Knights have gone with the houreh, to take care of the other potentially hostile forces in the city. They'll act once we've finished here."

"If you're going to have a party, you should always invite the interesting people," Yago mused. "Otherwise it becomes ever so dull."

"Try Tanis," Sanojé said.

"Thanks, but no." Neva shook her head. The gryphon rider stretched her long legs with a creak of leather. "Though there're times, rare, one admits, when being bored could be a diverting change of pace."

Yago shouldered his sister. "You'd go raving mad without something to do. You're a bloody nightmare when you're bored. All this excitement almost makes you tolerable."

"Oh, look!" Neva pointed to the gap between the pillars of the Tyr-Jahavān, where it ended in a precipice over the bowl of the city below. "Somebody needs you over there."

Yago pantomimed a laugh, then stopped abruptly to shoot his sister an obscene gesture.

Mari smiled. If a person could be measured by the company they kept, Mari counted herself as fortunate. *How does my father think to lead when he surrounds himself by the basest people he can find?* She craned her neck to take in her brother, a man stepped from their father's shadow to shine in the sun. *Surely Father must see himself reflected in those who serve him, and wonder why he fails to inspire anything but dread?*

"How will you save those who've been bound to a marsh-puppeteer?" Mari asked Sanojé.

"*If* we can save them," she whispered back nervously. "We'll try to force them out of their hosts, which will be painful for the host, but hopefully not fatal. I've done it a few times with similar parasites when we've come through the Drear."

"Did they live, the people you helped?" Neva asked.

"Not as often as we'd hoped," Belam said grimly.

"My hexes, and the Stormbringer's canto, will hopefully cause the malegangers to withdraw, to preserve their own lives," Sanojé said. "They're smart, if unpredictable. If we can't force the malegangers out, then we'll be left with no choice. They may stay bound, slaves to their violent nature, causing as much damage as they can before they die."

"Sounds like fun." Yago's tone was dour.

"Not remotely."

The doors to the Tyr-Jahavān closed with the sound of finality. The Neyudin—the ceremonial guards of the counselors—took station at the exits, tall spears and hexagonal shields held at parade rest, their plaited beards bound in silver wire. They were a near-invisible fixture of the Tyr-Jahavān, less skilled than the Feyassin, who had once defended the Asrahn, before her father had them disbanded. Mari did not remember the last time a member of the Neyudin had been required to shed blood. Not in her lifetime. Today they would have the chance for history to remember them as something more than an anachronism.

Ajo walked to the center of the room, his cane clicking on the floor. Padishin rapped his sheathed dionesqa on the floor for silence. Ajo thanked the Secretary-Marshall, then bowed to Rosha and Siamak as was their due. A perspiring Osman looked nauseated and out of place. Ajo turned to the place where the Asrahn should have been seated, his frown not quite theatrical. He raised his cane and pointed to the empty place, until the silence was uncomfortable.

"I have petitioned the Teshri before to consider the mistake we made in electing Erebus fa Corajidin to the highest office in Shrīan," Ajo said. There was no response from the counselors. Everybody knew why the session had been called. "A growing number of us doubt the Asrahn's fitness to govern in these troubling times. Shrīan stands upon a precipice, and we have an Asrahn who seems intent on pushing us off the edge." A few shouts of support and applause, some of derision, and uncomfortable shuffling. Or the lack of response from those who should have spoken loudest in Corajidin's defense.

"And here we are," the Sky Lord continued. "Members of our society abducted at Corajidin's order—an incontrovertible fact—the ban-kherife abusing their power, ambassadors fled the country for fear of their lives. An Asrahn who has exceeded every authority and occupied the prefecture of a fellow rahn, without the permission of the Magistratum, or the sanctions our own codes of sende provide us. An Asrahn who is busy waging his illegal military action, rather than being here to govern the country he is sworn to protect, and to serve."

"We know the story, Ajo." Padishin smiled to take the harshness from his words. "Raise the motion again, and be done."

The Sky Lord acknowledged the chuckles from around the room with a good-natured wave. "As you will, Secretary-Marshall. As Sayf-Avānweh, Arbiter of the Change, and member of the Teshri am Shrīan, I call for a vote of no confidence in Erebus fa Corajidin's leadership."

"I so second." Siamak's voice rang around the Tyr-Jahavān. There was not a rational person in the chamber who could gainsay him the right.

"Since we've been down this road before," Padishin said, "I'm invoking an open vote." There were some murmurs of surprise, but no opposition. It was Padishin's right to ask for transparency in the voting process. "Those in favor of the motion to remove Corajidin from the office of Asrahn, please make yourselves known."

Mari did a quick head count as hands were raised, the colors of their House or Family in evidence. Given the political climate, not every counselor had attended, and there were no absentee votes. Of the seventy counselors present, plus the members of the Magistratum, twenty-seven voted in support of the motion. There were some Mari had expected to be compromised by marsh-puppeteers who voted in favor.

Padishin waited for any more hands to be raised. He vocalized the count, and the junior secretaries made notations in their journals. Padishin cleared his throat. Mari tensed. Femensetri and Sanojé had said they would act immediately, once the potential targets revealed themselves.

"Those who oppose the motion to remove Corajidin from the office of Asrahn, please make yourselves known."

Hands shot into the air as one, though others rose slowly, as if the counselor was not entirely sure of their position. *We have you.*

Femensetri and Sanojé rose from their seats, as did a handful of other people in the shorter over-robes and coats of the middle-castes. Sanojé chanted her hex, her Aspect of a six-armed hag made of the flotsam and jetsam of shattered bones a nebulous thing, as if she did not want to manifest it. Femensetri crooned her canto, her mindstone a whorl of black on her brow. Other scholars' voices joined hers. Mari felt the air thicken, heavier as it pressed onto her skin and hair.

Within moments, the bodies of those counselors who had voted against the motion took on a dirty corona, the formulae and hex illuminating within the bodies of their hosts and revealing the pus-colored phantom of marsh-puppeteers. Tendrils shone throughout the majority of the counselors' bodies, where the parasitic marsh-puppeteers had spread throughout the head, torso, and limbs. It was not only the counselors but their personal guards who were so afflicted, which made their enemy more numerous than expected.

Mari dashed forward, Belam, Neva, and Yago at her side. Around the chamber the warriors aligned to their cause wielded their sheathed swords like clubs—the purpose here was to render senseless, rather than kill.

The Neyudin leveled their spears, stoic in the face of danger. They joined ranks in squads and marched forward, until Padishin ordered a squad to escort the rahns and allied sayfs from the chamber and protect them at all costs. The others were to hold the doors. The ceremonial guards looked confused, but were trained to obey.

Mari sprinted on light feet, drawn Sûnblade burning bright in one hand, her scabbard in the other. She dropped and slid on her knees as an enemy swung at her. Mari hammered a blow across the man's abdomen as she passed under his attack. She turned as she came to her feet, the man barely perturbed by a blow that should have doubled him over in pain. Mari spared a glance for her comrades to see they all faced similar problems. Those inhabited by the marsh-puppeteers were stronger and faster than they had been as people; they also did not react to wounds. Despite dislocated shoulders, limbs bent at wrong angles, or other damage, the enemy was undeterred.

About her the Tyr-Jahavān was a place of turmoil. Counselors cried in terror as they tried to escape under the Neyudin's protection, in stark contrast to the battle cries of the warriors, or the crooning scholars whose skin and eyes shone bright as lanterns. The floor was smeared with the blood of warriors who had used less-than-deadly force. The marsh-puppeteer counselors snapped bones, or tore throats out in sprays of viscera. Femensetri's cantos and Sanojé's hexes had failed, and subduing their enemies was not an option.

"Lethal force!" Mari yelled. Without hesitation the warriors drew steel. Belam glided through the press like a dancer, every movement precise and beautiful. Neva moved lightly, her spear spinning, striking, parrying, her brother Yago completing their web of steel. Padishin joined the fray, his two-handed dionesqa handled with all the skill of his years as a soldier. Kiraj was by his side, swordwork precise, clinical.

Femensetri and Sanojé stood amid the melee. The Stormbringer had dropped her over-robe to reveal a sapphire-scaled gauntlet that covered her right arm from fingertips to shoulders. Lightning arced across the scales, burning blue-white. There was lightning, too, in her hair, and the phantom images of storm clouds whirled about her. She reached into the empty air and pulled from nowhere a tall spear, a single length of metal that blazed from tip to tip. The Stormbringer flung lightning and caused her enemies to dance an unsightly death jig as they cooked. Sanojé summoned flaming serpents who coiled, crushed, and immolated their targets.

Their enemies took their toll. Kiraj fell, his face collapsed under the hammer fist of a counselor. Padishin, surrounded, was knocked to the ground and stamped to death as he went to aid his friend. Neva was savagely backhanded, her body sliding across the blood-streaked floor. Yago shouted in anguish, his spear a blur as he cleared his way to his sister's side, only to have his back broken with an audible snap when one of the enemy counselors kicked him. Yago fell to the ground atop his sister, their blood mingling.

"Bensa!" Mari screamed. Bensaharēn the Waterdancer was tracked with blood. One eye was swollen closed. Clumps of his hair had been torn from his head. He swung his red-stained amenesqa with speed and skill, yet those fueled by marsh-puppeteer strength were not easily put down. Missing limbs, they fought on. The Poet Master swayed, flowed, and seemed to pour into the empty spaces between his attackers. Still he was pummeled, and struck with weapons taken from the fallen. He fought with blade, fist, and foot, yet was pushed back toward the open space between the pillars of the Tyr-Jahavān, and the space beyond.

Mari cut the head from one opponent. Both arms at the elbow from the next. She fought her way toward Bensaharēn: With each step her Sûnblade severed and cauterized flesh, slowly closing the distance.

The Stormbringer hurled lightning. Sanojé guided her flaming serpents, a puppeteer fighting the puppeteers. Belam and Nima fought like men possessed, their bodies streaked red. Though the floor was littered with the dead and wounded, the marsh-puppeteers neither gave, nor asked, for quarter. It had become less a battle, more a cull, as the odds slowly turned in the favor of Mari and her comrades.

Bensaharēn had been forced to the edge of the Tyr-Jahavān. One counselor, then another, and another, flung himself at the Waterdancer, weighing him down. Another added her strength. Then another. Bensaharēn was pushed farther back, his technique heartbreaking for all that its beauty did no good. He roared in defiance, teeth bared in a bloody mouth.

Mari was within arm's reach, when the press of bodies became too much.

The Waterdancer, her teacher, along with the handful of counselors who attacked him, toppled off the side of the Tyr-Jahavān.

Mari threw herself to clutch at one of the Poet Master's hands. For a moment they held together. She was dragged toward the edge, but held on regardless.

"I will not let you fall!" Mari screamed.

Bensaharēn hacked the head from one of his attackers. It was not enough. He smiled at Mari. "Tell Valaji I love him, am glad I married him, and will wait for him . . ." With deliberate care, he let go of Mari's hand.

Clutching his attackers to him, Bensaharēn sailed through the darkening skies to the cradle of Avānweh, hundreds of meters below.

❊ ❊ ❊

Mari gave orders through her tears, her voice as hard as her grief. Belam and Nima had gone into the city with their surviving Anlūki, in the hopes they could help maintain the peace, obsessed with making amends for Corajidin's failings.

The compromised counselors had been vanquished. The floor of the Tyr-Jahavān was littered with the dead, the dying, and the wounded. Healers had been summoned; Femensetri, Sanojé, and the other Sēq prioritized their patients and used the energies at their disposal to save whom they could.

Ajo approached Mari, his expression stricken as he stared at the scholars who kneeled over his grandchildren: not dead, though not far from it. "Mari . . . we can't—"

"Continue with the vote, Ajo," Mari snapped. She looked down at her hands, dried blood caked in ox horns around her nails, or wedged under them. *It goes on much more easily than it comes off.* "It's what we came here for. Don't make so much death worthless."

The Sky Lord nodded mutely. He addressed his colleagues, themselves stunned but attentive, their allies in the Teshri saved, for the most part. Mari did not hear the words. The raising of their hands—all of them this time—was something she barely paid attention to.

Mari wiped the tears from her eyes with her bloodied thumbs. The floor was smeared with red. The wounded cried in pain. Healers crooned, or chanted hexes, hard marble in place of soft beds for the stricken. Such is the price of liberty. She wished it had been otherwise—they had tried for it to be otherwise—but this was a road one saw to the end, or did not walk at all. This is what it means for the few to protect the many.

30

"HOPE AND EXPECTATION ARE NOT THE SAME THING. BOTH WILL
LEAD TO DISAPPOINTMENT. EXIST IN THE MOMENT, ACCEPTING ALL
THINGS AS THEY ARE, NOT AS YOU WOULD HAVE THEM BE."

—from the Nilvedic Maxims

DAY 83 OF THE 496TH YEAR OF THE

SHRĪANESE FEDERATION

Corajidin huddled in his over-robe at the entrance to the bustling command pavilion, his wrist, eye, and back aching. Snow-
flakes whipped out of a mustard sky, long streaks of late afternoon
light staining the stew of mud and camp filth. He was thankful for
the cold and the way the ground froze hard in the night, as it kept
the reek of the camp at bay.

He crushed the scroll in his hand, then dropped it into the
stew at his feet: Narseh was dead, an ally gone. Erebus only knew
what her heir was going to do; his message had certainly been non-
committal. *Do all my sins remembered and forgotten come for their
retribution now? It would be typical, for the world to take from me as*

much or more than it gives. Soon it will be over, one way or another, and perhaps I will know peace of a kind.

"What are you thinking, Jidi?" Mēdēya asked.

"Endings, beginnings . . ." He looked at his wife, Yashamin so close to the surface. *How much are you Yashamin, how much Mēdēya, and how much the voice of the Emissary?* "I stole your grace from you, my love. Is it too late to give it back?"

"You steal the grace from everything about you." At the sound of the Emissary's rusted croak, Corajidin's hearts stuttered, and Mēdēya jumped back, startled. The Emissary stood at Corajidin's other shoulder, hooded and cloaked. Yet she was no longer in silver-shot gray: Her attire was a sullen mix of bruised hues. Her sword was changed, a long curved weapon with an ornate bell guard shaped like an octopus, its tentacles forming an interwoven basket. "It's what we ensured you were made to be, so you'd be in this place, at this time, doing this thing for us. Never doubt that you're indeed an agent of destiny, Corajidin. Take comfort that most everything you do suits a purpose."

"Where have you been?" Mēdēya breathed. Corajidin's mouth tasted sour at Mēdēya's relieved tone.

"Indris killed me." The Emissary's tone was bleak.

"Indris is alive?" Corajidin choked. "How long have you known?"

"You were dead?" Mēdēya asked sympathetically. Corajidin glared at her interruption.

"For a time. I've hung in and on darkness, drowned in the will of my Masters, and punished for my failures. Yet they're not done with me. The Masters are never done." The Emissary glanced at Corajidin's prosthetic hand. Craned her neck to stare into the *kirion* ball that replaced his missing eye. Her smile was cold. "Seems I'm not the only person somebody tried to kill. At least Indris is neat about these things." She used her stiffened fingers to pantomime a sword stab. "He even kills with love. One cut. Right through the heart."

"One would assume this changes your position on whether he lives or dies?"

The Emissary's head cocked to one side in what Corajidin took for confusion. "Why? He was defending himself and those he cared for: one of the things that draws me to him. Neither my own nor my Masters' need for Indris has changed. He'll grow into what he must be."

"And my daughter?"

"That's a different matter entirely. She has taken something from me. I mean to have it back, over her dead body. You've lost her, Corajidin, to a cause she loves more than yours. And your golden Widowmaker, who came close to showing such promise. Tamerlan is fallen. The Dowager-Asrahn taken by the sea. Jhem slain at Mari's hands, and Nadir captured."

Had I understood what Belamandris was going to do, would I have stopped him? "How do you know this?" Corajidin whispered. An old pain settled in his chest as his hearts faltered in distress.

"I witnessed it."

"And there was nothing the great Emissary of the Drear could do to prevent this?"

The Emissary pressed her hand against Corajidin's chest. His hearts hammered more erratically, his pulse an off-kilter staccato. "Do? My husband saw me for what I have become, and killed me at Tamerlan. Would you like to share the experience of my death, my epiphany, enlightenment, and my resurrection?"

Corajidin found it hard to breath. His hearts beat so rapidly that his body shook, and his skin became fever hot. He could not form words, so he shook his head rapidly from side to side. The Emissary held on. His pulse was a whirring of hummingbird wings in his ears. His vision dimmed. He collapsed to his knees in the filth, then to his side, curled in a ball. Contact broken, his hearts slowed. It took many minutes for Corajidin to find his breath, all the while lanced on the Emissary's gaze.

"I thought not," she murmured. The Emissary looked at the last of the siege engines being hauled aboard a wind-galley. Soldiers struggled with the weight, faces red. The storm-cannon lumbered upward, so heavy it barely swung in the wind. Feyd stood at a safe distance among his officers, though Baquio stood almost directly beneath his creation, as if he could coax it upward through hand gestures, vocal encouragement, and will. At the far end of the camp, Prahna oversaw the loading of her precious cargo: lined crates filled with fire water, medicines, fuel crystals for the Salamander Lances, exploding powder, and other items best not damaged during the journey to Fandra.

"You're going to fight Indris from a fixed position?" The Emissary shrugged. "I suppose your Master of Arms knows what he's doing."

"Of course he knows what he's doing!" Corajidin snapped. Her tone rankled, the ensuing silence more so. "Why? What would you suggest?"

"Run? Surrender?" The Emissary was not smiling. "I'd not want to face him. My husband is a smart man, Corajidin. Smarter than anybody you've met. He made a career in the Sēq by delivering improbable solutions to complex, virtually unwinnable situations. He'll let you think you're doing well, right up to the point where he has you realize that not only are you beaten, but you've been playing the wrong game."

Troubled, Corajidin stalked across the compound to Feyd. The Master of Arms bowed to Corajidin, pretending the Emissary was not there. A report on progress was given promptly and in detail, much as Corajidin expected. Fandra had been occupied, the remaining townsfolk incarcerated so they could not spread word of the Erebus deployment or of new weapons. The force moving in from the south had maintained its approach, gaining strength as it passed. According to Feyd, the enemy commanders followed sound tactics and coordination. If they remained as disciplined in the field, the Erebus and their colors would be grateful for the protection Fandra had to offer, as well as the additional strength delivered by the witches, and the weapons of the artificers and the alchemists.

"Have you heard anything from the ruins?" the Emissary asked.

"Not for some hours," Feyd replied.

"Maybe you should check on their status," Corajidin suggested.

"As you wish." The Master of Arms called for one of the witches on intelligence duty.

"What word from the ruins?" Feyd asked her.

"Nothing since high sun today," she replied. "Ikedion wanted to reduce the number of sendings, as the hexes agitate the local fauna. We're finding the same thing here: Creatures are drawn to the power we use. We had a dhole come within a kilometer of the camp. It took a dozen witches and almost forty soldiers to kill the thing."

"Contact Ikedion now," Corajidin said. The witch muttered her hex under her breath, eyes rolling back so only the whites were seen. After a minute the witch's eyes rolled back down, her brow lined by a frown.

"There's no response, Asrahn."

"No witches to speak to?"

"No, Asrahn. Nobody at all."

Corajidin snapped orders to ready the first available ship to fly to the ruins. "Where is Kasraman? Or Wolfram? They need get out there and report back to me."

"Pah-Kasraman is in Fandra, overseeing the positions for the last of the siege weapons," Feyd said. "Wolfram was with Ikedion, at the ruins."

"You can blow your people at the ruins a kiss good-bye," the Emissary jibed.

"Oh, for . . ." Corajidin clenched his teeth in frustration. He was reminded of the Emissary's words, not too long before. Was this Indris? Was he this close? "What about Tahj-Shaheh?"

"With the sky fleet, Asrahn," Feyd replied. "I can have the witches recall her."

"No. Have her scout Wolfram's position, then report immediately." He pointed at Feyd. "Hasten the installation of the siege weapons at Fandra. I want the city as defensible as possible, as soon as possible."

"As you will, Asrahn." Feyd turned and shouted orders for his officers to join him in the command tent. The Emissary's chuckle was wet. Corajidin shot her a glare.

"You should rest, Jidi." Mēdēya's voice was firm. "You're not recovered—"

"I am well enough."

"No, you aren't. You can't fight, you're half blind, and your back wounds are not fully healed." Mēdēya placed her hands on his chest. "The energy in the Rōmarq is healing you faster than I would have thought possible, but—"

"So much so that you don't use my potion," the Emissary added. "Perhaps you should relocate here? Live amid the muck and mire. I'm sure your sins would find the scenery to their liking."

Corajidin rested his palm on the hilt of his knife, an unfamiliar gesture with his left hand. "Emissary, unless it has escaped your recollection, this is all being done in order to unify my people, so I can pay off my debts to you. You should rejoice that I have the strength I do, to execute your will. And, Mēdēya, I will be well enough. I do not intend to take part in the fighting." *What use would I be? How has this changed my dream, of facing Indris on the Ast am'a Jehour? I never saw how that encounter ended.*

The Emissary glanced at Corajidin's prosthetic with a smile. "I can make you whole again, Corajidin. All you need to do is ask."

"Another debt?" The lump of his artificial limb became the center of Corajidin's attention. He pulled the sleeve of his over-robe down to hide it. When he looked up, the Emissary was gone. Her cold chuckle came from nowhere, until he turned his head. She had moved into his blind spot. *But that is where you have always been, neh?* "I don't know that I'm wealthy enough to pay what you'd ask."

"You always have something to give, Corajidin."

❊ ❊ ❊

Corajidin stalked the camp, plagued by the Emissary's offer to make him whole. Though he had rejected her overture, he could taste the lie on his lips. Mēdēya walked with him, her fur-lined over-robe dragging in the slurry. She had said nothing since they had left the Emissary at the command pavilion, the weight of her silence growing with each step.

"What?" Corajidin rounded on her as they entered his pavilion. "You have something you want to say, say it!"

Mēdēya's gaze was fixed on Corajidin's hand. "Jidi, if the Emissary could make you—"

"Is there anything that woman says that you do not agree to?"

She looked baffled, and reached out a hand to tap his prosthetic. "You are my husband. And the most powerful man in Shrīan." Her expression became ferocious. "You deserve better than this cold lump, where a warm hand should be!"

"The Emissary cannot be trusted, as I have learned through bitter experience. There is always a price for her help, Mēdēya. And always the price seems reasonable in the moment of anguished acceptance, yet the shine soon wears off her gifts, and the depth of the hole one has dug becomes all too apparent. I can barely see what is around me for the darkness of the debt I am into her, and her Masters."

"And was my reincarnation such a tarnished gift?" Mēdēya's voice was sharp-edged with rage. "Have I not given you everything? I, who helped you plan the war against Far-ad-din? Was it not I who helped you murder your second wife, so that we could be together? And was it not I who died at Vahineh's hands, because you killed her father? You owe me much, Erebus fa Corajidin!" Her eyes welled with tears. They trembled on the ends of her long lashes, bright as chips of diamond. "You dragged me from the Well of Souls, made me a Nomad in a country that can't abide me. I hide in another woman's flesh, speak with her voice, while you look into her eyes and ravage us both—"

"Enough!" he cried. His hands trembled and pain blossomed in his head. "Please, enough. I loved . . . love you more than any other woman I have known. I see you, Yashamin, in Mēdēya. It is you I love, not the flesh. But there is more in you than Yashamin. Something that speaks with the Emissary's voice."

"There is only I, Jidi. Only Yashamin. If it happens that you hear the Emissary's voice in mine, it's perhaps because I agree with her. She's given much, and it's fair she asks much in return. We've demanded the same of others, and our hands are far from clean.

"Do I think you should let her make you whole? Yes! I don't want to be touched by that awful excuse for a hand for the rest of your life. Do I think your daughter is an ungrateful bitch who has betrayed her House, and should be used however is best to repay her debt to her bloodline? Yes! Put her in the Torque Spindle! Make her part of the Feigning! She was born to be used. The world is ours by right of conquest, my love. Such was clear to you once. Put aside your doubts about me, about us, about right or wrong. Lead your people the way they need to be led. You are Avān, and you were made to rule this world."

Corajidin sat down hard on his couch. Were the room darker, he would have sworn the person before him was Yashamin in all her temper. The cadence and timbre of her voice, her stance, her words, were Yashamin's.

He explored the cold thing that replaced his hand. *For the rest of your life* . . . To able to see properly again, rather than live half in darkness. To be able to face Näsarat fa Roshana and show her that she was powerless over him. He could still recover what had been taken from him.

Mēdēya curled at his feet, her head in his lap. Such a strong sense of Yashamin in the posture. Her hands were sure on his flesh with the years of their experience. "Do this for me, Jidi. I've lost the body I was born in, returned in this flesh that I'm still learning the feel of. But your body is yours. Make it whole again, for me. It's your real hands I want to explore me, your real eyes I want seeing me. Please, Jidi."

"Find the Emissary, Mēdēya," Corajidin whispered. "Let us learn what her price will be, before I say no to something I may regret for the rest of my life."

Mēdēya kissed him. Corajidin resisted at first, yet the movement of her hands, her lips, and her tongue, as well as the passion of her words, broke his reluctance. Still, he held part of himself back. Doubt lingered within him. Something only time, success, and the absence of the Emissary from his life would assuage. Mēdēya disengaged, her face a series of curved planes framed on backlit curls. "I shan't be long, Jidi!"

She raced out of the pavilion.

Corajidin crossed the carpeted floor to where his writing desk stood. The carpet squelched under his feet and released a faint hint of must. As he sat he felt the legs of his chair sink a little. Corajidin perused the scrolls and journals that accounted for his war effort thus far. The novels and serials he had brought with him from Erebesq. And a copy of his first book, *Our Destiny Made Manifest*. It was a jingoistic piece, written when he was younger and filled more with piss and vinegar, rather than with the fire of his experiences. Beside it a leather-bound folio, the pages less yellowed with age, titled *The Road to Tomorrow*, which was supposed to have been a more mature narrative on the greatness of the Avān, and the benefits of militaristic and economic imperialism. He cracked the folio open, to little more than one page of dogmatic blather, then a vast and empty vista on which he should have written more.

Should have, would have, could have. "Will do," he murmured.

The ceiling of his pavilion was backlit by a ball of lightning. There came the snap, crackle, and hiss of Disentropy Spools and Tempest Wheels. The ceiling of his pavilion sagged from the pressure as a ship flew low overhead. From what little Corajidin could see through the pavilion entrance, it was flying sideways, its stern wavering. He hurried outside in time to see the craft jerk in the air, then plow a deep furrow through the soupy ground. Its progress was arrested by tent ropes and several feet of flapping cloth. Soldiers assembled around it, weapons drawn.

Wolfram staggered to the rail of the skiff, helped by battered soldiers. Together they fell overboard into the mud. The Angothic Witch clutched at his head, then vomited into the filth.

"What happened?" Corajidin yelled. More soldiers had arrived. A squad boarded the wind-skiff and within moments the lightning flares stopped, wheels and spools spinning down into silent darkness. Two of the soldiers hauled the bloated carcass of Ikedion from the ship, the man's figure slick with blood. It took one look to know his fate: No man bled so much and lived. Corajidin stood by the heaving Wolfram. "What. Happened?"

"The Rōmarqim," Wolfram spat. "One of their advanced war parties. They came quiet out of the marsh, caused as much damage as they could, then disappeared before we could muster an effective resistance."

"We knew this would happen," Feyd said. "The armies are still too far away to cause us any harm. These skirmishes are to divert our attention. But I suggest, Asrahn, that we get you installed at Fandra sooner rather than later."

Corajidin grabbed Wolfram's shirt. "Tell me you managed to retrieve the treasures from the Rōmarq! Tell me this was not a waste of time, and that all may not be lost!"

"The Havoc Chair was already on its way to Fandra, Asrahn," Wolfram said. "We sent as much as we could ahead of us. All is not lost."

"But some?"

"Nothing that we can't retrieve once we're victorious, and nothing that I believe will give our enemy an advantage in the war to come."

Corajidin glared into the night. Best to take no chances. "Feyd? Order Tahj-Shaheh to expand her patrols, and retake the dig sites. The marsh beggars of the Rōmarqim will have fled back to their mud huts, no doubt content with their small victories. Tahj-Shaheh is to engage with prejudice when she has the chance, clear any opposition, but not to take any unnecessary risks. Soldiers can be replaced, but I will not tolerate the loss of a single ship. Somebody get me a wind-ship and crew. I would be in Fandra, to oversee the last of our preparations. And have somebody collapse the tunnels to the Weavegate. I'll not have them used by the enemy, and we can clear the rubble when we need to use them again."

Indris is behind this. Let him come. This time I have the advantage, and I will ensure that he does not walk away from the shot that should kill him.

"I AM WHO I AM BECAUSE IT IS ALL I KNOW HOW TO BE."

—Mahj-Näsarat fe Malde-ran, the Empress-in-Shadows, and
last monarch of the Awakened Empire

The trees sheltered Indris and his comrades from the wind, the
ground to the north of the forest pale with frost. False dawn lightened the horizon and made the rest of the world darker for it. The
warriors gathered around small pedestals of firestones, and huddled
in their over-robes.

With his Awakened sight, Indris gazed out across the breadth
of the Rōmarq in wonderment at the columns of energy that shot
skyward from it, ghostly columns like the phantom ruins of a city
nobody else could see. The ahm fountained upward in other places,
curving gracefully through the air like a phosphorescent rainbow, to
then splash back to the ground. Ahm shone from everything about
him: The leaves of trees were backlit stained glass. The snow was

fistfuls of diamond dust strewn across a blanket. The energy of the people around him flared and faded with their heartbeats. Their voices carried on the wind, resonant and heavy with meaning—

"Indris." Chaiya turned to him, a jade-hued phantom etched in black ink. *"You're Awakening whether you like it or not."*

"I know." Indris felt his new power coiled like a serpent up and around his spine. It ignited his energy centers. He glanced at her and the other Nomads that drifted between and through the trees. Friends both long and recently dead. Some he did not know at all. *"Now that my eyes are open, there is part of me that desires this. But I'm becoming what I can't be, and I don't think I can stop it."*

"Most likely not," Ariskander said. The man portrayed the image of himself in the prime of his life: lean, strong, and regal. *"But it was meant to be this way."*

"Why have you come?" Indris asked. "There's no need for the Nomads to be involved."

"There are Soul Traders about," Chaiya said grimly. "Traitors to their own kind. We will take care of them for you—you can rest assured the souls of your slain will not be harvested by them today. There is a tide of shadows rising in the Well of Souls, and the dead fear it greatly. We would have some answers from those we believe know more."

"What do you think's happening?" Shar's question jarred Indris back. The leaders of their forces were with her. The Nomads remained, superimposed on the world, but silent, watchful, and unseen by any save him.

"Corajidin will know the Rōmarqim are on the offensive," Morne said as he and Kyril walked up, hand in hand. "It's a logical thing for them to do, and Corajidin's generals will see it as such. If there'd been no reprisals, it would've raised suspicions. Last night was about giving him confidence he's in control. Our allied forces have assembled at the Anqorat Bridge and on the Fandra Road, days away. He sees that our strength gathers, and should be confident that he can outmatch it."

"Can we keep him confined?" Ekko asked.

"Breaching city defenses isn't ideal at the best of times," Kyril replied. "But it's just as hard to get out of a fortified position as to get into it. He'll realize that soon enough."

Indris nodded in agreement. "Once he and his officers are in custody, the chain of command will fall to those less interested in dying for Corajidin's cause."

"And the treasures he's stolen from the Rōmarq?" Ojin-mar looked surprisingly mundane in his weathered earth hues. He, along with He-Who-Watches, had been among the dozen or so who had been able to understand the translocation formula in the time they had available. "We'll need to make sure what he's taken from the Rōmarq is accounted for."

"And returned to its rightful custodian, Rahn-Siamak," Shar said.

"The Sēq will want—"

"Shar is right, Ojin-mar," Indris countered. "The Sēq are a long way from demanding anything. If you want to play with Siamak's toys, you'd best ask nicely."

"And the hostages?" Morne asked. "From what we've heard, there are still civilians in Fandra."

Indris glanced at Ojin-mar and He-Who-Watches. The tribesman was swaddled against the cold, only his pale eyes visible between the folds of his taloub. Indris pointed back into the forest with his chin. "How many Sēq Wraith Knights did you bring from Amarqa?"

"Twenty-three have gathered, in different simulacra," He-Who-Watches replied. "They're all war-shells, ranging in size from crows and hawks, to foxes, wolves, and mountain cats, to knights and armored warhorses. There are also twenty Iku, and about as many

Katsé. The Iku and Katsé were deployed into the Rōmarq under the cover of darkness, and have been marking patrols all night: no contact, as ordered. We've a good idea of troop numbers, rotations, entrances, and exits. They're ready to move against Fandra when we are."

"Send in the smaller Wraith Knights and have them find the hostages," Indris said. "If they get the opportunity, have the wraiths free them and lead them north out of the city. If they can't free them without exposing us, have the wraiths hold position until we arrive. Once in the Rōmarq, I doubt many of Corajidin's warriors will be keen on giving chase."

"Can we attack all our targets at the same time?" Kyril asked. "We're relying on the distraction."

"Ojin-mar? He-Who-Watches? Are your scholars ready?" Indris asked. Both Masters nodded. Indris tried to relax. Kyril was right: Their timing would be critical. "The Sēq Knights will coordinate the attacks, and we'll be in communication with each other. Each of them will lead small units of elite fighters from the Houses and Families, and cause as much disruption as they can at Corajidin's excavation sites."

Ojin-mar said, "Knowing he has days until the allied army arrives, we expect Corajidin to reinforce his dig sites in order to continue his tomb raiding up until the last minute. This will reduce the defensive capabilities of Fandra. He-Who-Watches and I will hide our own wind-ships behind illusions, and remain on over-watch over Fandra. If things turn ugly, we'll be ready."

"Can you maintain the invisibility charms around the fleet?"

"It's a short enough distance," Ojin-mar said. "If all goes to plan, they'll not see us. But if we have to fight, we'll not be able to hold the illusions in place for long. We'll be focused on battle formulae, and protective wards."

"If we have to fight," Shar said with a grin, "you won't have to be invisible."

"It is a win-win, when you think about," Ekko rumbled.

"I do believe you're right." Shar nodded solemnly.

"I'll lead the retrieval team to capture Corajidin," Indris said. "Morne and Kyril, you'll lead the strike teams. Once inside, you and your crews from the Immortals are to take and hold the siege weapons. Please avoid killing if you can. Who else will lead your teams?"

"Leonetto and Tamiwa," Morne said without hesitation.

Indris looked at those gathered about him, both the living and the dead. "Go to your teams and finish your preparations. Air crews to the wind-ships, strike teams to their commanders. Protect your scholars! They're the ones who'll get you in, heal the wounded, and get you out again in an emergency. And please, no heroics! You being here is evidence enough of your caliber. There's nothing more for you to prove."

He walked with the others a short way into the wood. They came to a clearing where the Immortal Companions were sharpening weapons, attending to armor, and breaking down the camp. Warriors made their way to their staging areas, with three wind-frigates in a nearby field and a larger destroyer and two corsairs deeper in the forest. Others from the Houses and Families assembled about their brown-robed scholars.

Shar and Ekko joined Indris as he took up his Scholar's Lantern. He missed Changeling already, used to her shape, weight, and length in battle. Yet his lantern would serve well enough as a weapon, as well as a focus for his disentropy. With his Awakening growing more pronounced, energy poured through his body like never before, making him restless.

The Nomads assembled, scores of spectral shapes invisible to the others. "*We are with you, Indris*," Ariskander said. Hayden, Omen, Chaiya, Vashne, Daniush . . . and a host of others all nodded their assent.

Indris accepted the offer silently. He looked to Shar and Ekko, armored and armed. "You don't need to do this. You've done enough, and Shrīan isn't even your country. I'd not see you killed, and there's a chance none of us will walk away from this."

"You say that all the time," Shar said. "But if I'm going to join the wind spirits, I'd rather my last moments be with the ones I love. Besides, we've come too far together to do something like this apart. I do wish Hayden and Omen were here, though."

Both Nomads smiled. *They are here, Shar.* Indris kept quiet; to say the words might cause her pain.

Two squads of warriors joined them: warrior-poets of the Rōmarqim with their shamshirs, reed sandals, and long ponytails; Lamenti in their phoenix-embroidered over-robes and armor; Anlūki in their blacks and reds; the gold-armored warriors of the Sûn; and the lion and lotus of the Selassin.

"Ready?" Indris asked.

"Always," Ekko replied. Shar nodded, her skin and eyes flickering with radiance as she prepared herself for what was to come. The other warriors shifted nervously, but nodded all the same. His crew formed a circle that faced outward, weapons drawn, Indris at its hub.

Indris made eye contact with the leaders of the other crews, and sent a thought to the Sēq scholars.

Now.

❋ ❋ ❋

Indris folded space. A rainbow bridge ignited in a riot of color. It spanned a place of monochromatic streaks: dimensionless, dizzying, silent, numb, airless, freezing.

They stepped forward and were swept from there to—

The roof of the governor's villa in Fandra. Dust swirled away in tiny spirals. The air smelled scorched. Translocation had not been as strenuous as Indris had feared, and both Changeling and the Scholar's Lantern trickled energy back into his system. It flowed into the widening channels of his existence, where what had been streams became rivers.

Indris was barraged by the layered hexes, and the unruly Disentropic Stains of the witches who cast them. Indris probed lightly and detected not only witches, but also the presence of arcane siege weapons, and artificers' and alchemists' creations. There were presences that stood out above all others, powerful individuals like stones in a strong current, as well as a device that stank of militant purpose. Those people and the device blazed with the untamed, tainted energy of the Rōmarq. Indris's gentle use of disentropy had given him a sense of euphoria, and he wondered what those others felt, having been swamped by it for longer. Changeling purred. *I'll need to be careful to not let myself go.*

Indris gathered his crew close. "Corajidin is our target. Anything else is a bonus. Am I clear?"

The crew nodded their understanding. Voices sounded in Indris's head as the other Sēq reported successful translocations, and were proceeding with their assaults. Ojin-mar and He-Who-Watches had arrived, and floated unseen above the city, within striking distance of Corajidin's sky fleet. So far, so good.

From the roof of the villa, Indris had a commanding view of Fandra. The city was comprised of forums, interconnected by winding roads and narrow lanes, and wide canals where the shadows of small boats rocked against the banks. The city was not well lit, though lantern light made a haze of the parts of the city occupied by the Erebus forces. Wind-ships had been grounded in parks and forums—whatever spaces had been large enough to hold them. The larger military vessels, frigates, a couple of destroyers, and an enormous dreadnought hung heavy, the light of their Disentropy Spools and Tempest Wheels bright on the rooftops. One decrepit vulture of a ship made him cringe, held aloft on spools of blood and shadow. It was toward this ship that Ariskander and Chaiya led the Nomads. The Nomads streamed through the city streets like a jade mist. They passed unsuspecting guards who marched on patrol, their lanterns swaying, red-robed witches of the Mahsojhin scattered among their number.

Indris looked to the walls of Fandra. There were two major gates, a number of smaller ones, and a large river gate of thick bars. Soldiers patrolled the walls, though more were huddled around braziers, spears and bows leaning against the battlements. What need was there for caution? Their enemy was days away.

Movement caught his attention. A small group of black-clad warriors crept up on a guard position and the ornate cylinder of the storm-cannon they crewed. There was a brief flurry of activity; then only the warriors in black—the Immortal Companions— were left standing. Indris watched as this happened twice more, the cynic in him aware that it was only a matter of time before somebody discovered what was happening.

Indris flicked a thought to the Sēq Wraith Knights in the city. *Are the captives safe?*

Almost. We're leaving Fandra now, General, with none the wiser. Do you need our assistance?

Not at the moment, thanks. Once the captives are out of the city, return to the gates with the rest of the Wraith Knights. There are witches and arcane engines that need to be dealt with, and I may need some help before we're done.

Shouts rang from the city. Horns blared and whistles pierced the night. Crews boarded the grounded wind-ships as pilots prepared their craft for takeoff. Raised voices reported that the excavation sites were being attacked. Within a few minutes, two of the wind-frigates—Selassin, by the lion figureheads—and a number of smaller wind-boats flew north at speed.

Indris felt the ahm currents stir as the witches in Fandra wove hexes. The color and shape of the ahm warping spoke to communication hexes, as well as those of protection, and scrying. There was so much disentropy that Indris had difficulty maintaining his control: The urge to let his powers free, to see exactly how powerful his Awakening body, mind, and soul had become, was close to overwhelming. His Scholar's Lantern pulsed with the beating of his heart, and Changeling growled with the need to be unleashed. Indris rested his palm on Changeling's hilt, and found she burned with an unfamiliar warmth.

With Morne's crews at work, Indris ordered his own team across the rooftop. Shar and Ekko went first, along with one of the Anlūki, and a Rōmarqim who had lived in Fandra. The four of them kept to the shadows, and emerged only to neutralize the guards. Wan cries stuttered in the darkness, each one causing Indris to clench his teeth, dreading the sound of alarms. It came closer than he would have liked when one of the guards proved to be a witch. Indris felt the witch draw energy to weave a hex. He leaped forward and stretched his Disentropic Stain, the power of his aura confounding that of the guard, silencing the hex long enough for Indris to put the witch in a stranglehold. He lowered the unconscious man to the ground with a sigh of relief.

The crew moved to the door that led down into the building. Indris rested his hand on the latch, when the raucous sound of alarms split the night. A hue and cry came not long after. Indris spared a glance for the walls, and saw Morne's Immortals in a melee with the Erebus soldiers. Morne's crew were holding their own, their scholar invoking layers of battle wards to provide additional protection. Indris felt the tug of the ahm from the scholar's formulae, as the witches of Fandra would.

Are you close? Indris thought to the Sēq Wraith Knights. *Morne and the Immortals need help.*

We're on the way, General.

Moments later Indris saw the shapes of hawks and crows rise from beyond Fandra's walls. They flew faster than their *kirion* and witchfire wings beat, moon-tinted light shining from between their feathers. The small gate to the north of the city boomed. Boomed again. Erebus soldiers ran toward it. It buckled. One more strike, and the door exploded inward as a massive metallic stallion, eyes shining like lamps and fire tracing its hooves, thundered into the city. The armored knight on its back struck with a massive hammer, leveling anything it hit. Other shapes bounded in—foxes, wolves, and mountain cats. Massive armored knights with helms shaped like jackal heads, birds of prey, and daemons of legend. The crow-faced Iku and the vulpine Katsé ran with them, weapons drawn. The Iku cawed and the Katsé gave their high-pitched yapping barks as they spread through the city, and Sēq Wraith Knights chanted their canto in unearthly dirges.

"So much for being sneaky," Shar observed.

"Stealth is overrated," Ekko replied. "Besides, we were going to be discovered sometime."

"And time is something we're short on. Follow me." Indris opened the door and raced downstairs, his crew with him.

They met soldiers on their way through the governor's wing. Where possible, Indris's crew subdued them. Where it was not, deadly force was used. Blood flowed on both sides. As they moved from room to room, the press of bodies against them grew. Swords belled. Shields crashed. Armor broke. Skin opened. The fallen screamed. Still Indris pressed forward, his crew working as one.

Indris's thirteen became ten. Ten became seven. Those warriors too wounded to continue remained to guard the rear. Those who died were left, in the hopes their bodies would be reclaimed after the red work was done. Shar and Ekko stood at Indris's shoulders, their weapons a glittering net of *serill* and steel. Ekko roared, and

Shar sang terror into her enemies, while buoying the spirits of her comrades. Both warriors were scored with cuts, the shoulder piece of Shar's *serill* armor chipped, with long shatter marks down its length. Ekko's mane was slick with blood, the fortune-coins in his mane dull with it.

A witch in the Aspect of a bull-skulled giant, with flayed skin and torrents of pus for blood, smashed through a doorway. Anlūki and other Erebus warriors were at its side. They were joined by a flaming squid of improbable proportions that lashed out with tentacles as hard as steel. Indris snapped out a canto and invoked layers of the defensive wards he had learned at Isenandar. Spectral panels of glass spun, fractals of light whirring between them to absorb the energies the witches hurled. Indris formed tiny points of light that grew, shone like gold, and turned into wasps the length of his finger. The wasps swarmed around the witches and the Anlūki, as his own wounded crew joined the battle. Indris drew the larger of his two pistols and fired bolt after bolt. When it was spent, he drew the smaller one and fired until it, too, was out of ammunition. He leaped forward with his Scholar's Lantern, the *serill* head as bright as a star. Side by side with his crew, Indris traded blows until the Anlūki and the witches were beaten. On death, one witch reverted to a woman who may well have been a schoolteacher. The other witch reverted to a grossly obese man with skin stretched to the point where it looked ready to split.

The double doors ahead of them slammed to a close. Erebus soldiers turned to face the new threat, their faces etched with dread. Ekko and Shar descended on them. Blades whirled and danced in a furious exchange. Shar used her voice as a weapon, a series of shouts stunning her opponent until he fell to his knees, and she struck him unconscious. Ekko snarled as he held his enemy over his head, then dropped the man flat; he lay on the ground, dazed.

Ekko faced the doors, fangs bared. Indris felt the upswell of energy as a powerful hex was thrown up around the doors.

"Ekko!" Indris thundered. "Don't—"

The lion-man kicked the doors with all his strength.

And roared in agony.

Lightning flared, holding the thrashing Tau-se in the air. A vortex appeared about him, gaining speed as it swirled. Ekko shrank on himself as he withered. Indris felt the tug of the malignant hex, and cast layer upon layer of wards about Ekko. About himself, and what remained of his crew. Plants curled and dried. Carpets aged and rotted. Paint peeled from walls and the air turned stale and musty. The outer layers of Indris's wards flared through the spectrum and puffed out of existence. The middle layers were slower to succumb, but succumb they did. The inner layers held, tinted with blue and purple from the damage they had taken. When the vortex played itself out, the room looked as if nobody had lived in it for more than a century, save what Indris's wards had shielded.

Ekko fell to the ground with a dry, brittle sound.

Shar streaked forward, crying out denials. Indris came more slowly, his senses peaked. Changeling had made its way into Indris's hand, the weapon oddly quiet. Ekko lay twisted, emaciated. His fur had turned white where it had not fallen out in tufts when Shar stroked it. The leather straps of his armor had rotted away, the steel rusted. Indris reached down to Shar, who slapped his hand away. He could not meet her eyes for the pain in them.

The sound of armored feet reached him. Indris saw dozens of Erebus soldiers: Anlūki, enormous Iphyri horse-men, the raggedy mountain Jiharim, and as many witches entered the room behind his crew. The doors where Ekko had been killed rattled. Sawdust and paint flakes fell from them. The hinges creaked as the doors slowly opened.

"It's over, husband," the Emissary said.

✳ ✳ ✳

Indris's mind reeled. He felt a hollowness in this chest, and his stomach sank. He clenched his Scholar's Lantern tighter in his fist for balance.

Behind the Emissary, Corajidin was much changed, his right eye a polished ball of *kirion* set amid angry scars, his right hand a horse-headed prosthetic club. Indris saw the artifact Corajidin sat on, and knew the grip of despair. *A Havoc Chair! If he knows how to use it, he could kill everybody in and around Fandra in moments.* Beside the chair stood Wolfram, Kasraman, and a beautiful young woman that Indris took to be Mēdēya.

Lurking in the shadows were a half dozen emaciated phantoms in ragged gray finery that had seen its day centuries past. Some wore coronets in memory of their station in life. All had dulled jewels and baubles around their necks, their fingers, or at their ear—and each of them carried an annulus with a swirling web of light at its center. *Soul Traders, I presume?*

The Emissary drew closer. "Do you not have an apology for me, Indris?"

He stood straighter. "I apologize for not killing you, if that's what you mean. It's a mistake I'll not make twice."

Her face contorted with anger. "As my husband—"

"We're not husband and wife," Indris said. "The woman I loved is dead."

"I'm here, Indris!" Under the light of the Scholar's Lantern, she could not take on Anj's face. "This is me!"

"What you are is dead to me."

The Emissary struck a blow across Indris's face that rattled his teeth and caused his knees to bend. *She is so strong!* His ears rang, and he tasted blood from his split lip. The Emissary came close and hissed, "You'll come to appreciate the sacrifices I made. Even as the

Masters tore me apart and remade me in their image, it was my love for you that let me hold on to what I was. Don't take that away. I'm the same Anj where it counts: the woman you loved enough to defy the Sēq. Love me again, and I'll give you the chance to make your defiance mean something, now and forever."

Indris probed one of his teeth with his tongue. "That's one of the most pathetic things I've ever heard."

The Emissary struck at Indris again, but this time her hand slammed into the Scholar's Lantern. There was a sizzle and a crack: the mixed smell of burned flesh and rotten seaweed. The Emissary shouted with as much pain as surprise.

"I'm here for Corajidin," Indris said. He allowed his left eye to burn bright. The Erebus forces gathered around him murmured nervously. "You know who I am. Have heard what I can do. There's no need for anybody else to die if you surrender and give Corajidin over to me."

The man in question laughed bitterly. "They are sworn to me, and my vision. What mercy will the Teshri show them? None! So stop your bluster, drop your weapons, and I may show the leniency the Teshri would never have shown me."

"Indris is mine," the Emissary said. "No matter what you want, Corajidin. I'll be taking my husband with me. Alive or dead, my Masters will find a use for him."

From where she knelt, Shar gave voice to a concussive sound-wave that smashed the glass in the windows and caused the walls to vibrate. The Erebus forces clapped their hands over their ears. Corajidin's head slammed back against the Havoc Chair, but the air before Wolfram, Kasraman, and Mēdēya glittered with passive wards that Indris had not detected. *Good to know.*

The Emissary rocked back, infuriated, as she wiped green blood from her nose and ears. Shar uncoiled from the floor, sword a blur as it flashed across the Emissary's throat. It left a faint scratch that oozed dark blood. The Emissary cocked her head, clearly unamused. Shar struck again, but the Emissary slid to the side and backhanded the Seethe woman. Shar flew like a rag doll across the room and crashed into the wall. Wood splintered. Plaster cracked. She slid to the ground, limbs twisted, blood gushing from her nose and mouth.

"That for your broken little bitch!" the Emissary grated. "It's nothing compared to what I'll do to Mari when I get my hands on her."

"That was a mistake," Indris murmured.

The room went silent.

Grief and anger, guilt and resentment, threatened to choke him. He translocated the last of his crew out of the villa, to the decks of the allied wind-ships that floated invisible above Fandra. Indris invoked dense layers of wards around Shar's and Ekko's bodies, to ensure they would not suffer any indignity from what he was about to do. He fixed their broken bodies in his mind.

Now there's only me, and those who oppose me. And nothing left to hold me back.

The Emissary drew her sword with its abhorrent tentacled guard. The Scholar's Lantern flared. Changeling sent vibrations up Indris's arm. Images flashed across his mind, with revelations of numbers in multidimensional formulae that Indris did not think possible. His Dragon Eye burned hotter. The serpent coiled around Indris's flexed spine, growing into its power. He looked at the still forms of Shar and Ekko. Hatred and vengeance hung like low-hanging fruit, tempting, possibly satisfying. Indris left them where they were. Sorrow, yes. Anguish, yes. Love, yes. Conscience. Honor. Justice. Duty. These were the things that fueled him. The expanded pathways in his body, mind, and soul channeled greater energies than Indris had felt before. His right eye, previously dormant, now smoldered. Air wavered as the heat from Indris grew, and he felt the dragon in him rouse itself from slumber and stretch its wings around him.

Erebus soldiers fled the room in a panic. Mahsojhin witches manifested in their Aspects, hexes spun as quickly as they could. The Aspect of a bloated shadowy spider shuddered, then vanished. The witch within it did not have time to shriek before she was incinerated. Her ashes swirled in the superheated air, soon joined by another, and another.

"Leave, or die!" Indris rapped his lantern against the floor. There was a peal of thunder. Glass fragments skittered. The floor rolled beneath his feet. Walls groaned as they exhaled. Needing no further encouragement, the witches fled.

The gates had been opened, and the Rōmarq flowed with energy. Changeling and his Scholar's Lantern thrummed with it, as they poured ahm into the vessel Indris had become. The lantern burned brighter, blazing with revelations. Changeling's croon became a clear note of ecstasy.

He was the eye of the maelstrom. The Emissary invoked her wards, strangely tuned things in hues of coral and the wine-dark sea. Layer upon layer she built, only for Indris's rapid-fire canto to demolish. Wolfram added his power, the great goat-headed shadow of the Black King of the Woods manifested around him. Cantos and hexes blistered the air, weakening the villa around them. Part of the ceiling collapsed, ground to dust by the Emissary's war formula. The wall exploded outward when waves of power met, and found the path of least resistance when irresistible forces met, and would not relent.

Corajidin, eyes rolling with madness, gripped the Havoc Chair. Indris lanced the man with a canto. Corajidin's body spasmed once, and his head lolled. The temptation to kill him, and be done, was strong. A deadly canto vibrated in his throat, silenced at the thought of what Mari would think of him.

Consequence damped his ire. He collared the dragon, and though it lashed its coils, Indris held on.

With calmer eyes, Indris saw the truth of the Emissary: the darkness and depth to her, and the umbilical of the soul that joined her with her dread, and watchful, Masters. They saw through her eyes, and heard through her ears, and would remember what they saw. Corajidin, too, was laid out before him: broken and poorly remade, a wreck collapsing under his own rot and the weight of the hatreds he hoarded—yet too insatiable to stop. In Mēdēya he saw Yashamin, peering from behind the body of a stolen woman, clinging jealously to life, and a world of selfish ambition, sensation, and power. And Wolfram, who wore the Aspect of the Black King of the Woods, a true believer in the old powers who had nonetheless had his faith shaken, yet knew no other way. Yet perhaps the only one who missed cleaner days.

Indris turned his attention to the chill specters that lurked in the corners. The Soul Traders were what they appeared to be, foul reapers of the dead, thieves of souls. Indris would have none of them: They did not belong here. A canto shattered their annuli, and freed the souls that had been snared in them. The freed souls sang for joy, the sound turning dark as they rounded on their captors. Indris voiced a basso chant, and sent the Soul Traders shrieking, broken and displaced, to the Well of Souls. Their former captives hounded them like cattle dogs.

Indris and Kasraman shared a long look. The Erebus heir disguised his true nature behind powerful hexes, and colossal self-control. He stood at the edge of the light of truth, the few radiant bars that touched him hinting at his strength, and at the Aspect beneath. Kasraman was, perhaps, in some ways, Indris's tarnished reflection. Indris saw visions of what Kasraman was capable of: broken earth, cities in flame, islands sunk beneath the waves and new ones risen, armies so vast they boggled the mind, the cries of those who had forgotten the taste of freedom as they bent their knee to a dark and terrible Mahj who would rule them for eternity—

"No!" Indris whispered. "That's not what I'll become!"

Indris drew his power in. Awakening tested his resolve, and defied his will. It had taken root, and the dragon had caught glimpses of Indris's mind, and soul. Unity called, the myriad voices of the world called to him, the strength of wild animals, the patience of ancient trees, the slow and deliberate mind of—

"Kill him!" Kasraman's voice cracked with panic. "In Erebus's name, kill him now!"

"He sees the truth too late," Indris murmured.

The Emissary raised her sword and struck, dark tears staining her face.

Indris raised Changeling by reflex. Her purr became a contralto hum. Indris's soul channeled through her, and manifested as a slender blade of starlight, trapped in wavering haze. He parried the Emissary's blow, her sword booming like the surf. She stared at him, and at the soul blade that Changeling had become. Her face betrayed her fear as she leaped back.

From the corner of his eye, Indris saw the withered and broken forms of Ekko and Shar where they lay. His wards were dull around them, almost spent. Indris held back a cry of relief when Shar cracked open a bloodied eye, grimaced, and shook her head. *No.*

Wind gusted as a Näsarat wind-destroyer descended, its port bank of storm-cannons leveled at the governor's villa. Beyond it could be seen the shapes of other wind-ships under the command of Ojin-mar and He-Who-Watches. The presence of scholars, the Wraith Knights, the Nomads, Morne's soldiers—all assembled around the villa. Watching. Waiting.

Vibrating with power, Indris drew himself up. He dulled the light of his lantern, and with a great effort of will extinguished Changeling's blade. His recent efforts had left him shaking, his skin flushed, head pounding, and light sparking behind his eyes. He felt the onset of a mindstorm—or worse, an ahm-stroke—but stood as best he was able. Indris leveled his gaze on Corajidin, who had regained his faculties, and snarled back, unrepentant.

"Rahn-Erebus fa Corajidin, by the power granted me by the Arbiter of the Change, by the Teshri am Shrīan, and by the unified will of the Great Houses and the Hundred Families, I place you under arrest for treason, regicide, and murder."

"The Teshri have no authority over me, boy!" Corajidin said. He gripped the arms of the Havoc Chair once more.

"It's over, Corajidin. Don't make me kill you."

"But you won't!" he gloated. "Not if you don't want to lose my daughter, with her misguided love."

The Emissary whispered to Kasraman. The two of them, and Wolfram, stepped clear of Corajidin. The old Angothic Witch stared at his Asrahn forlornly, hands wringing his oft-mended staff. Indris saw the way he glanced about, searching for escape.

"I'd not, were I you," Indris warned.

"But we're not you, are we?" the Emissary said. "Nobody can be."

"The Teshri will give you a fair trial."

"Can you promise that, Indris?" Kasraman asked. "Or will I be tarred with the brush of my father's failed ambitions?"

"That's for the Arbiter's Tribunal to decide," Indris said. "You're surrounded. Submit, before there's more bloodshed."

"I rather think not." Kasraman smiled urbanely. "Until I know whether it's silk sheets, or salt-forged shackles, that await me."

Something not quite a hex, and not quite a canto, crested from the ahm. Indris grabbed for it, tried to disrupt it. The grip of his power slipped, like trying to hold a greased fish. The Emissary, Kasraman, and Wolfram lost depth, then faded from existence, the air snapping with a small thunderclap into the places they had stood. Indris flung a seeker hex after them, but it, too, had nothing to latch on to.

Corajidin looked shocked, then furious. He bent his head in concentration, a frown cracking his brow. His left hand flexed on the arm of the Havoc Chair in a death grip.

And nothing happened.

Corajidin tried again, his eyes wide with panic. Then frustration. Then realization. He railed against his failure, his prosthetic hammering against the chair, his head shaking left and right in impotent rage. Tears welled in his one good eye. Reduced to sobs, he held open his arms for Mēdēya, who came to him with a look of pity, and love, as she settled into his arms.

The former Asrahn, and would-be Mahj, stopped his sobs. He gathered what remained of his dignity and sat upright in his chair, a lord of nothing.

32

"WE RARELY GET THE HAPPY ENDINGS IN OUR LIVES THAT WE THINK WE DESERVE. IT'S WHY WE HAVE THEM IN OUR STORIES, FOR REAL LIFE IS NOT AS FORGIVING AS FICTION."

—Nasri of the Elay-At, Shrīanese dramatist
(495th Year of the Shrīanese Federation)

DAY 85 OF THE 496TH YEAR OF THE

SHRĪANESE FEDERATION

Mari huddled in her over-robe, holding her balance on the cold bronze sphere that passed for the seats of the powerful in the Tyr-Jahavān. She let the voices of the Teshri wash over her. She had nothing to say, in turns numbed by ambivalence and grief, or wracked with nervous tension. Most of the Teshri seats were empty, many of the sayfs killed in this same room not two days earlier. Others, who had taken the field with her father, had been captured and were awaiting judgment. Some remained absent, fearful for their lives.

As you rise, so can you fall: the lesson learned, forgotten, and relearned by her House over the generations.

The clocks chimed the hour, though Mari did not bother to count the chimes. Each hour tolled was one less between her father and the declaration of his fate. With the death of Arbiter-Marshall Kiraj, the Arbiter's Tribunal had sat in emergency session to elect his replacement. After an hour's deliberations, it had been the conservative Arbiter-General Yauri, daughter of the Sayf-Emshara, who was elected. Her father had been blended with a marsh-puppeteer and killed in the purge. Now the young woman had to face the funerary rites for her father, her ascension to the role of sayf, and the added burden of becoming Arbiter-Marshall.

Rosha spoke for the Crown: a predictable choice, being the polar opposite of everything Corajidin had stood for. The counselors of the Teshri orbited Rosha and her closest advisers in Siamak, Ajo, and Ziaire, the four of them sharing the burden of power in the interim government. Osman said little, Nazarafine's rahn-elect looking like he was going to expire from anxiety each time he was asked his opinion. There were grave doubts that Nazarafine would survive, and Mari had heard the grim whispers about the lack of confidence in Osman. Corajidin's recent deposition, and the end of the Great House of Selassin, had set dangerous precedents.

The remaining sayfs talked, demonstrated, or donated their worth in the hopes of being noticed and elevated to the rank of Great House. The Selassins were gone. The fate of the Erebus unclear. There had not been such opportunity since the fall of the Awakened Empire. Similarly, the most influential of the middle-castes made their cases, seeking elevation to the ranks of the elite-caste, and the Hundred Families.

From the confident way Rosha managed the Teshri, Mari doubted there would be an election for Asrahn: She fully expected that Rosha would walk into the role, the uncontested monarch of Shrīan, just as Corajidin had always hoped he would be. Awakening was a topic that buzzed around the Tyr-Jahavān. There were no Awakened rahns in Shrīan, and those who had been Severed had a long road to recovery before they could be re-Awakened. That Indris could re-Awaken the rahns was a tightly gripped hope, and had done wonders for the perceived usefulness of the Sēq. Their grip on the throats of the Teshri was all but reestablished: Like black-lotus addicts, those who sought power in Shrīan craved Awakening. It was such an ingrained attitude, linked with ancient power and prestige, that even those who had been cured of their addiction hungered for the taste of more.

Femensetri stood behind the seated Rosha, her attempt at humility like a poorly fitted robe. The Stormbringer had been invited to attend the Teshri in an informal capacity, though the ancient scholar ensured her voice was heard at every turn. Though the Sēq were the wardens of the Awakening that the Teshri desired, the counselors had not forgotten the recent, and bitter, lesson in honesty the Sēq had taught them. To Femensetri's obvious anger, Rosha had dangled the trappings of political office before the leaders of the Zienni and the Nilvedic, as well as Sanojé on behalf of the witches. The latter name came with some stigma attached: Sanojé's reputation as an Exiled, and her association with Corajidin, offset by her recent efforts. Baquio of the College of Artificers and Prahna of the Alchemist's Society had also been offered seats on the Teshri. Femensetri scowled as Baquio waved his contracts with the Crown and State in the air like a folded paper fan, citing promises of ongoing support, and freedom of trade despite Femensetri's call for fierce restrictions. Teymoud made matters worse for the Stormbringer by citing the commercial advantages to be gained in making what the alchemists and artificers had available on the market. Even with Corajidin in custody, the lure of gold remained.

The more change that people endured, the more tightly they held on to the comfort of that which was familiar. Mari clenched her teeth and left the Teshri to its devices. She raced down the stairs, out the Crown Gate, and along the windy Royal Way to the gondola station. Mari wore a plain charcoal over-robe, atop the red and silver clothing of her mother's Family, the Dahrain. With her hood raised, and the over-robe masking the recurved length of her Sûnblade and her amenesqa, Mari passed without recognition as she sat quietly in the swaying gondola, flakes of snow clustered around the portholes. The gondola trembled and groaned as it reached her station. She strolled the quiet streets, the air redolent of eucalyptus and a hint of snow from the mountains. Nanjidasé stood with its doors open; candidates for roles in the reformed Feyassin huddled around braziers where there was no room for them inside the fortress. Mari smiled to herself. She had waited, as these others waited, for the chance to do something meaningful with her life. A chance to be something other than a Pah-Erebus or a bargaining chip in the great game of the bloodlines. A few of the hopefuls looked up as Mari passed, but she walked on by. It was not her place anymore. Nanjidasé and the Feyassin, bolstered by the surviving Anlūki, would be safe in Belam's hands.

The Nilvedic surgery and hospice was a small place, nestled in a crack in the mountain, and sheltered by a stand of ropy fig trees. The statues of a woman and a man in flowing robes, hands open with bowls of water on their palms in a sign of peace and hospitality, flanked the doors that never closed. Two Nilvedic scholars knelt at the door, clay bowls at their sides. Each had a long kahi flute across their knees, pronouncing them as see'jen, the Whistling Order: Nilvedic warrior-scholars and traveling healers. Both were bald, save for long braids at the back of their heads. Their brows painted with the High Avān glyphs shion and vah, the hearts of healing. Mari emptied her purse into the bowls. The see'jen bowed as she passed.

People walked and talked softly in the hospice, voices no louder than the whisper of robes along the floors. Mari made her way to the small room, well lit and clean, where Shar lay. Vases overflowing with colored lotus flowers brightened the room, their aroma heady. The exposed skin of Shar's face, shoulder, and right arm were mottled with bruising and recently healed abrasions. Symbols had been painted on her skin, and there was a long string of beads, seedpods, and flower buds wound around her wrist, another loosely about her throat. Indris looked up from the book in his lap, smiled, and gestured for Mari to come in.

"How is she?" Mari murmured.

"I'm not deaf, woman," Shar croaked. She tried to smile, a ghastly flexing of blue-and-black skin and swollen lips. "I'd be better if people stopped hovering over me."

"She's cranky," Indris said. "And recovering. Broken collarbone, broken shoulder, broken ribs—"

"I get it, Indris. I'm broken." Shar looked at Mari through bruised, swollen eyes. "Well hello there, you beautiful thing. Can I convince you to help me escape from here?"

"But she'll recover." The relief in Indris's voice was palpable. He pulled a seat next to his so that Mari could sit. He kissed her gently, his hand sliding from her back, to her waist, to her hip, to rest on her thigh as she settled. It felt good. "The surgeons think Shar will be here for another week or so. Even with all their skill, it was a close thing."

"I hear you came to visit me, Mari," Shar said. "You must have been very dull, since I don't remember."

"Yes. You were completely fascinating, lying there like a log. Between Indris and myself, Morne and Kyril, and Belam and Sano, you've had barely a minute alone." But no Ekko. Of all the faces in the world, that was the one Shar would have wanted to see most.

THE PILLARS OF SAND

Hayden. Omen. Ekko. The price the few had paid in blood for the many was high indeed.

Shar drew in a shuddering breath and swore with the pain. Indris held Shar up so that she could take her medicine, and smoothed the sheets around her when she lay back down again. The three sat and talked for the morning, until Qesha-rē ushered them out. It was time for her patient to rest, and to forget her troubles until she was better able to face them. Mari was glad to see the healer, who was more in her element here than in Tamerlan.

Mari took Indris by the hand and led him to the street. Columns of late-afternoon light pierced the clouds and moved across the dappled waters of the Lakes of the Sky. The mountains were capped in white that blended with the gently rolling clouds. Mari leaned in and rested her head against Indris's shoulder. He put his arm around her.

"It won't last," she said.

"What won't last?"

"Any of it," she said. "Everything is so . . . temporary. Is this what it's supposed to feel like, when almost everything you knew is gone? I can't help but think of what we've seen, what we've done, and wonder whether everything we fought for is actually what we wanted."

Indris rested his lips against her hair. "Sometimes it's hard to find the good, or the sense in it all. When night comes, and there's only you and your thoughts—your guilt, your doubts, your memories, hopes, and dreams—then you see most clearly. There's nothing left to distract you. It's then that you realize that you don't need expensive things, or false friends, or feigned love." He paused for a long indrawn breath. "And new things come to fill the empty spaces."

"Like people?"

"No, love. Never people." He touched her chest over her hearts. "They're always here, and there's always a place for them. We just need to make sure it's the right place."

"Does that include Anj?"

Indris looked her in the eye. "She and the Emissary are different people. I won't lie, Mari. Yes, the Anj I married will always have a place in me. Does that bother you?"

"Yes, it does." Mari patted away his worried expression. "But I understand it, and in time I'll learn how to accept it. The fact that she's out there somewhere with Kasra and Wolfram terrifies me. With you, even with Kasra, such power as you have has never frightened me. I respect it, admire it, but I'm not scared. The notion of the Emissary makes my blood run cold."

"And mine." He held her close against a gust of chill wind, and continued to hold her after it passed. "But is there anything I can do for you? I'm sorry I've been distant and distracted. Between Fandra, Shar, Ekko . . . I've not helped you like I should."

"We've each had things on our minds." Mari patted Indris's cheek, and her smile felt comfortable. "I love you, Indris."

"And I, you. Who'd have thought we'd be here to say it?"

"Never doubted it."

"Not ever?"

"Well, sometimes. A little. But then I remembered that I'm in love with the all-powerful Dragon-Eyed Indris." Mari paused at the expression on his face. "I'm sorry, Indris. I didn't mean anything by it. I was making light, is all."

Indris smiled halfheartedly, and Mari saw how both his eyes now had the orange-yellow tint to them, as if fires burned behind the irises. He held out his hand for her to take, and Mari joined him as they dawdled the almost-empty streets. The question of what else had happened to him at the Pillars of Sand, and at Fandra, hung between them like grapes too long on the vine. But Mari let their silence linger, the two of them alone with the sound of the wind and the clatter of the leaves.

"What are we going to do?" Mari broke the quiet with her question, only half whimsical. "We didn't break. We didn't die. But I don't think the places we know fit us anymore."

"All we are is everything I love, Mari." Indris pointed to the mountains. "Wherever we are. Over mountains, over seas, are places so beautiful and peaceful they're hard to leave. I've a small home on the beaches of northern Tanis, overlooking the Deep Salt. There are fruit plantations, and cane fields that seem to stretch forever, swaying and sighing in the wind. On summer nights the lightning flashes, and the rain falls after a hot day and turns to steam. It's too hot to wear clothes, so you lay naked on cushions and let the sea air dry the sweat from your skin, and listen to the surf crash on the beach."

Mari held her breath for the beauty of the vision. Indris had seen so much of the world, and she so little. Duty to others had consumed her, but as Indris had asked her once, what about her duty to herself? Large parts of her world were broken; it was time to take the pieces she liked and make a new one. "Tell me more."

"I've told you about the Nomad dancers and symphonies of Memnon," he mused. "And the villas in Oragon where you can look out over the Marble Sea, and watch as the old *ilhen* lamps from the Petal Empire still shine beneath the water, wavering like fireflies. There's the great migration of the zherba herds in Darmatia, where thousands of the most beautiful horses in the world thunder across a sea of emerald grasses, smooth and pale as mist in a gale, their horns shining. Eidelbon, the capital of Manté that they call the City of Masks, has relics of the Starborn that rise in towers amid ziggurats that are home to thousands of temple daemons in lapis, jade, and onyx. For years the Starborn towers have hummed, parts moving to follow the sun, or lights shining at night though nobody understands how.

"This is the world we can see, Mari. I've seen some of it, and there are places I love and loathe. But travel is more than half about the company, and the things you bring back with you—rather than what you take."

Mari took it all in, the wanderlust alive in her. But her life was not her own just yet. *Rather than what you take* . . . like the burden of her House and its uncertain future. The guilt of her father's crimes and the pain he caused, and the need to make restitution in some way to those people the Erebus had harmed. Would whatever penance her father paid ever be enough to wipe the slate clean, or would Mari forever feel as if she owed a debt to the nation Corajidin had split, and the lives he had ruined?

"Is it as easy as all that, do you think?" she asked. *Please say yes.*

"We can make it harder than it needs to be," Indris replied. "But we don't have to."

"It sounds incredible. And, yes, I'd love to see the world with you. But, Indris?" Mari stopped abruptly, Indris dragged to a halt. "Do you know what's going to happen to my father? Belam? My House?" What would be enough to sever her bonds?

The smile fell from his face and dragged the corners of his mouth down. That he needed to prepare himself made Mari's anxiety return. She knew her father had done terrible things . . . but he was her father. It was not until his illness that Corajidin had lost his way, the specter of his end making him dangerously desperate. For power, for glory, for salvation. "You can't take the burden for things you've not done, nor had any hand in," Indris said. "Mari, there's no weakness in letting go, or putting one foot in front of the other and moving on."

Moving on. Was it as easy as remembering, but packing the feelings away until time and distance had no further use for them? "Indris, tell me."

"Mari, I've not been involved in any of the—"

"Tell me. Now."

"Your father is likely to be charged with several counts of treason for starters," Indris said softly. He placed his hands on Mari's shoulders and locked her gaze with his own. His words were quiet, but relentless and monotone. "I'd expect them to make the charges of regicide stick, as well as more counts of murder and conspiracy than I care to think about. Your father went for the big prize, Mari, and made a mockery of sende, and the law, on the way. People won't forget it, and the Teshri and the Magistratum will want to make an example of Corajidin, so that nobody thinks about following in his footsteps."

"They'll kill him, won't they?" She was surprised at how even her tone was. *I expected this. I just needed to hear it said out loud by somebody I trust to be honest with me.*

"They'll kill him." Indris stopped, eyes distant as he considered. Before Mari could drag his next words out of him, Indris gave them up. "From what I know of the mood of the Arbiter's Tribunal, the Teshri, and their nervousness about the opinions of the foreign governments, the Arbiter-Marshall will most likely level the most severe sentence against your father that she can."

"Indris, they're going to kill him!" Mari said, exasperated. "What more can they do?"

"Under the laws of the Awakened Empire, most of which we still follow, the Arbiter-Marshall can call on the Magistratum to agree to confine Corajidin in a Sepulchre Mirror, a prison from which he will never escape."

Sepulchre Mirror? Why was that familiar? "A prison? You said they were going to kill him."

"Sepulchre Mirrors are eternal prisons for the soul, Mari. Similar to an Angothic Spirit Casque, which is what your father imprisoned Ariskander in. We retrieved a Sepulchre Mirror from the Rōmarq, before your father had a chance to use it on somebody else. It's here, in the possession of the Sēq."

"How?" Her mouth was dry, and she wanted to vomit. The thought of her father languishing for eternity was quite different from seeing him strangled, a clean death, his soul free to travel to the Well of Souls, his body planted in ashes.

"He'll be shackled to a chair, or a frame, and brought before the Sepulchre Mirror. A scholar—not me, never me—will Sever him from his Awakening. He'll face the mirror, and it will absorb his soul, like the annuli of the Soul Traders. But for him there'll be no escape. Not ever."

Mari laughed hysterically, then covered her mouth with her hand. She wanted to sit down, but in sitting wanted to stand. She wanted to run, or fight. Instead she settled for tears.

"Will he feel anything?" It was important that he did not.

"I don't know, Mari. There's no way of knowing."

Clouds passed before the sun, making the city dull, colors bland. The domes lost their shine. Snow became soiled gray: leaves on the streets litter, rather than beautiful. Between one stuttering breath and the next, the city was once more sun-kissed and bright. How things could change in a moment. How such a simple thing as the clouds across the sun could make the world seem so different.

Her father thought her a traitor—to him, she was. With the knowledge that he would be gone from her life forever—with no chance of a reconciliation in the Well of Souls, in the love of their Ancestors—the immediacy of his death weighed on her.

"Indris, can I meet you at the *Wanderer* later?"

"Of course. Good luck." He did not need to ask Mari where she was going.

She kissed him, then raced away as fast as she could run toward the gaol where her father was being held. Up sweeping flights of stairs, across bridges that spanned vast and empty depths, and along roads where the cold wind burned her face, Mari sped. She remembered the way to the gaol, having been a guest there herself not so long ago.

While Mari and her father had their differences, Mari had never stopped loving him. Belam had told her how their father had given him his blessing to go to Tamerlan and free Mari from the clutches of the Dowager-Asrahn. So much had happened, so quickly, that neither of them had the chance to sit together, to talk, and to remember what it was like to be father and daughter. She remembered their reconciliation at Amnon, how he had shared his secrets with her. What he had shared had made Mari more resolute, but the fact was he had loved her enough to open his hearts to her.

Mari would not leave the gaol until he had done so again. If she was lucky, she may even be able to help him remember at least something of the man he had been: the father she had loved, before the threat of death, and ambition, had blinded him.

The shadows had flooded the city by the time she arrived at the gaol. Out of breath, Mari rang the old bell. Then again when there was no immediate answer. She pounded and kicked at the door, and yelled to get the guard's attention. Eventually there came the rattle of the key in the lock, and the scrape of the bolts. The door opened to reveal a middle-aged man in the green coat, and taloub, of a kherife. He clutched a studded maul in hand, and looked very much as if he knew how to use it.

"Can I help you?" he asked, clearly irritated.

"My name is Pah-Erebus fe Mariam," she said. Best to dispense with all that now, and save time arguing. "I've come to visit my father, who I understand is being held here."

The kherife bowed when he heard Mari's name, and surreptitiously hid the maul behind his back. Mari cut his apologies off and walked past him. It was dim inside, and quiet. There were no other guards, which Mari found strange. She waited, but the guard did not move from the door.

"Will you please escort me to my father?" Mari asked. *I can't save him, but I can save what remains of us. Please hurry, damn you!*

She summoned an imitation of a smile, hoping it did not look as false as it felt.

"I'm not sure how to tell you this, Pah-Mariam," the guard said. Even those words were a kick in the stomach. She did not want to hear the rest, but he went on regardless. "The Rahn-Corajidin is no longer a guest here. He was moved three hours ago."

"Where?"

"I do not know, pah."

"Who?"

"They were . . . elite soldiers . . . of the Arbiter's Tribunal," the man stammered. Worse than the secret police, and harder than steel. The militant arm of the law. "They came with the Arbiter-Marshall and took your father away."

Mari nodded stiffly. She concentrated on her step as she exited the gaol, and marched like an automaton down the road. She was not sure when the tears started, or the sobbing. It was still happening when she reached Nanjidasé. The petitioners had gone for the day, but the Feyassin and the Anlūki all knew Mari. They looked at her, expressions gentle, as she walked into the depths of the place in search of Belam.

Her brother greeted her with a smile that the look in her eyes killed. Mari walked past him, and with steadier hands than she thought possible, poured them each a bowl of wine, filled to the rim. As best she could, Mari explained to Belam what she knew of their father's fate. He sat down hard in shock. They emptied their wine. Poured another.

Then brother and sister laughed, cried, and were silent by turns, as they did their best to remember the best of the man they would never see again.

"Inevitability is silent. It is the absence of a beating heart, the indrawn breath that never comes, or the cry for help that is never heard."

—Zamhon, Father on the Mountain for the Ishahayan Gnostic Assassins, and Master of Assassins to the Great House of Näsarat (259th Year of the Shrīanese Federation)

DAY 86 OF THE 496TH YEAR OF THE

SHRĪANESE FEDERATION

Corajidin glowered at the knuckles of his left hand, covered in dried scabs, and the dented headpiece of his prosthetic hand, both damaged in his fits of impotent rage against the moldy walls of his cell. The cell was taller than it was broad and deep: He was already familiar with the five paces by five paces of his accommodation. There was no natural light, only a few dirty *ilhen* to provide a jaundiced gloom. Nor was there was furniture, not even a refuse pot.

His new cell was marginally worse than the one they had moved him from yesterday. Silent warriors had placed a leather hood over his face, shackled him into a coat where his hands were bound behind his back, and unceremoniously manhandled him through a long, stumbling darkness. Before too long, they had thrown him into a conveyance of some kind. Corajidin had doubted it was for the transportation of people, given the miasma of animal feces and urine that pervaded the air. The soldiers had folded his legs up so that he was curled in a fetal position, then slammed the doors shut, bolts rattling loudly. His body had been wracked with spasms during the journey, his guts knotted, and he had thrown up a small amount into his mask, another odor he was forced to contend with, as well as the sour taste, and the sensation of regurgitated food on his face. He had wet himself twice when the conveyance had gone over a bump, and Corajidin had counted his few blessings that he had not voided his bowels, also.

The healing effects of the Rōmarq had faded almost immediately after his arrival in Avānweh. Between the sudden, violent relapse of his illness and his recent wounding by Roshana and Vahineh, Corajidin wondered whether he would survive long enough to attend his trial. Corajidin could afford the best arbiters in Shrīan. Even an advocate who hated him could be swayed to greater effort when given enough money to live the rest of their life in splendor. Such had always been Corajidin's way, to find the glittering lever of another's self-interest, and turn it until it pointed in the direction Corajidin most needed.

His lip curled as he paced. He had not been charged with any crimes, and they had breached all rules of sende in their humiliating treatment of him. But how best to approach his situation? A veneer of contrition, with an admission to being influenced by the forces of darkness, and a donation to the Crown and State for reparations? Perhaps an appeal to Roshana, Nazarafine, and Siamak, to think of the stability of the nation and to benefit from Corajidin's experience? If he could get a message beyond the walls of his cell, he could better prepare for his defense, and ensure the right people were motivated to act in Corajidin's best interests. Better yet, a bribe to the guard to help Corajidin escape. Once he was free, he could retreat, consolidate his strength, and resume his path to his destiny.

Yet no guards came. There was no sense of time, and the walls of his cell closed in with every count of his faltering hearts.

Agony seeped through his body as inexorably as his blood. He longed for the Emissary's potion, just a taste, to help abate the pain for a while. Lying in his own fever sweat, bile, and excrement, Corajidin wrapped his arms about himself and let the chills take him. Wolfram had told him that there were bends in the road to the future, and for Corajidin to die now was intolerable. He was the Thrice Awakened, the one who would usher in the new age of empire. To die now was more than intolerable: It was impossible. *Destiny will protect me from the lapses in fate. All I need is the chance to continue the work.*

For that chance, he needed help, and there was only one place where such help could come. Through dry lips he chanted the Emissary's name, and listened for her coming. She, his dark deliverer. She, to whom he owed debts that his death would never see repaid.

She left you for dead, he said to himself.

No! She left to save Kasraman, he argued back.

Kasraman left you for dead, too. Everybody can be replaced, Corajidin. The world so rarely makes one of anything: the concept of rarity, of the value of uniqueness, is the vanity of the civilized mind.

I need one more chance, that is all. I will not fail again.

Sleep came and went. His eyelids fluttered closed, to open again as he startled himself from his slumber. Always there was the same gloomy light that froze moments in place, so that time became an illusion. Neither food nor water was brought. Nothing to break the monotony of his claustrophobic little world. He slept again, his fever dreams filled with basso voices in the deep, the accompaniment of gibbering sopranos, shrill pipes, and wailing flutes. Tentacles writhed from the depths, decked in diadems of air bubbles. They coiled about, tossed him in the wake of their movement. Massive eyes that saw him, and saw through him. Flayed him of all veneers and misconceptions: to lay him bare, his failures made manifest—

He scrabbled to wakefulness, his sweat smelling like brine. A shadow loomed, and Corajidin screamed. He scuttled back on crooked fingers that refused to straighten, until his back and head slammed against the wall. There was not enough room to distance himself from the silhouette that filled so much of Corajidin's small space.

"I promise I will do better!" Corajidin heard the desperation in his voice. The silhouette cocked her head, leaned forward, and extended a hand. "Please, Emissary, I will do whatever you want! Kill whomever you want! I will topple the thrones of the world, and give to you the Twelve Stones of Avānisse. The Keys of Castavān. I will find the original Torque Spindle, and we will have a Feigning such as has never been seen.

"Just one more chance." And Corajidin bowed as best he could before the darkness. "Deliver me, and I will not disappoint you. I will serve you, and your Masters, in all things."

Light flared around him, and Corajidin held up his crooked hand to shield his eyes.

"I will deliver you, Corajidin," she said. But the voice was wrong. Corajidin blinked against the glare. His eyes focused on a compact woman, her hair pulled back in a severe tail. Her features were chiseled and stern. The gray over-robe over her white jacket and black trousers embroidered with the symbol of the scales of justice in gold proclaimed who she was.

"You remember me, don't you?" The new Arbiter-Marshall's lips were a slash in her face, her eyes remorseless pits. "Have no fear; you'll have your wish. You'll serve the people you failed."

Yauri stepped out of the room. Armored kherife barged in and laid rough hands on Corajidin, dragging him out of his cell. He tried to kick. Did his best to struggle. But even his shouts for aid, and his cries of indignation, sounded weak. His hand flailed ineffectually; his legs were unable to support his weight. The kherife bundled Corajidin into a bronze chair with a high back. His ankles and wrists were shackled. They blindfolded him, then strapped his head to the back of the chair.

The chair was lifted, and Corajidin carried away. Corajidin screamed for the Emissary until he was hoarse. When that availed him nothing, Corajidin yelled for Kasraman to rescue him. For Wolfram. He demanded to know where he was being taken, but the only answer from his guards was the sound of their heavy tread on stone.

Gripped by fear, Corajidin had no idea how long he was carried, from where, or to where. His pulse galloped, and his chest began to hurt. His fingertips tingled. His toes were numb. Bile threatened to come up again, yet there was nothing left in him to expel.

The chair was set down with a jolt. The blindfold was removed.

Corajidin's eyes focused on the gathered ranks of the Teshri, all in their formal robes of state. There were many that Corajidin recognized as people he had scorned: Roshana, Siamak, Ajomandyan, Ziaire, Teymoud . . . Femensetri! The Stormbringer stood grim as death in her worn black cassock, Scholar's Crook topped by a radiant, jade-hued sickle. There were others he did not recognize, and many he had influence over were absent. Corajidin struggled against his bonds, to no avail.

Yauri approached Roshana, Siamak, and Nazarafine—who looked like she would collapse without the support of her portly nephew, Osman. With a degree of ceremony that chilled Corajidin's blood, the Arbiter-Marshall handed Rosha a scroll. Rosha broke the seal, took up a brush, and wrote on it. The scroll was passed to

Siamak, who wrote without hesitation, and then to Nazarafine, who wrote slowly, the ink brush unsteady in her hand.

"What is this?" Corajidin winced at how weak his voice sounded. He licked his lips and repeated the question, the result little better.

Roshana answered. "The Teshri am Shrīan has been in deliberation with the new Arbiter-Marshall, the Kherife-Marshall, and the Scholar-Marshall—"

"That role was abolished, the Sēq cast out of Shrīan!"

"We reestablished it, and invited the former Scholar-Marshall to resume her place until we can hold elections."

"You don't have the authority!"

"I was given the authority when you crippled our damned nation!" Rosha thundered. She flung her arms wide to include the other members of the Teshri. "Ironically, it was you who showed us the way. We have the authority, together. And together we have reviewed the laws, and debated what it is that should be done with you."

Her voice was clear as a bell. She rose from her seat to loom over Corajidin. He sneered up at her, his dry lips sticking to his teeth.

"What is it to be? Who has the courage to end me, eh?" Corajidin rolled his eyes left and right to see the way some of the counselors shuffled their feet. *That's right! I still own some of you. Time for you to lick the hand that fed you, like the dogs you are.* "Who will tie the yellow silk around my neck, and strangle the life from me? Who wants my blood curse on their head? You, Roshana? Seems only fitting.

"Or do you realize that my life is more valuable than my death? That, though my judgment may be perceived as lapsed, and my actions ill considered in your eyes, I've experience and influence you need."

His rasping voice echoed from the close walls. Several of the Teshri leaned in to speak with one another. Then a few more. Corajidin smiled. *This is how it starts.*

Expression carefully neutral, Roshana stared down at Corajidin.

"All the wealth in Ïa won't save you from the fate you've made. I, Asrahn-Elect Näsarat fe Roshana do, as the voice of the Teshri am Shrïan, sentence the former Rahn-Erebus fa Corajidin to death for his crimes of multiple counts of regicide, treason, conspiracy, and murder." Roshana waved the scroll. "There's more, but frankly I'm sick of talking about all the wrongs you've done. Do you have anything to say?"

Corajidin glanced left and right, and saw the support he thought he had vanish into hard, cold expressions. "Where is my advocate? I demand a trial! And time to prepare for it. It's the law."

"A trial presumes you may be innocent," Nazarafine said. Her graying skin hung in a loose bag around her neck. "With the evidence arrayed against you, there was never any doubt that you were guilty."

"You end today, Corajidin," Roshana said. "Here, and now."

"Who brings you your evidence?" Corajidin's breathing was panicked. *I'm going to die!* "I demand to speak with my children!" Was Belamandris here? Mariam? There was much to say that could not wait until their reunion in the Well of Souls—provided the ancient powers of the Drear did not drag him down.

"Mari and Belamandris are better off away from you." Roshana gestured. The kherife dragged two bodies behind them. Mēdēya and Nadir. Corajidin bit down on his grief to see Yashamin-Mēdēya dead on the floor, her second life over before it had been lived. Both corpses had lengths of yellow silk wrapped around their throats, their faces dark with strangulation. *And I will be next . . .*

"I will see you in the Well of Souls, my love," Corajidin murmured. But Yashamin-Mēdēya only stared back with lusterless eyes. "We will be together again."

"No, you won't," Roshana said. She leaned forward and whispered in Corajidin's ear. "As you did to the father I loved, so I do to you, whom I despise!"

Corajidin's chair was turned around so that he faced a tall rectangular shape, hidden by curtains. Preoccupied, the terrible jarring he felt came as an unwelcome surprise. It was more than physical, more than mental, more than spiritual, yet comprised of all three: as if somebody had gone into him with a razor and excised parts of his memories. Some of his senses. Again. And again. Sharp, directed pain that had his one eye tearing. With each invisible wound he gasped and felt parts of himself get cast away.

"We Sever you from your Awakening, and leave you deaf, dumb, and blind to the power of the world you had been blessed to know." Femensetri's crook hummed, and fractals of light grew in size and brightness, until Corajidin had to close his eye. He heard her voice close by his ear. "And now we leave you to a fate more richly deserved than any you gave your enemies, Corajidin. May others look back on this day, and question themselves before walking in your steps."

Corajidin heard the counselors walk away. The doors closed. There came the hiss of curtains being drawn, and a sense of cold washed across him.

Silence. The light faded.

He gingerly opened his eye. It focused on the ornate and ancient mirror before him, the glass that gave no reflection as dark as any ocean. Pearlescent light seeped from the baroque frame, reaching out to him in spirals and arcs cold as ice when it touched him.

Corajidin screamed, voice rising in pitch as the lazy tendrils from the Sepulchre Mirror sank into his body. They coiled, flexed, and broke the anchors between the physical and the spiritual. His essence was torn from his body and carried back to the glass.

Corajidin floated like a man drowned in a glass box, but horribly aware. He saw his own slumped, broken body in the chair. It was a piteous thing, now that it was devoid of the life that had animated it. A sack of aged and diseased flesh. He hammered on the glass with his fists, but there was no sound.

He drifted, no pulse, no warmth, no voice—alone, silent, and powerless, as he would be forever.

34

"TRUTH, LIKE LOVE, SHOULD NEVER BE HIDDEN. YET TRUTH, LIKE LOVE, IS ONE OF THE HARDEST THINGS TO FIND."

—from *The State of Grace,* by Sedefke, inventor, explorer, and philosopher
(823rd Year of the Awakened Empire)

DAY 87 OF THE 496TH YEAR OF THE

SHRĪANESE FEDERATION

Indris disentangled himself from Mari's limbs. She mumbled a sleepy, drunken protest, and reached out for his missing warmth. Her hand fumbled around until it found the thick softness of the sheepskin blanket. With a dreamy sigh she hugged it to her neck. Indris sat on the edge of the bed in the blue-gray light, skin raised in gooseflesh from the cold. He ran a gentle hand through her tousled blonde hair, leaned forward, and kissed her.

He dressed quickly and quietly. Out of habit he reached for his weapon harness, then put it back on the rack. Instead, he slid Changeling's curved hilt through the sash at his waist and took up his Scholar's Lantern. As softly as he could, Indris made his way to the top deck of the *Wanderer*, where he paused at the wonder of the world, the night so bright it was almost blinding. The white-clouded ball of Eln shone, a radiant opal on a sheet of black velvet strewn with polished gems. The Ancestor's Shroud blazed against the darkness, the sapphire of its eye piercing Indris as if it could see him from across the breadth of the sky. Avānweh was marbled with the rainbow haze of the souls of everything that lived there: the fitful sparks of people, magnificent and flawed; the calm and deep-seated minds of trees and flowers; the thousands of nocturnal animals that darted here and there. And the mountains themselves radiated colors and textures he had no names for, other than peace, strength, and depth. Of them all, Īajen-mar shone brightest. Lines of energy flowed, the veins of the world carrying the precious Water of Life.

Indris heard his name on the lips of the world, a siren song that promised wonders, and gave hints of powers and secrets that Indris could barely conceive of. All he need do was let go . . . But he was already too far down a road toward becoming something that terrified him, and in no hurry to reach a destination he—and the rest of the world—might regret.

The clatter of metal drew his attention. A crow was perched on the rail. The glow from the Wraith Jar inside it flashed from between the metallic feathers, and lit the amber ball of its eye. Indris scowled at it, seeing the misty shape of the Sēq Wraith Knight contained within.

"Spying? Really?" Indris asked it. "How long till she gets here?"

"Not long," Femensetri croaked. The crow simulacra bobbed its head by way of an apology, then flew off into the night. Femensetri blazed with ahm, her Disentropic Stain a corona of energy currents that flowed around her. Indris closed his third eye and looked at his former sahai with his physical ones. "Didn't think there'd be much that would drag you from Mari's side."

"She's sleeping, and will have the mother of all hangovers tomorrow. Corajidin's death, and the manner of it, were hard on her, and Belamandris."

"So where are you off to at this time of the night?"

"Thought I'd take the chance to settle a few things before we leave Shrīan."

"So you're going to ignore your duty, and leave the country in shambles?"

Indris waggled his finger. "I'll not let you goad me. I've done well by Shrīan, by the Great Houses and the Hundred Families, and by the Sēq. Now I have to do well by myself."

"Listen to you!" Femensetri laughed, clear, soft, and without the mocking tone she usually carried. She leaned on her crook, and gazed out into the night. "You have done well, Indris. And you do deserve the chance to do what you need to do. And to be happy. I'll not apologize for what we did. Suffice to say we had larger concerns, and still do. Had we to do it all over again, we'd do exactly the same."

"As would I," Indris replied. "It's why I'll never return to the Sēq. And why all those scrolls and letters of offer that are sitting on my desk will stay unopened."

"Do you have any idea what you're being offered?" Femensetri gazed at Indris with something close to envy. "You've shown the Teshri, and the Sēq, a glimpse of what you can do. Indris, many of us would follow you—"

"I know. And that's part of the problem. The rahns have been at me to re-Awaken them, but they're not ready yet. It will be some time before they are, I think. For now they'll have to rely on their own experiences and instincts, like any other leader. The world will turn well enough without Mari and I, but I'll know if things take a turn for the worse. You always said my love was a weakness. If things go badly here, you'll understand how wrong you were."

"Kasraman is out there, Indris." Femensetri's voice was hard. "And Wolfram. And Anj—"

"Anj is dead, sahai. The Emissary is who you should fear, more for what we don't know about her than what we do. Corajidin was tied to her, but she abandoned him to help Kasraman escape. Morne has said that he met others who called themselves the Emissary, in service to the Dynasty of the Ivory Masks, in Eidelbon. The Sēq would do well to enlist what aid they can to assess the threat they represent."

"Where will you be, while you leave this mess with us?"

"Mari wants to go somewhere warm."

"Not surprising, after Tamerlan," Femensetri snorted. "But you're not going somewhere warm. You're going to translocate to Amarqa, aren't you? You're going to open that damned vault. I told the Suret that letting you in there was a mistake. Some of them are blind to what you are. Others refuse to see it."

"But not you?"

"Never me!" Femensetri looked fierce. "There are others who share my view that you are the answer to a lot of our questions."

"I don't know anything about that. But it's time I found out who I am."

Femensetri rested a hand on Indris's shoulder. The tenderness in the gesture made Indris apprehensive. "I don't know that there's ever a time to discover what you're about to learn. Suffice to say, there's a reason it was kept a secret by a few, for so long."

Indris swallowed his questions, with a large portion of trepidation. "Take care of the place while I'm gone. I didn't work so hard just so you could break it some more."

"It's pretty broken, but we'll try."

Numbers cascaded through his mind in overlapping, multidimensional formulae. He reached out for the space where the Black Archives stood, linked the energies around it to the place he stood, and brought them together in his mind. A rainbow bridge opened across the monochrome nothingness. He took a step out—

Crossed the silent, airless, absence between—

The tiny hammer blows of snow struck his face. Wraith Knights in their rimed simulacra turned their gazes on Indris, but made no move to bar him.

It took merely moments to solve the puzzle door, the pieces collapsing like toy blocks. Indris strode through the archive. Ancient artifacts resonated as he passed: Scrolls and books glowed, weapons flared beneath thin layers of dust, writing on the walls displayed second, and third, layers of characters. Fixed on his purpose, he opened the door to the central archive, climbed the stairs, and came face to face with the *serill* vault with his name on it. The lock had reset itself, but Indris answered the questions one after the other.

The final questioning on Awakening was part of him now. It was not a question he could have answered in words, rather something he demonstrated. Indris opened the barriers he had erected one by one, and allowed the question to examine him. With each barrier Indris dropped, the question flowed deeper into him. It merged with the metaphysical serpent that coiled around his spine: filled his body, rose into his mind, then trickled like warm water through his soul. Indris closed his eyes, overcome by the peace that pervaded him. He did not know how long he stood there as the sensation in him faded. When he opened his eyes, the door to his vault folded in on itself, over and over, until none of it remained.

Inside, a gentle light shone on a faceted crystal egg over half a meter long. The egg was striated with rainbow glimmers that swirled in circles and arcs, in straight lines and waves. He looked closer at the patterns of light, to see they were comprised of thousands of tiny glyphs. Indris recognized High Avān, Maladhoring, the characters of the Time Masters, Hazhi, and three other languages he guessed to be those of the other Elemental Masters. The last character set that made him dizzy as the characters looped in, around and through each other, their shapes erratic in composition and movement.

It was a Feigning Egg, such as was produced by the Torque Spindles of old. Indris racked his memory for what he had been taught about the Feignings, where disparate living things were brought together to fabricate, or forge, life. Only the Great Feignings used eggs, where the disparate elements of many lives had been used to create something powerful and unique. That which was made would remain in the egg for months as it grew and the different elements bonded. Most of the Great Feignings failed, and of those that survived the process, most went mad and died—but only after being the sources of great tragedy and sorrow.

Who is in here? And what have they to do with me?

The vault was otherwise empty, save a jade disk ringed in glyphs in different languages. As Indris reached in to take the disk, his arm brushed against the Feigning Egg. It chimed with a crystal note, and a name coalesced on its surface.

Ia fa Näsarat fe Malde-ran yai Sedefke fa Amon-Indris. Indris, son of Sedefke and Malde-ran, son of the Näsarat, son of the world—

Speechless, Indris stumbled back as the egg split into two hemispheres. Inside it was stained blue and gold, edged in a mosaic of polished stones that blazed the hue of ruby and sapphire, amber and diamond. Indris tried in vain to control his breathing when he saw the vacant, fetus-shaped space at the center of the egg.

"And now you know," the Herald said.

Indris leaped at the Herald, pushing him back. He pointed at the egg. "No! That's not me! I was born, not—"

"Made?" the Herald said softly. "Is that which is born not also made, a miracle of elements coming together to create life? In this case, your parents sought to take away the randomness, and give to the world what it needed."

Numb, Indris slumped to the ground and held his head in his hands. The answer to the question of why he was never told was apparent. How do you tell a child such a thing? Indris barked a laugh. How do you tell an adult?

"You are no different than what you were before you knew, Indris." The Herald's many voices, each laid over the other, were gentle.

"The children of the Feignings were all massively flawed," Indris replied. He looked at his hands and thought of the things he had done with them. "And now there's an Awakened one! Ancestor's teeth, I almost underwent Unity! Feigning children were all mad, power hungry, tragic things. And they all died the way they lived—by violence, brought down like rabid animals."

"But you are none of that. Of all the children of Feigning, you were made by ones who saw into the heart of creation. They understood the mind of Ïa, heard its lullabies, nurtured it, and protected it. Even Malde-ran's Great Heresy was done out of desperate love, and the need to protect her people. She never intended what happened. Understand that Awakening is about understanding, nurturing, and compassion. The power Awakening provides was never intended to cause harm."

"I understand power well enough, and that it's only as benign as the person using it."

"But you fear it," the Herald said. "You respect it. You've never sought it out for its own purpose, or yours—"

"That's a lie. You were here with me when I made the decision to Awaken myself so that I could open that damned vault. That's as much for my own purposes as you can get."

"And even learning what you did, you turned your back on an incredible power. You are what Sedefke and Malde-ran promised us. A light that we all could follow." Indris cast a glance at his Scholar's Lantern. The Herald caught the gesture. "Yes! Of all the things you could have made, you made something that shows truth. You need to trust in yourself, Indris. Knowing what you are, why and how you are, is one thing. But you define who you are."

Do I? Or will madness and hunger for power shape me? Indris felt sick. "How am I supposed to react to this?"

"However you deem appropriate. Who else can react for you?"

Half-truths, events, and conversations fell into place. Indris looked inward at the ephemeral walls of the Anamnesis Maze around the kernel of his mind, a barricade to memories kept from him. Even Awakened, the shadows of the maze were bewildering, hinting at a mind more vast than his own. Was it Sedefke who had done this thing?

Sedefke . . . Father. Malde-ran . . . Mother. One vanished for centuries, the other centuries dead but not in her grave, the greatest heretic of the Avān. The last—and current—Mahj. And Indris was her heir. No wonder the Sēq wanted to control him so badly, and Ariskander had tried to make Indris his heir. It would have been an easy step from rahn, to Asrahn, to . . . He let the thought drop.

Indris rose unsteadily to his feet, reflection rippling in the Herald's mask. He reached into the vault and took out the disk: another riddle that needed answers. The Feigning Egg he left in place. The vault door restructured itself, leaving no sign Indris had ever been there.

"What will you do with what you know?" the Herald asked. "There are many who would seek to raise you as the Mahj. Others, such as the Soul Traders, would relish the chance to tear your secrets and your power from you."

"I don't know," Indris said. There were too many secrets. What else had he seen that required his memories to be locked away so thoroughly? How much danger was he, and those close to him, in? "I'll not be yelling it from the rooftops, if that's what you want to hear."

"Such is a wise course, I would think. Where will you go?"

Indris thought of Mari, curled in their bed, and her words to him.

"Somewhere warm, where the sun shines, I don't have to wear much, and can both think and worry less."

It took seconds to translocate himself to the Manufactory, where the completed *Skylark* waited. He started the spools and wheels spinning, and flew her out of the Manufactory and into the night sky. When he reached altitude, Indris folded space and went back to where he could have origins of his choosing.

❊ ❊ ❊

The late afternoon sun showed a happy face as family and friends gathered at the Lotus House, above the Garden of Stones, to say farewell to the hallowed dead. Snow glittered like diamonds on a white carpet across the vale, and the sound of horn and pipe, sonesette and voice, echoed in a heartbreaking paean. Every tear was a tribute. Every smile, and laugh, and hug, and kiss, in honor of those who suffered no longer, but dwelled in the peace of those who had gone before.

Throughout the morning, the Master of the Dead had observed the rituals, Indris and Mari among those who had born witness. They had melted the amber for the Reliquary Masks. Etched the names of their dead on slivers of jade. All except Ekko's remains had been laid to rest in alabaster for their journey home, where they would be planted like flowers in fields of ash. Ekko had been bathed, his fur brushed. The fortune-coins were taken from his mane and replaced with colored beads and tokens that spoke of the greatness of his heart, his honor, his courage, and his deeds. Kembe, the High Patriarch of the Tau-se prides, had sworn to return Ekko to his people, with all the glory and ceremony a hero deserved. Indris held the silk bag with Ekko's fortune-coins in his hand, a gift from Kembe to those Ekko had chosen to spend his last days with.

Indris held Mari close and thought of those they had lost: Ekko, Hayden, and Omen. Bensaharēn. Nazarafine had lost her fight with her illness, and passed away in the twilight hours of the morning, leaving a bereft Osman in her place. Ariskander. Vahineh and her Family, the Great House of Selassin, at an end. The long list of dead counselors of the Teshri, and the warriors who had fought for ideals on both sides. The innocents who had lived in times that should never have been allowed to pass, and died for no good reason. Sende was supposed to have protected them, the warrior-caste and the upper-castes sworn to ensure sende was observed. So few had failed so many. Yet eyes had been opened, and questions asked. The world would not be the same for any of them.

For Mari, there was the combined grief and guilt at the loss of her father, as well as her friends. No matter what Corajidin had done, Mari had tried her best to save the father she loved. By her own tearful, drunken admission in the shallows of the morning light, that man had died long ago. The Corajidin who had died was somebody she barely knew. In that, she and Indris shared a common loss.

There was joy to be had. Neva and Yago had been released from their beds, brought back from the brink of death by Femensetri's will until healers could attend, still much the worse for wear. Ajo stood guard over them, expression fierce. Belamandris and Sanojé stood together, yet now there were many who spoke with them, and smiled, and pressed their hands to brows, lips, and hearts in gratitude for what they had done. Morne and Kyril were hand in hand, battered, bruised, but alive.

Rosha and Siamak, Ziaire and Teymoud, along with their allies in the Teshri, talked quietly among themselves. Rosha gestured for Indris to join them more than once, but he held his drink up in salute, smiled, and remained where he was. Femensetri, too, had tried to engage Indris, but he had avoided her, uncertain of what to say now that he had the context of the truth.

Shar stood on unsteady legs, her eyes a vivid orange in her grief. She had tried to sing her loss away, but her voice had betrayed her at the last, and she had mouthed the words to a song only she knew. Indris and Mari let the tears flow as they took Shar in their arms and guided the recuperating woman to a couch.

"I think Ekko would want you to have these." Indris curled Shar's fingers around the bag of fortune-coins. Shar held them to her face for a silent moment. Then she laughed and wiped her eyes.

"He'd not want us to be sad, would he?" she asked. "He died the way he wanted, in service to others, his friends at his side."

"There's no sin in tears, Shar." Indris leaned down to kiss her brow. "I think Ekko would understand. He knows who you are, and loves you for it. As do I."

Shar flung her arms about Indris's neck and held tight. She looked at Indris and Mari with a sweet melancholy. "You're leaving, aren't you?"

"Yes," Indris said. Shar's expression fell at the admission. Mari nudged Indris with her hip and nodded for him to say more. "But we'll not be gone forever. And there's one more gift I have for you that may make us feel like we're a little closer."

Indris and Mari helped a bemused Shar to her feet. They walked from the Lotus House and clambered into a carriage. Indris whispered direction to the driver and for the entire journey resisted Shar's question, repeated almost every other minute, as to whether they were there yet. At one point Mari put her hands over her ears. When that did not work, Mari struggled with Shar in an effort to put her hand over her mouth. The two women laughed, rocking back and forth in the carriage, until Shar bit Mari's hand. Mari looked outraged, then broke into a smile as Shar took Mari's arms, leaned into her, and forced Mari into a hug that she did not try to escape from.

The carriage came to a halt, and the three friends climbed out. Indris gave the driver a handful of silver rings, more money than he would make in a year, and bid the thankful driver farewell. They stood at the gates to the Royal Skydock, high up on Star Crown Mountain. The air was cold and crisp, stands of pine trees and carved alabaster screens protecting visitors from the wind. The *Wanderer* sat at rest on a nearby platform.

"You're leaving now?" Shar gasped. "No! Surely you can stay another few days?"

"We can't," Mari said. "The Teshri is driving us insane with their overtures. I know they think they're being kind, but I will literally stab somebody if I don't get some peace."

"Literally?" Indris asked.

"Want to try me?"

"No, thank you."

Indris took Shar's hand and led her across a small bridge, through a water garden that was more ice than water, toward smaller platforms of the skydock.

At the center of the platform was the *Skylark*. Shar clapped when she saw it, admiring the graceful avian and Seethe-inspired lines. She ran her hands over the metallic feathers and stood on her toes to look at the pilot's station.

"You did it!" Shar's grin was wide. She came back and hugged him. "I'm so glad you finally built it. Thank you for showing her to me before you go."

"Why wouldn't I?" Indris said. He reached into his over-robe and took out the wind key, which he gave to Shar. "She's yours."

Shar looked at Indris, then at Mari, then back at Indris. Her eyes widened, and her mouth opened in surprise. Then she clutched the key to her chest and did a shaky pirouette of joy. Indris removed

THE PILLARS OF SAND

a small plate from the side of the vessel. Beneath was inscribed the wind-boat's name in Seethe: *Shar-fer-rayn*. The Dawn Skylark.

"It was always for you, my friend," Indris said, sad for their parting now that it was so immediate. "For years we've been companions, friends, and when we've both needed it, lovers. When things were dark, your lightness saved me from the worst of myself. You deserve to fly, Shar. For everything you've done, and for all you are to me, please accept her as your own."

"Oh . . ." Shar showered Indris with kisses, then Mari.

They stayed together, sheltered from the wind, reminiscing about all they had seen and done. Indris retrieved a bottle of wine and bowls from the *Wanderer*. Together they drank and laughed at Omen's fey strangeness, took pride in Ekko's limitless courage, and smiled at Hayden's rural manners and his fatherly concern. When the last bowl had been emptied, they smashed the bottle and the porcelain bowls.

"Can I come and see you?" Shar asked.

"Of course!" Mari replied. "You're part of our family, Shar."

"I love you both, you know," Shar said. "More than anybody I can remember."

"And we you," Indris said. "This is farewell, Shar. Not good-bye."

Shar stepped back as Indris and Mari boarded the *Wanderer*. Indris went to the pilot's station and ignited the Disentropy Spools. The wind-galley thrummed with life. The Tempest Wheels started to spin, giving off a snap and crackle, and the *Wanderer* rose into the air. Indris circled the skydock, where Shar was waving her arms madly in farewell. He smiled, and set course northward to somewhere warm.

✳ ✳ ✳

Indris watched Mari stride along the beach. The day was sunny, the waves crashing on the shore, the seas flecked with whitecaps. It was the first day of winter, but the northernmost beaches of Tanis were warmer than Shrīan, and a far cry from the freezing oceans that chilled Tamerlan.

He had told Mari what had happened to him: his Awakening and his brief glimpse of Unity. Of his origins, or as much as he knew of them. Indris tried to gauge her reaction, but Mari's face was still. She had told Indris she was going for a walk. There was no invitation in her words, and Indris made no move to impose on her thoughts.

It was a lot for her to hear, on top of the grief she carried. There had been neither hostility nor anger nor judgment. Only the kind of silence that came from shock, and the need to think about a response. Indris did not know what he would do if she decided that she wanted to return to Shrīan. Those were worries best left until they were real rather than imagined. But the thought of losing her caused his chest to ache.

Indris went back into the house and ignited the firestones to take the edge off the chill. Hoods came off *ilhen* lamps, painting the wooden floors and stone walls in a drowsy parchment glow. It was a simple place of sandstone and wood, the walls mainly shuttered windows to let the breeze flow through. A central room passed for a Hearthall, three bedchambers, a bath, studio, and an armory, long empty. It had been some time since Indris had been here, longer since there had been guests. At the back of the house was a large room with a veranda that overlooked the cane fields, a fruit plantation in the distance. Wind sent ripples through the grasses, and clouds to the south promised a storm.

He went to the armory. One wall was covered by an empty weapon rack, another wall with a rack for armor. There was a pedestal in the center. Indris raised his eyebrows at how large the room was. How much war can one man make?

With sure hands he hung his storm-pistols and his dragon-tooth knife. The Scholar's Lantern dimmed as he rested it on the wooden pegs, barely a flicker in her depths, the glyphs on the stave dull. He took Changeling from his sash, and the weapon purred loudly: something it had done since Fandra, when it had ascended, and became a soul blade. *Another thing I've no idea how I did. Or did I know, and Changeling helped me remember?* Indris was tempted to ignite the weapon, to see the spectral blade of starlight, but did not. Instead, he rested her on the pedestal, where she crooned in curiosity.

"We've come a long way, you and I," Indris murmured to her. "And I suspect we've some way to go before we're done. But for now, I need to walk without death at my side, if only for a little while."

Indris left and closed the door behind him.

He went to the front of the house, down the stairs, and sat in the sand. Mari walked the shore, crouching from time to time to pick up seashells. She brushed the hair out of her face and waved to Indris. After a long moment of stillness, Mari closed the distance between them and sat beside him on the sand: not touching, but not far away. They said nothing as they both stared out across the Deep Salt, an undulating expanse unbroken from the beach to the horizon.

"What's out there?" Mari rested her chin on her knees, her fingers raking patterns in the sand.

"Questions. Answers," he said. "The past."

"Dragons?"

"Absolutely."

"But we don't need any of those right now, do we?"

Indris turned his gaze away from the horizon, to the woman who held his hearts, sitting right beside him. He smiled at her. She smiled back, and moved a little closer.

"No," Indris said, and meant it. "There's nothing we need right now, other than what we have."

Even if it's only for a little while.

CAST OF CHARACTERS	
Indris	Avān. Pahmahjin-Näsarat fa Amon-Indris, formerly a knight of the Sēq Order of Scholars and now a daimahjin, a mercenary warrior-mage. Once commanded the Immortal Companions' nahdi company. Also known as Dragon-Eyed Indris; Indris, Tamer of Ghosts; and Indris, the Prince of Diamonds. Bears the mind blade, Changeling.
Ekko	Tau-se. Former Knight-Colonel of the Lion Guard First Company. Commanded the expedition to retrieve Far-ad-din after his escape. Now a kombe, travels with Indris.
Hayden Goode	Human. Deceased. Killed by Erebus forces in the Dead Flat.
Sassomon-Omen	Nomad. Became a Wraith Knight in the collapse of the Awakened Empire. Formerly an artist and philosopher, he became an infantryman with the Immortal Companions. Killed by Erebus forces in the Dead Flat.
Shar-fer-rayn	Seethe. War-chanter of the Rayn-ma troupe, reputed to be the last surviving member of her family. Met Indris in the slave pits of Sorochel, from which they escaped together. Now travels with Indris.
GREAT HOUSE OF NÄSARAT	
Ariskander	Avān. Deceased. Avān. Former Rahn of Näsarat Prefecture and Prefect of Narsis. Murdered by Corajidin.
Nehrun	Avān. Pah-Näsarat, once Ariskander's rahn-elect but now incarcerated at the Shrine of the Vanities.
Roshana	Avān. Federationist. Rahn-Näsarat of Näsarat Prefecture, and Prefect of Narsis.
Tajaddin	Avān. Pah-Näsarat and Ariskander's third child.
Anani	Deceased. Tau-se. Lion Guard. Killed by Erebus soldiers.
Baniq	Deceased. Human. Gnostic Assassin. Killed by Erebus soldiers.
Bensaharēn	Avān. Poet Master of the Näsé-sûk, the Phoenix School, in Narsis. Poet Master of the Great House of Näsarat. Also the Sayf-Näsarin, distant cousins to the Great House of Näsarat. Called the Waterdancer. Bears the amenesqa, Rain.
Danyūn	Human. Member of the Ishahayans, and Master of Spies for the Great House of Näsarat.
Maselane	Human. Sayf of the Family Ashour and Master of Arms for the Great House of Näsarat. Also Knight-General of the Näsarat Phoenix Armies.
Mauntro	Tau-se. Knight-Colonel of the Lion Guard.

GREAT HOUSE OF EREBUS	
Basyrandin	*Deceased. Avān. Imperialist. Corajidin's late father and four-time Asrahn of Shrian.*
Belamandris	Avān. Imperialist. Pah-Erebus, called the Widowmaker, and leader of the Anlūki. Corajidin's second son. Born to Corajidin's second wife, Farha of the Dahrain. Warrior-poet of the Erebonsûk. Bears the amenesqa, Tragedy.
Corajidin	Avān. Imperialist. Rahn-Erebus of Erebus Prefecture and Prefect of Erebesq.
Dhoury	Avān. No affiliations. Distant cousin of Mariam and Belamandris, living on Tamerlan.
Kasraman	Avān. Imperialist. Pah-Erebus and Corajidin's rahn-elect. Trained as an Angothic Witch by Wolfram. Son of Corajidin's first wife, Laleh of the Ars-Izrel.
Khurshad	Avān. Imperialist. Widow of the late Basyrandin, Corajidin's mother, and the Dowager-Asrahn. Khurshad is currently the Sayf-Tamerlan.
Mariam	Avān. Federationist. Pah-Erebus, called the Queen of Swords. Former member of the Feyassin. Born to Corajidin's second wife, Farha of the Dahrain.
Mēdēya	Avān. Imperialist. Corajidin's fourth wife, and the host for Yashamin's spirit. A woman of unknown ancestry, and formerly a resident of Avānweh.
Nima	Avān. Imperialist. Corajidin's nephew and warrior of the Anlūki.
Yashamin	*Deceased. Avān. Corajidin's third wife and former nemhoureh of the House of Pearl.*
Armal	*Deceased. Avān. Imperialist. Thufan's son.*
Brede	*Deceased. Human. Formerly a Sēq Librarian captured and turned by the Angothic Witches. Wolfram's former apprentice.*
Elonie	Human. Witch in service to the Great House of Erebus, released from the Mahsojhin.
Feyd	Exile. Avān. Imperialist. Leader of the Jiharim. Corajidin's Master of Arms.
Ikedion	Human. Atrean-born witch in service to the Great House of Erebus, released from the Mahsojhin.
Jhem	Exile. Avān. Imperialist. Sayf-Delfineh and Corajidin's Master of Assassins. Known as the Blacknake.
Kimiya	Exile. Avān. Imperialist. Youngest daughter of Jhem, and Wolfram's apprentice.

GREAT HOUSE OF EREBUS (CONT.)	
Nadir	Exile. Avān. Imperialist. Son and eldest child of Jhem. Before his Exile, Nadir was Mari's lover, and a former student of the Näsé-sûk.
Nix	Exile. Avān. Imperialist. Sayf-Maladhi and son of Rayz, the Ironweb.
Ravenet	*Deceased. Exile. Avān. Imperialist. Oldest daughter of Jhem. Killed by Mariam.*
Sanojé	Exile. Avān. Imperialist. Pah-Chepherundi. A Tanisian witch.
Tahj-Shaheh	Exile. Avān. Imperialist. Marble Sea corsair and daughter of Hatoub, the late Sayf-Näs-Sayyin. Corajidin's Sky Master and Master of the Fleet.
Thufan	*Deceased. Avān. Imperialist. Sayf-Charamin and Corajidin's Kherife-General and Spymaster. Prefect of Jafke. Killed by Erebus soldiers.*
Wolfram	Human. Angothic Witch and Corajidin's Lore Master, and rajir. Originally took service with Corajidin's grandfather, Rahn-Erebus fa Qarnassus. Corajidin's close friend and adviser. Kasraman's teacher in the arcane.
Yotep	Avān. Warrior of the Anlūki.
GREAT HOUSE OF SELASSIN	
Daniush	*Deceased. Avān. Pah-Selassin and Vashne's rahn-elect. Murdered by Corajidin.*
Martūm	Avān. The Selassin rahn-elect, and Vashne's cousin.
Vahineh	Avān. Rahn-Selassin and Vashne's only daughter. Third child of Vashne and Afareen.
Vashne	*Deceased. Avān. Rahn-Selassin and Asrahn of Shrīan. Prefect of Qeme. Murdered by Corajidin.*
GREAT HOUSE OF SÛN	
Navid	*Deceased. Avān. Pah-Sûn and Nazarafine's nephew. Warrior-poet of the Saidani-sûk, the Four Blades School. Navid was the commander of Nazarafine's Sûnguard.*
Nazarafine	Avān. Federationist. Rahn-Sûn of the Sûn Isles and Speaker for the People. Prefect of Qom Riyadh.
Osman	Avān. Federationist. Pah-Sûn, rahn-elect of the Sûn Isles, and eldest brother of Navid, and Riam. Warrior-poet of the Saidani-sûk, the Four Blades School, and graduate of the Zienni Scholars.
Qamran	Avān. Formerly a Knight-Major of the Feyassin.

GREAT HOUSE OF KADARIN	
Anankil	Avān. Federationist. Pah-Kadarin and Narseh's heir. Knight-General of the Yourdin, the elite Kadarin heavy infantry.
Narseh	Avān. Imperialist. Rahn-Kadarin and Knight-Marshall of Shrīan. Prefect of Kadariat.
GREAT HOUSE OF BEY	
Harish	Avān. Federationist. Pah-Bey and Siamak's eldest son. Karia of Ifqe, Master of Arms to the Great House of Bey, and leader of the Marmûn, the elite warriors of the Rōmarq and Bey Prefecture.
Siamak	Avān. Federationist. Rahn-Bey of Bey Prefecture and Prefect of Beyjan and Amnon.
Umna	Avān. Federationist. Pah-Bey, Siamak's eldest daughter, and rahn-elect.
Indera	Avān. Federationist. Poet Master of the Marmûn-sûk, and Poet Master to the Great House of Bey.
(FORMER) GREAT HOUSE OF DIN-MA (THE SEETHE DIN-MA TROUPE)	
Anj-el-din	Seethe. Pah-Näsarat. Far-ad-din's daughter and Indris's once-missing wife, now returned.
Far-ad-din	Exiled. Seethe. Rahn-Din-ma, deposed at the Battle of Amber Lake. Former Prefect of Amnon.
THE HUNDRED FAMILIES	
Ajomandyan	Avān. Federationist. Sayf-Näsaré and Prefect of Avānweh. Also referred to as the Sky Lord.
Bijan	Avān. Federationist. One of Vashne's and Ariskander's allies.
Cesare	Avān. Federationist. Sayf-Ashion and the Speaker for the People.
Chanq	Avān. Imperialist. Sayf-Joroccan and heavily involved in organized crime. One of Corajidin's supporters.
Dowager-Asrahn	Avān. Imperialist. Sayf-Khurshad of the Savajiin, Corajidin's mother, wife of the late Basyrandin, and governor of Tamerlan. Also referred to as the Shark of Tamerlan.
Eladdin	Avān. Imperialist. Son of the Dowager-Asrahn and a warrior-poet of the Erebon-sûk. Called the Sidewinder.
Hadi	Avān. Imperialist. One of Corajidin's supporters.
Karim	Avān. A merchant sayf with strong ties to the Malefacti, the various groups of organized criminals in Shrīan and abroad.
Kiraj	Human. Neutral, though generally allied with the Federationists. Sayf-Masadhe and Prefect of Masadhe. Arbiter Marshall of Shrīan. One of Vashne's and Ariskander's allies.

THE HUNDRED FAMILIES (CONT.)	
Neva	Avān. Federationist. Ajomandyan's granddaughter and heir. Commands the Sky Knights of Avānweh, and performs in the Näsaré Flying Cirq.
Rayz	*Deceased? Exile. Imperialist. Former Sayf-Maladhi, and former Master of Assassins for the Great House of Erebus.*
Teymoud	Avān. Imperialist. Sayf-Saidani and Magnate of the Mercantile Guildsman. Formerly one of Corajidin's supporters.
Yago	Avān. Federationist. Ajomandyan's grandson. A senior officer of the Sky Knights of Avānweh, and performs in the Näsaré Flying Cirq.
Zendi	Avān. Imperialist. Sayf-Bajadeh. Runs bordellos in competition to the House of Pearl. One of Corajidin's supporters.
Ziaire	Avān. Federationist. Sayf-Manshira and Prime of Amajoram in Avānweh. One of the most celebrated nemhoureh of the House of Pearl. Head of the newly formed Peace Faction within the Teshri.
THE SĒQ	
Ahwe	Avān. Sēq Magnate. One of the greatest of the Sēq, and one of Sedefke's first apprentices. Helped found the scholastic orders
Aumh	Y'arrow-te-yi. Sēq Master and member of the Suret.
Cennoväl	Avān. Sēq Master, also known as the Dragonlord, and the only scholar aside from Indris and Anj-el-din to have traveled to the Spines and returned.
Femensetri	Avān. Sēq Master and Scholar-Marshall of Shrīan. Formerly Indris's teacher. Also known as the Stormbringer. Member of the Suret and one of those who helped found the scholastic orders.
He-Who-Watches	Avān. Sēq Master and member of the Suret. An orjini tribesman.
Kemenchromis	Avān. Sēq Master Magnate and Arch-Scholar. Twin brother of Femensetri. Lore Master and rajir to the Empress-in-Shadows. Prime of the Suret. Helped found the scholastic orders
Ojin-mar	Human. Sēq Inquisitor and member of the Suret.
Sedefke	Avān. Founder of the Sēq Order of Scholars, who discovered the process of soul binding with the consciousness of Ía, otherwise known as Awakening.
Taqrit	Avān. Sēq Inquisitor and one of the Eight. Childhood friend of Indris and Anj-el-din.

THE SĒQ (CONT.)	
Yattoweh	Avān. Once, Sedefke's first and greatest disciple. Helped found the various scholastic orders.
Zadjinn	Avān. Sēq Master and member of the Great House of Erebus. Member of the Suret.
OTHERS	
Baquio	Human. Ygranian Master Artificer and dean of the College of Artificers.
Carmenya	Avān. Ygranian-born captain of the Immortal Companions.
Danger-Is-Calling	Warden of Isenandar.
Delfyne	Avān. Poet Master of the Grieve, also known as the Erebon-sûk, or the Stallion School, in Zam'Haja. Elder sister of Maroc.
Kembe	Tau-se. High Patriarch of the Tau-se tribes and Protector of Taumarqan.
Kyril	Human. Darmatian-born captain of the Immortal Companions. Married to Morne Hawkwood.
Leonetto	Human. Imrean-born captain of the Immortal Companions.
Morne Hawkwood	Human. General of the Immortal Companions nahdi company, and long time friend and comrade of Indris. Married to Kyril.
Navaar	Avān/Human. High Palatine of Oragon.
Prahna	Avān. Tanisian Master Alchemist of the Alchemist's Society.
Qesha-rē	Avān. Pashrean born scholar and surgeon of the Nilvedic Order.
Tamiwa	Human. Jiomise-born captain of the Immortal Companions.
The Emissary	Previously known as Anj-el-din, daughter of Far-ad-din, and Indris's missing wife. Now an agent of the Drear, in league with Corajidin.
The Herald	Adviser to the Suret, in Amarqa-in-the-Snows.
Tyen-to-wo	The Laughing Wind spirit of the Seethe.

GLOSSARY OF TERMS	
Ahm	Also referred to as disentropy, it is the energy created by all living things. Its most powerful source is the qua, the theorized center of all creation.
Ahmsah	The collection of disentropic effects taught to scholars. It includes the various arcane formulae, as well as the perceptions used by scholars to see entropic and disentropic effects.
Ahmtesh	The fluid space of the ahm, which connects all things together. This is where the disembodied kaj dwell, as well as a space being accessible to pséjhah, or psé-masters, where mental communication is possible over vast distances.
Ahoujai	Medallions, amulets, or jewelry made from salt-forged steel and the sand from burned-out arcane mandalas. Used as protection from the effects of the ahmsah.
Aipsé	The no-mind taught to warrior-poets.
Aj	Small-scale war, conflict, or feud.
Ajam	Large-scale conflict.
Ajamensût	War of the Long-Knife.
Amenankher	The Long Shadow, a pejorative name given to Amer-Mahjin by the people of Avānweh after the Scholar Wars.
Amenesqa	High Avān word meaning "long wave." From *amen* (long) and *esqa* (wave). The traditional weapon of the Avān during the Petal Empire and the Awakened Empire. It is a long recurved sword shaped like an elongated, flattened "s" from the pommel to the tip of the blade. The weapon has a long hilt and can be used either one handed or two handed.
Amer-Mahjin	The Deep (of the) Enlightened, the Deep (of the) Magi, or the Deep (of the) Wise; the Sēq cavern fortress built into World Blood Mountain.
Arbiter	A legal advocate and practitioner of the law. Generally works in conjunction with kherife, as the enforcers of the law.
Ashinahdi	A warrior of the elite-caste or royal-caste who has cut the ties to their Great House or Family, to pursue a course of action that might otherwise be contrary to the best interests of the family group. A person becomes an ashinahdi generally only after some great shame, or insult to the family, which the rules of sende would otherwise forbid. The separation from family exempts the greater family group from the consequences of the ashinahdi's actions.
Aspect	Terrifying illusory manifestations that appear around a witch when they use their powers.
Asrahn	The highest-ranking rahn in Shrīan, elected through the process of Accession, held every five years in Avānweh.

Avándhim	The first generation of the Aván to be created in the Torque Spindles of Avánisse, on the isle of Castaván.
Avánweh	The political capital of the Shrīanese Federation. Under the governance of Sayf-Ajomandyan of the Näsaré.
Awakening	The process whereby a person is given the potential to connect with the consciousness and power of Ĩa, as well as gaining the ability to access the unbroken line of their Ancestors in living memory. An Awakened rahn is able to affect the weather, see and hear vast distances, increase the speed crops grow, see through the eyes of birds and beasts, etc., in their prefecture. The process is solidified, and made stable, through the drinking of the Water of Life in the Communion Ritual, and the process of Unity.
Blade Master	A weapons instructor, subordinate to a Poet Master in skill and training.
Canto	The vocalization of a scholar's formula, used to create an arcane effect.
Catechism	The governing body of the witches, represented by the Mother Superiors and Father Superiors of the various Covens. The Catechism works closely with the ruling class of the Golden Kingdom of Manté and is reputed to have significant influence in setting policy across the Human nations of the Iron League.
Dai	A warrior.
Daikajé	Traveling warrior-ascetics, thinkers, and monks of the various orders of philosophy across Southeastern Ĩa.
Daishäri	The sects of the warrior-poets, including their traditions, heritage, and measure of conduct.
Daimahjin	A warrior-mage who is no longer a member of the Order that trained them. Such people have been released from service and given the freedom to exercise their skills on behalf of suitable employers, though they are forbidden to pass on their teachings to others. Most are also highly sought-after nahdi.
Daul	An esoteric pain amplifier and concussion weapon favored by Sēq Inquisitors.
Dhar Gsenni	From the High Aván term for "the good of all," the Dhar Gsenni are an ancient sect of Ilhennim that work within the Sēq.
Dilemma Box	A complex metaphysical puzzle box, used to bind elementals and other spirits.
Disentropy	The power of creation, manipulated by scholars using the formulae of the ahmsah, or by witches using their own Arcanum. The use of disentropy is known to cause rapid decay of those materials that it comes in contact with, including living flesh. Metals that decay slowly are generally used in the construction of arcane devices powered by disentropy.

Drear, the	The darkest and most malign depths and reaches of the ahmtesh. Source of dark desires and dreams, as well as the dwelling place of ancient beings from the old world. A place where one forgets all the good things about themselves, and sees only the dark, bitter melancholy that pools in the most hidden depths of the soul.
Ebrim	Nomads who take artificial simulacra in which to interact with the world.
Ephael	The purest of the Nomads, who exist as pure spirit.
Ephim	Nomads who live symbiotically with a host.
Erebon-sûk	The Stallion School of warrior-poetry from Erebus Prefecture. Currently under the governance of Master Delfyne of the Zam'Haja.
Eshim	Nomads who take possession of others against their will; the *ephim*, who live symbiotically with a host; the *ebrim*, like Sassomon-Omen, who took artificial simulacra in which to interact with the world; then there were the *ephael*, who took no hosts at all.
Esoteric Doctrines	Various schools that articulate how the Ilhennim perceive and stimulate natural energy to supernatural outcomes.
Exalted Name	Famous people who have gained a name, epithet, or other title as the result of their actions.
Extrinsic Precept	Within the Esoteric Doctrines, a method of mysticism that uses external forces as a conduit. The method has little restraint, or control, and is not as reliable as the Intrinsic Precept.
Feigning	The process whereby new individuals, or a small group of powerful beings, are created by consuming the essence of a thing, or things, in a Torque Spindle.
Feigning Egg	The gestational crystal required by a product of a Feigning to mature. Simulates the womb and allows for the merging of the various elements used to create the new life.
Font, the	Central point from which the ahm flows. Theorized by scholars to be the center of all the worlds in space and time. Some scholars have posited that the Font is not a point, but a long axle around which an almost infinite number of worlds exist.
Formulae	The calculations scholars use to cause an arcane effect in the world around them.
Gnostic Assassins	A group of highly trained assassins of Mar am'a Din, the mountain range separating Shrīan and Pashrea. Highly sought after as killers for hire, the Gnostic Assassins are taught a series of physical, mental, and other disciplines that make them formidable spies and killers. Also known as the Ishahayans.
Grieve, the	Also known as the Erebon-sûk.

Habron-sûk	The Heron School of warrior-poets of Avânweh. Currently under the governance of Master Nirén.
Hex	The method for witches to cause an arcane effect.
Houreh	Versatile entertainer companions.
Human	Also referred to as the Starborn, the Humans are the predominant power behind the Iron League. Once the vassals of the Seethe, then the Avân, the Humans were the architects of the Insurrection which saw the end of the Awakened Empire.
Huqdi	From the High Avân term for "street dog." The huqdi are generally common bravos, freebooters, and soldiers of fortune, sometimes criminals, without the sense of professional ethics of a nahdi.
Ilhennim	The illuminated, a general term used to describe the various types of mystic.
Intrinsic Precept	Within the Esoteric Doctrines, the way power is channeled, focused, and exercised from within. Based on the repeatable, predictable effects of formulae.
Isenandar	The Pillars of Sand. Formerly the greatest academy of learning for scholars.
Ishahayans	Gnostic Assassins.
Jhah	High Avân word for Master.
Jhi	The stigma. A physical manifestation known to have appeared in the most powerful of the ancient scholars and witches.
Jombe	Tau-se warrior who has chosen to travel beyond the protection and guidelines of their tribe. Generally outcasts who have committed crimes of honor, in search of redemption.
Jûresqa	High Avân word meaning "short wave." From *jûr* (short) and *esqa* (wave). The name for the Pashrean and Shrîanese recurved short sword.
Kaj	High Avân word for soul.
Kaj-adept	A scholar who has mastered a suite of complex spiritual disciplines. A kaj-adept is also able to speak with Nomads, as well as perceive Nomads who have not manifested a physical body, or who inhabit a simulacrum of some kind.
Kajari	Soul blade, as used by some Sêq Masters who have attained the level of insight and power to create one. A kajari has no blade in its passive form, the blade being created as a manifestation of the scholar's soul, harnessed and focused by their mind.
Kaj-jhah	A Sêq, or other Ilhennim, who has died and returned to life, bringing back with them the memory of how to climb the ladder of their consciousness and interact in the ahm.

Kanbōjé	"The falling sapling" is a two-handed maul. Usually made of wood or iron, it is covered in thick stubs or spikes.
Karia, the	The elite military force of Mediin, comprised of both living and Nomad warrior-poets, warrior-mages, and other soldiers.
Kherife	An enforcer of the law.
Khopesh	The long Tau-se sickle sword.
Kirion	A rare metal smelted from meteors, also called star metal. It is usually black in color, shot through with a rainbow hue when seen in direct sunlight.
Krysesqa	High Avān word meaning "quick wave." From *krys* (quick) and *esqa* (wave). The name for the Pashrean and Shrīanese recurved long-knife.
Lament, the	Also referred to as the Näsé-sûk, or the Phoenix School of warrior-poets, from Narsis in Näsarat Prefecture. Currently under the governance of Master Bensaharēn of the Näsarin.
Lore Master	A mystic who has been appointed to a Great House or Family as adviser to a mahj, rahn, or sayf. Traditionally Lore Masters have been members of the Sēq Order of Scholars, though it is not unheard of for Zienni Scholars, Nilvedic Scholars, or witches to assume the role.
Magistratum	Senior officials who represent the holistic interests of the Crown and State, led by the various Officers Marshall. The Magistratum is a neutral body, with a number of portfolios created to represent the common good, each managed by a senior officer. Examples of portfolios in the Magistratum include education, law, the military, finance, and trade.
Mahj	An Awakened Emperor, generally one who is a fully trained Sēq Scholar. The last Mahj was Mahj-Näsarat fe Malde-ran, currently known as the Empress-in-Shadows, in Mediin.
Mahjin	Title or honorific given to one of the Ilhennim.
Mahjirahn	A rahn who is also a trained mystic. These were quite common in the Awakened Empire where the Mahj was also a fully trained scholar, generally of the Sēq Order.
Mahrahn	A Coven-trained witch who is the rahn of a Great House. Almost became synonymous with mahjirahn.
Mahsayf	A Coven-trained witch who is the leader of a Family. When the Great Houses were formed, they were also referred to as Mahrahn.
Mahsojhin	The great university of the witches in Avānweh. Closed by the Sēq at the end of the Scholar Wars, then reopened again by Corajidin.
Maladhoring	The arcane language of the Elemental Masters.
Marmûn	The elite warriors of the Rōmarq and Bey Prefecture. Most are graduates of the Marmûk-sûk.

Marmûn-sûk	The Marsh Hawk School of warrior-poets, from Bey Prefecture. Currently under the governance of Master Indera.
Marsh-puppeteer	Also known as malegangers. A parasitic species from the Drear that virtually kills its host, then takes control of it. Malegangers share a hive mind: What one knows, all know.
Master of Arms	The highest-ranking military officer and strategist in a Great House or Family.
Master of Assassins	The commander of the assassins assigned to a Great House or Family. This role will include the responsibilities of the Master of Spies.
Master of Spies	The commander of the spies assigned to a Great House or Family. Generally used when a House or Family does not usually have assassins in their permanent employ.
Master of the Fleet	The highest-ranking naval officer of a Great House or Family.
Master of the House	The role of managing all the financial, mercantile, and other administrative tasks required to run a Great House or Family. Quite often the role is also that of secretary to a rahn or sayf. Sometimes the role also assumes the responsibilities of a rajir.
Nahdi	From the High Avān word meaning "iron dog," a nahdi is the name for a mercenary or other professional soldier unaffiliated with a Great House or Family. Nahdi generally operate with a strict code of professional ethics.
Näsé-sûk	Also known as the Lament.
Nayu-adept	A scholar who has mastered a suite of complex physical disciplines.
Nemhoureh	Gold Companion of the House of Pearl. A prized courtesan and entertainer who engages only with the upper-castes and the most affluent members of society.
Nilvedic, the	An order of scholars famed for their expertise as healers, herbalists, and alchemists. Known for their dark yellow robes, they are not a militant order.
Nomad	The Avān term for the undead.
Officers Marshall	The most senior officials in the Magistratum. Some are representatives from the Hundred Families or the Great Houses, though many are representatives from the merchant-caste, warrior-caste, or the freehold-caste, which includes artisans, farmers, and other tradespeople.
Pah	High Avān word for the child of a rahn.
Pahavān	The highest-ranking members of the Avān in a country where there are no Awakened rahns.
Pillars of Sand	See Isenandar.

Poet Master	The head of a Poet Master academy, teaching the ancient arts of the warrior-poet.
Prefect	The appointed ruler of a city. A Prefect is always a rahn or a sayf, where the title is inherited. Where a Great House or Family is Exiled, or otherwise removed from the roles, a new Prefect from a different House or Family will be appointed.
Psé	High Avān word for "mind."
Psé-adept	A scholar who has mastered a suite of complex mental disciplines.
Pséd	A field of study in the Esoteric Doctrines that focuses on mentalism, reputed to have been taught in the lost university of Khenempûr.
Psédari	High Avān word meaning "mind blade." From *psé* (mind) and *dari* (blade). Used by some Sēq Knights and Sēq Masters who have the skills and disciplines for creating such weapons. A psédari can only be wielded by the person who made it.
Pséja	The marriage of minds, used by mystics to work in concert and maximize effectiveness.
Qadir	A palace.
Qua	Also referred to as the Font.
Rahn	Leader of one of the Great Houses. A member of the royal-caste.
Rajir	Closest adviser to a rahn or sayf. Usually a Lore Master, Master of Arms, Master of Spies, or other senior officer in a household.
Sahai	High Avān word for "teacher."
Saidani-sûk	The Four Swords warrior-poet academy of Sûn Prefecture. Currently under the governance of Master Jarrah.
Sayf	Leader of one of the Hundred Families. A member of the elite-caste.
Sende	The collection of policies, codes, measures, and other behaviors that the Avān use to regulate their social interactions.
Sēq, the	Scholastic order that teaches a combination of physical, mental, and spiritual disciplines.
Serill	The drake-fired glass of the Seethe. *Serill* is lighter and harder than steel and can be made into almost any shape. Often colored, *serill* is popular with the Seethe in the making of armor and weapons.
Shamshir	The typical weapon of the Avān. It is a long, single-edged curved weapon with a hilt long enough to use in either one or two hands.
Shan	The unofficial title used by the heads of influential tribes or clans. Generally used by the mountain peoples of the Mar Jihara, the Mar Ejir, the Mar Silin, the Mar am'a Din, and the Mar Shalon. It is also sometimes used by affluent families with a military tradition.

Soul Trader	Nomads, though sometimes living beings, who harvest the souls of the dead in order to sell them to others.
Starborn	Humans.
Sûk	A school.
Sût	High Avān word meaning "knife."
Teshri	The government leaders, representatives of the Crown and State. Members of the Teshri are sayfs and rahns, though senior members of influential consortiums are also appointed such as the leaders of the House of Pearl, the Banker's House, the Mercantile Guild, Alchemists Guild, etc.
Unity	The process whereby an Awakened rahn travels their prefecture, communing with the consciousness of Īa. Successful Unity provides the Awakened rahn with the ability to share, harness, and leverage from the vast natural forces of Īa.
Vayen-sûk	The Lotus School of the warrior-poets, from Myr in Selassin Prefecture. Currently under the governance of Master Tarshin.
Warrior-poet	Arguably the most dangerous weapon masters in the world, a warrior-poet is trained in various weapons, strategies, unarmed combat, and military history and philosophy. They are also trained in the creative arts of writing, poetry, painting, and sculpting, as a means to offset the violence of their core teaching and to gain an understanding of the value of life. A warrior-poet lives according to the tenet "The one will fight, so the many do not have to." Once trained, they are contracted out as bodyguards, champions, and military leaders to the Great Houses, the Families, and to the various large syndicates such as the Mercantile Guild, the Banker's House, and the House of Pearl. The Feyassin, the personal guard of the Mahj (or the Asrahn, in the case of the Shrīanese Federation) are entirely comprised of warrior-poets from the various schools.
Water of Life	Also known as the World Blood, the Water of Life is a rare and vital source of water, enriched with a high content of disentropy from where it has flowed through areas where the border between the physical world of Īa and the ahmtesh are tenuous.
Witch	The first group of the Ilhennim, mystics who are able to harness a vast array of natural forces to affect a supernatural outcome. A more dangerous, and less predictable, set of practices than those used by scholars. The first scholastic orders were created by witches.
Witchfire	A natural ore with the mineral properties to more effectively channel disentropy, without being destroyed in the process. Often alloyed with *kirion* for greater strength, though can be alloyed with other metals.
Zienni, the	An order of scholars that focuses upon mental discipline and philosophy. They are capable practitioners of unarmed combat, though tend not to engage in violence. Known by their gray overrobes. Also known as the Wandering Order.

CULTURES	
Avān	A species originally made by the Seethe in Torque Spindles from Seethe and Human specimens, as well as samples from predatory animals. The Avān were originally used as peacekeepers in the Petal Empire, though they rose up against the Seethe. Rather than release Humanity from their servitude, the newly formed Awakened Empire kept Humanity as a vassal race for the next millennium until it was toppled as part of a Human revolt.
Dragons	One of the Elemental Masters species, Dragons are also known as the Fire Masters. They call themselves the Hazhi. Rarely seen in the modern world, they are known to spend much of their time in slumber as part of the Great Dreaming, with only a small percentage of their population awake at any one time.
Fenling	A race created by the Seethe in the Torque Spindles, the Fenling are the merger of giant tool-using rats and the Avān. They are a race of scavengers who rarely deal with non-Fenling, and are known for their cannibalism and carrying of virulent diseases.
Feyhe	One of the Elemental Master species, the Feyhe are also known as the Sea Masters.
Herū	One of the Elemental Masters species, the Herū are also known as the Earth Masters.
Humans	Also referred to as the Starborn. The most populous species on Ia. Once a vassal race to the Petal Empire of the Seethe, as well as the Awakened Empire of the Avān, Humanity is now independent. The largest Human faction in Southeastern Ia is the Iron League—composed of Atrea, Jiom, Imre, Manté, Orē, and Angoth. Humans are known to live in almost every nation.
Iku	One of the species of the Bamboo People. An ancient and enigmatic race of avian-like humanoids, with strong ties to the Sēq Order. They are rarely seen outside their mountain retreats, and generally people mistake their appearance for a disguise. For the most part the Iku are daikajé, traveling warrior philosophers and teachers. Sometimes associated with bad omens.
Katsé	One of the species of the Bamboo People. Also referred to as the fox-folk, they are a vulpine race who live in the forests and mountains of Ia. The Katsé are known for their cunning, and nature as tricksters.
Nomads	The undying or undead. Generally, they are without physical form and need to inhabit a physical shell in order to interact with the physical world. Seen as abominations by the Ancestor-worshipping Avān.
Rōm	Also called the Time Masters, the Rōm predate the Elemental Masters. There is very little documented about the Haiyt Empire of the Time Masters.

Seethe	One of the Elemental Master species, the Seethe are also known as the Wind Masters. The founders of the now fallen Petal Empire, they are effectively immortal, though they can die via sickness and violence. As Seethe mature, they undergo a physiological change where their bones thin and they grow wings. Seethe elders are capable of flight. The Seethe live and travel in extended family units known as troupes. They can be found in many cities across Southeastern Ia, though most dwell in the floating Sky Realms, which drift around the world, propelled by the winds.
Tau-se	The lion-folk of the Taumarq, originally made in the Torque Spindles by blending Humans and lions. They are collected into a tribe-based patriarchy, though it is the women who run businesses and households. The Tau-se are sought after as mercenaries.
Y'arrow-te-yi	A reclusive species reputed to be descended from earth elementals.

ACKNOWLEDGMENTS

The creation of these three novels in the Echoes of Empire series has been such a consuming part of my life for the past couple of years. Writing them has been a tremendous experience, not without its lessons learned, its joys, and its sacrifices.

To my family and friends who've been so very patient, putting up with infrequent visits, and my social absences. Thanks for being there, and understanding how important this is for me.

To John Jarrold, who was always there with his advice and experience, and who has been so passionate about my work. I look forward to working with you on my next books.

David Pomerico and the 47North Author Team, you've proven time and time again that you believe in me, and the Echoes series. There's so much work behind the scenes, and you made it all flow as smoothly as I could've hoped for.

To my editor, Juliet Ulman, for your guidance and attention to detail.

Matt Patin, I appreciate how hard copy editing can be. Thanks for all your hard work, and trying to make my stories a better experience for the reader. And to my proof editors, Elaine Caughlan and Chrystal Nelson, my gratitude for your professionalism and care.

To Stephan Martiniere, you've given me the most amazing cover art for these stories. I'm blessed to have had your vision as the first thing people see about my books.

My humble thanks to you all.

ABOUT THE AUTHOR

Mark T. Barnes was born in Sydney, Australia, in September of 1966. A strong athlete, he was also drawn to the arts at a young age, penning his first short story as a seven-year-old. He worked in finance and advertising and eventually landed satisfying work in information technology, where he continues to manage a freelance organizational change consultancy. In 2005, when Mark was selected to attend the Clarion South residential short story workshop, he began to write with the intention of making it more than a hobby. Since that time, Mark has published a number of short stories, worked as a freelance script editor, and has driven creative consultancy for a television series. *The Pillars of Sand* is Book Three in the Echoes of Empire series, which also includes *The Garden of Stones* and *The Obsidian Heart*.